Deadly Request

Rod Canham

Deadly Request/Rod Canham —— 1st ed.

ISBN: 978-1-7338423-4-1 print book
ISBN: 978-1-7338423-5-8 eBook

History——World War II——Scuba Diving—Shipwrecks——Adventure—— Mystery ——1944-1994——Fiction

This is a work of fiction. Any errors are the sole responsibility of the author.

To my precious wife, Kath -
life would not be
the same without you

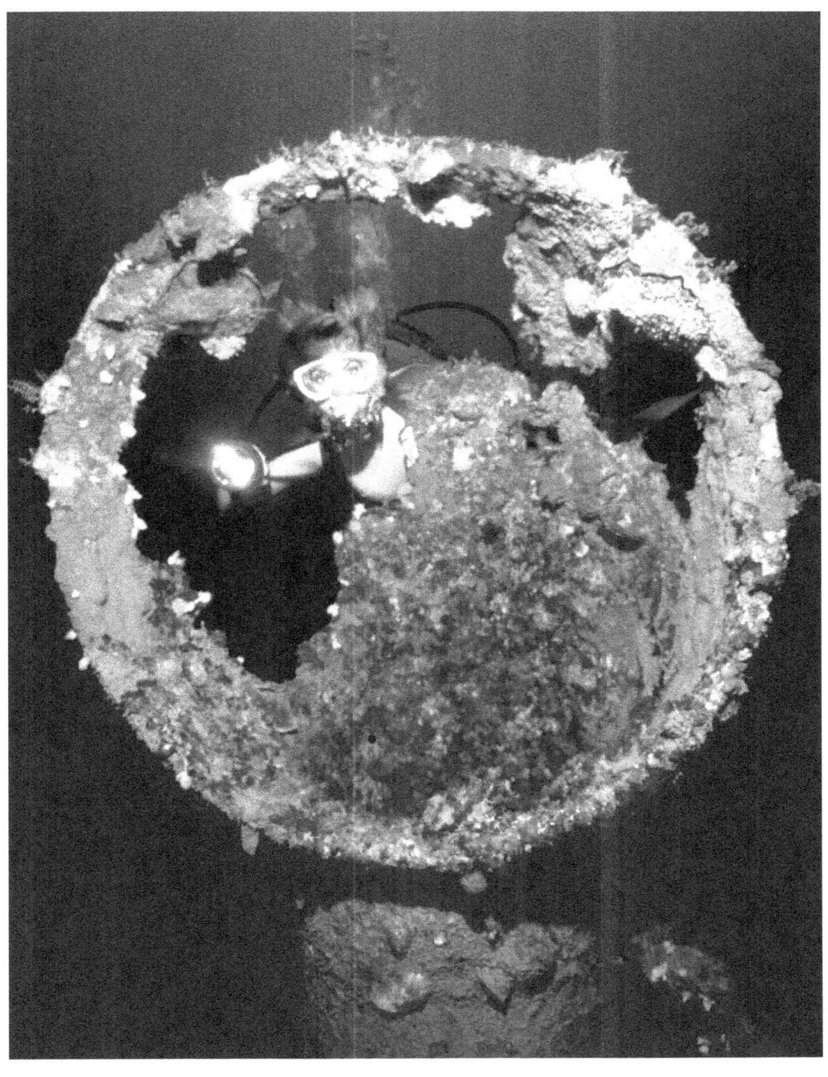

Table of Contents

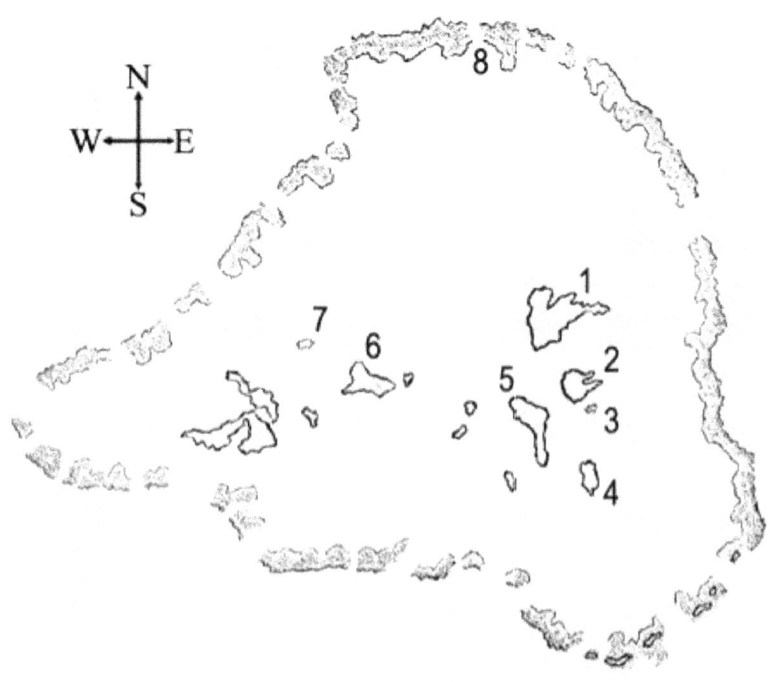

Map of Chuuk (Truk) Lagoon

1 - Weno (Moen)
2 - Tonoas (Dublon)
3 - Eten
4 - Uman
5 - Fefan
6 - Udot
7 - Romanum
8 - North Pass
9 - Neoch Atoll

Prologue:
Opening Salvo

17 February 1944
Fourth Fleet Anchorage
East of Dublon Island
Truk Lagoon, Micronesia

Yoshizo Nakamaruo senses the bitter realization that today will most likely be his last. Early morning pandemonium has dragged the fifty-seven-year-old freighter captain from the privacy of his comfortable stateroom.

In any other season of life, duty at this tropical atoll would be a welcomed respite from the normal rigors of life in the military, but this is war. The cacophony of battle shatters the paradisal atmosphere.

He adroitly sidesteps panicky junior officers to a vantage point outside the *Aikoku Maru's* navigation bridge for a front-row vista of the deadly panorama: to his southeast, the *Reiyo Maru* is in flames from detonating munitions stored beneath her bridge, the specter of drifting black smoke cloaks *Nagano Maru's* struggle, while the *Momokawa Maru's* inferno generates towering clouds which block his view of yet another freighter, the *San Francisco Maru*, ablaze since earlier in the morning.

From the north, the violent shock wave from a nearby explosion compels Nakamaruo to thread his way through the crowded bridge to the ship's opposite rail. Pedestal-mounted binoculars presage his soon-to-be-realized destiny——the

Nippo Maru backlit by rising flames from expanding pools of oil on the water's surface.

Vaporous currents carry the acrid stench of burning fuel and cordite while concealing the heart-wrenching details of the *Nippo's* intrepid crew losing the battle to save their ship. Nakamaruo shutters when a deafening explosion and intense flames fling hapless sailors overboard. With each subsequent burst, the crippled vessel moves closer to extinction. As water envelops her searing hot decks, blankets of steam roll over the oil-blackened dead. The survivors struggle to avoid the floating infernos as they're uncontrollably tossed about by swells of air escaping from submerged compartments.

He helplessly witnesses the stricken *Nippo* slowly settle into the lagoon. *This is a forerunner of what awaits my ship … my men.* It's only been four months since he assumed command of the *Aikoku,* but her loss looms imminent.

Reconfigured as a heavily armed merchant raider by the Imperial Japanese Navy, the four hundred and ninety-eight foot-long liner is as yet untouched. To him, she's an imposing vessel; to the allies, she's a plum target.

Engrossed in the scene playing out before him, the captain is interrupted by his first officer, a newly-minted lieutenant commander whose face reflects the sobering reality of their fate. The two men do what they can to carry on a conversation while dodging determined seamen who rush along the companionways to their battle stations and damage control assignments.

Deep down the young officer already knows the answer, yet seeks reassurance from his mentor. "Any chance we can escape this, Captain?"

With his hand clenched tightly, Nakamaruo pounds on the side of his hip. "They waited too long to give us the fuel we needed to rejoin the convoy," he laments.

Waves of U.S. Navy aircraft fade into the distance, but the skies are filled with so many more. The battle inexorably closes in on their position. Nakamarou notices the younger man's eyes drawn skyward and does what he can to reengage his subordinate. "Commander!" he shouts. The startled first officer anxiously forces his gaze back to his superior. "Have the gunners manned their posts?"

"I will check immediately, sir."

"Confirm with the engineers their assessment of our fuel reserves, and ask how long before they can work up steam. I'll be on the bridge. Report to me as soon as possible." His anxiety troubles the captain. "Keep in mind the men need our reassurances we can get through this. Now move."

A short time later, flushed and struggling to catch his breath, he returns to update his superior. Unnerved by the advancing drone of the next airborne wave, he can't help but glance up. Reacting to the inbound threat, he secures a firm grip on Nakamarou's upper arm and yells, "Captain, please, we *must* take cover," then forces him down as the first bomb strikes the officers' wardroom. The tumultuous impact violently slams the two men into the compartment's rear bulkhead.

Running true to target, another bomb-strike shudders throughout followed closely by a third. Deafening explosions rip through bulkheads with lethal, white-hot shards of steel peppering everything in their path and swiftly igniting fires. Shattered bodies of crewmen are fiercely thrown about their compartments, while others are blown off companionways into the lagoon, and more into the ship's deep cargo holds.

Regaining their senses, displaced gunners atop the *Aikoku's* superstructure reclaim their seats astride the anti-aircraft guns. Subsequent detonations amplify their fear of onboard fires prematurely cooking-off their nearby ammunition.

The rhythmic *thump-thump* of the twin auto-cannons jar the two senior officers to a befuddled awareness. Despite aching stiff knees, the first officer manages to pick himself up from the deck. Staggering with every jolt, his head swirls with incessant ringing from the concussive explosions. Through his own pain and disorientation, he instinctively shields his severely broken wrist while he makes a futile attempt to help his commander regain his footing. Still on his hands and knees, the bewildered captain does his best to shake off the blasts' effects.

A single Navy TBF Avenger breaks southeast from the next inbound air wing to continue its role in the sortie alone. The pilot, a popular young lieutenant from Georgia, is torn between the welfare of the two he's crewed with since reporting aboard the *Intrepid*, and the success of their mission. He warns them to brace themselves as he banks inbound to begin the bombing run through an intense hail of anti-aircraft fire.

The sight of the inbound aircraft terrifies the *Aikoku's* bridge crew. They point at the craft with hopes their panicky yells will somehow ward off the approaching menace. Nakamaruo raises himself up for a better view forward.

Through incessant land-based and shipboard gunfire, the plane continues its run. Seconds into its turn, a loud explosion severely shudders the aircraft. A shore-based artillery battery gravely cripples the rear stabilizer forcing the pilot into a battle of maintaining control and remaining on course.

With the drop-point fast approaching, the pilot reaches ahead to pull down the bomb bay control lever, and prays the doors are still functional. Even though he's already heard and felt them, the red jewel light signals the doors are locked in the open position. Despite shifting forces on his vibrating craft, he deftly toggles the release switch atop his joystick. The delivery of the heavy payload gives the craft a temporary lift, but when the pilot attempts to pull out of the run, he discovers he no longer has control.

The youthful bridge crew is initially encouraged when the battery on nearby Dublon Island scores its strike, but their momentary hope abruptly shifts to despair when its four, 500-pound bombs are deployed true to target——the ship's foremost cargo hold filled with munitions.

Nakamaruo instinctively ducks behind the bulkhead seconds before the crippled Avenger crashes immediately below the *Aikoku's* bridge.

After the bombs reach their mark, superheated air from the primary and secondary explosions radiates into a massive expanding globe that vaporizes the forward two hundred plus feet of the ship, and takes with it the lives of not only the three American aircrew, but everyone aboard the *Aikoku*, seven hundred and forty souls, save one.

The resultant mushroom cloud, filled with smoke and particulate, is propelled thousands of feet skyward. When the upward thrust loses its momentum, steel, aluminum, and wood rain throughout the site in a mile-wide circumference. Dissipating smoke reveals no sign of her existence other than roiled waters, flotsam, and pools of burning fuel.

The once proud vessel's remains settle into a newly formed cradle two hundred and thirty feet below, minus the entirety of the ship forward of its smoke stack. There she remains, upright and undiscovered for the next twenty-eight years.

April 1994
Chuuk (Formerly Truk) Lagoon, Micronesia

Jon Hall hovers over the leading edge of the *Aikoku Maru's* superstructure, one hundred and forty feet below the water's surface. The vision of an abyssal blue void, where the front half of the ship once existed, captured his interest on his first trip to the lagoon. Since then, he's returned frequently, first with his beloved wife Patricia, and yearly after her death from cancer.

While guide Brent Edelson leads a couple from the charter on a fast-paced, pre-planned route throughout the wreckage, Jon drops over the rim to view the torn, mangled sheets of steel framing its sides, and marvels at the unbridled power of destruction. *What unfathomable terror those men must have gone through until the cataclysmic finale of their lives.*

All too quickly, the sound of Brent's signal forces Jon from his reflections. Time has run out and he has to begin his ascent. By the time he reaches the superstructure, Brent and his charges have already started up without him. He checks his instrument console to calculate his dive profile and begins forty-two minutes of stage-decompression stops on his way to the surface.

During the dive boat's return transit, Brent, never one to socialize, chooses a place to sit by himself while Jon joins the couple and shares an enthusiastic discussion about their discoveries and the island's history.

After a quick shower, Jon enters the hotel's recently refurbished lounge, a popular hangout where divers relax, refresh, and talk-story. He's pleased to find his old friend and bartender, Salpasr, a long-ago transplant from the neighboring island, Pohnpei. He's dependable, extremely patient, and his ever-busy wait-staff enjoy working with him while realizing there's a line with him they'd best not cross.

"With all the changes, Sal, it's nice to see a familiar face."

The usually taciturn man cracks a genuine smile and extends his hand with a warm greeting, "Welcome back, Jon."

"How 'bout a——" Before he can finish his order, Sal pops the cap off a Heineken, straddles a glass over the top and hands it to him. "Good memory," he says and reaches for his wallet.

Sal holds ups his hand. "First round's on the house, my friend." Jon tips the bottle in appreciation. They've known each other since Jon's first trip to the islands with his wife. Sal was one of the few who reached out to him after her passing.

The lounge is L-shaped. The smaller more popular seating area is lined with floor-to-ceiling mirrors that reflect light and visuals from the outside wall of solid glass. Contemporary furniture line both sides, and provides patrons an unimpeded view of the lagoon.

When the sun has fully settled and the light-show in the heavens fades, recessed lights enhance the interior's ambience. The din of conversations and laughter, a light curtain of lingering smoke, and the aroma of freshly grilled ahi hold fond memories for Jon of earlier visits.

After a short greeting and conversation, he tactfully begs out of an invitation to join the couple from the charter to find a secluded booth away from the view and the crowd. He takes a sip of his drink, lights up an unfiltered Camel, and scans the surroundings. The new motif is complimented with beautiful paintings and stunning underwater photographs. Each has a business card attached near the frame's lower right-hand corner:

Aqua Views
by Steve Mitchell
Orders on request

Jon has known Steve for many years and makes a mental note to give him a call.

He finishes his beer and is about to order another when his hopes for solitude are cut short. Brent Edelson approaches balancing two beers in one hand and a gym bag in the other. He slides one of the moist bottles toward Jon, and carefully places the bag on the carpeted floor. Jon reluctantly pushes out the opposite chair with his foot and gestures he sit.

"At least you're not empty-handed. What's the occasion?"

Brent points to Jon's pack of cigarettes. "You willin' to give up one of those?"

"Help yourself." When he moves the pack and lighter within his reach, he intercepts Brent's outstretched wrist and turns his arm face-up for a full view of a relatively fresh tattoo. "This looks new." It's a photorealistic black-ink rendition of an octopus that covers the entire underside of his forearm with tentacles that curl around the top of his wrist and hand. "It's odd that I never noticed it before. Looks expensive. I presume you didn't get it done here?"

Brent self-consciously pulls his arm back, and lights up one of Jon's cigarettes. "About a month ago, I got a tip on a good artist in Manilla and took some time off to check her out."

The two quietly sit together enjoying their smokes and beer with nothing of consequence to share until Brent props himself up. "I've dived the *Aikoku* scores of times, and to me it never changes. What's the fixation you have with this wreck?"

Jon stares at his former employee critically. "I'm getting a vibe you're sorry you moved here."

Brent mulls it over longer than either expected. "Guess I haven't given it much consideration."

"Think maybe you're burned out? I've noticed your dispassionate approach to exploring the ship. You're always in such a hurry to lead tourists along the same path with no variation." Jon remembers Brent's enthusiasm when he led dives for his charter operation, and the steady stream of compliments he received from his customers. "Have you ever considered diving on her when you're not at work? You might discover something new to reignite the flame you once had on Maui."

Brent reacts as if Jon's lost his mind. "Hell, no! Why would I want to spend my off-hours out there?"

"I'm sorry you've lost the joy of the experience. I imagine your divers must sense it too."

"I don't hear any complaints," he quickly shoots back.

Uncomfortable under the judgmental gaze of his former boss, he takes a draw from his beer, and nervously flicks the ashes of his cigarette into an empty bottle.

Sensing Brent has heard enough critique about his work ethic, Jon changes the subject. "People who get inked usually have a story to go along with the artwork. What's yours?"

Brent takes another glance at his arm, and deflects the question by reaching into his gym bag. He pulls out a jar filled with oily sea water and casually lets it drop onto the table with a dull *thud*.

"This here holds a different kind of 'story' you and I need to discuss."

Jon holds the jar up to the light and stares at the viscous fluid suspended in the clear container. "Help me make sense of this. You say you collected this seepage from a wreck in the lagoon?"

"Yeah, the *Sankisan*."

"And the concerns of visiting divers and ecologists have somehow reached the governor?"

Brent sighs heavily. "Again, they've led him to believe the wrecks' deterioration will lead to unimaginable oil spills from ruptured fuel tanks and storage drums, which will kill the marine life on the wrecks, endanger the divers, destroy the fishing industry, and over the course of time, our tourism."

"What I have a hard time with is the belief my government can do anything to prevent this 'ecological disaster'. What does he expect us to do about it?"

"For starters, firms are needed to draw the oil out of the wrecks. After that, scientists have proposed their own theories on ways to slow down the deterioration, but all these proposals require substantial funding."

"Why has the governor asked for *my* help?"

"Not you exactly. You're just the first person I thought of."

Jon smirks. "How did *you* get involved?"

Brent's taken aback. "You're surprised I have some standing in these islands?"

"Actually, yeah," Jon chuckles. "Heads of government do not have a history of seeking help from dive guides."

Brent's sudden rise nearly knocks over his chair. "This is a legitimate request. If you're going to be an asshole about this, I'll look for someone who may be willing to help." He doesn't control his agitation as he gathers his belongings.

Jon waves both hands in surrender. "You're right. I'm sorry. Sit back down and I'll buy the next round."

Brent pauses until Jon signals the waitress. He quickly helps himself to another one of his smokes. After a moment, he spits out a strand of tobacco, and points the lit end toward Jon. "The governor sent one of his men to meet with my boss, and despite *your* harsh opinion of me, Andon steered him my way."

Nursing his beer, Jon deliberates and stumbles for words. "I get it, Brent. I do. As an expatriate, you're his best chance. Well, it's plausible, I guess, but you do remember I'm nothing but a smalltime businessman. I imagine the governor would be better served through diplomatic channels."

"I'm just spit-balling here, man. I don't know if you can help, but it's at least worth a try."

When Brent retrieves his bag, Jon says, "Before you go running off, give me some time with this."

Brent reaches over the table, grabs another cigarette, and lights it with the stub of his old one before he settles back down.

Jon stares into the distance. "Come to think of it——," he stops himself short. "I might have someone in mind who could at least point me in the right direction."

Brent leans forward. "Yeah? Who?"

Jon shakes his head, "Oh no, I'm not going there."

"What? You're going to leave me in the dark on this?"

"No. I'm quite serious. Try to understand, it won't happen overnight, but I promise when I get back to Maui, I *will* make inquiries."

"When? A week? A month?"

"You remember I have a business to run? I know patience isn't your strong suit, but in order to make this work, you'll need to abide by *my* timetable. I don't want to set this whole thing up only to discover you've sourced it elsewhere."

"What should I tell the governor?"

"I don't care," he snorts. "Tell him whatever you want. What I can promise you is when I know, you will too."

"Why the sudden buy-in?"

"I prefer to keep the reasons to myself."

Brent hesitates when he stands, "By the way, you haven't mentioned that little daughter of yours. What's Keira doing with herself?"

He smiles. "I guess it has been some time. She's all grown up, and ..." Jon's attention drifts, his mind takes him in an unexpected direction.

Brent taps the table with his knuckle. "Where'd you go?"

"Don't interrupt me," Jon scolds. He mutters to himself, "I should try to get her involved ... admittedly there's a few obstacles to overcome, but——"

"You mean you'd be able to bring her here? To the islands?" With renewed enthusiasm, he says, "If *she's* your reason … I'd love to see her again."

Jon glares at Brent coldly and finishes his beer. "There's no guarantee. She's pretty much kept to herself since she left for college."

"You *do* know you have only yourself to blame——"

"Don't push your luck, boy. You tell your friend the governor what we talked about and I'll be in touch. Now, beat it. I need some time to myself."

Brent takes a last pull before he stuffs the cigarette down the newly emptied bottle. He grabs his bag, gives him a mock salute, and walks off.

Jon orders another beer and reaches for his smokes, only to discover the pack is empty. He wads it up, tosses it in the ashtray, and loses himself in thought again. *Hopefully, she'll return my call.*

Brent stops by the receptionist's desk in the hotel lobby. Anaria's dressed in a colorful tropical shift and wears her long dark hair pulled back into a tight bun. She consistently tries to present herself as pleasant and co-operative almost to a fault, but tonight her ever-present smile masks her resentment. "What now, *Mister* Brent?"

"Call me a cab."

She stares at him without moving.

"Please," he adds snidely.

She glances at the wall clock. "What you need cab for this late at night?"

He retrieves a long knife from his back pocket, opens the blade, and deftly twirls it between his thumb and fingers.

"It's not that late, and I'm in a hurry. Please make the call."

She's unsettled by the swiftly moving blade.

"Cabbies tell me they no longer want business with you no more."

"And did they say why?"

"They do," she confidently nods. "Kasian say you *never* tip and you run out on your fare last time. Made him go to Mr. Andon for his money. Both not happy about it."

"And didn't he dock my paycheck … besides I was drunk. I haven't over-indulged tonight."

Fixated on his blade, she barks, "Put that thing away! It

scares me!"

After he complies, she gives him a broad, toothy smile and beckons him with her finger. When he succumbs to the lure, she leans over the counter, sneaks a quick but emphatic sniff and pushes herself back.

He wonders what's on her mind. "What're you doin'?"

"I think maybe you not true with me, but I'll call them for you this one more time. You behave yourself," she wags her finger, "or you get me in trouble."

"Whatever. Better if you not tell them who the call's for." Brent retrieves his knife, takes a seat, and resumes his twirling.

Anaria is writing herself a note when the cab pulls up. The driver's less than happy at the sight of Brent in the lobby.

"It's a lovely night out, isn't it, Kasian?" she coos.

He glares at Brent, shakes it off, and turns his attentions to her. He tempers his irritation. "Don't you ply your charms on me, sister. I've told you we don't want his business."

"Good for you, I think, but *I* must do what the customer say."

Without looking, Kasian waves his hand toward the lobby. "Since when has *he* become 'customer'?"

She taps her teeth lightly a couple of times with the pen and aims it toward Brent climbing into the back seat. "Looks to me like right now *he* is."

Kasian does a double-take, points at her accusingly, then gives her a halfway flirtatious glance as he takes his leave. By the time he turns to face the car his countenance has soured.

The cab is a twenty-year-old sun-faded brown Chevy station wagon which has gone through a couple of owners before Kasian. Though dated, the car is spacious and comfortable, with a working air conditioner as it's best feature. It's hard on gas and burns an excessive amount of oil, but 'in season' when tourism is at its heaviest, the increased frequency of fares more than makes up for the added expenses.

When Kasian slides behind the wheel, Brent adds to his aggravation. "The governor's home … and make it fast."

Kasian adjusts the rearview mirror to make eye contact. "Don't you pull none of your monkey business on me tonight."

"Can we get started. I'm running late."

Kasian slams the car into gear, and pauses to calm himself before he releases the brake. It's a slow-paced drive on the straight gravel lane that leads through the hotel grounds to the main road. The poor conditions of public roads, especially at night, require drivers use extra precaution. The added transit time adds to Brent's agitation. He's concerned about the governor's reaction to the late hour.

In anticipation of his visit, the gate to the circular driveway is left open. When the cab comes to a stop, a slightly-built man dressed in island-casual opens his door. "Glad you could spare the time, Edelson."

Brent climbs out. "Yeah, well, hello to you too, Tino." He points his thumb back to the cab. "Cover the fare for me. Thanks."

Without so much as looking back, he walks toward the house. Tino scowls, but reaches into his pocket and pulls out a roll of bills to pay the cabbie.

"Mr. Brent believes he 'Mr. Big Shot' now with the governor," remarks Kasian.

Tino follows Brent's movement with his eyes while he blindly hands the cabbie his money. "Take your fare, and never you mind about what goes on inside this house."

He counts the cash, no tip. "Must be contagious."

He spits out the window, guns the gas pedal and screeches hot rubber as he makes the severe left turn into the dark.

At the entry to the manse, an intimidating individual opens the oversized front door for the arrival. Brent has to look up to make eye contact. "Thanks, BG. The governor still awake?"

"He's expecting you."

"What kinda mood's he in?"

BG thumbs the way inside. "Kinda late for a lotta chit-chat. Don't keep the man waiting any longer than you already have."

Before Brent can add to the discussion, Tino prods him in the small of his back. "Quit stalling, and get in there. The governor's an impatient man."

Brent mutters, "He's not the only one."

Tino follows him closely, but stays by the door.

Brent's forced to wait. It's a ritual the governor likes to put visitors through to inflate his own importance. The circular great room has a high peaked ceiling of exotic wood which radiates from its apex. Thick, tinted windows reach from the tiled floors to the ceiling.

He spends the time viewing the recovered artifacts confiscated from divers who liberated them from the wrecks and are now displayed in well-lit custom-built glass cabinets. Brent recognizes the recently cleaned ship's bell the governor tasked him to personally salvage from a deep-water wreck. He believes it was a test for his prospective employment.

While Brent continues to nose around, the governor monitors him through the security feeds to his office. When he finally enters the room, he tersely admonishes his visitor. "We expected you earlier, young man." Before Brent can respond, he adds, "I hope the wait's been worth it."

From his perfectly coifed hair, to his brightly polished shoes, the governor presents the image of a well-heeled politician. Tino assumes a place to his right.

Brent's intrigued by the relationship these two men have, but puts his thoughts aside for the moment. "I found our way in."

The governor folds his arms. "Continue."

After Brent recounts the highlights of his conversation with Jon, the governor nods. "You've done well. But don't blow this by running your mouth … not to anyone. We have others we answer to, and it's important they be kept happy."

"Whadya mean by 'others'?"

"The Consortium," Tino interjects.

Brent's confused; the governor's annoyed.

"Try to picture a sort of 'brotherhood'——"

When Tino tries to involve himself in the greater discussion, the governor shoots him a disapproving gaze. "Is this your discussion, or mine? Remember your place." Tino backs away.

Brent remains resolutely mute and listens with his usual degree of skepticism.

"It's important you realize, if you play this right, it could make you a rich man."

"To be sure we're on the same page, he warned me it could take a while."

"Yes, yes, I understand. The wheels of big government turn ever so slowly. Go home now, and remember to contact me if and when you hear from this 'well-connected' friend of yours."

The governor glances at his subordinate. "Tino's anxious to go home too," he flicks his hand toward the door, "so you both scurry along now."

Brent angrily pushes open the front door with Tino close behind. He turns toward him. "What was that all about?"

Tino ignores the question. "Good night, Edelson."

"How about calling me a cab."

Tino shakes his head. "They won't be back out here this evening."

"Why not?"

Tino faces him directly. "You possess an uncanny gift of annoying people."

Brent points toward the garage. "How 'bout a lift in your car then?"

Tino snorts, "I'm *also* one of those people you shouldn't annoy. Yet, you do." He gestures toward the darkened skies with a smile as expansive as his outstretched arms. "Besides, it's such a lovely night for a brisk walk. It should only take you what? A couple of hours?"

"Gimme a break will you. You could get me there in

twenty minutes easily. It's right on the your way." Tino scoffs at the suggestion.

Disgusted, Brent clumsily unzips and reaches into his gym bag.

Tino worries, *This can't be good.*

He pulls out the jar of oily water and quickly lobs it toward Tino who bobbles the container before he secures it.

"What's this?"

"A reminder of why you brought me in on this."

Brent starts to walk away when Tino yells, "The next time you come out here, Edelson, you make sure you have your own fare."

The governor views their exchange through the window, and shakes his head when Brent flips-off Tino.

Back inside, he holds up the jar. "You still believe he's the right man for this?"

The governor eyes Brent as he ambles down the road and out of sight. "I understand your skepticism, but for now, he's our connection to the dive operation and," pointing to Tino, he adds, "you need to fix this. As far as he's concerned, we're all on the same side."

Tino timidly interjects, "You remember we do have another working on the inside who, in my mind, will be much more compliant."

"I *know* that," he snaps. "But he's a boy and doesn't have the stateside connections Brent does."

After a pause, the governor turns his gaze to BG, "Going forward, I expect you two to maintain a close eye on him and remember to keep me informed."

Half an hour later, Tino spots Brent a couple of miles from the governor's. He slows his late model Toyota and pulls alongside. "Hop in."

After Brent buckles in, Tino offers him a smoke which he gratefully accepts. He hands him two. "Light one up for me. I have to keep a close eye on these roads after dark."

As he lights them together and hands Tino his, then asks, "Tell me more about this 'Brotherhood' you mentioned."

31

February 1995
Baltimore, Maryland

After the unexpected call from Jon Hall, agency Director Jay Johnson replaces the phone in its cradle. *I haven't been called, 'J.J.' in some time, and now this. It's been several years since we last spoke, yet it feels like only a few days. Interesting how friendship has the ability to melt away time and distance.*

Seated directly across from him, new-hire Eric Woods constantly shifts around in the well-worn leather chair to familiarize himself with the surroundings. Older than most recruits, he nevertheless makes an impression: tall, articulate and equipped with the self-discipline common to those with an extensive background in law enforcement.

Director Johnson retrieves a metal case from his jacket pocket, and discretely slips a tablet under his tongue. After a couple of minutes he takes a gulp of his cold coffee and grimaces.

Eric attempts to break the ice. "Headache, sir?"

He lightly taps on his sternum and dismissively answers, "A slight case of indigestion." He gestures toward the phone. "I apologize for the time, but it's been awhile since we last spoke. He's an old and dear friend."

He abruptly grabs his cane that's propped against the wall in back of him, uses it to stand, then makes his way to the adjacent side of the spacious office. He focuses on several maps mounted high up, one atop the other similar to rolled-up window shades. Using the crook of his cane to latch onto the uppermost chrome handle, he pulls down an oversized map for the Central Pacific region. He works his finger over the area until he locates the spot he's seeking, and glances back at the new man. Eric picks up on the cue and immediately joins him.

Pointing to a speck in the blue expanse, Johnson asks, "Have you ever heard of Micronesia?"

"Yes sir, in several books about the Pacific Theater during World War Two."

"A war buff, huh?"

"A bit."

"You're going to have a chance to do more than read about it," he says, then discusses the substance of the call. "We have a new assignment and I have a lot of arrangements to make before your departure."

Eric inquisitively raises his eyebrows, "My departure, sir?"

"Yes. Your assigned team is on holiday in Canada. I believe you've already met Agent Gerhart?"

"I have, during the interview process."

"Good, because I need them back here right away." He retrieves a contact sheet from the center drawer. "Looks like you have a long drive ahead of you." He hands the information to Eric. "Go get our boys." His chair groans as he swivels it around to check the clock behind him. "I expect you back here by daybreak Monday."

Eric checks the time, *it's after three——rush hour*. He hasn't learned agency protocol yet, but is about to get his first lesson. "You realize I'll be on the road all night."

The director peers up from his paperwork and says matter-of-factly, "Then I suggest you get started." He retrieves his personal directory and turns his attention back to the calendar.

"See you in a couple of days, sir." When the director doesn't lift his head or respond, he leaves.

After the door closes, Johnson reaches for the photo propped alongside the model aircraft which usually collects dust on his desk. He stares at the crew posed in front of the P-3 Orion they manned while hunting Russian submarines thirty some-odd years ago. Through his heavy, black horn-rimmed glasses he glances at his reflection in the picture frame and compares it to the one in the photograph. In those days he wasn't encumbered with a cane, glasses, or a waistline he self-consciously hides with loose-fitting clothes. His shock of blond hair is now pure white and he's grown a full beard which he keeps well-trimmed. He focuses on the image of Jon, and says aloud, "I hope you can handle what you've gotten yourself into old friend."

New to the agency, it takes Eric longer than usual to sign out an unmarked van from the government motor pool. Before he's handed the keys, there's a pile of paperwork to complete accompanied by a lecture recited by rote from the desk clerk. By the time he turns in the forms, it's half past five on a Friday afternoon.

Eric pulls into the first convenience store he runs across to load up on high-energy snacks, the tallest black coffee they offer, and a good road map. He pours over the map in the front seat, and traces a direct route to the Georgian Bay, a hundred and eighty-five miles northwest of Toronto. The bypass around Baltimore will add some distance to his trip, and he'll need to clear customs in Buffalo. With the probability of adverse weather in Canada this time of year, he's facing at least twelve hours of road time one-way.

After he's negotiates the Buffalo/Niagara Falls metro-area traffic, it's a straight shot into Hamilton at the westernmost point of Lake Ontario. From there he follows Canada's Route Six North to the tip of the Bruce Peninsula. The road is long, straight, and bordered by flat, white fields shrouded in darkness. His only visuals are the banks of plowed snow and the reflective markers which divide the two lanes. On the plus side, wintertime traffic this late at night is nonexistent. When scanning the FM radio dial he runs across an oldies rock station out of Buffalo to keep him company on the lonely drive.

Tobermory, Canada

The event planners selected a location fifty yards from the heavily pined shoreline. To create a point of entry for the divers, a motor-driven auger, equipped with an eight inch diameter bit, requires two men to drill three holes through the thickset ice in a triangular pattern spaced three feet apart. A chainsaw with a four-foot guide bar connect the holes. As soon as the heavy block is pushed beneath the new opening, the water rises level with the ice. As the point of entry is the only way in or out, fifty foot straight radials are shoveled in the foot-deep snow to provide a visual guide for the divers' return in case they lose their orientation. From below, the pattern resembles the spokes of a child's bike converging at the exit.

At the northern limit of the Niagara Escarpment, the limestone limnology and still waters ensure a minimum of siltation. Despite the added layer of snow, there is plenty of light below, and lateral visibility is exceptional. Their destination is a two hundred and fifteen foot freighter, victimized by the region's unpredictable weather which foundered her on shallow rocky shoals. Over the next couple of seasons the derelict was completely stripped, scoured of fuel and potential snags, and towed to deeper water where she settled with a thirty degree list to starboard. It's fifty feet down to the wreck's stern——its closest point to the diver's entry.

Paul Gerhart was invited by his old friend and fellow agent, Timothy Dax, who has made dozens of dives in these conditions. Even though this is Paul's first time under ice, he's a seasoned pro with over a thousand hours below, and never one to turn down an opportunity to get wet.

The bulk of his drysuit, the extra weight it requires, and the attached tether lines, which restrict them from penetrating the wreck, serve only as a distraction. There is much the two can explore outside.

Communicating with the surface is accomplished through a series of pre-arranged tugs on the line held by a tender at the entry where a fully-geared diver stands by if they run into trouble. Safety is everyone's top priority.

Thirty minutes after submerging, Paul and Dax get the dreaded hard tug, the signal from the surface it's time to start their way back. They acknowledge with a double-pull on their respective lines, and begin their turnabout. As the divers approach the exit, tenders take up the slack in the lines and carefully coil them separately.

The only open gas station in the village is Eric's first stop where he has the van topped off. As soon as he exits the vehicle, the frigid breeze informs him he's underdressed for the conditions. The station has a variety store where he buys three thermal containers of hot coffee, a heavy knit cap, and is given easy directions to the dive site from the clerk.

Close to thirty warmly dressed locals stand on the solid surface——family, friends, divers back from their excursion, the next team in line, tenders, and the curious——all to view the spectacle and help where needed.

Eric arrives at the gathering near the time Paul and Dax surface.

Paul pulls back the hood of his drysuit, and recognizes him among the crowd. "J.J.?" he asks. His exhalations condense into a plume of icy mist which rapidly dissipates in the breeze.

"If you're referring to the director," Eric nods emphatically, more from the cold than Paul's question.

Once on solid footing, Paul says, "I heard he was bringing you on staff. Welcome aboard. You'll have to come out with us next time."

Eric scoffs at the suggestion, "Uh-huh."

After Paul and Dax hand off their roped harnesses to the next pair of divers, they carefully drop the heavy weight belts, and receive help with their compensator vests and scuba rigs.

Paul approaches the new man with an extended hand. "Seriously. It's unbelievably peaceful down there and the water temps are a balmy thirty-two degrees."

Eric coughs as he swats his arms around his chest in a vain attempt to keep warm. The slight breeze has pushed the wind-chill way past the thermometer reading of twenty degrees below zero Celsius. He's wearing a lighter coat than needed, rapidly losing body heat, and anxious to seek shelter from the weather. "Well, it's neither balmy nor thirty-two out here. So if the two of you would kindly hurry it up I have this nice *warm* vehicle with even *warmer* liquid inside, set to take us back." Nearby observers smile at Eric's predicament before they turn their attentions back to the team's prep for the next pair of divers.

After Paul efficiently exchanges his drysuit and heavy liner for layers of warm, dry clothing, he invites Dax to join them.

"You haven't had a chance to meet my friend, Timothy Dax."

"Nice to meet you, Tim."

Dax stands four inches shorter than Eric and tries to makes up for it with a hard grip. "Likewise, but please call me Dax," he says in a strikingly high-pitched voice.

"Sorry, I should have mentioned it straight out," Paul adds. "He prefers we use his last name, but we don't hold it against him."

"So, the director has managed to transfer you here already?" Dax jests.

"Fortunately, only for the day."

Disappointed they have to break away from the group sooner than planned, the men express their regrets to the sponsor, help load their rental equipment into the bus they rode from Buffalo, and climb into Eric's van for the return.

During the drive down the peninsula, Eric throws out for discussion, "I don't get the attraction. You're immersed in crippling cold water with no light, and limited visibility."

Fighting fatigue from the day's physical demands, Paul takes a draw from the thermos of hot coffee. "This hits the spot, Eric, thank you." After another gulp, he says, "Let's start by setting the record straight. Almost every word out of your mouth is wrong."

Eric's quick to take up the challenge. "Okay. Start with the visibility."

From the back seat, Dax answers sleepily, "Close to a hundred feet."

"Who're you trying to kid?" Eric scoffs.

"He's not exaggerating," says Paul.

"You're under three feet of ice covered by another foot of snow. How much light penetration could you possibly have?"

"Try to picture yourself suspended in a vast cathedral of crystal-clear green water," answers Paul. "Before us awaits a wreck and the whole place to ourselves."

"Impressive," he responds sarcastically.

"You're right about one thing, though," concedes Dax, "it is cold." The three men chuckle. "This place is special," he continues. "Enthusiasts from all around North America make the trek to Tobermory to enjoy what the area has to offer."

"In this deep freeze?"

"Well, not so much this time of year," Dax concedes. "But this is where Lake Huron feeds into the Georgian Bay. Numerous unpredictable storms have left a myriad of shipwrecks in their wake, which offer the best cold-water wreck diving anywhere."

"It's ironic you raise the topic," responds Eric. "The director has an assignment for us, and from the way he puts it, we'll have our fill of wreck diving, but in conditions where the land is more green than white, the waters are blue, not green, and do *not* require a chainsaw to enter."

Paul glances at him, "I haven't heard about any new assignment. Do you know when it came in?"

"J.J. took the call while I was in his office, mid-afternoon yesterday. He mentioned Micronesia, but gave me no other specifics."

"Try not to refer to him as 'J.J.' anywhere within earshot," warns Dax. "You may wind up here … permanently."

"I'm surprised he'd divulge …" Paul catches himself. "Let me rephrase that. He's usually pretty tight-lipped … especially with new people."

"Can one of you tell me … does J.J., excuse me … *the director* have a heart condition?"

Dax leans forward. "Why do you ask?"

"When he got off the phone, he tucked a tablet under his tongue, and waited a few minutes before taking a drink of coffee. It goes with rinsing out the bitter taste of nitroglycerine."

"I guess we can add 'observant' to your already significant list of qualifications," adds Paul.

"Years back, my dad dealt with a bad heart until it eventually took him out."

"Sorry," the two respond in unison.

He responds quietly, "It was a long time ago."

To avoid the crush of traffic and crowds at Niagara Falls, they continue south to clear customs and cross into the States at Buffalo. Once Dax takes his shift behind the wheel, Eric sprawls out in the back.

"Thanks for the invite, buddy," says Paul.

"I figured you'd have a good time. With your experience, I'm still surprised you ended up in this line of work. Wouldn't the underwater world have suited you better?"

"I did check into some prospects years back. Except for some commercial work, there's no serious coin in it."

"What, you're in *this* racket for the money?"

Paul concedes the point. "I've talked to a few oil rig vets who told me the extended repetitive deep dives wrecked them physically and the pay was not what they'd hoped for, especially considering the expertise they needed to develop, the risks they take in a hostile environment, and the beat-down their bodies go through."

Excited about Eric's news, Dax changes the subject. "Can you believe Micronesia? How lucky can we get! You ever been there?"

"Kind of a hot-button topic with the wanderlust in me, especially since I'm no longer tied down."

Dax immediately regrets reminding Paul about his new reality since Hannah left him. She was Dutch, blonde, beautiful and self-obsessed——alas, a professional casualty.

Paul ponders the question before he responds. "Years back I visited the island of Yap for training. Nothing recreational though. You have a favorite go-to?"

"My only proviso is to walk off my back porch and get wet."

"You can do that now."

"Maybe when my lawn sprinkler's on."

After an extended silence, Dax asks, "Any idea how many dives Eric has under his belt?"

"I'm certified, with over fifty hours," he interjects as he sits up and yawns, "But not all of us can lay claim to being trained by Navy Seals."

"True, but don't discount your time in the Special Forces, though I imagine not as much in the water."

"But, water is where we're headed."

"Don't worry," says Dax. "When we're below, we'll keep an eye on you … wherever we end up."

Baltimore, Maryland

The director invites the three men to make themselves comfortable.

"Where to this time, boss?" asks Dax.

J.J. makes his way to the map he'd pulled down earlier. "Right there." He taps his finger on the chart, "Micronesia."

"Puh-leeze tell me we're headed to Palau," interjects Dax.

J.J. turns to him. "Why? What's so special about Palau?"

"It has the reputation as a showcase of diving's best. It offers the most diverse variety of diving anywhere I've read about," when he turns towards Eric, he adds, "without the need for the chainsaw you mentioned."

The director dismissively shakes his head. "You'd better get *that* notion out of your mind right now. This isn't a vacation. You're tasked with validating the need for a substantial investment requested from our government."

Paul walks over to the map. "Micronesia's a pretty big place. Where to, exactly?"

J.J. pulls down the glasses from atop his forehead, examines it closer, and relocates the dot hidden in the boundless blue of Oceania, then tracks over to the corresponding inset. "Right here ... the Chuuk Island group." He examines the map further. "It's about 3,500 miles west-southwest of Honolulu."

Paul sighs. "Lotta flight time ahead of us."

The director agrees. "We'll send you to Guam, with a couple of stops along the way to pick up passengers."

"Other agents?" asks Paul.

"Not this time. Our main contact is an old friend of mine." He returns to his desk and passes around the framed photo of his old flight crew. "He's the one to my left."

After Paul and Dax take a quick scan, they hand it to Eric who stares at the picture for a few minutes. "Which one is you?"

The other two try to suppress their laughter. The director smiles along with them. "Is that some kind of dig at my girth?"

Flustered, Eric responds, "Oh no, sir. This picture is … well … *old*."

The laughter intensifies as the director snatches the frame out of his hands. "This isn't exactly a tintype."

"Welcome aboard, Eric," says Dax, slapping him on the back. "Better start shopping for your cold-weather gear."

Amused, the director points out his friend. "His name's Jon Hall. He lives on Maui."

Paul says, "You mentioned making 'a couple of stops'."

"Jon requested his daughter accompany you," which elicits groans from both Paul and Dax.

"Now hold on. He's not only a good friend, but convinced me she has expertise germane to this assignment. Your first stop is Los Angeles——Long Beach to be exact."

He retrieves a set of packets from his desk and gives them to the agents.

"Familiarize yourselves en route. Your bags and equipment are already on the plane. Supplemental equipment should make it to the islands within a day or so of your arrival. We'll message you an ETA. Wheels up in an hour gentlemen."

When everyone stands, the director taps Paul's shoulder. "Please stay seated for a few minutes."

"That can't be good," mutters Dax as he coaxes Eric into the stairwell.

Eric secures the door for privacy. "Have you had much experience diving on wrecks?"

"Any and every chance I could get. It's why Paul and I went to Tobermory, and for the opportunity to go for it under the ice. You?"

"'Fraid not. Our instructor mentioned it requires specialty training. Regretfully I didn't take the time or the opportunity. What should I expect?"

"I'm sure we'll have daily briefs, and they won't be limited to the three of us."

"Dax sounds pretty excited about all of this," says Paul.

"I gathered as much. You have a rigorous assignment ahead of you. Your cover is spelled out, but the packet isn't comprehensive."

"It rarely is," Paul comments.

"All kidding aside, your team's role is part of a much larger operation."

"How so?"

"This reaches far beyond the islands of Chuuk. It stretches throughout the Micronesian chain and into the Marianas. Though you'll have your hands full, I'll need you to serve as my eyes and ears out there. Keep in touch."

"Will do. By the way, where did you source the intel on this?"

"From Jon Hall. He'll be onsite, and with the expectation *he's* in charge." Paul eyes him curiously. "Don't worry about him. He insists his daughter——"

"You seriously expect us to babysit——"

The director holds up his hand to interrupt. "It's a legitimate request. Her education and background dovetail nicely with the assignment, and will provide you with a credible cover."

"How old is she?"

He taxes his memory to come up with an answer. "A bit younger than you ... gotta be late twenties by now. Sadly there's a history of estrangement, and he warned me she can be 'a handful'. Your first job will be to convince her to accompany you and hopefully cooperate."

"And if she refuses?"

"I'll leave that up to *your* area of expertise. Oh, and the new man——"

"Eric?"

"Yes, Woods. He has a lot of experience, but——"

Paul interrupts, "I already went through his file——impressive background——Army Rangers, detective, and top cop in Denver before we got him."

"We are fortunate, but I didn't find any information about his diving background."

"We asked him on our way back from Tobermory. He has basic certification, with a minimal number of hours under his belt."

"You think he'll work out?"

"We'll keep an eye on him."

The director stands to signal their meeting's over.

After the aircraft reaches cruise altitude, Paul emerges from the cockpit and holds up his packet. "Time to hit the books, fellas." Included in their mission brief are archival records of Truk's history which pre-date World War II, and dossiers with photographs.

As Paul scans the packet of prints, Dax reaches over his shoulder and taps one of them, the daughter.

"She is pretty, but J.J. warned me she's also high-strung."

"What do you think he meant?" asks Dax.

"Not sure, but …," he pauses for another glimpse of her photograph, "I always enjoy a good challenge."

45

Long Beach, California

The research institute where Keira Lynn Hall works is tucked into a modest industrial development a few blocks from the Long Beach Airport. The spacious atrium reflects the funding generated since its inception——a facade of smoked-glass, European tile, imported wood paneling, contemporary furnishings, and a stylish receptionist named Evangeline.

The agency recruited Keira straight out of Stanford University. She holds advanced degrees in geophysics and oceanography with specialized studies in marine biology, environmental disasters and methods to mitigate their impact.

In her spacious second floor office, she analyzes data from the loss of a supertanker in waters over two hundred and twenty feet deep off the coast of Scotland. She's well-connected professionally and draws upon several years of experience for this type of assignment.

The wall facing her desk displays two sizable bathymetry maps of underwater topography flagged with pins which highlight areas of concern. Stacked atop her desk, over-stuffed binders are filled with accident reports, messages from the South Queensferry Coastguard, transcripts of radio traffic, inquiries from the National Counter Terrorism Office, and analyses from the Scottish Environmental Protection Agency. A clipboard sits under her phone with a list of agencies, both government and civilian, and key personnel associated with the disaster. The adjacent table holds a collection of blueprints sent from the South Korean shipyard that built the supertanker. The ship's photograph with the twenty-eight crew members' names who lost their lives in the disaster serves as a daily reminder of the real loss. Two men survived.

Keira tosses her leather bag under the desk, drapes her jacket over the back of her chair, and starts to sift through the overnight message traffic. She mindlessly retrieves a new bag of black jelly beans to nosh on while reviewing her planner. She's lived on the phone for the better part of the last four days in attempts to draw on the goodwill and cooperation of everyone affected by the tragedy. The eight-hour time difference between the two countries means she either has to come in way too early or stay very late. Today's agenda necessitates her four a.m. arrival.

She's on her third coffee when the clear acrylic intercom button on her telephone lights up. Her close friend, Angie, usually calls about this time for lunch. Keira picks up the receiver but hesitates several seconds before she connects the line. She takes a deep breath, and pushes the button. "I can't right now, sweetie, I'm up to——"

"Oh, hello to you too, snookums." It's her boss, Zack. She's about to hang up in disgust when he adds, "I need you down here right away."

She lets out a frustrated groan.

"This isn't a request, Keira. Don't keep us waiting."

"Us?" But he's already hung up.

Keira slips into her shoes, and neatly tucks her stylish linen blouse into her sleek black pants. She tosses the balance of candy into the desk drawer, retrieves the peach lip gloss out of her bag and calmly refreshes her look. In a fit of pique, she kicks her wastebasket halfway across her office. Wadded balls of paper litter the flight path.

By the time the elevator reaches the ground floor, she wants answers and approaches Evangeline, whose phone Zack used to summon her.

"Any idea what going on?"

Angie tilts her head toward the four men standing in the alcove at the atrium's far end. Zack glares at Keira with a would-you-hurry-it-up look. "What's this about?"

"I'm not sure," Angie whispers to her, "but after he got off the phone, he seemed ticked-off."

"Thanks for the warning." She lets out a huff and walks toward the conclave. Her heels echo loudly on the tile floor.

The men's conversation grinds to a complete halt when she approaches. Her photograph did little to prepare them. She is stunning——tall, graceful, and angular, with wavy auburn hair that flows below her shoulders. She's a natural beauty with full lips, a lightly freckled face and piercing green eyes that express her discontent.

"Keira, I'd like you to meet Agents——"

"What's going on, Zack? You're aware of what I'm involved with right now." She quickly scans the men in his company. "Am I in some kind of trouble here?"

The visitors laugh. She's unamused.

The tallest steps forward. "My name's Paul Gerhart."

She shakes his hand limply, avoids eye contact, and keeps her attention on her boss, with hopes he'll get her out of the trap she senses about to be sprung.

Zack announces, "Let's go to the conference room where we can fill you in."

Her puzzlement matches her reticence to follow. "Fill me in on what? Why can't we discuss this here and now?"

"Keira, please!"

Though Zack appreciates her contributions to the institute's success and prestige, he's constantly forced to balance them against the stress of confronting her volatile temper.

They take the elevator to the third floor meeting room lined with wall-to-wall glass overlooking a manicured terrace. The agents arrive first and are seated by the time Zack and Keira enter. He lays his folder on the table before he sits; she remains standing.

It irritates him he has to lean back to address her. "These gentlemen are with the government and have requested your assistance by name."

She has buried herself in her work since joining the institute and the Scotland incident weighs heavily on her.

"Nowhere in my job description does it mention I'm available for contract or field work." She turns to Paul. "I've never met you people, so how did you get *my* name?"

"Give us a chance to explain," says Paul.

Keira stares back quizzically.

"The Governor of the Chuuk Island group has requested help from our government."

"What does that have to do with me?"

"Your father requested you accompany us."

"Jonathan?"

Paul nods.

"Huh,' she muses. "He often talked about going there when I was younger … wanted to uproot us and move, but mother put a stop to it. She had built a successful career as an attorney and did'nt want to pull us out of school to trade one paradise for another, less lucrative one." She stares at him with curiosity. "What's your association with *him*?"

"Your father's connections with certain individuals both on Chuuk and within our government have made him an integral link to this assignment."

"You realize we haven't spoken in years."

In fact, except for her mother's funeral, she hasn't returned to the islands since she left for school. Her father blamed her for her brother's death, which left her bitterly resentful. *Here I've built a career where I feel secure, comfortable, and I thought free from Jonathan.*

"This is absurd, Zack. Don't I have any say in this? What if I refuse?"

Paul matter-of-factly points out, "Much of your research, Miss Hall, as well as that of the institute's, is funded through government-sponsored grants, which *will* dry up if you don't fully cooperate."

"That's coercion!"

"Call it what you will, but our instructions start with bringing you with us."

She wants Zack to cover for her. *You better help me out of this you little weasel.*

He squirms in his seat. "Keira, this is only a temporary assignment. The wreck in Scotland isn't going anywhere. Take advantage of the opportunity to get out of your office."

She is not appeased.

"You've done an excellent job laying the groundwork for this institute's participation. I can easily slide Terry Venier into your slot until you return. He's more than capable——"

She snorts derisively. "Don't be surprised when he doesn't——"

Zack quickly stands. "Keira. We've got this!"

Now toe-to-toe with him, she whines, "I have no time——"

He clears his throat to summon a rarely used authoritative voice, "Like it or not … you do now."

Her eyes track to Paul. "When does this so-called 'assignment' of yours start?"

"Now," he states firmly. *J.J. sure hit that nail on the head. I'm already sorry we made the stop.* "Get what you need from your office. We have a car outside to take you to your apartment. Our flight leaves as soon as you're ready."

"A flight to where?"

"Maui."

"I presume to pick up Jonathan."

Paul stands and checks his watch. "Gentlemen, Miss Hall, we have a plane waiting."

As Keira watches the runway drop beneath her, she remembers her last trip to Maui to bury her mother. It would not have been her first choice to attend, but she knew her mother would not have approved; she needed the closure.

As soon as they're cleared to walk about, Paul heads

directly into the cockpit to confer with the flight crew. Keira hasn't moved from her seat. She continues to stare out the window lost in her memories until Paul interrupts her by sitting in the adjacent seat. She scans the rest of the cabin. "Couldn't find another place to sit?"

"I'm sorry for the immediacy of all this, but we're up against——"

"You mean the kidnapping?"

"You know, you could make this a lot easier——"

"Look, I don't care what you're 'up against', and I don't give a damn about making this easier on you, Jonathan, or this assignment. Who do you think you are dragging me away from my life?"

"I am sorry for *your* inconvenience, but I have my orders!"

He's had enough with the back-and-forth. When Dax gestures toward the cockpit, he quickly and gratefully responds. Paul closes the door behind him. "What?"

"Thought you could use the break."

Paul appreciatively pats his friend on the shoulder before Dax slips back to the cabin.

Keira catches a glimpse of Eric staring at her before he quickly turns away. His jet black hair has streaks of gray; he's older than the others, but projects some uneasiness.

When Paul steps back out, she sizes him up. *Rugged good looks, mid-thirties, well-defined jawline, and those disarmingly deep blue eyes. He obviously keeps himself in shape, but so do the other two. Must come with the job. Dax is different though. He's cute—curly blond hair, short, powerful, but his voice. I guess it's why he keeps to himself.*

Paul walks over to her, but stays standing. "We'll land at the Kapalua Airport on the west side of Maui——"

"Yeah, yeah, Jonathan's place overlooks Honokahua Bay … what *don't* you know about us?"

He takes a deep breath before he sits back down. "It may surprise you——"

"Which means?"

"Your father lives alone in a house way above his pay

grade. Since your mother passed eight years ago, other than her funeral, you haven't returned to Maui for over ten years."

"My father and I haven't spoken since."

"It isn't difficult to do the math when you've avoided any return to this slice of paradise."

"Paradise," she scoffs. "I don't get why you need *me* on this."

Paul shrugs. "To tell you the truth, neither do I. I'd as soon leave you as not, but your father insisted."

"You admit you don't know everything. At least it's a start."

Paul holds up both hands as if to throw in the towel. "Can I get you some water? Soda? Peanuts? … Perhaps a parachute?"

She tries to suppress a grin. "Thanks, but I'd like to catch a nap."

"Suit yourself." He returns to his original seat.

Eric's rereading the dossier when Paul joins him.

Nodding in the direction of Keira's seat, Eric says, "You've obviously got your hands full."

"I'd rather change the subject."

Eric sets down his packet. "What can I help you with?"

"How will you handle these separations? We'll be away at a minimum of two weeks, and our time estimates are usually 'fluid'."

"My wife and I talked this through before I applied for the position. My only concern centers around our children."

"How so?"

"They're getting older and she feels they need me around more."

"What's the age spread?"

"Fourteen to … well, we recently celebrated our youngest's fifth."

"Are you worried they might become a distraction?"

"Time will tell. How does your family handle it?"

When Paul doesn't answer, Eric picks up his packet. "Guess it's time to hit the books."

Paul returns to his seat, and mindlessly leafs through the documents. *What could I have done differently with Hannah.*

After a turbulent approach through a low ceiling of rain, the aircraft touches down five hours after liftoff. When the ladder moves to the cabin door, Jon, who's parked on the tarmac, exits his car. He tosses the stub of his cigarette onto the wet asphalt where it quickly sizzles out.

Keira follows Paul down the ramp. Jon shakes his hand, and steps in front of his daughter. "Hello, Keira Lynn."

He leans in to kiss her, but she turns her head aside and steps back.

"Want to fill me in?"

"We'll talk when we get home."

"Home," she mutters as she sidesteps him to retrieve her luggage.

The house hasn't changed since she last visited——thirty-nine hundred square feet, professionally decorated and immaculate throughout, with glass reaching from the floor to the vaulted ceiling, which takes advantage of the panoramic overlook. The three visitors exchange glances with raised eyebrows.

"How do you manage to keep this place up?" she wonders aloud.

"With help," Jon answers dismissively.

He flicks his finger toward the hallway. "You'll find your room the way you left it."

"Gentlemen, if you'll follow me, I'll show you to your rooms."

Keira throws her bags on her bed and drops down next to them. Nothing has changed since the funeral. A flood of memories and emotions hits her in waves. She remembers how her father ostracized her after her brother's death and the nights her mother tried to comfort her in an attempt to assuage the guilt Jonathan unloaded on her. Now, she's gone too.

David's room is two doors down from hers, sealed by her father after his death. She walks down the hall and grips the French door handle——locked.

"You know no one's allowed in there."

She turns to face Jonathan. "You still won't let him go, will you?"

"I can't."

Her lips start to quiver.

"Now what?"

"You wouldn't understand——," she struggles to hold herself together.

"Comprehend what?"

"You didn't lose one child that day. You lost both of us."

He remains adamantly stoic.

She throws her arms out to her side. "And *why* haven't you given up this … this palace of yours?"

"There's too much of your mother here. She's as much a part of——," his voice starts to crack.

"She's just another ghost to keep you company," she says bitterly, and angrily bumps his shoulder on the way back to her room. She slams the door behind her.

Close on her heels, he loudly raps on the door then barges in when she doesn't respond.

Still standing, she faces him with crossed arms. "Tell me why I'm here."

"Because we need you for this project."

"That's a load of bull, Jonathan!"

"We've got an important job ahead of us over the next several weeks. Your expertise and cooperation could mean the difference between success or failure."

"I doubt it."

Frustrated, he reaches for a smoke, but reconsiders. "Some old friends and acquaintances on Chuuk have asked for our help."

"'Old friends'?"

"You remember Brent?"

"Edelson?"

"One and the same."

"Talk about pulling a name out of the past."

"Apparently some highly placed government officials contacted him. Their shipwrecks date to the mid-40's, and according to him, have disintegrated to the point where the release of fuel threatens the lagoon … at least it's what he used to make his point. I'm not convinced."

"And yet we're here," she scoffs. "Why did they contact him?"

"I asked, but never got a straight answer. From what I could tell, they hoped he might have the necessary connections. As such, he'll be their liaison."

"How long ago did he leave Maui?"

"Around the mid-80's … about the same time Micronesia became the Federated States. He got a job there as a dive guide. When he contacted me about this, I thought of you first."

"Tell me. What's supposed to be my role in all of this?"

"Survey and document the wrecks, determine the feasibility of drawing off the oil, and evaluate the validity of their concerns. This should fit nicely into your wheelhouse, an area you've uniquely trained for."

She points toward the lanai where the agents congregated after stowing their bags. "Who are these men you sent to shanghai me?"

"Come on, Keira that doesn't help."

"Answer my question," she insists.

"They're from an agency which provides oversight, evaluation, and security for requests such as this."

"'Security'? Why? Are we in some kind of danger?"

"I don't believe so, but our presence may make some people nervous the more deeply we get involved. I've already expressed my concerns."

Keira shakes her head. "Brent Edelson of all people. Tied in with the government?"

"The *goverNOR* … and as I'm led to believe, closely."

"How times have changed." Realizing the futility of her resistance, she throws up her hands. "Okay. I give up. Count me in."

Jonathan reaches out to put his hand on her shoulder, but she gently brushes it aside and walks out to the lanai, leaving him alone in her room. The three government men have settled in to share a bottle of pinot and take in the view.

Pointing to the table, she asks, "Anything left?"

They all jump up in unison and laugh at how ridiculous they look. They defer the honor to Paul. After he pours her a glass, he waves the bottle in a gesture to take in the lavish home. "How'd your father get this fat?"

All eyes are now on her.

She's hesitant to respond. "Well, there's family money on my mother's side, some good investments, and I can only presume a healthy life insurance payoff."

After some small talk and questions about the islands still visible in the fading light, Paul checks his wristwatch, and gestures to the others. It's time to turn in.

When the three of them leave, Keira settles down to relax and appreciate the solitude. It's her first opportunity since she arrived for work in Long Beach some sixteen hours ago. But she's not alone. Paul returns with a newly opened bottle.

57

Paul scans the label. "Your father has excellent taste in wine."

Keira remains stoic.

"Lost in thought?"

She slowly peers up from her reverie. "You uncomfortable with silence?"

He sets the bottle down, pulls his chair close, and surprises her by sliding hers around to face him.

"You have my attention."

"You've cut a pretty wide swath since we first met. Why the hostility?"

"You're kidding, right? My 'recruitment' includes: threats to withhold grant money from my place of employment, kidnapping me to a region I've only heard about, and forcing me to work with my estranged father, a relationship, by the way, you know nothing about. I'd be disingenuous if I said, 'I'm so sorry. We're good'."

"At Long Beach you mentioned 'estrangement'. Would you be care to elaborate?"

She redirects her eyes toward the overlook, takes a drink from her glass, and slowly shakes her head in disbelief. "You fancy yourself some kind of psychologist?"

"Consider me a friendly ear."

She finishes her wine. When he offers a refill she covers it with her hand. "I better not."

After a very long pause, her voice softens, "Jonathan and I used to be close. I fell in love with the ocean at an early age. My parents recognized and encouraged it. When I earned my scuba certification, I immersed myself in the study of marine life … whatever I could get my hands on. I knew then that I wanted a life which included the sea.

"Fifteen years ago, my brother, David, returned from school on the mainland. We tagged along with my father's charter to dive *First Cathedral* off Lanai. After Brent, one of his crew, secured the anchor, David and I entered the water well before the charter group got underway——"

"This Brent you mentioned. His name sounds familiar."

"Brent Edelson. You'll get to meet him soon enough."

"He used to work for your father?"

"Do you want to hear about this or not?" she snaps.

"Oh, sorry. Please go on."

"We hoped to put some distance between us and the tourists and quickly descended to fifty feet. We took the opposite direction from where we knew the guides would go, and followed a route between two house-sized lava seamounts which frame a six foot-wide sand channel."

She vacantly stares into the distance. "David usually carried a catch bag and a dive light. We'd use them to search the crevices and holes known locally as *pukas*. Over the years he amassed an enviable collection of shells, so we took our time. The pace reminded me of an adage our father continually drilled into us——'It's about the journey, not the destination'. We encountered a green sea turtle at rest in a recess. It had a three foot carapace with patches of moss and a few scratches. The turtle nonchalantly eyed the two of us, indifferent to our presence."

Keira pauses and her face brightens with the memory. "I love interacting with marine life … any size … really doesn't matter. I'd frequently buy a pack of frozen squid to feed the turtles and moray eels. I knew where they lived, and many by name——Garbonzo, Scratch, Miss Piggy. I wanted to spend more time interacting with the turtle, but David grew impatient. That's when we separated."

She turns toward the horizon and gestures with her hands as the memory plays out before her. "The seamount to my right ended close to a patch of reef densely populated with butterfly fish. I gravitated toward an especially active area. The fish sought refuge when a six foot-long white-tipped reef shark started to swim lazy figure-eights over a coral head. I was mesmerized. I had encounters with sharks at Molokini Crater before, usually at rest under overhangs of lava, but I'd never observed this kind of behavior. Directly beneath the focal point of its path, an octopus weaved itself further into the recess while camouflaging its skin tone and shape.

"I tapped on the bottom of my tank with my knife to get David's attention, but he was out of sight. The shark stopped and hovered, totally focused on its prey. It worked its way up and down the head of coral until its shovel-shaped nose made contact with the base. It firmly anchored its pectoral fins on two lesser growths in the coral apron. I wanted to get a closer view and found a place to lie down a couple of feet from the shark. Its tail slowly drifted up while its nose stayed firmly planted beneath the holdfast. It started to wave its tail side-to-side." She demonstrates the exaggerated movement with her outstretched arms. "Its thrusts increased in speed and amplitude——back and forth, back and forth.

"There was still no sign of David, and if I left to find him, I'd miss the moment.

"The shark's undulations eventually loosen the coral, and with a loud *POP*," she slaps her hands together, "it gave way and collapsed. The octopus took off for safe refuge. It released a dense cloud of black ink before it rapidly dropped straight down. With a lightning quick thrust, the shark nabbed it and immediately started to rake it across its rows of tiny teeth. It continued to swim while it regurgitated and minced the carcass repeatedly until the pieces were the right size to swallow. The shark started a gradual glide to the depths followed by an escort of two smaller sharks and other fish which competed for the morsels passing through its gill slits. I swam alongside totally enthralled, oblivious to the depth.

"Eventually I retraced my path, anxious to find my brother, but couldn't." Her tears flow silently as she struggles to continue. "When I surfaced, Daddy waved me in, visibly angry because we'd held up the charter group. No sign of David. We searched for his bubbles anywhere in the vicinity, but the surface chop from the early afternoon trades made it impossible."

Her demeanor hardens and she stops referring to her father as 'Daddy'. "Jonathan told Brent and me to gear-up and he followed suit. He wanted me to retrace our route. Charlene was left in charge while the three of us dropped to depth.

"We easily found the seamounts and took a faster pace along the channel. When we reached the point where I turned right, Jonathan followed but Brent held back. We soon heard him tap on his tank. He waited by the entrance to a cavern under the seamount to the left of where David and I had separated. The opening measured fifteen feet across and four feet high. Brent scanned inside the expansive recess with his light. Toward its far end," she physically points to the area as she visualizes it in her mind, "the powerful beam found David lying face down, no bubbles, motionless. He appeared to be asleep. We knew otherwise.

"Apparently he'd gotten wedged between the cavern's erose overhead and the silt bottom. Jonathan started to go in, but Brent caught him mid-way into the entry. He swatted his arm aside, but Brent reestablished a tighter grip on his b.c. and gestured for him to wait. He knew the close quarters and signaled he'd go instead. Jonathan relented.

"Brent approached David carefully to minimize siltation. He secured a grip on his b.c. and strained to free him. In the act of dislodging the body, the resultant cloud of roiled silt expanded until we lost sight of them. Brent turned off his dive light for signs of ambient light to guide him out. Eventually he emerged with the body. David's regulator mouthpiece bounced along the silty bottom.

"When he reached us, Jonathan made a desperate attempt to resuscitate David. He forced the mouthpiece of his back-up regulator between his slack lips and purged the water, but it dropped back down to his side. Jonathan hugged him closely before letting go."

She turned coldly clinical. "David must have smashed his head on the overhead. The faceplate on his mask was cracked, and he'd suffered a terrible cut on his forehead. Anoxia turned his complexion blue. His eyes wide open.

"Jonathan towed David's body back to the boat, turned him over to Brent, and boarded before he gestured to hand him up. A couple of men from the charter jumped in to assist. By the time I was helped aboard, I was an emotional wreck. Someone took my gear, while Jonathan turned away without a word. He needed to make arrangements for David's body and didn't want to create a scene in front of the customers. Most remained silent while a few quietly cried.

"Brent radioed in the call. The coroner and police awaited our arrived at the slip. The authorities escorted the customers off the boat and away from the dock before they took David away. I didn't believe I was at fault, but I tried to apologize to Jonathan. He wouldn't acknowledge me.

"Mother met me at the door with red, swollen eyes. She gave me a compassionate hug. We sat together on my bed, while I told her all I remembered from my perspective. She encouraged me to take a nap, but I couldn't sleep.

"Jonathan came home late. He'd been drinking. I stayed in my room listening to their conversation, which rapidly escalated into an argument. I expected him to check on me. Instead, his heavy footsteps passed my room, followed by the door to David's being forcibly shut.

"When I opened it, Jonathan was on David's bed. I'd never seen him cry before. He yelled at me to leave him alone. I wanted to put my arm around him, but he intercepted it, forcefully pushed me out, then slammed and locked the door." She rubs her arm as she recounts the memory. "I'd lost my footing and took a hard fall. I was hysterical when my mom helped me up and into my bedroom. Afterward, she went to have it out with him. I became a pariah."

"Any attempt at a reconciliation?"

She stands. "It's been an exhaustive day, and thanks to you, I'm led to believe we're facing another one tomorrow. I'm turning in."

Paul stands with her. "Good night, Keira," he says softly.

Paul wants some time alone to reflect on what she shared, but his respite is short-lived. Jon takes the seat next to him. Paul notices the empty glass he's holding and offers him the bottle.

He holds it up to the light, and drains what little is left.

Paul scans the view. "You're a lucky man, Jon."

"This isn't the home life I once envisioned."

"Oh?"

"Since the loss of my son, my wife, and Keira's self-imposed exile, it gets lonely."

Paul reckons, *If he's not willing to acknowledge his role in their estrangement …*

"J.J. has fond memories of you."

"I've appreciated his friendship through the years."

He points to the sideboard in the great room. "The photograph of your flight crew … he has the same one on his desk at the agency."

"Huh," Jon mumbles.

"He took action on your request immediately. There isn't another person he's ever accommodated this rapidly."

"Thanks. From what I gathered he has a special place in his heart for you too."

"He's never let on."

"He tells me you've had some pretty harrowing experiences in the Navy Seals."

"How much did he——"

"Enough to assure me we're in good hands."

Paul relaxes as the two enjoy the quiet.

"Keira brought up an interesting question about our involvement. She wants to know if we'll be safe." Paul doesn't respond. "Well, will we?"

"I believe so, but whenever there's large amounts of money involved——"

"Listen, I can't have Keira endangered, not in any way. Do I make myself clear?"

"She'd be more assured if she heard it from you." He stands to turn in for the night when Jon grabs his arm.

"You haven't answered my question."

"To put your mind at rest, Jon, my number one priority throughout this assignment will be her safety, as well as yours, Dax's, Eric's, *and* mine. Good enough?"

"And the others ... at Chuuk?"

"You tell me. I've never met them."

Paul glances at his watch. "It's time to turn in. Try to get some sleep, Jon. Tomorrow's going to be a long day."

Paul reflexively ducks when he enters the cabin of the government's C-11A jet for their predawn departure from Kapalua. The aircraft is configured with twelve plush seats in a variety of roomy configurations.

Dax takes a seat next to Eric and engages in conversation about their respective backgrounds. Throughout the flight the two continue an unfiltered exchange, and emerge with a newly minted friendship.

Paul is disappointed to find Keira and Jon have seated themselves at diametrically opposite ends of the cabin, not a word or gesture passes between the two. It does, however, leave an opening for him to do or say something to thaw the ice between them. Pointing to the seat next to her, he asks, "Mind if I join you?"

"You bought the tickets."

"Why don't you tell me about your work at the institute."

"You mean the one you forced me into leaving?"

Oh brother, glad I opened this bag of worms.

Her demeanor grows much more animated. "Now that you mention it, why don't you tell me about you. Who are you people?"

"Friends of your father," he says weakly.

"That doesn't honestly work in your favor, does it? How do you even know him? Why am I really here? What is my role supposed to be? And who are you? Not your agency, but *you?*"

Paul smirks, but does nothing more to answer her.

"When you decide we can have a two-way conversation," she scoffs, "with honest answers, then come back and try again. Otherwise, I prefer to be alone."

He moves to a seat were four people can talk face to face, props his feet on the empty chair across from his and closes his eyes. *If the project doesn't kill her, then maybe I will.*

It's a short layover in Guam to refuel both the aircraft and passengers. After a quick bite in the terminal, Paul ducks into the message center to retrieve an anticipated telex from Baltimore, regarding the logistics of a planned shipment. *I'll have to get back to J.J. with a list of anything we haven't already thought of. It'll give me something to mull over on the next leg of this endless odyssey.*

Their trek is concluded with a final ninety minute flight to Chuuk.

Weno's airport sits like a cap on the northwest corner of the island. The jet begins its descent to their final destination southwest of the 6,000 foot-long runway. The passengers in the starboard seats get glimpses, then a full-on overview of the largest city in the Federated States. Those on the port side take in the view of the lagoon's gorgeous clear blue waters. Rusted wreckage breaks the surface nearshore and serves as enticements to new arrivals. The craft touches down on runway four, ten feet above sea level. Its turbines wind down after it taxies past the port of entry sign:

CHUUK INTERNATIONAL AIRPORT

Four vehicles await them on the tarmac: three late-model Jeeps for the passengers and a well-used, modified Datsun pick-up for the luggage and equipment. The governor stands between his unlikely ally, Brent Edelson, and a uniformed custom's agent who is instructed to give the arrivals a wave-through.

Jon exits first, followed closely by Paul.

Brent strides over with an artificial smile. "Thought I might have heard from you sooner, Jon," he mutters through clenched teeth. He stands a couple of inches shorter than his former boss. As usual, his hair is dirty and longer than Jon remembers. A wispy mustache, along with a scruffy goatee are Brent's latest attempts to find an identity. He's outfitted in khaki twill cargo shorts and well-worn black flip-flops. The drape of his islander shirt highlights his weight loss. The ever-present reek of nicotine accompanies him.

Jon opens the introductions. "It appears you've gotten more acclimated to life here, Brent. Meet one of my associates, Paul Gerhart."

The two nod but dispense with the handshake. Brent says, "Let me introduce you to the Governor of Chuuk."

When Dax and Eric wander over, introductions are made all the way around. The middle-aged governor is handsome and well-dressed appropriate for the climate. His dark, tanned skin shows few wrinkles. His only concession to age is his full head of black hair laced with threads of grey.

Keira captures everyone's attention as she starts down the ladder. Brent hits Jon on his upper arm. "Who's the babe, she's absolutely——," he stops short when he realizes who he's standing next to.

Jon smiles at his dilemma. "Go ahead, Brent. She'll be happy to see a familiar face."

Keira greets him warmly, "Of all the places, I never expected to run into you here."

When she sidesteps his attempt at a hug, he places his hands on his hips and gives her a once over. "Keira Lynn Hall in the flesh. You sure turned out …," he mutters something unintelligible.

As an aside, she points to his sunglasses. "Aren't those the same pair of Maui Jims you had in Hawaii?"

The popular glasses not only protect his eyes, but partially hide the severe facial scar and drooping eyelid. A faded neoprene sleeve wraps around his neck to secure them. He ignores her remark.

"Would you be willing to answer some questions for me?" she adds.

The suggestion dovetails nicely with his aspirations of time alone with her, so he readily agrees.

The governor flags his attention and taps on his watch. "We have a lot to get caught up on, but right now I need to get your group and baggage checked into the hotel. How 'bout dinner tonight? Give us a chance to get reacquainted?"

"Just the two of us?"

"There'd be fewer interruptions that way."

She adds the stipulation, "Dinner only … at the hotel. Agreed?"

"Yeah, sure," he concedes.

Paul tracks their interchange from a distance until interrupted by the governor, "Shall we go? We have a lot to discuss. Brent will take the others to the hotel along with your baggage."

"Where to?"

"My home. We can relax in an atmosphere much more enjoyable than the hotel; it'll be quieter, with fewer distractions."

"Lead the way, sir."

The main route from the airport to the hotel runs five miles due south along the western shoreline. Once past the commercial district, the narrowing roadway is bracketed with tight clusters of four-room houses, several littered with early model vehicles, most with their last mile wrung out of them. It takes thirty-five minutes to negotiate the route from the airport to their destination.

An expanse of lush green grass surrounds three, two-story

interconnected buildings which face the lagoon. A dense population of palm trees enhance the tropical ambience and provide much needed shade.

All five in the team have individual rooms grouped together on the main building's second floor. Brent directs the unload and helps carry Keira's luggage to her room.

She inspects her accommodations while Brent stands in the open doorway. The amenities are dated, but adequate. Too tired to care, she slides open the door to the balcony and pauses at the rail to take in the view of palm-lined grounds and azure blue waters.

He plans to propose a more intimate night out when Keira interjects, "I'm exhausted, Brent, and I need a nap. Can we meet in the lobby at say … six?"

He checks his watch and reluctantly acquiesces.

She quickly closes and locks the door behind him. He loiters in the hallway until he hears the *snick* of the deadbolt.

She remembers the times spent underwater with Brent after David's death. Over the year they logged dozens of dives together, an opportunity not open to him before. Despite their ten-year age disparity, he tried many times to impress her with his skill set, knowledge, and interaction with marine life. In his mind, her youth, vulnerability and teen-aged naïveté might lead to … but Keira was intelligent and perceptive for her age. Even though she sensed his creepy vibe she continued to use him as a means to dive. As an adult, she can imagine his expectations and shudders. *I'll have to set some clear boundaries over dinner.*

Tossing her bag atop the bed, she notices an envelope with a note written on hotel stationery. She stays standing to read it.

> *Miss Hall,*
>
> *I understand you're due in today and from first-hand experience, you've already dealt with a grueling marathon of flights. If you wish, I can offer some assistance with your assignment. After you get some rest and settled in, the hotel operator knows*

how to reach me.
Steve Mitchell

She flicks the note onto the dresser, and lies down.

When the governor's car stops at the main entry, there's a colossal individual waiting for them. Paul and Jon get a better perspective outside the car. He towers over both, impressive when one considers Paul's six foot four frame. He has tight black hair, and recessed, inscrutable eyes. By the scars on his face, Paul guesses he's had to defend himself more than a few times. He has no sign of a neck, and his broad shoulders taper to a trim waist. He's dressed in lightweight cotton slacks and a tightly tapered polo shirt which accentuates his considerable physique.

When he stoops to open the governor's door, Paul notices he's discretely armed. Last to exit, the governor introduces him, "My associate, Benjamin Gumataotao, gentlemen."

Paul withholds offering his hand with concerns it may get crushed. Without breaking eye contact, he gives him a half-hearted nod, and fumbles in his attempt to pronounce the man's name.

Benjamin condescendingly adds, "My friends call me 'BG'".

When the governor invites them inside, BG strides ahead to effortlessly open the heavy main door, and smiles at the guests as they enter. His teeth are disproportionately small for the size of his head. Paul stifles a grin.

BG walks back to the car, directs the driver to the garage, and follows him on foot. The two observe him walk away.

"I'd hate to run into him in a dark alley," mumbles Jon. Paul nods in agreement.

The manse stands in stark contrast to the others in the neighborhood. It's obvious the governor has done well for himself, which raises the first of many red flags.

They initially admire a refurbished bronze Japanese Tao commercial diver's helmet. After submerged for decades, the helmet is now mounted upright on a polished stand of dark wood designed for display.

"An impressive piece," says Jon.

"A photograph of it appeared on the cover of one of your country's dive publications," the governor responds, "and shortly thereafter disappeared from the *Fujikawa Maru*."

"How did it end up here, and in such great condition? It's beautiful."

"Word reached the police from a fisherman who observed a private boat anchored over the wreck at night. The police inspected the boat the next day, confiscated the helmet, and cited the divers. They pulled anchor and left before their court appearance."

Paul points to the helmet. "How——"

The governor interrupts, "We contacted the magazine's publisher, who's done much over the years to promote diving in these islands. He arranged with the airlines to ship the helmet to him, had it professionally refurbished, built the mount, and returned to present it as a gift to the people of Truk. It received some good press, and I felt that for now, it'd be safer in my home."

As both men silently inspect the artifact, the governor voices his frustrations. "We do what we can, but despite the adage, 'take only photographs and leave only bubbles', we do not have the resources or manpower to deter poachers. I issued an amnesty to recover items already pilfered, with no penalty to anyone who voluntarily returns them. Otherwise, we're limited to customs officials, who screen baggage for items about to leave by air, and the police, acting on tips from fishermen, to recover the artifacts, but we lose them on a weekly basis."

A collection of beautiful blue and white Noritake china: platters, rice bowls, and saké cups displayed in a well-lit cabinet, gathers their attention. "Those came from the *Momokawa Maru,* again taken by people aboard privately owned sailboats, and subsequently confiscated."

The cabinet also holds a score of dark blue medicine ampules from the *Sankisan Maru*.

As the men continue to inspect the displays, Paul asks, "Don't your dive operators and live-a-boards police their own charters?"

"Sure, it affects their livelihood too. We hope one day to have a museum to display several of the recovered artifacts for everyone to enjoy——divers, non-divers, *and* our native peoples. If we return them to the wrecks, they remain vulnerable to theft, thus a fruitless endeavor. In fact, there's a storeroom with several documented relics waiting for the right venue to display them properly."

Paul says, "Governor, you've requested our assistance. What can we do for you?"

Brent waits in the lobby until Keira makes her appearance. Her hair hasn't dried from the shower and humidity, so she wears it straight. She's dressed in a light blue scoop-neck t-shirt, white cotton twill capris, and her favorite black, low-cut sneakers with bright white laces. The entry to the dining room is adjacent to the main reception desk and nearly filled with guests.

Brent gives her another up-down. "You're looking …," he stops himself short. "You have to agree the noise in here will make conversation difficult. There's a quiet restaurant not too far——"

"We're good here, Brent."

"Figured as much," he mutters. "I reserved a table by the window."

She notices her father sharing a table with the three agents. Jon stands and gestures they join them. She ignores him and follows Brent.

The interior's decor is standard fare, but augmented by a spectacular view out the windows. Beyond the expanse of thick green grass, graceful Kotop palm trees sweep over the water, and are frequently backlit by the wondrous sunsets commonplace to these islands.

When the waiter approaches the table, Brent suggests some wine.

"We agreed on dinner only, Brent."

He rolls his eyes. "In some cultures, wine is considered——"

"A bottle of cold water will suit me fine," she tells the waiter.

They place their order for the featured catch and are left to themselves.

Brent gazes at the window. The angle of glass gives him a clear reflection of her face. He catches her staring at his tattoo.

"This is new."

He sniggers at the irony. "Your father said the same when he first noticed."

"Do you mind if I take a closer look?"

Without waiting for an answer, Keira turns his arm for a better view. "It's really beautiful, but the sun can fade out the detail if you're not careful."

"It brings to mind when we dove *Second Cathedral* together," he smiles. "Remember?"

She groans in mock disgust and pushes his hand away. "Don't remind me."

Paul notices Jon staring at Keira and her escort. "Tell me about Brent."

Jon re-engages with the three men. "We've known each other for years. I initially met him when he approached me for a job on Maui. He seemed down on his luck, but surprisingly open about his circumstances. While stationed at Hickam Air Force base on Oahu, he got into trouble and was given his traveling papers with a medical discharge."

"What kind of trouble?"

"He fell in with the wrong crowd on Oahu, went off-base to go clubbing, and got involved in a knife fight with some rivals."

Paul runs his finger over his eye. "His scar ... I didn't want to stare——"

Jon interrupts, "After awhile you don't notice. It kinda fades behind his personality. It did come up during the interview, and I appreciated his transparency. The damage had impaired his vision; thus his departure from the service. I wanted to give him a chance, so I hired him to run the air compressor and help load tanks for the charters. He eventually worked his way onto the boats as a dive guide. A darn good one, too. Our customers constantly paid me compliments about him, so I trusted him to dive with Keira after her brother's death."

Paul's surprised.

"When we lost David, she no longer had her brother for a dive buddy. It was a pretty rough time for her and she needed to get back in the water. I sent her out with the charter groups a couple of days a week to dive with the customers and hang close to the guides. A woman named Charlene worked for me and I paired them up, but when I caught wind of her complaining about Keira getting in her way, I let her go, which left Brent. They dove together on alternate weeks. I basically paid him to go have fun."

"What happened?"

"His issues always centered around money. He was constantly broke and continually dabbled in schemes to make himself a couple extra bucks. Maui's an expensive place to live. Young people who move to the islands for work and adopt 'the life' are often surprised with the reality of cost versus paychecks. Compromises need to be made, so whenever we spoke, I expected Brent to raise the topic of a bump in his pay. Despite what he brought to the job, I felt relieved when he left."

"When Keira cut off her relationship with me, no matter what I tried, she'd keep me at arm's length. When she left for school in California, we completely dropped out of contact."

"Did she and Brent … you know——"

"Not ever," he quickly responds. "If any hint got back to her mother, I'd have quickly gotten an earful. She did not agree with the arrangement from the start."

"What brought him here?"

"What inspired you to move to these islands?" Keira asks.

"I suppose I can pretty much blame it on your father. His conversations often centered around the trips he and your mom took here in the eighties; it planted a seed. When she passed and you dropped out of his life, he started to travel here on his own. After our charter boat came out of dry dock in Seattle, we'd sail it back to Maui together, and off he'd go for any number of weeks. After I read so many articles about Truk, and questioned transiting divers, I decided to make the move."

"Did he ever mention me?"

Brent shakes his head. "He made it a point to not answer my inquiries, so I eventually stopped."

Keira's eyes start to well up. Brent reaches over and lightly touches her hand. She hastily grabs her napkin. "You didn't finish telling me about your move."

"Jon's stories seemed too good to believe. I wanted to make more money and needed his help to obtain a captain's license, but he never showed any interest. He left me little choice. I had to seek alternatives. When I suggested the relocation, he made some inquiries, gave me a glowing recommendation, and got me this job."

"Did you visit the islands beforehand?"

"I couldn't afford it. I trusted his opinion and stepped out on my own."

"Are you happy you made the move?"

"Initially yeah, big time. After a while … I don't fit in here. I feel like I'm on the outside looking in. So I guess I'm still adjusting."

"What do you mean?"

Brent finishes his drink and signals the waiter.

"The islanders are poor. The locals do what they can to eke out a livelihood, either in the fishing, diving or hospitality industries——retail clerks, wait services, cooks, housekeepers, but the unemployment rate is exceptionally high. I have no prospects for a relationship, and am forced to live in a modest studio."

He stares out the window. His mind starts to drift.

"Brent?"

He reacts as if she jolted him awake. "Oh, sorry."

"Do you plan to move back?"

"Not right now. I'm exploring a few interesting prospects."

"What do you mean by that?"

Brent realizes he's said too much, returns to his gaze out the window, and clams up.

Paul breaks Jon's fixation on the other table. "In all honesty, should we trust Brent?"

He reluctantly shakes his head.

"Okay. We'll keep our eyes on him."

"I need the three of you to listen to me." Jon hesitates until he has their undivided attention. "When you're in the water together, it's like a second home to him. He's a lot more resourceful below than you imagine."

"Thanks for the caution," says Paul, "but we can handle your friend there."

Jon holds up a finger. "Allow me to make one more point with you. He has this habit he does with a knife."

"What kind?"

"It's a pocket knife, and constantly with him. He amuses himself by rolling it around his fingers, and adroitly juggles it. I believe he does it to settle his nerves, but he's gotten surprisingly good at it."

"Thanks for the warning," Paul smirks, "but really, how dangerous … I mean, come on, it's a pocket knife, right?"

"Okay," concedes Jon, "but don't say you haven't been warned."

Keira continues to question Brent. "How did you get involved in this enterprise?"

"The governor sought my help to get some answers to our problem. Your father came to mind first. Jon made the call, and here you are."

"I don't get it. Who's my father's connection with enough influence to put this together?"

"I asked, but he never said."

"That reminds me, do you know Steve Mitchell?"

Brent turns from the window to face her, somewhat astonished. "How did you come up with *his* name?"

"Who is he, Brent?"

"An ex-patriate who's lived in the islands for well over a decade."

"What does he do?"

"He's an artist. When he first arrived, he did private dive charters for well-heeled clients, made his money, and retired. Now he pursues his craft full-time."

Brent motions to the waiter. As he delivers a couple of flutes and an ice bucket with a bottle of champagne, Brent makes a clumsy attempt to reconnect with her hands. She pulls them away quickly, glances at the waiter holding the bottle then glares at Brent.

"I'm sorry. I figured——"

"What? You and me! It'll never happen, Brent. *Never!*"

After her outburst, the embarrassed waiter quickly leaves with the bucket, bottle, and glasses.

"Can't blame a guy for trying," he mutters.

Ignoring her complaints, he lights up a cigarette. Despite her efforts to pick his brains, he has shut down. Keira realizes their time is done. With a curt, "Good night," she leaves with no more pertinent information than when the evening started.

She checks out the table where her father sat, but the men had already left.

A knock on Paul's door awakens him. He opens to find two local men.

"Yes?"

"You Mr. Gerhart?"

"I am."

"My name is Solomon Enap."

He is neatly dressed in a dark polo shirt, tan slacks and top-sider shoes. His black hair is trimmed short, and worn combed over. Horn-rimmed glasses frame his dark, friendly eyes. He greets Paul with a genuinely warm and enthusiastic handshake.

He keeps his grip on Paul's hand, and adds, "I'm here with my half-brother, Elias Kohper."

Kohper scans the hallway while the two exchange their amenities and reacts with surprise at the mention of his name. He is in a wrinkled khaki shirt, green shorts and leather sandals. His demeanor is half-hearted and his handshake is quickly withdrawn.

Paul steps aside, "Gentlemen, please, come in."

Paul invites them to sit in the two stuffed chairs, and pulls one over from the table. "I received the message about your visit tonight," nodding to the lieutenant governor, "but I didn't expect——"

"Let me explain. My brother is the Chief of Police. When I mentioned the reason for your visit, he invited himself for our initial meet. It's a good idea. You may be working together at some point."

"Okay," Paul turns his attentions to the officer.

"How should we address you?"

"Thank you. People rarely extend the courtesy. Please call

me Chief or Chief Kohper when I'm around my men. When we're alone you may use my Christian name, Elias."

"How many work for you?"

The chief grimaces toward his brother, who answers, "'It's somewhat of a sore spot. He has three full-time officers and two others he calls on when needed."

Elias adds, "Our island is small, and our financial resources are stretched to the limit. If problems arise beyond our ability to handle, I have reassurances I can phone the department on Pohnpei for assistance. So far, no need."

"What are you and your men usually called out for?"

"We're here to give assistance to residents, domestic disturbance and the infrequent emergency. More often to answer requests for help from tourists. Why I'm here tonight is to get some clarification about *your* group's involvement."

Paul takes some time to collect himself.

"Unofficially, we're going to take advantage of some of your wreck diving we've been told is 'unparalleled'."

"And officially?"

"I'm really not at liberty …"

The chief gives his brother an 'I-told-you-so' expression. "I had hopes for a bit more cooperation," he adds, with a scowl toward Enap.

"Well, sir, I'm under strict constraints regarding non-disclosure," says Paul.

The chief stands and glares at his brother. "This is a waste of my time. I'm outta here. I'll wait for you in the car."

Without acknowledging Paul, he leaves.

Enap runs to the door, and shouts, "Elias, please", to no avail. He sheepishly turns back.

Before Paul can apologize, Enap stops him. "No, I'm the one who is sorry. He doesn't feel he's taken seriously. I've told him he needs to have more patience. This could be a good job for him and I want him to succeed."

"When did he take over?"

"Hmm," he starts to mumble to himself, "nineteen ninety … three years or there about."

"My boss forewarned me you contacted him."

"When the governor told me of your upcoming trip, I messaged him outside normal channels."

"What brings you here?" asks Paul.

"We need your help."

Chapter 7
Steve Mitchell

Paul greets the team in the lobby and directs them to the hotel's conference room on the main floor, which has been reserved for their daily briefings. The staff set up a buffet table with platters of fresh fruit along with the main attraction——a tray of Moen donuts, the hotel's renowned high-calorie, high-fat, glazed to perfection, deep-fried pastry which melts in the mouth. A smaller table is off to the side with an urn of coffee, and iced trays of bottled water.

With refreshments in hand, they amble to the chairs facing the dais. Jon arrives accompanied by a native islander. "Mornin' everyone. I'm happy to introduce Andon Labonne, the owner of Micronesian Divers. He started as my dive guide many years ago when I first came to the islands. His operation is located a short walk from the hotel's west end. He has two brand new boats reserved exclusively for our use which will be at the dock adjacent to his shop. While his crew will supply the tanks and weights along with any support equipment, you're responsible for your personal gear."

Andon's in his mid-thirties with a full head of dark wavy hair, wears a disarming smile and exudes Micronesia through and through. Keira thinks, *This guy is beautiful. I wonder if he'll dive with us?*

Paul prompts Andon, "Why don't you give us a rundown on what will be made available and *your* expectations."

"No problem." He's totally relaxed, and soft-spoken, when he begins. "Our waters offer a variety of wrecks. Some relatively shallow, others not so much. Before I can release the deeper ones, we'll need to assess *your* diving skills on a couple of relatively shallow wrecks. I'll get feedback from my staff and make my decisions from there."

A low groan circulates around the room. They collectively resent the idea of 'intro dives'——descending individually with a guide down a line in shallow waters for a skills review—— real 1-0-1 stuff.

Jon stands. "Okay, settle down. This will not remotely resemble your certification training. The evaluation will be based on how safely you conduct yourselves on the initial dives." The grumbling continues, so he makes one more attempt, "Trust me. You're in for an extraordinary experience. These wrecks are adorned with artifacts and marine life beyond your wildest imaginations."

Andon checks his watch, and peers out the door. He turns to face the group. "Any questions?"

Keira's quick to raise her hand and stands. "Will you dive with us while we're here, and can I buddy up with you?"

He's humbled and a bit embarrassed. "I may go along on some of the dives, but I'm afraid I have other responsibilities which require my personal attention."

With all eyes now focused on her, the men chuckle and let out a collective, "Aww."

She sits back down in a huff.

Andon double-checks the door. "I'm sorry I had hoped to introduce——"

"I'm here," pants a young man as he pops into the room. He gives Andon an apologetic shrug, and whispers, "Sorry. Couldn't be helped."

Andon pulls the reluctant young man up to the podium, and gives him a familial pat on the shoulder while he makes the introduction. "I want you to meet Alou, my sister's youngest. He's assigned as your boat captain for the majority of your visit."

"Hello, Alou," the group says in unison.

Self-conscious about his tardiness, he sheepishly flashes a flawless smile and half-hearted wave. He's a good-looking kid and appears much younger than his twenty years.

Jon asks, "When did you start working with your uncle?"

He's reticent to speak, and glances toward Andon, who answers, "Alou's hung around the shop since he turned ten. I put him to work doing odd jobs after school recess. He's earned his way on crew since turning sixteen and as a boat driver for a couple of years now. He has a good instinct for negotiating the waters, locating the wrecks, and has my complete confidence."

Dax notices his discomfort and decides to have some fun with the taciturn youth. "Would you care to add to the discussion, Alou?"

The lad laughs uncomfortably and again wants Andon to bail him out. "We better call it a day. Don't worry, you spend any amount of time together, it'll be difficult to shut him up."

Jon grins as he takes the dais again. "I'll stay in close communication with Andon throughout our assignment. Together we'll do what we can to ensure everyone's safety … and enjoyment."

When Andon excuses himself and leaves with Alou, Keira indiscreetly follows him with her eyes until he's out of sight.

Anaria catches sight of Andon and Alou as soon as they leave the conference room and postures herself as they pass by her desk.

"Come back soon," she offers.

Neither man responds.

"Who do you think she's talking to," says Andon.

"I think she means me."

"So, 'couldn't be helped', huh?" Andon presses as they pass through the doors.

"I made it here in plenty of time," he pleads, "but she

collared me as soon as I entered the lobby."

"About what?"

"Oh, she made this to-do about how much I've grown, and wants me to call on her daughter."

"What did you tell her?"

"You needed me at the meeting, the sooner, the better, but I couldn't get away from her."

"Have you dated Kaysha before?"

"Who?"

"Anaria's daughter."

"You mean, Kayana?"

"Whatever. I can't keep 'em all straight … well?"

Alou reddens when he says, "No."

"Why not?"

"Too young."

"How young?"

"Not her," Alou answers, "me. I'm not ready, yet."

"I take it I should mind my own business?"

Alou grins. "Thanks, Uncle."

Jon concludes the meeting. "Today's a day for rest and prep for what's ahead. Have your gear at the dock and ready to load no later than seven a.m. sharp."

He makes eye contact with Keira and signals she hold tight. Dax and Eric pick up his cue and quickly vacate. Paul stays behind.

"Attractive guy, isn't he?" Jon says to her.

Before she can answer, he adds, "Never mind. I've made an appointment for you to meet with Steve——"

She turns her attentions away from the door and faces him.

"Mitchell?"

"Have you two met already?"

She fishes out the envelope and hands it to her father. "I found this note in my room when we checked in."

He reads it and hands it back. "Don't worry. I've known him for over twenty years. He spent a couple of nights at our place on Maui some twenty, twenty-five years ago."

"You're right, I don't remember."

"He said he'd meet you in the lobby right after lunch."

Paul butts in, "Before either of you leave, I have a packet for you."

He retrieves a bound report from his shoulder bag and hands it to Keira.

She leafs through its pages. "What's this?"

"An answer to your questions about your role within our team." Pointing to the report, he adds, "The governor gave me this last night. It's the justification for his request and our presence."

Jon and Keira start paging through the eighty-six page document, filled with surveys, photographs, charts, line drawings, and scientific text. While Keira takes her time reading through the summaries, her father nudges her. "Does this make sense to you?"

"Of course it does." She taps the open page. "The tuition from mother's trust didn't completely go to waste."

She closes the booklet. "May I keep this, Paul?"

"Of course. We're here to validate their government's claim, and need you up to speed to sign-off on their proposal."

"This will certainly help, but I'll need time to go through it. When——"

Paul's halfway out the door. "Glad we had this chat. Meet you at the docks in the morning."

Confused by Paul's behavior and quick exit, Jonathan questions her.

"We kinda got off on the wrong foot."

Steve is waiting when she comes down from her room. "Miss Hall?"

"Please, call me Keira."

"Okay, Keira it is. I'm Steve."

She gives him a half-hearted handshake, and says, "Nice to put a face behind the note you left."

"Actually, we first met on Maui when you stood about this tall." He holds his hand three feet off the floor.

"Jonathan reminded me earlier," she says, "but I don't remember——"

"I can imagine. You were in primary school," he rubs his bald head, "and I had a lot more hair back then."

He's noticeably shorter than her, trim, deeply tanned, and wears a heavy mustache.

He gestures toward the lounge. "May I interest you in some coffee?"

She shakes her head. "If I have any more caffeine, I'll be wired all day. I would like some water and if you're willing, a stroll around the hotel grounds?"

"Sure," he holds up his valise and says, "I'll leave this with Anaria out front."

They stroll the heavily-shaded north side where it's relatively cooler.

"What brought you to these islands?"

"My then-wife, Cecilia, and I came here on a dive vacation and discussed setting up a private charter operation. She shared my enthusiasm, and a year later we sold our belongings to make the move. I bought a boat, and with my connections in the States, invited several friends who spread the word to help kick-start my business. The plan worked well for me, but Cece never got into the rhythm. She became chronically bored and presented me with an ultimatum—— follow her back to the States, or stay here alone——I chose to stay. After she relocated and settled down, the divorce papers followed."

"I'm sorry," says Keira.

"It's okay ... really. We had no children, and parted as friends. She has since remarried, had a couple of kids, and I'm living my dream."

"What do you do now?"

"When I made enough to live on, I shut down my charter business to practice my art full-time."

"What kind of medium do you work in?"

"I initially wanted to do a book about the islands related to the history and wrecks. I also considered video production, but ended up creating pen and ink drawings and oil paintings——primarily underwater. The diving offers an infinite number of subjects to practice on."

During their walk, Keira notices a dark lump hanging from the low limb of a tree ahead. "What is that?" She approaches more cautiously as she nears the tree.

"It's a bat."

"Ew." She stops and backs up a few paces. "A bat?"

"Yeah, a *fruit* bat."

"Is it dangerous? Will it bite?"

"The locals consider them a delicacy."

"Oh. Guess I'll have to look more closely at the 'fresh catch' option on the hotel's menu. All kidding aside, your note said you could help. What do you have in mind?"

"Your father mentioned you're here to conduct surveys. I have developed resources——."

"What kind?"

"Well, detailed line drawings of several wrecks. I've gone on to paint most of them. They're not blueprints, but they should help orient you below and give you an idea of what you can expect. Not to sound too self-serving, but I'm probably as familiar with these sites as the professionals or locals on the islands."

"Uh-huh," she responds skeptically.

Steve stops cold in his tracks. "Your father warned me you could be a bit frosty around the edges." Before she can react, he continues. "So that we're on the same page, I'm here to help … but *only* if you want it. There's no pressure from me. If you're not interested, give the word and I'll back out."

"I'm sorry. I'm a bit on edge from all the uncertainties."

"No worries. Let's head back. I'll get my notes on the way to the conference room."

"Please don't take this the wrong way, but how are you involved with this?"

"Because your father asked, and because he paid me handsomely to make my drawings available for you."

Steve retrieves his case with a wink for Anaria, and escorts Keira to the meeting room.

"When will you plug into our schedule?"

He doesn't answer right away, and lays out some of his sketches on the table. "First, you'll dive on the *Shinkoku Maru*. It's a perfect introduction to these waters. You'll follow that up with a dive on the *Sankisan*." He taps on each drawing as he names them. "Both ships settled upright in relatively shallow waters——not too many demands, nevertheless beautiful in their own right."

He hands her a couple of books. "These should help. They contain backgrounds on the ships and info on the sites."

"Are these mine to keep?"

He shakes his head, "Sorry, but no. They're from my personal library and I'll need them back by the end of your stay."

"I will treat them as I would my own."

"I'd appreciate it. After you get your bearings on the relatively easy wrecks, you and I will dive together on the more complicated ones."

"What do you mean by 'more complicated'? And why only the two of us?"

"Several ships settled on their sides or on slopes, and can easily disorient novices."

"Where does Brent fit——"

Steve holds up his hand to interrupt. "Please, let me first give you my take on Mr. Edelson ... he keeps a lot to himself. We believe he's moonlighting, but nobody's sure. He isn't always available and I'm the one they call when he isn't."

"Why does Andon let him get away with it?"

"I'll concede Brent is good at what he does. Despite his frustrations, Andon doesn't feel he can afford to let him go."

"Tell me where you fit in?"

"I'll lead the group on a couple of dives and the balance with you exclusively. The latter will be much more to your liking."

"How so?"

"You'll have exposure to things the others won't, and with less crowding. We'll then use the opportunity to talk about our experience without interruptions or interference from the others."

"Jonathan used to talk a lot about the *Fumizuki*."

"That site's earmarked for the two of you to dive together. It's an opportunity to spend some quality time on a wreck special to your folks. They were in the islands when researchers from Japan discovered the destroyer."

"Will the others dive with us?"

"They didn't come up in our discussions."

Steve retrieves his research binders filled with maps, line art, notes and photographs. His drawings range from primitive, stick-figure outlines to more elaborate works which highlight damage and point out significant artifacts.

"These are impressive. What did it take to put this collection together?"

"I've continued to work on it since I moved here. It started when I ordered the photographs from the National Archives in Washington."

He puts on his glasses. "Andon and his crew helped me with the maps. I needed them to locate the wrecks."

She points out a couple of photographs. "I've seen these before, in Jonathan's collection."

"I'm not surprised. They've appeared in numerous publications. I want to plant a seed with you, before you start these 'surveys' of yours."

He hands her a magnifying loupe, much the same as jewelers use when examining precious stones.

She examines the unfamiliar device. "What's this for?"

He selects a print from the attack. "Here. Lay the photograph flat on the table and place the loupe directly over the area you wish to study."

She spends more time with the highly magnified image. "This is cool. It pulls out so much more detail."

"Try to focus on any one of the ships."

She takes the magnifier, and reexamines the print.

"What am I looking for?"

"Choose the closest one with the sharpest image and check the waterline of its hull."

She examines the photograph with five ships at anchor, taken during the attack. "I don't get what you want me to——"

"Take your time."

She sighs and resumes her search. She leaves the loupe in place and points to the shot. "This one sits relatively high in the water? And ..."

"Wanna take a guess at why?"

"It's empty?"

"Right. You'll eventually come to appreciate Japan's struggles with their supplies, *especially* petroleum. The ships at anchor received their fuel at the same time as their departure orders, not beforehand, which applies to the majority of those caught here."

Keira does another scan.

"And while you're at it, consider this; Andon's father witnessed the attack and spoke about the oil which coated the shorelines for weeks afterward, but when you go below tomorrow, you'll experience a dazzling underwater paradise."

The potential for what's ahead, gives her a buzz of anticipation.

He hands her a magazine. "This organization sent a renowned scientist here to conduct research having the exact date marine life started to develop on the wrecks. Her feature mentions the seepage of two different types of fuel: one used by the ships which percolates from the wrecks so slightly the droplets dilute in the currents. The other, aviation gasoline, disperses when it breaks the water's surface."

"You have such a good handle on this, why am I here?"

"When your father told me about the governor's request, he failed to mention the three agents you brought along to oversee your surveys … which, by the way, I could have *easily* conducted for them."

"They're auditors, not agents."

"Guess again. Those men are much more than accountants. Obviously you have an important role to play. Keep your eyes open, do the reports, and exercise caution. I'm interested in how this plays out."

"You have any theories?"

"I do, but I don't want to influence you." He picks up on her confusion. "Don't let it bother you. We'll continue to touch base as the surveys move forward."

"So, one last item," as she leaves the room, "'frosty around the edges', huh?"

His eyes follow her until she passes out of sight. *This ought to make for a couple of interesting weeks.*

93

Chapter 8
First Dive
Shinkoku Maru

North of Fefan and West of Weno Islands

Andon's latest acquisitions are reserved for the exclusive use of Jon's group——two brand-new thirty-three foot white fiberglass boats, sleek and utilitarian. Each is equipped with two rows of cradles which snuggly hold scuba tanks, secured with a bungie cord looped over its valve. Passengers sit on hinged benches, which open to storage bins large enough for guest's personal gear as well as the boat's support equipment. Eight, six foot high aluminum poles support a taut white canvas tarp used for protection from the tropical sun. The pilot's console stands five feet from the bow fronted by a molded wrap-around bench for passengers who prefer to soak up the rays. At the stern, an articulated four-step ladder can swing down from the transom to facilitate boarding after the dive. A forty-four gallon hard-rubber barrel provides a fresh water rinse for diver's equipment.

On the morning of the first dive, it's agreed by all to hold the briefing onsite rather than in the conference room.

Keira sits alone on the unshaded front bench. It's been awhile since her last dive, and she admits to herself she's a bit anxious, but the combination of calm waters, fresh air, and steady drone of the boat's engines, brings her a degree of serenity she's rarely experienced the last several years. She closes her eyes and turns her face skyward to bask in the sunlight. Her attempts to push back memories of her brother do not succeed, *David would have loved this.*

When a shadow blocks her light, she opens her eyes to the silhouette of her father holding a dive bag.

He carefully places it at her feet. "I put together some equipment——"

"I brought my own," she interrupts.

"Nevertheless, you'll need a full wet suit for——"

"Aren't the waters here close to ninety degrees?"

"Not to put too fine a point on it, but you'll enjoy an iso-thermic eighty-three degrees throughout the islands."

She points to the mesh bag. "Then why do I need all of this?"

"For your protection."

"From what?"

"These wrecks have subtle hazards which can snag, abrade, scratch, burn, or cut. As careful as you are with your buoyancy control, full wet suits are a welcome precaution."

She gives him an appreciative gesture, and slides the lightweight bag aside with her foot to resume her sunbathing.

"Before you get too settled in," Jon roots around the bag and fishes out a slate with an attached grease pencil. It displays detailed graphics of points of interest including the hole in the port-side rear-quarter where a bomb sent the *Shinkoku Maru* to the bottom. "I had Steve do these for you. He made different slates for each wreck, which include paper copies in multiple aspects to help you take detailed notes for your reports after the dives."

She quickly scans through them. "Thanks. These will be a great help."

When she stows the extra gear under the bench, Jon glimpses a corner of a purple bag in with her dive gear, which triggers a laugh.

"What's so funny?"

"Looks like you haven't outgrown your jelly bean obsession."

She self-consciously tries to hide them by quickly closing the lid, pauses, then raises her hands in resignation. "Busted."

He takes the seat next to her and puts his hand gently on her shoulder. "Keira, can we——"

Alou throws the boat's twin motors in reverse signaling their arrival at the site.

They make anchor directly over the wreck sixty-six feet below. The waters are so clear they're able to visualize the expanse of the ship, which openly invites them to reach down and touch it.

After Brent secures the anchorage, he calls for the group's attention to review their dive plan. As soon as he begins, Paul immediately interrupts him, "Why don't you start with the ship's background."

Brent's does nothing to hide his annoyance at the interruption.

"Whose brief is this? Mine or yours?"

"Start by telling us what led to the ship's sinking," Paul suggests.

While the two men continue with their back-and-forth, Keira takes the opportunity to lean over the railing for a closer view of the wreckage. She notices minuscule globules of oil breaking the water's surface in diffuse streaks of red, green, and brown. *Do these foretell the ominous ecological disaster they're predicting?*

Jon feels the need to step in and refocus the group's attention on the upcoming dive. "Listen up. The *Shinkoku Maru*'s a five hundred foot-long oiler, the second largest ship in the lagoon. It was pressed into service at the outbreak of hostilities to support the Japanese war machine. She made anchorage in Truk three days before the Navy's attack, and transferred the balance of her oil to the *Tonan Maru*."

Paul faces Brent. "Wasn't so hard, was it?"

When Jon notices all eyes not on him, he decides to hold future briefs at the hotel each morning. For now, it's, "Let's get wet."

In short order, the team's gear-up and make their way to

the transom.

Paul stops Eric to double-check his set up. "Let me give your gear a quick once over."

"You *do* remember I went through certification classes."

"It's a good practice for everyone, and too often overlooked. It's not unheard of for divers, in their excitement, to forget to turn on their air or check the tank's status."

He does a quick, thorough inspection of his system.

"Is this really necessary?"

"He pats the tank. Come on, you're ready to go. I'll help you with the rig."

Eric gives him a patronizing thumbs-up.

"Sorry, but that reminds me of one more thing." As he returns his thumbs up, he adds, "This is the signal to surface. Remember to give us a closed circle with your thumb and forefinger to say you're 'okay'."

"Thanks, Dad. Don't forget to sign my log book when we're done."

"What's a log book?" Paul deadpans.

After Paul dons his equipment, Dax gives him the okay, and Paul reciprocates.

Dax taps Eric's arm. "Forget something?"

"*Now what?*" He snaps.

Dax holds up his dive light.

"Here?" He takes an exaggerated scan, first skyward on down to the wreck. "This isn't exactly a night dive. Have you noticed the visibility?"

"True, but the interior compartments have little to no ambient light. And when you're exploring the outside you'll want a light to highlight the fullness of colors offered by the marine life." When he gets no reaction or response from Eric, he adds, "Trust me."

"Whatever," he mutters on his way to retrieve his gear bag.

The three eventually make their entries and follow Brent down the line.

Keira's enveloped in the warmth of the tropical waters. Her regulator constantly feeds her air at ambient pressure, which adapts with the changes in depth. It feels cool, moist, and a little salty. The familiarity of the sensations are a visceral reminder she's back in the sea. The bubbles from her exhalations caress her cheeks as she begins a headfirst descent; the ceaseless crackling of shrimp immediately displaces the mechanical sounds of her breathing.

She has extensive experience scuba diving, but she's a neophyte when it comes to wrecks. *Steve sure got this right—the* Shinkoku's *a perfect introduction.* But his line art did little to prepare her for the plethora of organisms which have readily adapted to the man-made substrate. A wave of emotions sweep over her from the panoramic profusion of life to the variety of colors. The wreck humbly presents itself with the placid beauty of spectacular artificial reefs, sessile communities which have grown into inexpressive splendor. *These aren't iron hulks rusting into oblivion, they're dazzling microcosms of life.*

While Brent leads the group to an entry into the interior, Keira stops. For her, it'll wait. She's determined to explore the outside first. She wants to use this dive to take in the aquatic wonderment without the distraction of a group. *If Steve's right, the surveys will follow.* She leaves the team and continues around its exterior alone.

The wreckage is a pageant of movement. A rainbow of tropicals—angel-, damsel-, and butterflyfish continually hunt and peck throughout the reef-wreck in a perpetual quest for food, community, and protection.

With a slight scissor-kick of her fins, Keira glides effortlessly above the wreck, trying to absorb all the visuals she can. Fields of decay best describe the decks' surfaces, layers of gray chips—dead *Halimeda* algae intermixed with muted orange flakes of decomposed steel, pock-marked with minuscule, occupied recesses.

Encrusting sponge, and hard corals compliment the orange patinas of decaying steel. The ship's masts, rails, davits, funnels, and deck guns have morphed into the marine architecture.

The four-story superstructure's upper-most level has disintegrated and collapsed exposing the ship's compass, binnacle, and telegraph with easily identifiable controls frozen at the last command sent to the engine room. Remnants of the framework appear fluid——rotted steel bulkheads reanimated by countless thousands of tiny silver opal sweepers——schools of fish aligning themselves with the flat upright vestiges, gracefully move in tandem. Their behavior resembles a living aperture, as they make way for larger species, be it predators or explorers, to pass along the wreck's heavily encrusted companionways.

Sizable gorgonian fans and sponges, both tube and encrusting, decorate the hull in festive colors. At several locations throughout, exotic *Dendronepthya*, soft tree branch corals, present breath-taking displays. Using her dive light, a close inspection reveals a tapestry of polyps segregated by color——bright oranges, vivid reds, muted pinks, and radiant yellows. Each grow from a near translucent white trunk intricately threaded with white spicules which serve as both reinforcement for the coral and a prickly repellant to predators.

As Keira progresses from one area to the next, she regrets how she foolishly fought to avoid this underwater paradise. *I still resent Jonathan, but I have to admit without his insistence I would never have come here on my own.*

She's distracted by the familiar metallic tapping from a knife handle on the base of a scuba tank. Experienced divers are fluent in several means of communication. Jon emerges alone from the cargo hold and signals his daughter a second time. She makes her way toward him. When he gestures her to follow him inside, she gives him a thumbs down. He taps her slate and removes his mouthpiece to yell into her ear, "Follow me". Through his bubbled exhalations the vibrations of his words clearly transmit his message. She repeats her thumbs down. When he reaches to take her wrist, she yanks her arm away. Annoyed, he signals to surface. They start up together.

Jon surfaces first as Keira stops to take in one last panorama of this paradisal vision. When she breaks the surface, Jon spits out the mouthpiece of his regulator and props his face mask on his forehead. "Talk to me, Keira. Tell me what's going on inside your head."

She ignores his remark, works her way out of her b.c. and swims the equipment to Alou, who's leaning over the transom. She glances at her father, removes her fins, and climbs aboard. Jon follows suit.

When she walks away from the rinse barrel, he grabs her elbow. "You can't ignore me this entire trip."

She angrily yanks her arm away, and takes her seat. It's hot to the touch, so she retrieves her towel to drape over the bench. She grabs a bottle of water from the cooler for herself.

"You *do* remember why we're here?"

Keira earnestly stares at him. "I want to——"

"Then you——" he interrupts.

"Let me finish!" she snaps, struggling to keep her emotions in check. "I didn't expect any of this." Her demeanor softens. "I can see why you and mother loved this place so much." She gently adds, "Thank you, Jonathan, for including me."

With no more wind in his sails, he drops heavily on the bench next to her. "Is David's accident why you don't want to go inside the wreck?"

She lies to him with a nod.

"You won't be alone, and the passages are easily navigable." He taps her slate. "This will also help guide you. Since you've already acquainted yourself with the wreck's exterior, how 'bout we make this our second dive as well. We'll take our break here, spend some time outgassing, and start over, this time with the interior."

"I don't want to dive as part of a group when I do the penetration," she insists, "at least not my first time in. Can't I go it alone with Brent?"

"You and Brent, yes, but I want Paul along with you."

"Why?"

Now it's Jon's turn to be less than forthright, "He hasn't made many wreck dives, and I want you two to feel more comfortable together underwater."

She gives him an, 'Oh, come on … really!' expression.

"It's not that. You two need to get familiar with each other's capabilities. I can't maintain the pace the project demands and will need to pass on some dives——especially the repetitive, deeper ones."

The crew hands out box lunches——a modest sandwich, cut up fruit, and fresh coconut juice served straight from the husk. While Dax and Eric pepper Brent with questions about their last dive and what they can expect on those to come, the other three gather at the opposite side of the boat.

Keira shares her observations about the rivulets of petroleum and its dispersal in the currents. Jon reiterates it's what they're here to ascertain. She aches to tell him about her conversation with Steve Mitchell, but figures he's well aware.

Paul enthusiastically joins them. "What a step back in time," he exclaims. "I'm stunned at the condition and diversity of artifacts we came across."

He turns his attention to Keira, "Lost track of you though. Have any problems?"

"No, but tell me, how'd Eric do?"

"Why would you ask?"

"You treated him like he's a novice."

"I suppose," he concedes. "He's recently certified. When we penetrated the wreck, he focused all his attention on what his instrument console told him rather than the sights themselves."

"How can I help?" asks Jon.

"I'm hoping he'll relax as he gains more experience. In the meantime, I'll buddy him with either Dax or myself."

Jon lightly nudges Paul to the side to talk over his revised plan for the day.

Without asking, Brent wedges himself next to Keira. She huffs at the need to put some space between them.

"We're going——"

Jon overhears and interrupts him. "You'll revisit the same wreck for your second dive, but this time with Keira *and* Paul."

Brent's chagrined at the change of plans. "So, what's on your mind, boss?"

"As Keira didn't make a penetration on the first dive, I'll need you to take her through the interior with Paul. Concentrate specifically on the engine room followed by the storage compartments."

"I'm okay to lead Keira on a private tour inside," Brent points his finger at Paul, "but whadda we need him for?"

"Experience. I want him to get a better handle on doing penetration dives."

"Uh-huh."

From the edge in Dax's voice, Paul realizes he's upset about sitting out this dive. He leads him back to the transom and points to an unusually sleek yacht at anchorage.

"I need to give you a task while we're below."

"Give it to Eric. I doubt he'll mind sitting this one out."

"I'm asking you."

"Why can't I do whatever it is *after* the dive."

Paul doesn't react.

"Okay, what?" Dax huffs.

He points to the black craft. "Use Eric's binoculars to monitor the activity around her. At this distance, it appears to attract an unusual amount of traffic."

"Yeah … sure … okay. What does it have to do with us again?"

Paul grabs his upper arm, "I get you're not happy about this, but trust me, I promise you'll rack up plenty of bottom time while we're here."

Dax gives him a skeptical gaze. "I'm going to hold you to that."

Chapter 9
Second Dive
Shinkoku Maru

As the three start their descent, Paul points out several black-barred gray sharks. They patrol the periphery, yet keep their distance from the intruders. He gently folds into Keira's hand.

Brent impatiently waits at the entry. Keira shakes loose of Paul's grip to give him an "okay" sign. Paul repeats the gesture. Brent ignores them both and slips into the interior.

Keira pauses at the opening. There's no dangerous creatures, ghosts, or spirits, only memories of a lost brother. Entering the first compartment, she's initially taken with the blanket of silt that seemingly coats everything. To minimize stirring up the particulate, Brent and Paul rely on their skillset to keep themselves neutrally buoyant——suspended off the bottom. She follows suit by tapping her power inflator valve to add a bit of air into her compensator vest.

They glide by a surgery table stacked with artifacts collected by earlier visitors and left on display for passersby. The next compartment contains the bathhouse——a tub covered with a paltry skin of white tiles, and filled with silt which resettled after the earlier team passed through the confined space. Along the opposite bulkhead, a bank of white porcelain sinks awaits the swipe of a cloth to put them back into operation. There's much to slowly take in, but Brent pushes the pace and leads them through a different exit to the ship's deck.

The remaining aft superstructure has slanted skylights behind the single smokestack standing directly over the engine room. Keira points out the globules of oil trickling from the cylinder bank. She follows one upwards until it finds an escape through a break in the compartment's overhead. To her the leakage appears minuscule and not a threat.

She effortlessly propels herself into a compartment adjacent to the engine room. With no outside light source, it's pitch-black inside. Her light becomes her new "dive buddy". Its beam directs her eyes to two tiers of oil drums stacked next to the furthest bulkhead. She notes their quantity and location before moving on.

Brent crosses his arms while he hovers midwater near the exit hatch. He notices Paul examine the seepage, and with Keira gone, wedges himself inside the hatchway. It only takes a slight effort to kick up a blinding cloud of silt which completely envelopes Paul.

With visibility compromised, Brent rejoins Keira deep into a well-lit stowage area. A school of harmless pinnate batfish, each the size and shape of a dinner platter, startles Keira as they pass her from behind. She subsequently flinches when Brent unexpectedly taps her shoulder, then notices roiled-up silt spill onto the deck from the open hatchway and dissipate as it spreads out.

Paul has yet to emerge. *Could he be lost? Stuck? Confused?* She glares at Brent and signals they go back for him, but he shakes his head and starts to lead her further away. Keira stops, pulls out the slate she uses for notes and writes "PAUL", and jams the sign flush into his mask so he can't avoid her message. He responds with hand signs, "He's okay." When he tries to physically lead her ahead, she forcefully shoves him aside, and returns to the cloudy entry alone, peeks inside the blacked-out compartment to listen, but hears nothing. Her dive light is useless as its beam cannot penetrate the dense cloud of silt.

Puzzled why Brent won't go back inside with her, she signals they surface. On their way out, they follow the hull's outer edge to the anchor line. All during their return and ascent, Keira scans for streams of bubbles, a telltale sign of Paul's whereabouts. Nothing. The terrible memories of her brother, and the retrieval of his body from the cavern, dominate her emotions. She cannot abide reliving that horror.

When Keira breaks the surface, she yells for her father while she doffs her scuba gear. As she hands up her tank and vest, Paul reaches down to give her a hand.

"Paul, where——"

"Sorry, but it got so murky down there I lost sight of you. I had to back-track until a patch of light pointed me to a gaping hole in the hull, so I made my exit. It's all good."

She boards the boat and hugs him, then punches his chest. "You scared me. I thought we'd lost you," surprising them both with her physicality. She awkwardly drops her arms and laughs it off.

"I guess Brent and I will need to straighten out our signals," he answers.

Without making further eye contact, Keira mutters, "Good idea," and walks away, visibly shaken.

Jon tails Keira to her seat to check on her. "I'm rattled right now, okay," she barks. "That brought back too many terrible memories. For a moment down there, it was David all over again."

When Jon doesn't respond, Keira replays the dive for her father. He tries not to chuckle.

She's exasperated, "What? Of all people, *you* find that funny?"

"Paul told me about Brent's ruse and I believe he's come up with an appropriate solution."

When Brent surfaces, he's surprised to face Paul waiting at the transom.

"Let me give you a hand with your equipment."

Brent doffs his scuba rig and hands it up. As if nothing happened below, he passes his mask and fins to Paul, before he starts his way up the ladder. Paul blocks his progress at the top rung, gets a good grip on his fins, and with an, "Oops. Clumsy me," flings them far overboard in opposite directions. He answers Brent's incredulity with, "You better hurry before they sink. Figure you'll need them for the swim back."

"Whaddya mean?" he yells before diving in.

"Better save your energy. As I recall we're a marathon's distance from home base."

He adds, "Oh yeah, I guess you'll need this, too." He flings Brent's mask well over his head.

"You and I *will* have words when I get back."

Yes, we will, Paul says to himself.

Brent easily retrieves the mask, but the boat is far enough away that by the time he turns back, the anchor's pulled and they're underway. He flips off Paul, and shouts a loud stream of obscenities the boat's motors drown out when they kick into gear. A smiling Alou starts their return to the dock without Brent.

An hour after the boat's unloaded, a second pulls alongside with Brent onboard. Paul stayed to help Alou with the unload and hose down the boat. As soon as Brent catches sight of him, he drops his gear in place and yells, "Stay where you are, Gerhart!"

He runs directly toward Paul and throws a clumsy roundhouse punch, which he easily sidesteps. As a result, Brent's completely off-balance. With a light shove, he stumbles face-first into the gravel. Startled, Brent quickly stands, brushes off his cheek, gathers himself, and throws a left cross. When he completely misses, Paul intercepts his arm and in one motion folds it into a half-nelson and takes him back down. He continues to twist the hold until Brent yells, "Okay,

okay, enough already!"

Paul tightens his grip causing Brent's face to dig deep against the sharp stones. "Let me up," he screams. "I'm sorry, okay?"

"We need to better define our relationship, Brent."

"We ain't gonna def——"

He turns the hold until Brent lets out another yelp.

"It must be you think I'm blind, otherwise I might get the impression you intended to do me bodily harm."

"You sonofa——"

He clamps down with more pressure.

"Listen closely. Brent. We will conduct our investigations safely … and by 'we', I mean you, too. Clear enough?"

Brent tries to move his head, but can't. "YEAH, YEAH!" he yells. "Now let me up!"

"There's one more item."

"WHAT?"

"If I suspect you of pulling a similar stunt, I *won't* send out a chase boat. Do we understand each other?"

"Okay, okay, no more funny stuff." Paul releases his grip, gives him a hand up, turns and heads to the hotel without looking back.

Brent slowly regains his footing while he works the circulation into his numb arm. He brushes off the gravel, gently rubs his sore cheek, and hopes no one witnessed his predicament. The boat drivers, Alou and Kristian, laugh openly at Brent's humiliation and pull their boats away from the dock to refuel amiably chatting with each other.

"We'll find out who has the last laugh!" Brent yells at them.

Jon and his daughter wait for Paul in the hotel restaurant and wave him over when he enters.

Keira greets him warmly. "How'd it go?"

"I believe we've come to a mutual understanding."

Jon hands him the extra menu. "Let's go with the fresh fish."

Keira tries to shift the focus onto a topic other than Brent. "I understand you're pretty well-traveled. How does this compare to some of your other adventures?"

"I have to admit this place is truly unique."

Jon adds, "And we haven't scratched the surface yet. There's so much more down there. Wait 'til we dive the *San Francisco Maru.*"

"Didn't you say you'd pass on the deeper dives?" responds Keira.

"Someone's done her homework," Jon grins at Paul. "The *Aikoku* and *San Francisco Marus* are two wrecks I won't pass on."

"Okay, I have a question for you, Jon," says Paul. "Whatever happened to the bodies? I expected to come across some remains."

"Unfortunately you will on some deeper wrecks, though they're nothing but remnants of bones; they've recovered a good percentage already."

"Why haven't they retrieved the rest?" notes Keira.

"It's a sticking point between the two governments. Japanese officials have petitioned for their recovery, but so far unsuccessfully.

"Japanese tourists come to the islands annually to venerate their veterans who died here. Their government has lodged protests. They claim it's a source of distress to the entire country, but the local powers understand if they remove all the bones, tourism will take a hit."

"So what it boils down to is money," Keira shudders, "it's ghoulish."

"I doubt all the bones could, or would ever be recovered," Jon adds. "There's still too many. They're either too deep or under the cover of siltation, and would require a dredge—dangerous and expensive work. We all need to stay sensitive to the fact we're diving on much more than underwater museums."

"On a related topic," Keira pauses until she has their attention. "You make such a to-do about the artifacts, yet for me, the real treasure is the marine life. I'm fascinated by how a relatively few traces were able to gain an anchorage on bare steel and eventually overtake the remnants of war. The profusion and variety are astounding."

Jon responds immediately. "I understand your attraction to the marine life. You grew up with that deep connection, but the historic significance of these wrecks and artifacts shouldn't be dismissed. We get to step back in time to an era which changed the destinations of both our countries——a time when men fought and died to remove a threat to freedom the entire world feared."

Paul shares his thoughts. "I haven't found many places in the world with the living museums offered here. Nothing below separates us by glass and a pristine note identifying objects we either can't touch or only given time enough to catch a glimpse, all while following a docent who has to stick to a tight schedule."

"What do you consider Brent?" she quips.

"Good point," he chuckles.

"I hear what you're saying," she enthusiastically responds, "and you're correct to appreciate their importance, but you place too high a value on relics used by men who did their best to kill each other while you overlook the incomparable diversity of marine life staring you right in the face.

"On the first dive, I floated over a ladder adorned with plate corals, sponge, and the eerie saw-toothed smile of cock's comb oysters, which reminded me of carved jack-o-lanterns. Nearby, the ship's starboard lantern rested on the deck; its green lens intact in its frail brass housing. A hatch, propped open for fifty years, hosting tall purple tube sponge with an underside encrusted in orange, a colorful invitation to enter below.

"I saw bright blue chromis dart in and about the calcareous branches of hard corals that encrust the rim of a cartridge box filled with eleven of its twelve 4.7-inch shells.

You see artifacts of war and death. All I see is life."

After a pause, Paul makes a suggestion. "Have you ever considered teaching, maybe marine biology or ecology? You could infect your students with the same enthusiasm you have for the sea and raise a whole new generation of avid explorers in love with the oceans and aware of what they need to do to protect to them."

Keira doesn't respond.

Jon points to the couple. "It's getting late. Unless either of you can come up with a reasonable objection, I'd want you to buddy up together as much as possible."

"You're in charge," Paul says as he stands to leave.

Astonished, Keira says, "Wait a minute. Don't I have any say in this?"

While Brent pays the cabbie, Tino joins him. "I thought you might visit us tonight."

As the cab quickly pulls away, Tino forcibly grabs Brent's chin and turns his abraded cheek to the side to inspect the damage more closely, and is pleased with what he finds.

"We heard you ran into a bit of trouble today."

Brent does not appreciate the familiarity and slaps his hand aside. Tino's not as tall as Brent, but wiry strong, and carries himself confidently. Brent knows him as an 'insider' from the Marianas, who frequently visits the island under a "diplomatic passport". Somehow they're linked via the 'Consortium', though in what capacity, he hasn't a clue.

"May I go in now?"

"He's expecting you, but before you do, we need to talk."

Brent stops and faces him, "About what?"

"We have a certain method of dealing with people who get in our way ... and *you*, young man, are inching dangerously close."

"You want to explain your remark? Should I take it as some kind of a threat?"

"Possibly."

Brent sloughs him off, and walks away.

The governor enters the main parlor to greet his visitor. He stops ten feet short and asks a rhetorical question, "What brings you here tonight."

How could they have already heard about the incident?

The governor impatiently goads him. "Well, how do you account for yourself?"

Brent's distracted by Tino's reappearance who assumes a place slightly behind his right shoulder.

"It's about the agent with Jon's group, the one they call Paul."

"Gerhart," the governor clarifies.

"Yeah, him."

"What's your problem?"

"He's experienced, dangerous, and I believe he's suspicious of us."

Brent hesitates and glances back at Tino before he adds, "And I want him dealt with."

"You 'want him dealt with'? You fool." The governor makes eye contact with his associate, and before Brent can argue his point, Tino slashes the damaged side of Brent's face with his pistol, sending him down to one knee. He tries to stand up, but reels back to the floor and lands on his haunches. His cheek throbs and he spits blood onto the tiles.

He wants to lash out at Tino, but the sensation of cold steel against his forehead shuts him up. While Brent struggles back to his feet, Tino clicks the hammer in place.

"Enough!" yells the governor.

Tino backs off.

Though distracted by the stream of blood dribbling onto the front of Brent's shirt, the governor walks directly up to him.

"Pay attention, boy." He tightly grabs onto Brent's throbbing face and pulls him closer. "You have to realize by *your* reckless actions and ties to us, Gerhart might start to investigate *our* activities. If so, it would bring about a terrible consequence for you."

He pushes his face away, staggering Brent.

It takes him several seconds to collect himself. He wants to yell, but his voice fails him as tears fill his eyes. He angrily sputters, "You don't have to worry about me. I've got ..." the words catch in his throat, "... I'm the best diver out there."

Lifting his arm, Brent flinches at the sight of Tino's gun raised to strike him, until the governor waves him off.

"It's not your skill level I'm worried about. It's your judgment." His voice starts to elevate, "Do you believe his government will grant us a single penny if even one of their representatives meets harm in any way while they're here?"

He tries to taper down the intensity by speaking with a more business-like voice. "We play our cards right *and* if all of us do our job," he nudges him in the chest, "especially you, we're in for a sizable payday. If this team from the states approves the grant money, your retainer with us will smack of pocket change. Do you really want to throw it all away?"

Brent wipes the side of his mouth and sheepishly answers, "No."

"Good. Now get out of my sight and do what you need to make this right with our guests."

Outside the house, he wipes away another trickle of blood, and glares at Tino. "What the hell!"

"Consider yourself lucky this time."

"Lucky!" he yells. He holds out the waistline of his blood-stained shirt. "You call this *lucky*?"

"If the Chairman had gotten wind of this, you'd of had to answer to people other than us and trust me, it would not have gone as well for you."

"Who is this 'Chairman' you keep bringing up?"

"He's the Consortium's head honcho and you'd better hope you never have to meet him in person." Tino speaks to him empathetically, "You've had a difficult day. Why don't you let me give you a ride home?"

Brent glares at Tino making the offer while holding a cocked pistol at his side. He spits his response on the entry stoop before he begins the trek back to his studio.

115

Chapter 10
Sankisan Maru

Off the Western Shore of Uman Island

While the team continues their surveys and explorations on the relatively shallow-water wrecks, Brent is forced to take several days off to give his face time to heal. No one in the group objects. Jon invites Steve Mitchell to lead their dives during Brent's absence.

Before Steve begins this morning's brief, he places an enlargement of one of his detailed prints on the easel. It represents the front half of a wreck.

Dax takes an empty seat next to Keira, who asks, "Where's Paul?"

He scans the room before he quietly answers, "Been wondering that myself."

When Steve begins his talk, Keira interrupts, "Shouldn't we wait for Paul before we begin?"

Jon addresses his daughter, "He wanted to get an early jump on his prep this morning and is down at the boat."

Steve's anxious to begin. "So, if everyone's ready, let's get started. This is the *Sankisan Maru*, originally a three hundred and sixty-seven foot cargo hauler. Her bow rests at eighty feet. An explosion tore the ship in two and carved a crater a hundred and fifty feet below where the stern settled upright. A point we will not visit today.

"In stark contrast to your experience on the *Shinkoku*,

where one clean bomb strike served her death knell, the *Sankisan's* demise came about from either a single catastrophic explosion, or a devastating series of secondary explosions which set the stores of ordnance in the ship's after-holds ablaze." Pointing to the chart, he continues, "The first three cargo holds, foremast, and kingpost remain intact, but the superstructure crumbled, either from fires or collateral damage from the explosions which tore her in two.

"There's a lot of speculation about her final days, unfortunately no records exist to fill in the gaps. It is known the ship arrived here four days before the attack on February 17th. She's located at the Sixth Fleet Anchorage, off the western shores of Uman Island. Five Navy SB2C Curtiss Helldivers attacked her with strafing runs and a 1,000 pound bomb strike. Unfortunately, we have no photographic evidence or confirmation from after-action reports about the ship's demise and nobody came forward as a witness. After the attack, the only evidence of her existence was a lingering oil slick.

"Despite the extensive damage, you're in for another visual spectacle. The *Sankisan* combines an extensive variety of marine life with a varied collection of artifacts. As such, this wreck has rightfully developed into one of our most popular destinations."

Keira's excited about the possibility of encounters similar to her previous experience.

Paul's compelled to thoroughly inspect their equipment before the team arrives from the brief. He'll get a rundown from Keira during the transit. When he arrives at the dock, he notices an airline-sized baggage cart close to the dock's ramp filled with scuba tanks. Alou's handling them by himself.

Paul drops his bag and hurries to help. "Let me give you a hand."

"Thanks, but it's my job."

"Come on. It'll go a lot faster with the two of us."

Alou smiles. "Okay. Thanks."

Alou boards the boat, and Paul carries the tanks to him, two at a time. While Alou secures them in the cradles, Paul retrieves the next round.

"Where are the others?"

"At the hotel for the brief."

"From Brent?" he scowls.

"No. Steve's leading the group today."

"Good," he mutters.

"I take it you have some issues with Brent?"

Alou checks to ensure they can speak freely. "I do," he bitterly declares, "I *hate* him."

"Kinda harsh isn't it?"

"Ever since Andon set me up as a boat driver, Brent has made it a point to disrespect me."

"How?"

"He doesn't listen. He won't help with the crew duties, and laughs when I need him to give me a hand."

"Have you spoken with your uncle?"

"He said to give him a chance to adjust to my new role."

"Have you?"

"I don't know how."

"You're now in a position of authority over him, so step-up and give *him* a hand with the workload."

Alou returns a blank stare.

"When he believes you're not coming across as better than him, he'll come around."

Alou rolls around his advise for awhile.

"Can I ask you a question?"

"Sure."

"How'd you learn to handle Brent so easily."

Paul uses the time while he grabs the next pair of tanks to formulate an answer.

"Before I did this kind of work, I served in the military. They taught me how to defend myself."

"I've never seen anyone here fight like you."

"Have a lot of fights on Chuuk do you?"

"Not a lot, but occasionally."

With the next round of tanks, Alou continues his inquiry. "Would you teach me?"

"I'm afraid we won't have enough time."

Alou drops his head. "Oh."

"But I can show you a couple of moves to avoid anything serious."

Alou's face brightens up. "Thanks. I'd appreciate it."

The team's arrival cuts their conversation short.

"Could we talk more about it some other time?"

"You bet, my friend. Anytime."

It's a long transit to the site and a good opportunity to relax. The ship's foremast rises above the surface to provide an easy tie-off for the anchorage. The group splits into two teams. Keira and Paul go with Steve while Jon leads the others. Both teams try their best to avoid each other. The descent will follow the kingpost's stanchions to the deck.

Lateral visibility on the wreck pushes a hundred feet. Keira's enthralled by the conditions and profusion of growth. She hopes to spend some of the dive observing the lush diversity of marine life.

A sizable red tomato anemone dominates the kingpost's upright. Two clownfish perform a hide-and-seek ritual using their bright orange bodies offset by a distinctive white vertical stripe to allure prey into the anemone's paralyzing tentacles. The symbiotic relationship provides a food source for both, as well as protection for the immune clownfish. When they sense no threat from Keira, they resume their provocative dance. Experience has taught her to take in the whole ritual without touching.

She slowly continues down the kingpost noting the encrusting sponge and cup corals, whose polyps retract into calcareous casings during the daylight and resemble a collection of orange puckered lips.

Keira wants to stay outside rather than root around the dark, silty cargo holds, but Steve taps on the bottom of his tank to have her follow. She doesn't really care about the surveys, but did make the commitment. Up until now she has used the slates to make notes about her observations, while back in her room she pours through the books on marine life, as she completes her cursory reports.

Steve leads them into a hold which contains radial aircraft engines, originally shipped as replacement parts for the squadrons on nearby Eten Island, but left to decay in the depths after the attack. Eight trucks lie scattered about the ship, their thin-gauge steel bodies have dissolved to the frames. She notices odd parts survived the ravages of salt water and time: the steering wheel and gear linkage, rubber tires mounted on their wheels still affixed to the axles, and surprisingly readable manufacturers' imprints on the radiators——Toyota and Isuzu.

When they drop into the number one hold they're greeted by the surreal sound of tinkling glass, as if someone is running their fingers through a chandelier's crystal prisms. Keira points her light into the cargo hold beneath them which illuminates countless empty vials of deep cobalt blue, light amber, and clear glass. They used to contain medications for the hospitals and first aid stations. When their stoppers eventually dissolved, the contents assimilated into the lagoon's waters. Over time, the original cardboard and wooden containers broke down and unleashed the vials throughout the hold.

Keira's wonders, *How did these survive the explosions?*

After the penetration dive on the *Shinkoku*, she resolves to keep her hands to herself. She notices Paul slip a blue bottle into his vest pocket. *Interesting. People, especially him, have repeatedly warned us not to pilfer from the wrecks.*

The hold also contains mounds of 7.7 mm ammunition, countless thousands still in their brass casings. Several are jacketed in five-round stripper-clips fused together in rusted black sleeves, reminders they're diving on ships-of-war, and a popular temptation to divers who seek souvenirs. With the ban in mind, Keira watches for Paul to add to his collection, and puzzled when he doesn't.

The next point to inspect is the number two hold, filled with depth charges, anti-invasion beach mines, and twenty mm anti-aircraft shells.

In the engine room, Keira's enthralled by the sight of a six foot orange sea fan which spans the gap between two boilers. Its reticulated branches link them from top-to-bottom with a two dimensional web of brilliant orange, and presents a natural screen against any passage. She enthusiastically signals the others, and outlines the coral's expanse with her arms. When she points out the size contrast with a nudibranch slowly negotiating the web-like growth, Paul and Steve move on unimpressed. *What those two don't get about this place. Must be a guy thing.*

On their return to the main deck, they pass over the windless with its anchor chains in place which lead over the bow to the stocks. The port anchor's tucked into its hawse, but the deployed starboard chain hangs straight down. One of its massive links has broken off midway from the bottom. Heavy layers of marine growth have yet to disguise the individual links within the coiled mound.

An hour after their initial descent, Steve signals it's time to surface. Keira checks her pressure gauge for her remaining air——nine hundred p.s.i.——nearly a third of a tank. Though she has a more efficient rate of air consumption than the men do, she nevertheless has to go through the same decompression requirements before she can surface. As she hangs at ten feet for a safety stop, she catches sight of a school of bigeye trevallies as they pass by the port side. *The parade never ends.*

Keira interrupts Paul as he packs his dive gear. "Careful

you don't break the pretty bottle."

Embarrassed and defensive, he replies, "Keira, you don't——"

"Will you add it to your souvenir collection?"

"Don't be coy. You know it's against the law."

She waits for him to continue.

"It may tie-in with what I heard about the day we arrived. Don't worry, I'll return the artifact to Andon for safekeeping before we leave."

She waits for him to explain, but he retrieves his b.c. from the rinse barrel and continues to pack.

"For a minute there, I hoped you'd reveal at least a tidbit of info. Stop trying to keep me in the dark, Paul. Talk to me."

He continues to drain the water out of his vest and carefully rolls it tightly before he stows it.

"I hate this secret crap. You whet my curiosity with some hint of intrigue, only to go mute."

He stays on task until she briskly steps onto the dock and heads to the hotel in a huff. Paul empathizes with her frustration, but has to let her deal with it on her own.

Steve runs to catch up with her.

"Yeah, yeah, follow your lead and stick close to you," she mocks without breaking stride.

He gently grabs her arm and forces her to a stop.

She pushes his hand away. "I don't like that!" She exhales heavily to calm herself down. "Nothing about these wrecks scream ecological disaster to me, Steve. What're we doing here?"

He does a quick three-sixty and speaks quietly. "I totally agree with you, Keira, but for now, you need to play along—— do the dives, collect the data, and continue with the surveys."

She's puzzled, "But the other day——"

"Be patient. I need to collect proof, make my analysis, and once I can make sense of it, we'll talk with Paul and your father. Until then, try to appear cooperative."

"If you say so," she concedes. "Can I buy you a beer as a peace offering?"

He readily agrees.

From the dock, Paul monitors their interaction. *She definitely has some intrigues of her own.*

Alou quickly scans the corridor before he knocks on Paul's door. No answer. He tries a second time more emphatically and continues until he hears a response.

Paul yawns as he opens the door.

He regrets waking him up. "I'm sorry. Should I come back another time?"

"I'm awake now. What's on your mind? "

"Can we talk … alone?"

"Yeah, sure, come in and find a seat."

Paul leaves the door open behind him as he walks to the bathroom to throw some water on his face. Alou steps in, closes the door, and claims the larger chair.

"I hope you're not here to learn more about fighting," Paul states.

Alou's head hangs down as he quietly responds, "That's not it."

"You have my attention."

Tears roll down his cheeks. "I'm in trouble. I'm in over my head and I don't know what to do."

"Have you tried speaking with your father about this?"

"He walked out on us several years ago," he bitterly answers. "He lives on Pohnpei now, with his *other* family."

"How 'bout Andon. Can't you go to him."

Alou shakes his head more emphatically. "Him … last of all."

"Why don't you start at the beginning."

"Can I trust you won't tell my uncle, or anyone?"

"I promise, whatever we talk about will never leave this room."

Alou hesitates to work up the courage. "It started a while back. A couple of guys I grew up with contacted me one night after work. Damon and Miguel asked if I would do a job for the same people who hired them. They needed an inside contact."

"'Inside what?'"

"The dive shop."

"Go on."

"When they heard about your arrival, they told me to keep them informed of your activities, and offered to pay. The money would come from an associate of the governor. He works for some outfit called 'the Consortium'."

"What did he want?"

"He wasn't real specific. Whatever I could tell him."

"Can you give me an example?"

"I told them about your encounter with Brent?"

"And …"

"Nothing, I promise. It's the only time I ever called."

"What did they give you for the information?"

"They gave me some money."

"How much?"

Alou reaches into his pocket and slides an envelope across the table with a couple of hundred in twenties.

Paul counts the cash. "Did you speak to the governor directly."

"No." He pulls out a creased card with a hand-written phone number. "Take it."

Paul, scans both sides.

"It was folded in with the money. It's the number I'm supposed to call. But I won't do it no more."

"Who did you speak to?"

"A man who calls himself 'Nededog'?"

"You asked if you could trust me when you came in. It's my turn. Same question. Can I trust you?"

"I promise I won't call them again. Not ever."

"You have to realize, Alou, by accepting their money, they expect a return on their investment."

He pushes the money back toward Paul. "You keep it. I don't want it."

Without a response, he puts the money back in the envelope, seals it, and drops it into the dresser drawer.

"What can I do?" Alou buries his face in his hands and sobs.

Paul gives him time to work through it.

"Should I tell my uncle?"

"It was good you came to me first. I'm afraid Andon will take steps on his own and possibly put himself at risk."

"Will *you* help me?"

"When the time's right, but listen … you'll have to wait. Anyone else in on this? Brent? Anybody else in the crew?"

"I don't think so."

"Good. If these people follow-up with you, tell me right away." He pauses until he has Alou's undivided attention. "Not the next day, or the following, but right away."

"I will, I promise. Will you forgive me?"

Paul warmly answers, "There's nothing to forgive."

After dinner, Keira strolls the hotel grounds with a bottle of water. A line of palm trees fringe the shoreline. She eyes a man's silhouette against the night sky. He's seated on the trunk of a palm which grew horizontally before it turned skyward, forming a natural bench. She doesn't want to disturb him and starts to walk away.

"Come sit with me, Keira Lynn," Jon gestures to the spot next to him.

She stands in place with her arms folded across her chest. "Stargazing, Jonathan? Memories of your time here with mother?"

A deep sadness overtakes him. "Your mother and I loved this place. It evokes some tender memories of a special time together. She never missed a dive, seemed as much at home below as … well, as you do." After a pause, he begins to add, "I'd hoped——"

She interrupts astonished. "Hoped what?"

He frowns and impatiently shakes his head. "I hoped to share the joy of this place with you. Hoped you might come to love these waters as much as I do … as we did … somehow, someway, you might put our past mistakes behind you."

"*Our* past mistakes!" she yells. She fights back her own tears and frustrations. Especially since he will not admit David's death wasn't her fault. He's still incapable of granting her the absolution she so desperately seeks. "I love you, Jonathan," her voice cracks, "but you hurt me. All these years I've had to carry the guilt," her voice rises, as she points an accusing finger at him, "that *you* encumbered me with. You never took one step to ease *my* loss." She angrily jams her thumb into her stomach. "Yes, *my* loss!" Her voice quivers with unsuppressed rage, "I'm thankful at least mother understood, but I especially needed yours. I felt like my presence reminded you … whenever you looked at me … that you wished …" The words stick in her throat. Before she can say anything else, she runs to the hotel in tears.

127

While the crew congregates around the coffee urn, Paul breaks away from his conversation with Dax and Eric to start the morning's brief. He tracks down Jon and an unusually subdued Keira, who sit on opposite sides of the room. "You two doing okay?"

"A bit tired," concedes Jon.

"But looking forward to our dive," Keira adds.

"Jon, can I presume you've made the necessary arrangements with Andon?"

"We're all set."

"What?" interjects Dax. "You two going off on your own?" he asks, then looks back to Paul. "What's *our* plan today?"

Paul answers his friend directly, "Actually, the three of us have other commitments."

"Oh?——"

Paul interrupts, "It's about J.J.'s directive. I'll talk to the two of you alone after we break up here."

Jon leans toward Dax. "Sorry, but my daughter and I have reservations for a dive which holds some personal significance, yet contributes nothing to our mission."

"Well, aren't you *special*," Dax responds.

"Stow it," Paul interrupts, before he impatiently adds, "as a matter of fact, let's take this into another room … now."

Keira eyes the three until Paul closes the door behind them. She turns back to Jon. "He hates missing a dive doesn't he?"

"Before we go, I want to talk with you about last night."

Paul leads Eric and Dax into the hotel's lounge. It's closed to the public at this hour, but handy for an uninterrupted conversation.

As soon as the door closes, Dax presses, "What's going on?"

Paul responds, "We have a busy day ahead of us. Our jet left Guam early this morning. J.J. messaged he's shipped us two crates."

"So, I can assume there's no diving today … at least for us?"

Paul hands Dax his room key. "Two of Andon's people brought the hotel's pick-up to give you a hand getting the containers from the airport and up to my room. Please give them a generous tip, but under no circumstances should those crates be opened. After they're secured, close off the room with a 'Do Not Disturb' sign. I don't want maid service snooping around."

Eric's curious. "Why? What's in them?"

"We'll have a chance to open them together soon enough."

Paul singles out Eric. "As for you, the two of us have a house call to make."

"Oh?"

"I need to put some of those vaunted detective skills of yours to work."

"What about me?" asks Dax. "I like playing detective, too."

Paul quips, "Not this time, Sherlock."

Alou's childhood friend, Kristian, has done menial jobs for Andon around the hotel and the dive operation with the hopes of eventually working his way onto the boats. Alou constantly pestered his uncle to let him join his crew. As today's charter is limited, Andon gives him a green light. He'll get a good idea of how they operate without a lot of expectations.

Alou steps up to greet Jon and Keira. "Where's everyone else?"

"They have other commitments today."

"Paul too?"

Keira steps closer to Alou. "What can we help you with?"

Alou's eyes are focused on the hotel. "I wanted to continue a conversation Paul and I started yesterday."

Jon nudges Keira. "We need to set-up our equipment."

Alou returns to the console to finish his preparations. When Kristian joins him, Alou asks, "You remember Damien and Miguel?"

"Yeah. Why?" he responds skeptically.

He catches the judgmental tone in Kristian's voice. "Forget it." He points to the stern. "Get ready to cast off the lines."

Kristian works his way to the aft cleat. "We're not finished with this."

Paul tosses Eric the keys to the Jeep. "Easier if you drive. I'll give you directions as we go."

Twenty minutes later Paul nudges him to pull off to the shoulder, deep in the residential district south of town.

Leaning against the vehicle's fender, Eric takes in the house and the grounds: a modest-sized, tin-roofed, cinder block house with several layers of bluish green paint. Fallen palm fronds litter the sandy grounds. An old tire swing hangs limp from a steel pole suspended between the house and a nearby tree. A rusted, but still functional washing machine is nestled on the building's lea side next to a clothesline. There's no car in sight. He checks the road in both directions, and confirms the time. "You sure someone's at home?"

"From what I gather, the husband works, while the woman we're meeting stays homebound," Paul responds. "We're a bit early and I expect another party shortly."

On cue, a gray pick-up pulls in behind their Jeep. "The husband?"

"No. Come on, I'll introduce you."

Paul greets Kohper. "Thanks for taking the time, Chief."

"Yeah, sure," he shakes Paul's hand limply, and acknowledges his partner.

"My associate, Eric Woods … Police Chief Kohper. He arranged this interview for today."

As they walk to the house, Paul adds, "If it's alright with you, Chief, I'd like Eric to lead the questioning."

"It's your show." He raps on the door.

They wait about a minute before it opens slightly. Beyond the security chain, a disembodied voice says, "Yes. Who is it?"

"Mrs. Hetiback?"

"Who is this?" she demands.

"It's Chief Kohper. I'm here with the men I spoke about earlier."

"Give me a minute."

The door closes and it remains silent. Kohper answers Eric's inquiring look with, "Give her time."

Moments later they hear the chain slide and the door open. Covered with in a light pink housecoat she appears to have crawled out of bed to answer the door. She's in her late-thirties, slightly overweight, with a shock of prematurely graying hair which frames a pleasant face. She gives the visitors a faint smile, self-consciously strokes back her hair with both hands, and bands it into a knot. "I'm sorry. I didn't expect you so soon." She opens the door completely. "Please come in. Would you care for some coffee?"

"If it's no problem, thank you," answers Eric.

"I'll put on a pot. We can sit at the kitchen table."

As the water heats, she takes a chair. "What can I help you

with?"

"Chief Kohper shared a bit about the encounter you had with your son."

She rises from the table, and without a word walks into a back room and loudly closes the door.

Paul glances over to the chief who's trying to sneak a peek at his watch.

"You sure we're expected?" whispers Eric.

"Patience. She assured me we could make contact anytime."

When the coffee pot beeps it's ready, she steps out, fully dressed. She lays a hand-sized bottle flat on the table and sets up four cups. "What do you take with your coffee?"

"Black is fine," says Eric.

"Same here," echoes Paul.

She smiles back. "Call me Lorleen."

"How 'bout you, Chief?"

"Sure."

"You have a lovely name," adds Eric.

She smiles.

His attention shifts to the cobalt blue bottle with Japanese lettering molded into the glass. It's rectangular, flat, about four inches tall, and tapers to a narrow neck.

"What can you tell us about this?"

"When I repacked my son's dresser with his clean laundry," she breathes deeply before she continues, "I came across the bottle. I dug around his drawers and discovered a substantial amount of cash hidden under his shirts. As you can see, we don't have much. It was more money than I'd ever seen at one time. My boy …," she slowly shakes her head, "the change in his behavior shocked me. When I held it up to him for an explanation, he got so angry with me." Her tears flow freely. She feels the need to apologize.

"It's okay, Lorleen," Eric reassures, "you're amongst friends."

"He grabbed the money from me and said it's his. I wanted to reach for his arm to calm him down, but he pushed me against the dresser and stormed out. He slammed the front door so forcefully, I didn't dare go after him."

Kohper empties his cup and goes to the stove for a refill. Familiar with her story, he leans against the counter to listen and observe.

Paul records her answers in his own notepad. "Did he tell you where it came from?"

She shakes her head. "Not right away."

Paul points to the bottle. "May we keep this?"

She hesitates before she nods. Kohper glares. "That's evidence."

"I'd like to run some tests," he tells the chief. "I'll get it back to you."

Lorleen slides the bottle over to Paul and continues, "My husband got home the same time he usually does. When I told him what happened, he insisted the two of us go through the rest of his dresser. When we checked his closet, we found the gun."

"A gun!" shouts Kohper. "Why's this the first I'm hearing about it?"

She turns her attention directly to the chief. "I was afraid of what you might do to him, Elias."

"A handgun?" Eric clarifies.

She cringes in agreement.

"What did you do?"

"My son returned late that night. As soon as he came through the door, my husband backed him against the wall, pressed the gun against his nose, and pulled back the hammer. He threatened to use it if he lied to us. The gun wasn't loaded, but it frightened him … and me, too," she cried. "He admitted he worked for somebody I'd never heard of and needed the protection. How he ever got hooked up with *them* …" she bitterly remarks.

Eric picks up the blue vial. "How does this fit in?"

"He told me the governor's men gave it to him. We assumed he's dealing, so I went to the chief here."

Kohper startles her. "Where's the weapon now?"

She measures her response. "My husband prefers to fish on his day off, so he forced my son, Ryley, to spend the day on the boat with him. When they got into deeper waters, my husband flung it overboard."

Kohper's astonished. "He threw it away! That's evidence."

"I didn't want it anywhere around this house or my son!" she snaps back.

An uncomfortable silence takes over the room.

Eventually Eric reengages Paul. "You wanna jump in here?"

Paul stands. The others follow. He holds out his hand which she takes lightly.

"Thank you, Lorleen. I realize this wasn't easy for you to share with us."

"Is my boy in any kind of trouble?" She scans the three and stops at the chief. "My Ryley's a good boy, isn't he?"

He answers with a perfunctory, but disingenuous nod.

Eric does his best to reassure her. "Sounds like he's in good hands with his father."

"What will happen to him now?"

"If he keeps his nose clean, we've got no issue with him." Paul redirects toward Kohper. "You agree with me don't you, Chief?"

Put on the spot, he reluctantly nods.

Paul turns back to Lorleen. "Thank you for your time and transparency. We'll do whatever we can to get some answers."

Before Eric can open the Jeep's door, the chief rests his forearm on the roof and faces them. "Careful you don't overstep your jurisdiction. You're on my island and these are my people."

Paul quickly responds. "What's going on with you, Kohper? We're here to help."

He stares into the distance, then rechecks his watch.

"The entire time your mind seemed elsewhere, until she

mentioned the gun," Paul adds.

"I'm distracted, okay."

"About what? This isn't the first time you've checked your watch since our arrival."

He's embarrassed. "It's about the Consortium; something I have to deal with personally."

"I've heard that name twice already. Who or——"

"What's the best way to put this? They're a malignancy threatening to undermine our government and our way of life. I have to respond to another complaint my office recently received about them."

"Sounds serious," Eric adds.

"You ever hear of 'the Chairman'?"

Both agents shake their heads.

"I don't have time to get into this right now."

"How about the three of us meet for dinner, Elias. You can fill in the gaps, then we can toss about ideas on how we can give you some relief."

"Let me check my schedule. I'll get back to you."

By the time Paul and Eric settle into the Jeep, he's already driven off.

Paul speaks first. "Hope that doesn't have any negative repercussions. Any thoughts?"

Eric shakes his head. "If you're talking about Mrs. Hetiback, she's living every parent's nightmare. Where to now?"

"We better track down Dax. He's probably chomping at the bit by now."

"Awesome," Keira proclaims when she surfaces from the wreck with her father.

Jon remains uncharacteristically mute as he hands up his scuba to Kristian and helps Keira out of hers. After they break down their equipment, rinse and repack it, they grab bottles of cold water. Keira notices her father demeanor. He's visibly disheartened.

Alou starts the motor and inches the boat forward to take tension off the down line. When it's freed, Kristian pulls up the anchor, coils the line and gives Alou a thumbs up. He invites Kristian to the console and turns the controls over to him.

When she sits, Keira interrupts Jon who's deep in thought. "You doing okay?"

"I'm disappointed," he answers quietly.

"Why? This isn't the first time you've dived on this wreck."

"Your mother and I dove on her the day after its discovery."

"And?"

"It's changed."

"How so?"

"Back then, she was a pristine man-o-war, completely untouched. Now …," he stops to take a drink, "The first thing I see is the bow section torn from the ship and laying on its side."

"What do you think happened?"

He shakes his head. "I can only imagine. The deep furrow leading up to the break tells me a sizable anchor literally got dragged through the ship … I guess between its thin-gauge steel and the years of decay …"

As Keira never noticed the bow's displacement, she doesn't comment, but stays attentive as Jon continues.

"The ship's bridge resembled the size of a pilot house on our charter boats back home. Your mother found a couple of voice tubes connecting the bridge to the engine room. The date coincided with our anniversary and she used one to secret a note for me to discover." He dwells on the memory. "Now the entire structure's completely gone. It collapsed and slid off the port side into the flat pile of rubble we passed over. Your mother——"

He catches himself, and Keira puts her arm around his shoulder. He stares into her eyes. "You remind me so much of her. We … I …" He drops his eye contact.

"What, Daddy, talk to me."

When Jon glances at his daughter, she feels his shoulders slump. "I am so sorry. I never should have held you responsible for David's death. I just couldn't face losing him, and I admittedly resorted to self-destructive ways to cope." With tears streaking down his face, he sobbed, "and I lost you too."

Keira's shocked at the turn and starts to well-up.

"Daddy … I'm sorry, too."

"Why? You have nothing to be sorry for. This is on me."

"I was hurt, and bitter, but *I* made the choice to stay away from you all these years. I never gave us the chance to work this out."

"Can you forgive me, Keira … and can we try to put it behind us?"

He's lifted an unbearable weight from her shoulders. She gives him a tender hug and whispers in his ear, "Of course we can, Daddy. I love you."

Kristian turns his back to Keira hugging Jon. "A bit old for her, isn't he?"

"She's his daughter, you dope. They're really nice people."

"Oh. Tell me, why'd you mention Damien and Miguel?"

"I thought about them last night."

"Careful, brother.. I hear they're into some serious sh——"

Alou swats his chest. "Watch what you say around the customers."

"Okay, I'm sorry, but man, you need to stay away from them."

"Why? What have you heard?"

"For sure, nothing good."

Alou's aware he must govern his words with Kristian. He sends him off to make ready for docking.

Paul tracks down Dax in the lounge.

"We all set?"

"Two cases. All accounted for and under wraps in your room. How did your 'detective'-ing go this morning?"

Paul points to Eric, who answers, "Good."

Dax chuckles at the new man. "Okay. I get it. You've bought into the non-disclosure thing already."

He glares at Paul.

"What?"

"Hi. My name is Dax," he says with his hand extended. "I'm the new third-wheel around here."

Paul lightly swats his hand aside.

"So, what? Am I no longer in the loop?" After a pause he asks, "Did the chief show up?"

"He did," Eric answers.

"Tell me your impression of him."

"He's a bit of an odd duck and apparently under a lot of pressure, but the woman we met thinks a lot of him."

Dax glances at Paul who quickly adds, "Fair assessment. He did help pave the way for an open interview with her."

"What did you learn?"

Ignoring his question, Paul stands. "Before we head upstairs, I'm expecting the chief will call and take me up on an invitation to dinner, which will require all of us."

"What do you need us for?" carps Dax.

"I can assume you're still a member of this team, can't I?"

"Despite all the evidence to the contrary," he mutters.

Paul puts his hand on his shoulder, "Come on. We've got some work to do."

Dax leads them to the crates. "You have the manifest?"

Paul pulls the paperwork out of his pocket and flattens it out.

"Where shall we start?"

Paul points to the larger container. "I only want to check this one; the other's filled with munitions. It stays sealed for now."

When they break open the container, Dax carefully unloads it.

Eric tugs on a portion of unfamiliar equipment. "They didn't cover these in my dive class."

"Closed-Circuit Rebreathers fall into the 'speciality' category," responds Dax.

"Why do *we* have them?"

He points to Paul. "I don't know. Ask the boss."

Paul's drops his preoccupation with the enclosed paperwork. "They'e virtually bubble-free. Handy for stealth work. But they're expensive, and carry some limitations."

"I don't under——"

Paul interrupts to close the discussion. "Let's move on."

Eric stops questioning. *Guess I must sound pretty stupid.* "I'm calling it a night, gentlemen." He quietly closes the door behind him.

"His question's valid," Dax adds.

Paul stays glued to the manifest. "He's got enough on his plate already."

"Have it your way," and leaves Paul to himself.

Chapter 12
Trapped
Rio de Janeiro Maru

Their destination is the Fourth fleet anchorage off the east side of Uman island, and the wreck of the *Rio de Janeiro Maru*. During the lengthy transit to the site, Jon sits next to his daughter on the port-side bench near the bow. Keira discretely points toward Brent, who has isolated himself next to the transom.

"What do you think's going on with him today?"

"It's his first dive back in a while. Probably a little embarrassed. Give him time."

"Make sure he's nowhere near us while we're below."

"No problem. Paul's with us today; Brent will lead Dax and Eric. The wreck's large enough that we shouldn't cross paths."

"Good."

Built in the 1930's, the *Rio's* four hundred and fifty foot length, and sixty-two foot beam supported eight decks with a capacity to carry 1,140 passengers. The ship succumbed to a 1,000-pound bomb hit near the forward hold. Resultant fires torched stored munitions which tore the hull plates from the inside out, sending the ship down bow first to rest on her starboard side.

The wreck is accessible at the forty foot mark, and drops to a hundred and thirty at its deepest. Several access points to the holds and inner compartments contain artifacts unlike those found on other ships.

The three agents conduct their own discussion about the day's plan. Dax ribs Paul, "What do you think Brent has in store for you after your last adventure?"

Paul answers, "Not much I imagine. I'm diving with Keira and Jon today."

"Really?" Eric reacts.

"Oh, *boy*!" adds Dax with feigned enthusiasm.

Paul joins Alou at the console who needs Brent's help to secure the anchor. He reluctantly does so, before he works his way over to his two "buddies" as they prep their equipment.

"You about ready to go? We have a lot of area to cover, and I want to get started."

"Slow down, Brent," Eric complains. "We haven't gotten wet and you're already goading us to hurry."

"Stow the attitude and get ready."

Dax mutters, "Musta had a rough night."

Eric confronts Brent. "We're here to enjoy these dives. What's with all the pressure?"

He's several inches taller than Brent who realizes Eric has the same skill-set Paul personally demonstrated. Though Eric doesn't need the back-up, Dax stands next to him for support.

Brent throws up his hands. "Fine. Have it your way. You two give me a signal when you decide you want to head below."

Keira taps Paul and points to the trio. "Your boys aren't playing well together."

He interjects himself into their discussion, "What's going on?"

Brent peevishly responds, "It's a minor misunderstanding. No need for *you* to get involved."

Eric collars Paul. "I have no desire to dive with this clown today. May I buddy up with you?"

Jon responds. "We've got room."

Dax faces Brent in resignation. "Guess I drew the short straw."

"Funny," he sneers. "Soon as you're ready, we'll get started."

After they make their entry, the remaining four start to assemble their equipment. When Eric complains to Keira about Brent, Paul interrupts him. "Let's focus our energies on what's ahead of us. Dax can take care of himself."

"Good idea," agrees Jon.

They can make out the wreck directly beneath them, but are disappointed with the lateral visibility of less than fifty feet. The reduced clarity masks the wreck's expanse. As far as the divers can make out, they're immersed atop an immense field of steel.

Keira's first to notice the ships's name in both raised Roman letters on the hull, and above them in kanji. Though heavily overgrown, they're easy to make out. She's puzzled by the heavy copper cable strung along the hull——degaussing wire once used to demagnetize the ship and prevent inadvertently triggering magnetic mines.

Keira wants to take her time to observe the stony formations of table-shaped corals which thrive in the shallow water sunlight, each a miniature copy of a self-sustaining reef. Scores of humbug damselfish freely dart about their umbrella of protection. Their black and white vertical bands sharply contrast the backdrop of blue-green waters.

As they continue their journey toward the ship's bow, she notices pairs of longfin bannerfish and schools of IndoPacific sergeant fish. The color and variety of marine life continue to astound her.

Brent leads Dax on a fast-paced swim to the *Rio's* stern. Suspended in mid-waters at ninety feet, they pause to examine the port propeller, its immense blades are encrusted with orange sponge, gray tube sponges, green algae, and outcroppings of hard corals. The visibility reaches an estimated eighty feet; a marked improvement over the shallows.

The duo drift over to the raised letters on the stern before they continue into the aft cargo hold where several wooden crates used to ship bottled beer have since rotted away. The chaotic array presents a marked contrast to the adjacent wall, neatly stacked with the remainder of crated bottles.

They enter the engine room and its mix of control valves, switches, and white-faced dials. The convoluted arrangement is reminiscent of steampunk chic.

As Dax becomes engrossed in his discovery, Brent swims ahead to the base of the catwalk. He hasn't explored this section in some time, and notices the metallic structure's precarious balance on warped and decayed support struts. After he studies the instability, and confirms his dive partner's preoccupation with the machinery, he secures a grip on the rickety angle iron and powerfully swims toward the exit. The entire assembly begins to collapse.

The shrieks of dying metal alert Dax, who's startled by the catwalk, ladder, and support struts cascading toward him. He squeezes into a recess he hopes will provide some degree of protection. The rapidly collapsing metalwork careens off the bulkheads and screeches with metallic groans as it bends and tears apart until it reaches stasis. Completely blinded in a dense cloak of particulate, Dax searches for any sign of a way out, but the tug from his b.c. stops him cold. A jagged edge of metal has torn into his vest and physically pinned him in place. He's unable to move in any direction, much less retrace his path.

Self-satisfied, Brent starts to exit when he catches a glimpse of an intriguing artifact.

Jon initially directs his group to the 5.9-inch bow gun pointed downward toward the sea bed. Another cargo hold contains two rifled barrels salvaged from scrapped cruisers which were shipped to the islands to be repurposed as shore-based artillery. When they emerge from the hold they are greeted by a school of six pinnate batfish near the entrance.

Jon continues through the bridge's rusted-out overhead. The ship's telegraph now extends horizontally rather than upright. They continue aft to the immense smoke stack parallel to the lagoon floor, securely fastened to its original position on the deck by several steel cables, a surrealistic scape of disorientation.

Dax can't help but feel the grind of anxiety——a tight ball which can overtake a diver's ability to reason and lead to all-out panic. He stops to assess his situation. He reaches around with his left hand for the hose to his pressure gauge and places the dial flush with the front of his mask to read his air supply. He has eleven hundred p.s.i.——more than a third of a tank. He senses the increase in his rate of breathing. To avoid hyper-ventilating, he makes a concerted effort to slow down and conserve what air he has left. *Plenty of time.*

Tell-tale traces of light from the outside could lead to a possible exit, but the shroud of silt blocks any hint to guide him out. He knows he has to remove his equipment, a drill practiced dozens of times in his certification class, but never while pinned in place and blinded by particulate. The metallic wreckage limits his movements in either direction. Hampered by his restricted movement, he inches his hand down to the b.c.'s cummerbund sash, tears the velcro apart, and unclips the chest strap to release the last constraint. He drops his right shoulder, holds the vest in place with his right hand, and sidles to the left out of his rig.

His regulator pulls at the right side of his mouth until he loses the tug of war and lets his mouthpiece drop shifting his priorities to reestablish his lost source of air, doing so in the blind. Dax feels his way to where the regulator is attached to the tank's valve, then down the hose to its second stage. He securely bites down on the mouthpiece, exhales to clear the water, and breathes normally until his anxiety level settles. If he could break loose from his predicament, he understands without a clear way out, the option of abandoning his equipment and doing a free ascent to the surface is out.

He needs to unshackle his assembly from the collapsed metalwork. He does another check of his reserves. Seven hundred p.s.i. *I'm okay ... still in control.* He tries to reassure himself, but realizes his time continues to tick away.

The inability to orient himself on a fixed point does a number on his psyche. Like driving in a heavy fog with the high beams on, his dive light only amplifies the silt. He's desperate for a way out through the haze. He runs his hand along the bracket of metal which has him pinned down until he reaches its jagged end. Exerting with all the energy he can muster, he gains enough leverage to tilt the assembly up. The metal scrapes as he inches the entangled structure enough to release his b.c., all with the hope his exertions do not renew the collapse and pin him against a bulkhead with no air.

Free from the heavy metal encumbrance, Dax dons his assembly. His torn b.c.'s only use is as a harness for his scuba tank.

He checks his air, *three hundred p.s.i. Now use your head! Where's the exit? Maybe if I backtrack.* He turns and gropes his way around the nearest bulkhead which may or may not lead him to an exit point. With no other choice, he continues until he reaches the control valve assemblies. He's arrived at a familiar marker to get his bearings.

Now rid of Dax, Brent feels he has the freedom to follow up with the distraction he sighted earlier. He shines his light into the churned-up compartment, and though he can hear Dax's movements, he rationalizes, *He won't get out of this mess, but if he does, so what. I'll say I tried to find him and figured he already worked his way back to the boat.*

He refocuses on his own search. His light tracks down to

the spot where he made the observation. *Dumb luck!* The collapse has displaced enough silt to uncover a prized artifact. He carefully retrieves the item, and makes a quick exit to midwater where he can validate his discovery in better light. Away from the confines of the wreck, he fans a cupped hand to wave off the residual silt and confirms the remnants of a Katana Samurai sword! *How can I get this on board without the others noticing?*

In the forward hold, the other team's alerted to the metallic screech. It raises serious concerns with Paul. Toward the surface, he catches sight of a single diver making a beeline straight to the boat. In the reduced visibility, it's difficult to make out who. When the rest of his team starts up, Paul begins a slow swim aft.

He passes bubbles trickling from different openings along the wreckage until he makes out the main flow which rises from a slight gash in the hull adjacent to the engine room. From his present vantage point the visibility's inhibited, so he chooses a different tack and enters the same the rear entry taken earlier by Brent and Dax.

From his elevated position he can make out Dax moving hand-over-hand through the cloud of silt with his face pressed close to the bulkhead. Paul swims down, grabs the handle of his b.c. at the base of his neck, and tows him to clear water. When Dax struggles to twist himself free, Paul realizes he's on the verge of panic and releases his grip.

Once Dax regains his orientation and sees it's Paul, he signals he's out of air by running his fingers across his throat. Paul retrieves his back-up second stage with its own mouthpiece and hands it to him. The two begin their slow ascent toward the boat, both drawing air from Paul's tank.

On board, Jon sits by Dax.

"I'm okay now … thanks to Paul. I guess the catwalk in the engine room must have given way, though I never touched any of it. Nevertheless, I was caught up in the jumble." He points out the vest, cut beyond repair. All eyes turn toward Brent who is stowing his treasure under the bench seat.

Keira's incensed. "Why weren't you there for your dive buddy?"

Brent sets his gear down and begins to answer her, "I tried to——"

In one quick stride Dax has him on his back and presses his thumbs into his eyes. When Brent screams in agony, Paul steps in to quell the melee. He breaks Dax's hold, pulls him up, and places himself between the two.

"You don't learn, do you?" he shouts at Brent.

Alou, normally shy and quiet, adds, "He brought something from the ship and hid it in his towel."

Brent attempts to block Paul's reach for his bag, but is quickly flipped overboard with a light shove.

"What the hell!" yells Brent when his head breaks the surface.

Paul points at him with a warning, "Right now you're in the safest place possible. Stay there until we decide whether to let you back on board or if you'll need your mask and fins. Otherwise, I'll turn you back over to his care," pointing to Dax.

"Oh, please do," he mutters.

Paul lifts Brent's dive bag to uncover the rolled up towel and unravels his discovery. "I can understand why you hid this. If it's genuine, it may have some value, but it's not yours to keep."

"It's mine!" he yells while treading water. "I found it. Now let me back on board."

"You know about the law." Alou argues.

Brent stares down his accuser.

Paul offers the sword to Jon. "Will you make sure this gets into the proper hands?"

"I imagine Andon will be pleased to add this to the collection for the museum." Jon reaches over the side to soak Brent's towel in the water and rewrap the relic. "The air won't do this any good right now. What do you plan to do about him?" He points at Brent who wants out of the water.

Paul puts the question out to those onboard. "How about it folks?"

Jon and Keira give him a thumbs up. Dax, Eric, and Alou vote no. Paul makes the decision. "There's no other boat in sight, so I guess we'd better take him with us." Brent starts to climb aboard when Paul warns, "Hold on. You haven't gotten permission yet."

"Yeah, but you said——"

"You owe this team, especially Dax, an apology. If you're willing to do so, take a seat and keep your mouth shut."

Brent swears to himself as he climbs the ladder, avoids eye contact with everyone, and under his breath mumbles, "Sorry" to Dax. He searches through his gear. "Who took my towel?"

Paul informs him it's in use to protect the sword from deterioration.

"Perfect," Brent gripes, "I'm cold."

Paul points to the unshaded bench. "Take this seat. You'll dry out fast enough."

After tempers settle down, Alou asks Paul to help him disengage the anchor before they begin the trek back to Weno.

While underway, Brent turns to face Alou at the console, and leans in close. "Who will you hide behind after these people return to the states?"

Alou shoves him away. "Your threats don't scare me. My uncle will hear about this and he'll fire you!"

Brent innocently holds his hands out to his side. "What?"

Paul escorts him back to the stern. "Sit down, and shut up unless, of course, you choose to swim back. I'm sure your friend Alou won't mind if we leave you here."

Alou snorts his agreement and thanks him when he returns to the console. When Paul doesn't react or respond, he adds, "I really hate him."

"So you've said. Have you noticed a difference in the way the new boats handle?"

Alou's puzzled at Paul's response. "I'm going to demand my uncle fire him."

"I think it's best you hold off for now."

"Why?"

"I'm asking as your friend."

Alou curiously stares at him. "Only because you say so, but I don't understand why."

"You will. I promise."

Early that evening, the group has gathered in the locked conference room with a cooler full of bottled beer. The reason has nothing to do with the wrecks, surveys, or the marine life, but to clear the air about Brent. It's boisterous and heated. Each one has an opinion and the more passionate, the louder their contribution.

Paul remains resolutely quiet throughout the discussions while Jon serves as the mediator without expressing his. When the conversations die down, Jon turns to Paul, raises his eyebrows and addresses them as a whole. "You all know why we're here. Should Brent continue to crew with us, or do we banish him? State 'yea' or 'nay' and make your case. Do not worry about what the others think and please let each one express their opinion without interruption or editorializing. Understood?"

No one objects. "Good. Keira, let's start with you."

"He's changed. This isn't the same Brent we knew on Maui. I've had more than one person, both in this room and from others, who have told me not to trust him. So far, he's had an excuse for each incident. On the face of it, I don't think any of this would hold up in court, so for now, my vote is 'yea', he stays."

Eric's seated next to Keira and addresses her directly. "I'm not comfortable with him, and I don't trust him. I'd enjoy the diving more if he wasn't on the boat with us. I vote 'nay'."

When it's his turn to speak, Dax stands, glares at Keira, then shifts his attention toward Jon and Paul. "I don't understand why we're even having this discussion!" He struggles to keep his emotions in check. "Don't you get it! He's either trying to scare us off, or *kill* us. Based on today's experience, I believe he's dangerous to the lot of us!"

Jon senses the rise in agitation and calmly responds, "One more for the 'nay' column. We haven't heard from you, Paul."

He eyes his friend before he responds, "I'm sorry, bud, but we need to consider Brent's our sole connection to the governor. We toss him aside and we've closed off a potential conduit for information he could provide. An old, but applicable adage comes to mind. 'Keep your friends close, and your enemies closer.' I vote 'yea'."

"Appreciate the support, *'bud'*," Dax responds.

All eyes turn to Jon.

"I value your candid feedback. I tracked down Andon earlier, and posed the same question. He feels personally responsible for Brent's behavior. I'll try to paraphrase the gist of our conversation. Before our arrival, Andon received mostly positive feedback from his customers, and never any objections. Since hooking up with us, he has heard nothing but negative comments regarding his conduct. Alou has gone so far as to ask Andon to fire him outright. For all the reasons mentioned, Andon believes having Brent teamed with us is not a good fit.

"But …," Jon pauses before he continues, "I'll have to agree with Paul for now, with the proviso the two of us keep a closer eye on him below, yet remain open to a change if necessary. I want to thank you for your input. Let's call it a night."

No one is completely satisfied with the decision.

Dax stands, glances at Paul, and storms out, heading directly to the lounge.

Paul resigns himself to clear the air. He addresses Jon, "I

best go straighten things out with my friend, otherwise I'll see you in the morning."

Dax orders a beer as soon as he enters the lounge. Paul takes a seat next to him. Dax does not roll out the welcome mat. "What the hell, *buddy*. We're constantly at cross-purposes here. Do you trust me as part of this team, or not?"

The volume of his rant has started to draw the attention of other patrons. "Tone it down," pleads Paul.

"I think it sucks you're not backing my desire to black-ball Brent! Who, by-the-way, tried to *kill me!* Aren't we friends anymore?"

Paul faces his long-time associate. "Calm down, Dax, and buy me a beer. I need to talk to my *old* friend, if you can muster him up."

"Buy your own damn beer … and what do we still have to discuss?"

When Paul doesn't answer right away, Dax gives up and flags down the waitress. "Give us two more will you, sweetie … and put them on *my* tab."

"This better be good," he mutters.

Dax waits until the waitress leaves. "What's going on with you and the boy?"

Paul takes a drink, sets the bottle down, and shakes his head. "Odd question?"

"He obviously admires you."

"He needed advice from someone he feels he can trust."

"What about his uncle?"

"His problem concerns Andon, which's why he's come to me. Listen. I want your opinion, but need it kept between the two of us."

"Shoot."

"How do you think Eric's doing?"

"Well, he's dropped his obsession with his console, and has started to enjoy the scenery below. And I can see he brings a lot to the agency we haven't had 'til now. Why do you ask?"

"The deep dives start soon and I'm not sure how he'll handle himself," Paul adds.

Dax raises his eyebrows.

"Just feelings."

Dax huffs derisively. "Yeah, you should stay with them. They've served you well so far."

Paul laughs and takes another sip. "What do you think of Keira?"

Dax can't help but smile.

"What?"

"I've been waiting for the 'Keira' topic to come up."

"How so?"

"Come on. It's me you're talking to."

"You disapprove?"

"Well, other than her looks, intelligence, and diving skills, I don't get the attraction," he smirks.

"How about her volatile temper. Besides, rebound romances rarely work out."

Dax tilts his bottle in acknowledgment. "Should I reserve my tux?"

"I guess I'm being silly."

"Don't beat yourself up. You're a man, and she's ... one more round?"

"Last one though."

"Good. This one's on you."

Paul joins Jon in the dining room for an early morning confab over breakfast.

"Quite an animated discussion we had last night," Jon opens. "You straighten things out with your friend?"

"I did, thanks. So, you called this meet. What's on your mind?"

"Do you think I should send Keira home? With all that's going on, I'm more than a little concerned for her safety."

"You surprise me, Jon. She's ably handling the role we've set-up for her, and the 'danger' you mention is under control."

"I wonder."

"Have you talked with her about this?"

"Not yet. We've just started to warm-up to each other, and I'm conflicted with the thought of losing touch with her again."

"Then my advice is to let her be. She'll be fine."

Jon takes in a forkful of food, followed by a long draw of coffee. "What about Eric?"

"What about him?" Paul shoots back.

"Same question. Is he a danger to himself here?"

Paul takes a moment to collect his thoughts, and does his best to hide his annoyance.

"I don't know how things work in your world, but if he's sent back to the states before our mission is complete, that would be the end of his career with the agency. Why do you ask?"

"We're about to embark on several days of diving on the deeper wrecks. I don't want to see him get in trouble."

"I don't either. Dax did mention he's more acclimated to the dives now."

"You have had some concerns, then. This isn't an assignment he should be doing his training on."

"I'll tell you, and *please* pass this along to Keira. Eric is *my* responsibility, and I'll be the one to make the call. So enough about Eric."

"Okay, I'm not trying to step on anyone's toes here."

Paul and Jon are late for their morning briefing and surprised to find Brent at the podium. Jon motions he step outside. Brent reluctantly follows them out of the room.

When neither speaks, Brent snaps, "What is it this time?"

"*You* don't get to go on this dive," answers Paul.

"Whatdaya mean?"

Paul takes a step so he and Brent are face-to-face. "You speak English? You get to sit this one out."

Brent glares at both men and glances toward the room. When he turns, Paul grabs his arm bringing him to a stop.

Brent suppresses his urge to lash out, but with Paul, he's out of his league. He yanks his arm free and angrily heads toward the lobby. "Good. I can use the break!" he yells. "I haven't forgotten … you and I have a couple of scores to settle!" His departure is laced with curses.

Paul takes the seat next to Keira while Jon takes over the intro.

At the dive shop, Andon intercepts Brent pulling his dive bag from the storage rack.

"Where do you think you're going?"

Brent's incredulous. "Down to the boat. I still work here, don't I?"

"Not today. This is a *private* charter."

Brent spots Steve Mitchell at the dock assisting Alou with the tanks.

He turns back to Andon, who shrugs his shoulders. "As I said, 'a private charter'."

He drops his equipment bag where he stands. When he turns to leave, Andon advises him. "Before you go, I think it's best you periodically check your answering machine. I'll leave you a message if and when we may need you to help out again."

Somebody's going to pay for this, Brent thinks as he walks away from the shop and possibly his career.

"Sorry for the interruption," Jon addresses the group, "we had a bit of a mix-up on today's schedule."

"Yeah, right," Dax comments from the back, eliciting a few chuckles.

"Steve Mitchell will lead one team and I'll take the other."

The group collectively responds with an upbeat response.

Jon stands next to Steve's rendering, and begins with unbridled enthusiasm. "We're in for a special experience. The *Aikoku Maru's* my favorite wreck in the islands. I've made countless dives on her and with each one she presents me with a new delight. Not many ships here met such a spectacular demise which I'm reminded of whenever I visit her." He stops himself short when he drifts into his personal fiction of *Aikoku's* hopeless circumstances during the battle. "Let's start with the stern and work our way forward." He presents a thorough presentation on what they may possibly find. "I need to caution you, we will exceed safety limits for diving on compressed air. Monitor your instrument console, keep track of how you feel, and follow our lead when we give the signal to start the ascent.

"Because this dive's on a deep wreck, Andon is sending us out with two boats today. As we'll be going through our air faster due to the depths, two extra sets of scuba will be planted near the ascent line. Two more will be tied off at the forty foot mark, and six tanks, in their cradles on the boat, have regulators attached with extra long hoses lowered to the twenty foot mark. Andon's staff will be in the background to monitor our dive as a safety back-up. They'll keep a respectable distance, but will be on the alert and immediately available if needed. Questions?"

No one responds right away. As the team stands to leave, Eric looks around the room and reluctantly raises his hand. "Yes, Eric?" All stop to listen.

"I've never experienced nitrogen narcosis. What can I expect?"

"It's a good reminder for all of us. We need to take this seriously, so let's take the time to do a quick review." Everyone resumes their seats. "At extreme depths, nitrogen starts to act like a narcotic——you may start to feel the effects around the hundred plus foot mark, for others, it may be deeper; it's an individual experience akin to alcohol intoxication. Some may get giddy while others paranoid. It can be hypnotic to the point one may lose track of time and/or depth and not really care. Others may obsess about their personal welfare, which can lead to panic and result in dangerously bad decisions. While you're below, stay in tune with how you're feeling and notify your buddy if you experience a problem. Keep in mind, the effects will disappear as soon as we return to more shallow depths. Does that help?"

Eric masks his angst with, "Yeah, thanks."

The trip to the anchorage is on glass-smooth waters under clear blue skies. Both Jon and Steve anticipate excellent conditions below. Jon partners with Keira and Eric. Steve is with Paul and Dax. The six enter together. Lateral visibility is well over a hundred feet——perfect. At the eighty foot mark the first team can make out the ship's outline and drops off the line to the aft deck at a hundred and sixty five feet. Jon's team isn't far behind, but follow the line down until they reach the superstructure and take a slow swim toward its foremost edge.

Dax signals Paul to check out the prominent 4.7 inch deck gun mounted on a platform near the stern. Its seventeen foot-long barrel points skyward to the port. Paul, who has a special interest in shipboard artillery, speculates it's role against the attacking aircraft. Unrecognizably encrusted, the gun's not the ideal place to spend their precious bottom time. They move on.

Steve intends to lead the men on a penetration through the interior where hundreds of ground troops lost their lives in the sinking, but after Dax's recent experience on the Rio, he waves him off. Instead, they work their way along the port side deck. Beneath a kingpost, they pass the winch once used to recover shipboard aircraft.

A quick glance over the edge reveals the hull densely populated with sea fans, wire corals, and a few prickly stalks of tree branch coral. Each hosts its own community of residents. Dax points out a distant school of lesser barracuda in transit past the wreck. As they work their way toward the superstructure, Steve spots a single lion fish hovering dead-still near the foremost cargo hold. Its reminiscent of a miniature peacock, with a display of its beautiful, poisonous, red and white spear-like appendages.

At the edge of the superstructure, Jon has his team look into the void where the ship's first two hundred feet once existed, but neither Keira nor Eric appreciate the viewpoint's backstory.

Before exploring deeper, Jon wants to confirm both are doing well. She returns his okay sign, while Eric's feeling light-headed and engrossed in his console. Divers call it "getting narced." Jon stays close and signals they drop over the rim together, down another thirty feet along the jagged, torn plates of steel which frame the hull's edges. In the midst of the rubble, Jon signals the pair should start back up.

Reaching the superstructure, they continue aft, gliding by the collapsed smokestack, neatly folded over and resting next to the port side of its original mount. They drop down to the next level of decking, past the stumps of two intake funnels and the empty searchlight platform, its light dissolved from exposure and time.

Keira's familiar with spotted puffers from her years in Hawaii, but nothing matches the coloration or size of her next encounter——a mapped pufferfish which hovers near the base of the platform. Its pattern is completely unique——an array of kidney bean shaped black spots stand out in stark contrast to the backdrop of its white body. When threatened, the fish can ingest water and swell to a point where it becomes rock-hard. She follows it for a short distance, until a quick shake of its tail seeks refuge in a distant recess.

She taps Eric's arm to point out the puffer, but his head is pounding and his instrument panel reads eight hundred p.s.i., less than a third of a tank remaining. He ignores her and looks about for the ascent line to locate the extra tanks brought down to the wreck by the support team. Despite the narcosis, he has the wherewithal to capture a mental image of their placement.

Jon leads the pair to an improvised memorial consisting of an inscribed plaque. Like someone wiping the dust off an old relic stored in the family attic, he lightly fans the silt off the inscription:

"… THIS PLAQUE …

… COMMEMORATES THE BRAVERY
AND MANY LIVES LOST …"

Next to the sign, two skulls sit balanced atop leg bones next to a handful of plastic flowers tied together. Purists think the displayed collection is a desecration, but Jon believes it's a relevant remembrance to the men who died in the ship's cataclysmic demise.

Eric backs off. The sight of bones combined with his narcosis unsettles him. Jon notices the rate of Eric's breathing has increased dramatically, and checks his air supply. It's time to escort him up. At the approach of Steve's team, Jon quickly signals Keira to join the other two, then refocuses his attentions completely on Eric. He leads him over to the spare tanks, one of which Eric grabs in a bearhug and starts a rapid ascent. A beep from his dive computer warns him to slow down. Jon moves in close as a one-on-one escort to pace him up the line.

Steve's team, including Keira, continues forward past the memorial. Paul sights the easily distinguishable twin barrels of a 13.2 mm anti-aircraft gun atop the deck, and notes sessile marine growth has overtaken the emplacement.

When they reach the rim where Keira first observed the abyssal blue void with her father, she surprises the others by starting to descend. Paul quickly grabs her arm, checks her instrument panel, and holds it up to her mask. They're at the point where they need to start their ascent.

At the thirty foot mark, Jon and Eric stop for their first stage of decompression. He checks Eric's eyes closely and determines the narcotic effects have worn off, which leaves him free to focus on their remaining hang time. Eric drops his second stage mouthpiece and takes the one attached to the extra tank. He clears the regulator and breathes erratically at first, then calms to steady, even inhalations. *Close call*, Jon thinks.

Because they went deeper, Steve's team needs to start their decompression at forty feet and utilize the spare tanks mentioned in the brief. Keira joins her father and Eric while they out-gas.

Jon's team surfaces after they spend extra time at the ten foot mark, seven minutes over the called-for decompression profile——a safety factor he builds in to all his deep dives.

After the remaining divers board, Alou helps Steve with his equipment and does a headcount before he unties their boat.

Steve quietly pulls Jon aside to talk about Eric's conduct below.

Seated alone, Eric takes an introspective look at the dive and his role with the agency. *This isn't what I signed up for. If this team's responsibilities remain primarily below the surface, I'm going to have a sit-down with J.J. to reassess my future.*

After Paul confirms Keira is doing well, he joins Alou at the console and has the young man show him the controls. Alou's happy to turn over the wheel to him, but stays nearby to ensure they maintain the right path home.

They spend the next several days conducting repetitive dives on the deeper wrecks located in the 4th Fleet anchorage: *Nippo, Momokawa, Fujisan* and *Seiko Marus*. Keira teams with Paul and Dax to focus on her surveys. As promised, Jon sits out the dives, but does ride along to support the teams and help the boat crews topside.

Eric cornered Paul the night after the dive on the *Aikoku,* expressed his discomfort, and requested a different assignment during the deep water phase. With relief, Paul accommodated him by tasking him with conducting surveillance on the *Black Moon*, the yacht he had Dax monitor earlier. Eric takes to the new assignment with relish, sharing his findings each night with both agents.

Much to the relief of everyone on the team, they've conducted the dives without Brent or further incident.

The evening after their last dive on the *Momokawa Maru*, Jon has sent word to Paul to meet him in the lounge. Jon waves him over. He's sharing a table with Andon and Brent.

Still standing, Paul asks, "To what do I owe this pleasure?"

Jon pulls out a chair. "Please sit."

Andon speaks up first. "Brent has a request." When Paul doesn't react, he nudges Brent. "Go ahead and tell him what you told me."

"I need to rejoin the team."

Paul looks at Jon who's lost in thought. "You're considering this?"

Brent interjects, "Look, I'm having trouble paying my bills and I also think you need me."

"You think we *need* you?"

Andon speaks up. "This last couple of weeks has taken a cumulative drain on my staff and they could use the break. A couple have called out sick, and I'm starting to hear complaints about their schedule. Frankly, I *could* use the help."

Jon addresses Andon directly, "We aren't diving on the *San Francisco Maru* until the day after tomorrow. Let me talk with Paul about this and I'll get back to you."

Andon stands, pulls Brent up, and gestures toward the exit. "Let's go."

Jon looks to Paul, "Tell me what you're thinking."

Chapter 14
San Francisco Maru

Given clearance to lead the charter, Brent helps Paul and Alou with the pre-dive prep work on the boat. He's distracted as he mindlessly hands off a pair of tanks to Alou who yells when one drops on his foot. "Hey, watch what you're doing,"

"Oh, shut up and do your job," he responds.

Paul grabs Alou's shoulder and steps onto the dock from the boat. "Let me take it from here."

Brent doesn't respond, but bumps into Alou, and mumbles, "Twerp."

As Alou rubs his shoulder, Paul tells him, "Let it go. He's obviously having a bad day."

"He's *always* having a 'bad day'," Alou protests out loud.

Brent ignores them and grabs the hose to fill the rinse bucket.

Jon watches the team members reluctantly drag themselves into the conference room. Their first stop's the coffee urn, and ignoring the bowl of fresh fruit, their second is the soon-to-be emptied platter of Moen donuts. They are not used to the physical strains placed on their bodies from several days of repetitive deep dives, and once seated, remain unusually quiet.

Andon and Jon break off their conversation to assume their place on the podium. "Good Morning, everyone," opens Jon. There's no response from the group. "Lemme start over. Brent will lead one of our teams today." The statement brings about it's planned effect. Through mouths full of glazed pastry the group responds with muffled groans. "Now that I have you attention, I'll turn things over to Andon," he smirks as he takes a seat.

"Thanks a lot", Andon mutters. "Let's get down to business. By the sounds of things, the last couple of weeks have taken their toll. It's the same for my staff, and I need the help. The three of us met with Brent last night who requested to rejoin the group. I'm asking you put behind what's passed, and focus on what's ahead."

Andon acknowledges Eric's raised hand with a pointed finger. "So who will I, er … we team with?"

Dax pipes in, "Keep him away from me."

Jon stands and holds up his hands. "Okay. Paul and I spoke about this after our meeting. Dax and Eric will dive with me, Paul and Keira with Brent."

The overcast skies prompts Jon to ask Andon, "The weather forecast?"

"I hope last night's rainstorm didn't keep you awake," Andon states, "but you shouldn't worry about the conditions. Rains usually clear out quickly this time of year. If not, you're getting wet anyway, though the ambient light penetration may be reduced somewhat."

He places another one of Steve Mitchell's renditions on the easel. Andon continues, "Today's dive is on *San Francisco Maru*. It's nicknamed the 'Million Dollar Wreck', but the 'treasure' isn't in precious metals. It's the variety and volume of artifacts on board. The ship served as a cargo transport for twenty years before the war's outbreak. Despite her years of arduous service, the Imperial Japanese Navy pressed her into service. She carried bauxite ore from the islands to Japan for refinement into aluminum for their war production. The holds were cleaned and refilled with support materials for her return trips. On her last run, she arrived here on February fifth as part of a convoy and remained when the other ships continued on. As the Japanese command anticipated an assault by Allied forces, the ship was loaded with weaponry and munitions to help fend off the invaders. When it did begin, anti-personnel beach mines, three tanks, fuel trucks, staff cars, aircraft engines, artillery shells, small-arms munitions, and torpedoes had yet to be unloaded.

"Day two's attack brought bombs, fires, and more bombs which sent her to the bottom stern first. She came to rest perfectly upright, with the aft section in deeper waters. Stay on or close to our boat's anchor line while you descend; you can expect the ship to start coming into view around the ninety foot mark."

Andon points to highlights on the graphic. "We'll start at the aftermost holds which have cargo of specific interest to you Keira——several drums of fuel lay scattered throughout. It's a hundred and eighty feet to the afterdeck, a much deeper dive than you've experienced to date. We'll work our way to the foredeck during the dive. Keep in mind this will necessitate much longer decompression stops. Plan accordingly. We will provide the usual team of safety observers and all the extra air you may need.

"Jon'll pick it up from here."

"Though we'll dive as two teams of three, we'll stay close as one group. Brent and I will co-share the responsibilities of leading you through the wreck. Brent will lead, and I'll track our depth and bottom time from the rear.

"Because we will exceed the maximum safe dive depths on compressed air, you will need to track your own air consumption and dive computers. When either Brent or I signal the time to surface, you must begin your ascent without exception. As Andon touched upon, spare air will be available at the same points we had on all the deeper wrecks. We plan to spend twenty minutes at depth with decompression stops starting at forty feet on the way up.

"Let's talk about a couple of potential hazards. It's easy to get wrapped up in everything the ship has to offer. With the variety of artifacts onboard, the cargo holds beg for a closer inspection. You can easily lose track of your time and depth. Stay near your escorts.

"Toward the end, we'll run into the largest artifacts on the wreck, three Type 95 HA-GO land tanks fronting the superstructure's remains. Two settled piggy-back on the starboard side, and one on the port now straddles the side rail. If you peer over the side, you may spot another vehicle on the sandy bottom——the remnants of a steamroller. Because of water clarity, it's deceptively easy to go down to investigate, where you'd discover you're at two hundred and forty feet!

"The other danger relates to the munitions. Don't assume the extended exposure to the sea has rendered them inert. Many Japanese explosives contain a component called picric acid. In retrieving several mines from one wreck, reactant leaked from the canisters which devastated the surrounding marine life, confirming the experts belief they're highly volatile. The bottom line——hands-off."

When he finishes, Andon wants to wrap it up. "Thank you, Jon. Any questions?" Keira's hand shoots up. In anticipation he adds, "Alou and Nathaniel will cover the two boats today. I have to sit this one out." She drops her hand.

During the transit, Keira takes in the serenity of the lagoon and the inner peace she derives from it. *What could my life be like here? This isn't about Chuuk. Am I happy with my career? My life?*

When the boat slows for the tie-off, she thinks about her father. *Maybe we can start to rebuild our relationship through our kinship with the ocean.*

The site offers ideal conditions——clear skies and calm waters.

As soon as the group begins their descent, a circling seven foot-long tiger shark makes a fast, aggressive approach toward them, followed by an equally fast departure. Though there's no immediate danger, the encounter's enough to elevate the anxiety in some, and the level of excitement for others.

They clearly make out the hull's outline at eighty feet. A bird's-eye-view at a hundred and twenty feet reveals the deep depression in the deck encompassing the aft-most cargo hold. A bomb blast weakened the support structures, and time did the rest. The starboard side carries a noticeable split which extended below the water line.

Caught unloading during the attack, scores of Long Lance torpedo bodies, disassembled from their warheads, lay scattered about the deck. Stacks of wooden frames account for the balance of munitions in the cargo hold. It's filled with munitions in close proximity to the bomb blasts, including pallets of corroded artillery shells, crated twelve to a case. It's a miracle the ship did not disintegrate in a conflagration similar to the *Aikoku Maru*.

Paul points out the drums of fuel to Keira. She makes the appropriate notes on her slate, though somewhat illegible from her narcosis. He decides to keep her close until they reach more shallow depths.

Signs of severe fires ignited by the bombs, grab Keira's attention. *It must have been hell for them before the ship sank.* She remembers reading five crewmen died in the attack.

Brent directs the team into the number four hold. A tear through the port side hull combined with the fissure by the number five hold, must have overwhelmed the ship's crew. They weren't able to stem the rush of water and lost her stern-first. The beams that supported the deck hatch, no longer exist. Further in, they find more beach mines, detonators, and a variety of aerial bombs. Some crated, but others cast about, free from the confinement of rotted cases.

The engine room offers a remarkable amount of ambient light from five skylights still propped open. Dax makes sure Brent's nowhere in sight before he lightly fans the silt off the instrument panel to get a closer look at the white-faced dials. As they approach the exit, they pass by the catwalk with a variety of rusted fragments scattered about its grating, a sight which stirs visceral memories for Dax.

When they reach the main deck they work their way forward. Keira takes personal note the "Million Dollar Wreck" may be a ship filled with artifacts, but it has also developed into a healthy, vibrant reef with several species of fish she tabulated on other wrecks. A lone great barracuda rises out of a dark hold amidships, and gracefully joins a stream of yellow and blue fusiliers passing alongside the hull. The entire ship sports similar encrustations to those found on the more shallow wrecks, but not to the same extent. Delicate tendrils of white hydroids which remind her of hoarfrost on barren winter tree limbs coat the railings. Whip-like arms of wire corals punctuate each formation.

Paul points out an over-sized metal platter used to cook rice for the crew. He estimates it's three feet in diameter, but water does a funny thing to light——objects appear larger and closer from its refraction. The platter is coated with green, saucer-sized platelets of elephant-ear anemone, the same type which line the lip of the deck along the hull. When they reach a sizable colony of dark green sun coral, they traverse to the starboard companionway and pass by the ship's telegraph on its side, disengaged and fallen from the weakened superstructure.

They reach the three battle tanks highlighted in the brief. Though relatively small, each measures over fourteen feet in length, seven feet high and weighs seven and a half tons. They're designed for a crew of three: a commander, machine gunner, and driver. Initially used to support infantry, these machines were sent to Truk to augment their land artillery for the anticipated invasion. Each turret's armed with a thirty-seven mm gun which could fire either explosive or armor-piercing rounds. The swirling force of water, generated by the ship's sinking, lifted one tank atop the another. The upper tank's turret hatch is frozen open. A stalk of spiny tree branch coral with bright red polyps has taken root on the turret's right side.

Keira and Dax shine their lights inside the extremely cramped quarters. They can view the main gun's controls, but decades of accumulated silt filled the interior's void. Dax drops down the outside to inspect the Type 97 7.7 mm machine guns protruding through the fore and aft hatches. In their transit to the port to view the third tank, they overlook the truck next to the piggy-backed tanks, its body decayed to its chassis.

Their time to surface has arrived all too quickly. Paul has already started up the ascent line with Eric and Dax. Jon is distracted by a column of air flowing from the forward-most hold, he checks his air supply and swims toward the sight. The hold, one time filled to the brim with anti-personnel beach mines, contains only a fraction of the initial load. He illuminates the stacks of remaining mines stored neatly in their own casements. Each mine has two handles near the top, offset to allow easy transport by two men. As his beam of light penetrates past the eight foot inter-deck, there's more mines alongside ribbed metal cases of cordite——extruded filaments of explosives used in place of gunpowder.

Deep in the hold, Brent appears to be struggling. Jon enters to help, but stops to hover slightly above. Brent's instrument console has snagged in an empty casement. He fumbles his grip to free it and swipes Jon's waist. After he looks up to see who he hit, he turns his attention back to his entanglement. Keira catches up and easily clears the difficulty.

When Jon maneuvers upright to return to the main deck he feels his weight belt give way and slide down over his hips. The seemingly innocuous sweep from Brent's hand loosened the buckle of his belt. Jon tries to catch the weights, as does Keira, but the belt hits his fins before it plummets in-between the casements into the bowels of the cargo hold where it's swallowed up by the silt. Jon realizes he has neither the time nor the air to chase after the belt. At these depths, the loss of the weights is negligible to his buoyancy, but as they approach the surface, the gas impregnated in his full neoprene wetsuit will expand increasing the pull upwards.

Per their plan, they need to make decompression stops starting at forty feet and face another fifty minutes of hang time at various stage intervals. Jon remains easily in control at the first stop.

At thirty feet, a school of ten oceanic white-tipped sharks further test their nerves. The curious predators appear over eight feet long and not averse to quick, close passes. The sharks circle closer and closer, before they mysteriously leave. Keira makes eye contact with her father who isn't phased by the sighting.

By the twenty foot mark, he's fighting the upward pull on his body which would otherwise be offset by his weight belt. The added buoyancy from his near empty aluminum tank exacerbates his struggle to stay at depth. Keira holds onto his vest while he loops his ankle around the line to utilize the second stage regulator hanging from the boat. When he reaches for the dangling second stage, his ankle-hold slips and Keira loses her grip on his vest. She wants to chase after him but realizes it could place her in jeopardy as well; surfacing too soon means the nitrogen bubbles forming in her tissues may lead to paralysis, disablement, or possibly death. Jon's ascent is uncontrolled, out of reach of the nearly frantic Keira, and past the others hanging at their final ten foot stop. He completes his ascent upside down.

Jon manages to right himself from his perilous ascent, doffs the gear for Alou, and tosses up his fins and mask. He struggles to climb aboard. He's shaken and realizes it's only a matter of time. *When will the symptoms hit? And how bad?* Starting to feel light-headed as the fatigue grabs a foothold, he strips down to his swim trunks. Alou quickly helps him over to the bench seat and stows his equipment.

Paul surfaces thirty minutes later. "How's Jon?"

Alou points to him sprawled out on the bench. "I dunno. He hasn't said much since he surfaced, but I've kept my eye on him."

Paul hands over his gear, and checks in with Jon who appears asleep.

"Jon!"

He's startled when he opens his eyes.

"It's Paul. Tell me what you're experiencing right now."

He recognizes Paul's voice, but has trouble with his focus.

"I'm okay right now … little bit dizzy."

Keira's next to surface, frantic to rejoin her father. Without taking off her gear, she sits next to him and holds his hand. After helping her out of her rig, Paul moves to the transom to assist Alou with the others.

Jon warns Keira, "Pretty big storm musta moved in."

She's confused. "But we're on glass-flat waters, Daddy."

He points in the direction of Paul and Alou near the transom.

"Look," his voice is low-pitched and faltering. "They need take care in this storm, or they'll end up overboard."

Keira yells, "Paul, he's in serious trouble!"

Paul orders Alou to get underway immediately. He directs him to radio for an ambulance, and call the Divers Alert Network, to line up a recompression facility for a potential bends case.

He returns to Jon's side, while Keira stands close-by. She never takes her eyes off her father.

"Talk to me, Jon," says Paul.

"Get me to my feet. I feel nauseous."

"I'm not surprised."

They help him stand and lean over the rail.

When his knees buckle, Paul catches him, positions him on his left side, and places a dive bag under his feet.

"Any better?"

"The horizon's kinda flipped to a forty-five degree angle."

Paul looks at his eyes. They spasm to the right and back, repeatedly.

"Where's the nearest chamber, Alou?"

"Guam."

"It's another two hours by air!" he exclaims.

"Welcome to our side of the world."

Paul yells to Dax, "Give us a hand over here. Bring me the oxygen."

Alou points out the emergency storage. Dax fishes out the green cylinder from the rear bench, and straps the mask over Jon's nose and mouth. Paul notices his struggle to keep his eyes open.

"You have to stay awake, Jon. Fight this. We can't have you falling asleep."

Fatigue muffles his speech. "I get it ... you don't want me to go into shock ... I only need to rest my eyes ... only for a minute, please."

Paul notices his eyelids flutter, "No! You've *got* to fight it,

Jon. Do what you can to stay awake."

Paul grabs Keira's arm and gestures toward her father, "Make sure he stays engaged."

She puts on a good face. "Tell me about your best trip here with mom?"

When the first boat arrives, Andon and his entire staff have already manned the dock to do what they can to help. A few minutes later, a helicopter lands at the nearby pad. Two staffers wield a stretcher and off-load Jon onto the dock. One of the aircrew replaces the oxygen bottle at his side, before two others load him on the craft for a quick ride to the airport.

Keira climbs on board with him.

Jon appeals to Paul. "You'll keep an eye on my girl, won't ya?"

"Do what they tell you at the facility and get back to us soon."

Keira holds Jon's hand and does whatever she can to keep him alert and talking. Jon squeezes hers back. She places it on his cheek. "I love you too, Daddy." She can't hide her tears or her concern. *I can't lose him, too.*

When the helicopter lifts off, Paul asks Eric to bring the Jeep.

Andon and his staff pitch in to help the crew offload the boat, collecting all their personal dive gear followed by the tanks. He assigns two men to refill the cylinders, and the rest to wash down and refuel the boat, before he leads Alou away from all the activity. He wants to hear his take on the incident.

When the second boat ties off, Brent nonchalantly walks off with his personal dive bag. Andon's close on his heels. As soon as Brent secures his equipment in its assigned cubby, Andon wheels him around and slams him up against the wall.

"Tell me what the hell happened out there!" he yells.

"What're you talking about? The guy dropped his belt, and made an uncontrolled ascent. How's he doing?"

"Take a guess. What did you have to do with this?"

"Nothing," Brent pleads. "Why're you so angry at me? Apparently he forgot to do a safety check on all his equipment."

"As if you need to ask." Jabbing his finger into his chest, "I vouched for you. I put my reputation on the line for you ... 'Didn't do a safety check'? He's a professional!"

When Brent shrugs his shoulders, it takes every fibre of Andon's restraint not to lash out. "Why aren't you out there helping the others?"

"Because you brought me on as an independent contractor, remember? I'm not on salary, I get paid by the dive ... no benefits ... and no security. So you can use your salaried minions to your heart's content, but if it doesn't entail diving, I'm outta here."

"Don't plan on returning to the boats anytime soon ... if ever!"

Yeah, right, Brent smirks as he walks off.

A paramedic and a registered nurse await Jon's arrival. They leave him on the stretcher and rush him to the cargo elevator for the lift up to the government jet.

The governor's there with two men, both strangers to Keira. One's remarkably larger than the other two. The governor points to where Keira stands and leads them over to her.

It's difficult to communicate over the whine of the jet's turbine engines.

She has to yell to the governor, "Why're *you* here?"

"I monitored the chatter over the police band. What can I do to help?"

Keira looks up at his companion before she turns her

attentions back to the jet without a response.

The governor continues, "There *is* a favor you can do for me."

She looks back at him with astonishment. "Really! Now?"

He ignores her response and points to the smaller of his companions. "Mr. Hostino Nededog is a friend and a diplomat. He urgently needs to catch a ride to Guam and I would take it as a personal favor to——,"

When Keira looks away, the governor motions Tino to get aboard. He runs to the jet and up the ramp before it pulls away. Within minutes they're airborne.

From the tarmac, Keira shades her eyes as they lift off and stays until it's out of sight. She glances at BG but doesn't speak to the governor before Paul catches her attention. She runs toward the terminal while the governor and his remaining associate take a different track to avoid Paul.

Gently folding her into his arms, Paul tries to reassure her, "Don't worry. There's a team waiting for him on Guam who specialize in this. You've had a pretty rough day. Let me take you back to the hotel."

Afraid, she buries her head in his chest, and sobs.

A medical attendant is assigned to ensure Jon's comfort, and help him fight the overwhelming fatigue.

Tino keeps to himself in a seat near the front and uses the time to get his papers in order to get off the base, hopefully without any questions.

Ninety minutes after takeoff the jet touches down at the airbase on Guam where another team awaits. They transfer Jon's stretcher to an ambulance for rapid transport to the recompression facility.

As soon as it leaves the tarmac, Tino's ordered to disembark. He faces a long, hot walk to the main gate.

Jon's greeted by a man in a dark blue jumpsuit. He's the senior corpsman on duty with a group of three others. "Welcome to The Dive Locker, Jon. We're a state-of-the-art U.S. Naval Facility and we're here exclusively for you."

Jon feebly stands on his own and takes a couple of steps before he stumbles to his right. A couple of attendants catch him and help him back to the wheelchair.

"Get him inside," the senior corpsman orders. "As soon as our physician finishes his assessment we'll take you for a simulated dive in the chamber. When did you last eat?"

He answers softly, "Breakfast I guess, but I fed the fish over the side rail after the dive."

"Once you stabilize, we'll order up some food. We'll need you to continue to drink as much water as possible throughout your treatment."

The predominant feature inside the immaculate facility is the cylindrical recompression chamber. It's painted bright white and in combination with the white-tiled floors and fluorescent lights, amplifies Jon's visual discomfort. He weakly tries to shade his eyes. Despite his sensitivity to the harsh light, he does a visual scan of his surroundings. By counting the foot-long floor tiles, Jon estimates the chamber's length at approximately twenty feet by a width of eight feet, and eight feet tall. Mounted on a cradle of steel beams, pipes and wire harnesses connect the chamber to an eleven foot control panel and a cascade bank of tanks which provide compressed air and oxygen. The control panel's a maze of gauges, switches, dials, and instrumentation. A built-in lock-out is used to pass items in and out of the chamber while it's under pressure. Sophisticated communication equipment augments a black and white monitor to observe the patient and the onboard technician.

He's greeted by the duty dive physician whose in his mid-thirties and has a quiet confidence about him. A medical corpsman stands by with a chart to record his observations.

"Jon, my name is Doctor David Koonradt. Can you tell me

what you're feeling?"

As he lazily answers, the doctor checks his eyes dancing back and forth, and tells the corpsman, "He has nystagmus, loss of physical coordination, and overall weakness. What else can you tell me, Jon?"

"Other than my head feels like I'm on a carnival ride, my horizon looks like this." He holds up his shaky hand bent to a near forty-five degree angle. "I need to take a short nap."

"No naps! You must stay awake. We need you responsive and communicating with us throughout the treatment. Okay?"

He gives him a weak thumbs-up.

"We will simulate an immediate descent inside the chamber. You can expect this to last around five and a half hours as we reduce any nitrogen bubbles that may have formed in your body, to allow their gradual release from your system. One of our technicians will accompany you, track your vitals, and cover all your needs. We'll communicate with you through the intercom. Please drink as much water as you can possibly tolerate and then some. There's a honey bucket inside for you to void your urine, which will help eliminate more nitrogen."

"Do you think I'll get through this?"

"Don't worry. You will soon start to feel much better."

Tino flashes his credentials to the Marine guard at the main gate. The guard doesn't allow him to pass until he inspects his bag and takes a close look at his paperwork. He's eventually waved through and with directions from the guard, seeks a phone at the fast-food restaurant a quarter mile down the main strip. Fifteen minutes later, a late model Toyota with a single occupant pulls up to the curb. He climbs in. The two men talk for a minute before the car whisks them away.

Eric waits in the Jeep to chauffeur Paul and Keira to the Restaurant On The Wharf close to the airport. Paul tells Eric to allow them a couple of hours alone. They're shown a booth where they can enjoy some privacy.

"Hungry?"

Keira shakes her head. "I'm too upset to eat right now, but you go ahead. I could use some iced tea, though."

"I've heard the pizza's pretty good here. I'll order one, in case you change your mind."

"Maybe I'll try a slice."

After he places the order, Paul looks at Keira. "Tell me what happened."

The chamber's interior can barely accommodate Jon's tall frame, though he does little but sit. He hears the entry close as the hatch battens down behind him. The chamber contains a cushioned bench, which doubles as a cot, but he's encouraged to sit upright by the attendant while wrapping a blood pressure cuff around his arm.

"How you doing, Jon?"

He does his best to focus. "Okay, I guess. What's your name?"

"I appreciate it. Our patients rarely care enough to ask. I'm Petty Officer Harrington, but please call me 'Terry'. I'll take your vitals throughout the stages of your treatment. Tell me if you need any help."

Jon counts four small portholes fully occupied by observers on the outside. Doctor Koonradt gets the okay from Harrington and speaks over the intercom. "Jon, we will start to pressurize the chamber to simulate a depth of a hundred and sixty-five feet. It will take about seven minutes to get there. Make sure you clear your ears as we begin. You will start to feel cold which is normal. We don't want you to get so cozy you get sleepy. Thirty minutes later we'll start your ascent and stop at twenty foot intervals until we reach sixty.

Terry will strap on a mask with an oxygen rich blend until this cycle's over. You'll need to work around the mask to continue your water intake."

Jon acknowledges him and concentrates on countering the increasing pressure change he feels in his ears.

"This hits the spot." Keira pulls over another slice of pizza from the tray. "Who told you about this place?"

"You can thank Anaria from the hotel. You up for talking about the dive?"

"I don't know what I can add. We passed over the hold with all the mines, and found Brent struggling." At the sound of his name, Paul visibly tenses up. Keira places her hand on his forearm and leaves it there. "I believe it was an accident. His instrument console got entangled between two casements. In an attempt to free it, his hand slipped off and brushed Jonathan's waist. I guess the blow loosened the clasp on his weight belt. When we started our ascent, it plummeted into the silt at the bottom."

"Why do you continue to make excuses for him?"

She gestures with both her hands. "I *honestly* don't think Brent knew we were near him. It's unfortunate, but doesn't change the fact it's coincidental."

"Think about this: If exploring the cargo hold wasn't on the agenda, why'd he end up there? Tell me, how does a man, considered an expert on these wrecks, allow——"

He interrupts his own questions to answer them for her. "He set it up to lure you in and took advantage."

"I can't think of why he'd want to intentionally hurt my father."

"Did your father ever mention Brent's association with the governor?"

Shaking her head, she asks, "Speaking of the governor, who were those two men with him at the airport? One boarded the flight to Guam, and the other's the size of an ape."

Paul chuckles. "The 'ape', as you do delicately put it, is the governor's bodyguard, though he posed as a doorman when we first got here. Why he feels he needs one remains a mystery. The other man's new to me, but we've sent their photos to Washington for identification."

"He introduced himself as Hostino … whatever. It was noisy on the tarmac, and I was too distracted to catch his last name."

"Nededog?" interjects Paul.

"I guess that's it. What do you think Brent and the governor are involved in?"

Paul realizes in order to fill Keira in on their investigation, she'll expect more. *I'll give her a bit to gauge her reaction. If it works, I can let her in on more later.*

He starts by telling her about the visit from Lieutenant Governor Enap and his brother on the night of their arrival. He mentions the mother's concern for her son and his involvement with the governor. When he mentions the blue bottle, Keira responds, "Does it tie in with the vial you took from the *Sankisan*."

Paul nods.

"And you think Brent's somehow involved in this."

"Unfortunately."

"The night I had dinner with him, Brent hinted his prospects appeared hopeful. I don't get it," she states bitterly. "He never acted this way on Maui."

"In my experience, with sizable amounts of money …"

Keira thinks back to when she got back into diving after David's death and how Jonathan partnered her with Brent. She recounts all she can up to the point she left for school and dropped out of contact with him.

She muses, "You need to kick him off this project."

He pushes back. "I wish you'd reconsider."

"Why?"

"It's difficult, but we need him, Keira."

"You're right, I don't understand. We at least ought to

have him sit out the next several dives. The loss of income should make him reexamine his activities."

"I'll pass your suggestion along to Andon."

Keira polishes off her third slice.

"Should I order another pie?"

She looks at the empty platter and gives him a sheepish expression. "Oh … I guess I had more of an appetite than I thought."

"I'll keep it in mind the next time we go out."

"Oh, we're dating now?" she states with a sly grin.

Paul starts to fumble with his words. She pats his arm. "Relax, big guy. I'm having some fun."

Paul lets out an audible *"phew"*. "Speaking of Andon, we're invited to his place on Tonoas Island. He's hosting a cook-out, kind of a 'get to know each other better' thing. It should give you a good idea of how the other half lives."

Her eyes light up at the prospect. "Who'll be there?"

"Besides the two of us? Well … Dax, Eric, some of his staff, and I believe Steve will join us."

"Sounds fun. Nice to get away from the hotel for a change."

Paul catches the waiter's attention.

"Yes, sir. Room for dessert?"

Paul looks at Keira who holds up her hand to signal she's full. "You sure?"

An hour and a half after the treatment starts, Petty Officer Harrington grabs a bulky mask resembling equipment a jet-jock uses——a heavy black rubber cowl which fits over the nose and mouth with connections to the chamber wall by two heavy hoses.

Jon resists when he tightens the straps. "What is this thing?"

Terry answers as he continues the fitting. "It's called a BIBS mask. This line feeds you an oxygen blend to help purge the excess nitrogen in your system and the other vents your exhalations outside the chamber. I doubt you'll find it comfortable, but it's only for a couple more hours. The ascent will pause at ten foot intervals and remain at each successive level for longer periods."

"Doesn't this wear on you fellows?"

"It's a grind, but we rotate the duties so we're not in here for a successive run."

As promised, Terry removes the mask at the treatment's completion. The hatchway to the chamber is released to break the pressure seal and a rush of warm air displaces the chill inside.

Jon's wobbly when he stands. Some of his symptoms have returned and he needs help out. A couple of attendants walk with him into an anteroom where another doctor waits. The name tag on her white smock reads, Dr. Aahana Mitra. She's young, short, and grins at Jon's attempt to mouth the words. "Call me Doctor Ana, Jon. Do you feel any better?"

As soon as he opens his mouth projectile vomitus completely covers the front of her smock. After his convulsions subside, he turns his head to locate some paper towels. Even though he had no control, he's horrified. Despite the fact his head's swirling, he turns back to apologize. She's nowhere in sight.

Two orderlies enter the room. "According to the doctor, you're a pretty sick man and wants you to spend the night in our hospital. You'll be back here early tomorrow for your next treatment."

The ward in the nearby hospital is a classic government design——long, stark, featureless, and military clean. Jon doesn't care. Within minutes of his arrival he's in bed and fast asleep.

Jon wakes up tired and groggy. He slowly takes in the surroundings and notices the silhouette of a man seated by the window. "Glad you could join us." Jon's unable to focus easily, but the voice sounds familiar. "I heard you ran into some difficulties yesterday. How do you feel?"

"*You* ever try to sleep through a night in the hospital? It's impossible."

The visitor makes his way to the door. "From what I hear, you're in good hands with the people at The Dive Locker."

"Please forgive me, but who are you?" After a short silence, Jon opens his eyes. He's talking to an empty room.

A few minutes later the nurse comes in. "How'd you sleep last night, Mr. Hall?"

"If you don't count your staff's attempts to wake me up hourly to check on me and take a blood draw at an ungodly hour, I slept fine."

"I'm sorry for the inconvenience, but we want to ensure you're afforded the best care possible." She checks her watch. "The ambulance will arrive soon to return you to the chamber. What can I help you with?"

"Was there someone else in my room a few minutes ago?"

She positions the bed to help him sit upright before she answers. "There was, but I didn't catch his name. He said he's an old friend."

"Can you describe him?"

She's hesitant, and measures her words carefully. "He seems distinguished ... a dapper gentleman ... even though, in my opinion, he's a bit over-dressed for our humid climate. He's portly, wears a neatly trimmed white beard and walks with a cane."

"Hmm," Jon grins. "Thank you."

Tino's night involved numerous calls and entertaining a couple of visitors in his hotel room. The next morning, the same Toyota and driver wait for him at the curb.

He catches a forty minute flight aboard a Boeing 737 to Saipan. After clearing customs, another car and driver are available to shuttle him to an impressive complex in the northern suburbs of Kagman. The gated, manicured grounds overlook the island's eastern shore. Its buildings serve as the home base for the Consortium as well as the residence of its Chairman, and is patrolled by armed security.

After the guard at the reception table inspects Tino's valise, he's escorted into the room where several chairs are placed in a semicircular arrangement of three rows. The curtains are drawn and a table's set up near the front with an urn of coffee for today's arrivals. Tino acknowledges a couple of acquaintances, pours himself a drink, and gravitates to where they are standing. They have a bit of time for pleasantries before an impeccably manicured, gray-haired man enters the room. Immediately the conversations go silent.

"Thank you for your patience, gentlemen. Take a seat and we'll get started." With a voice roughly tempered by age, his countenance nevertheless demands their attention. Everyone sits.

His full name is Francis Xavier Vincenté, but to this group, he's addressed as "The Chairman". All the men treat him with respectful deference. They have a passing knowledge of his personal history——his meteoric and violent rise to the Consortium's top post. His excellent physical condition and youthful demeanor belie his advancing years.

When he gestures toward the door, two guards step out. "I ordered my security people to collect your weapons." With a slight smile, he adds, "I didn't want any untoward messes to clean up if you get into a disagreement." As if on cue, the men chuckle. "Okay, if you don't mind, we need to get started. We have much to get through today."

Jon's given a light breakfast at the hospital, and assisted with dressing before an orderly walks in with a wheelchair. "Good morning, sir. We have an ambulance ready to transport you to the chamber."

When he's wheeled into the facility, Doctor Koonradt stands to greet him. "Mr. Hall. Feel any better?"

"Please tell Doctor Ana I'm so sorry. I couldn't con——"

Doctor Koonradt waves him off. "Don't concern yourself. It comes with the job. Have you noticed any improvement in your vision?"

Jon hesitates while he sorts out an answer. "I guess my depth perception's out of kilter."

The doctor examines Jon's eyes and notes the same spasm as the day before. "Tell me more."

"Objects appear to be a lot closer than they really are and my footing's less than stable."

"Can you give me an example?"

"On our drive over here, I expected to get t-boned by a truck more than two blocks away, and reacted accordingly," he chuckles. "I'm not a good passenger to begin with. It's kind of a control thing——I would much rather drive than ride. So you can imagine what the driver had to put up with."

"Your symptoms will subside over the course of the treatments."

"'Course of treatments'? How many more chamber rides

will I need?"

"Today's run will last about an hour less than yesterday and we'll begin to decrease the times throughout the week as you continue to improve."

"Throughout the week?"

"You were in pretty rough shape when you arrived, Jon—— we believe it's bends related, but can't rule out the possibility of either an embolism or a stroke. We're required to treat you for the worst case scenario and continue to evaluate how well you respond to it."

"I guess I'm in your hands for as long as you need me, Doctor."

"Let's help you inside and we'll get started." The doctor signals the two in back of him. They assist Jon out of the chair and into the chamber. A new technician, Petty Officer First Class Sheila Ryan, is assigned to monitor his treatment. She's somewhere near her thirties, petite, with short brown hair and pleasant features. They make their introductions before the chamber is sealed.

A disembodied voice comes through the speaker. "Ready Mr. Hall? Please remember to clear your ears as the chamber's pressurized and continue to drink plenty of water throughout."

He takes a seat, hears the air feed into the chamber and feels the discomfort in his ears. He starts to clear them and repeats the process every few feet of simulated depth change until they reach the deepest level in the treatment. He glances at Petty Officer Ryan, who drops her hand from her nose and acknowledges him with an okay sign. He responds with the same before he sits back to tolerate the treatment.

After his second bottle of water he has to void his bladder, and self-consciously excuses himself. "I need to take care of this."

"No worries. No cause for embarrassment."

"All this water really necessary?"

She echoes the information from the day before. "It's one of several methods employed to expel excess nitrogen."

"Considering the amount of 'expelling' I've done in the last couple of days …"

She laughs. "You're doing fine, Mr. Hall."

"What's with all the formality around here, Sheila? Yesterday, everyone called me 'Jon'; today I'm addressed only by my last name."

"At our brief this morning, the commanding officer made a special trip here to tell us you are an important person from Washington and to make sure we give you our best care possible … even though it's standard operating procedure for *all* of our patients." She's aware that whatever is said in the chamber is monitored by those on the outside. She stays on script. "I could no more call you by your first name than I would our base admiral——too familiar."

"Where did they come up with the VIP stuff, which by the way, is total b.s."

"We understand someone flew in from Washington to personally meet with our base commander."

When they reach the sixty foot mark on the ascent, she hands him the BIBS mask. He scowls, but cooperates with her. It's bulky, uncomfortable, and loathsome on a personal level, but he concedes the necessity of its role in his treatment. Sheila adjusts the straps to ensure the mask's proper seating. Jon does not share his discontent.

After a four-hour session, the hatch opens and Doctor Mitra's there to greet him.

"Good afternoon, Mr. Hall." She holds up her hand. "David … Doctor Koonradt passed along your regrets about last night. Please, sir, do not be concerned."

"Nevertheless——"

"No, no. I will conduct another assessment to check your progress, before I can release you for the day."

"Back to your hospital?"

"No longer necessary. You have reservations at the Pacific Island Club in Hagåtña. I'm *sure* your accommodations will be to your liking."

"Can someone give me the number for a cab?"

"The base commander has made his personal car and driver available to you for the duration."

"Thoughtful, but who or what's behind all of this?"

She gestures toward the door to his left. "One more exam before I can let you go."

"In closing, gentlemen, thank you for your efforts on the Consortium's behalf." Chairman Vincenté pauses to frame the next statement carefully. "The reports from several island groups ... well, gratify. As you have heard here today, each of you has a unique and important role. So try to understand how dependent we are upon each other for our overall success."

Several men linger to renew acquaintances. Vincenté approaches Tino, "Mr. Nededog, a word with you ... privately, please."

The stragglers pick up on his cue and quickly vacate the premises. The last collects his weapon and leaves minutes later.

Tino notices the Chairman's face. His expression has turned dour.

"You worked your way aboard a private flight from Chuuk."

He's pretty well informed. "One diver got bent——"

"You mean Mr. Hall from the States," he interrupts.

Tino stammers, "I, I guess you already have all the details."

"We've heard some disturbing reports from your island."

"Why? Everything's under control!"

"Despite what I'm hearing to the contrary?"

Tino starts to raise his voice. "From who? I have a right to know who's spreading these lies."

Vincenté's eyebrows rise, "'Lies'? 'A right to'? Remember your place!"

"But——"

Vincenté slams his open hand on the table. "Enough! Let me speak!"

Tino's frustration now borders on panic. "But we're moving ahead——"

The older man's silent stare speaks volumes. He lets out a huff of disappointment before raising his hand to calm the agitated man down. At the window, the curtains open to a spectacular view of waves rhythmically breaking against the craggy coast.

Striving for mutual understanding, the Chairman draws a cigarette case out of his pocket, and reaches out to Tino who nervously helps himself. After he tamps down the end of his cigarette and lights up, he extends the offer, but Tino's hand shakes so uncontrollably he tosses him the lighter. The two stand in silence transfixed by the view while they enjoy the calming effects of nicotine.

After Vincenté snubs out his smoke, he notices Tino's hand continue to shake as he quickly disposes of the stub.

"I believe we've gotten off on the wrong foot. Tell me what you can about this Brent fellow."

When the car stops at the hotel's entrance, the driver swiftly walks around the vehicle to open Jon's door. He unfolds himself from the backseat, clad in scrubs, a lightweight robe, and slippers issued at the hospital. He acknowledges the driver, but before he can verbally convey his gratitude the hotel manager steps up to greet him.

"Mr. Hall, we are happy you've chosen to stay with us."

Jon eyes him skeptically as the car pulls away from the entrance. "Okay."

"We've set aside one of our nicest accommodations on the top floor. You will be well taken care of during your stay. Let me show you around our——"

Jon feels unsteady on his feet and reaches out to the man for support.

"Thank you, and I don't mean to come across as unappreciative, but I need to rest. May I have the key?"

"Right away, sir. Please let me escort you to your room."

Leaning against the glass, Jon takes in the view as the elevator begins it's climb. "What time do the stores close around here?"

"Is there anything you need?"

He fans out the robe with his hands in the pockets and gestures toward his slippers.

"I'm afraid I'm here empty-handed and at least need to pick up a change of clothes and some toiletries."

"You have a full assortment of each in your room——a nice selection of clothes both in the dresser and in your closet for you to use. Please feel free to keep whatever you need."

"Is this how you normally——"

He laughs. "Oh no, sir. A friend of yours has made the arrangements and has taken care of your entire bill." The muted chime signals their arrival. "Your floor, sir." The manager opens the door to his room with the pass key, and hands it to him along with his business card. "If for any reason our accommodations are less than suitable, you have the number to my direct line. Please do not hesitate to call me at any hour."

Jon's puzzled as he closes the door. He immediately goes to the curtained window, stunned by the breathtaking oceanfront view that unfolds before him. He checks the dresser and the closet. The room, the amenities, and the provisions live up to the promise. Jon has enough energy to use the new toothbrush before he collapses onto the bed.

The Chairman and Tino wrap up a lengthy discussion about the state of affairs on his island. "The other islands have not experienced the problems I've heard about from Chuuk. I'm counting on you to get things back in order. Otherwise, I'll be forced to send people who will. Stay near to the governor, keep a close eye on Brent, and be wary of others who may snoop around our operation. Have a safe trip back, Mr. Nededog." Tino leaves their meeting shaken, skeptical about having the Chairman's support.

Vincenté waits at the open front door until Tino's ride pulls away from the complex. He returns to the window which overlooks the ocean this time holding a glass of wine. He takes a sip, hears a different door, but keeps his eyes focused outside. "I presume you listened to our conversation?"

"I did," answers BG.

"Well, son, what do you think?"

Benjamin stares at his adopted father until they make eye contact. "Your concerns are legitimate, but Tino does have the governor's complete confidence."

Vincenté huffs, "The governor's a fool. Give me your honest opinion. Can Brent be controlled?"

"A reasonable question. He's operating out there on his own. It's his judgement which raises the most concern."

He places his hand on BG's massive shoulder. "What would you think about my coming to Chuuk in the near future to make my own assessment?"

"I'd love the opportunity to spend some rare quality time with you."

"It's not why I'm visiting, and we need to protect your cover until this gets resolved."

"Yes, sir." He masks his disappointment. "What can I do to help?"

"I can fill you in on the details once I arrive, but first I'll need to make arrangements with our people on the island. Will you be available to meet me at the airport?"

"You give the word, and I'm there."

"You cannot tell anyone, though. Absolutely no one."

"Yes, sir. Absolutely …"

"Good. In a few days then."

Three hours after Jon's head hits the pillow, he awakens with a start. He's not alone. He turns the light onto a familiar face in the chair next to the window.

"J.J.?"

"Good guess, young man. How about you get your butt up and we get out of this dump."

Jon scans his plush surrounding while he shakes off the cobwebs of sleep. "What's life like in your world, if you consider *this* place a dump?"

"Remember, I've spent time at your Maui home."

"Pat's funeral," Jon recalls.

"Painful times I remember, but how's life treated you since?"

Jon reaches for a bottle of water. "I miss her constantly. Everyday I need a reason to get out of bed, but each day I do."

J.J. pats Jon's shoulder, "You were fortunate for the time you had, and I hear Keira's grown into quite a woman."

"She's got her mother's looks and my love for the sea— both of which work in her favor." He lets out an exhalation and vigorously rubs the sleep out of his eyes. "But she also has my temperament."

"Oh, I *am* sorry to hear that. You two ever get your problems worked out?"

"We're moving in the right direction. I had to admit the blame's completely on me. I let this fester for way too many years." Jon laments. "You here to fix my dysfunctional relationships? Same old J.J. I've missed you, my friend. And by the way, I appreciate all of this, but how can you afford——"

"My department can take the hit. Don't worry about the cost. You up for some good food and a walk?"

"I'll try, but I'm still pretty shaky."

"How about a stroll about the lobby? We can take advantage of their restaurant——"

"I'm game," he interrupts.

He takes a quick shower, throws on some clothes, then glances at his profile in the mirror as he pats down the front of his shirt.

"Correct size, too. You're as thorough as ever."

"Paul rummaged through your room to get me your sizes."

"He's a good man."

"One of the best."

On the ride down in the elevator, J.J. inquires, "I've wanted to ask how the new man, Woods, working out?"

"Okay, I guess. I haven't spent much time with him."

"He brings impressive credentials to the agency, and comes from a good family, but I too haven't spent enough time to get a good take on him yet."

"I'll send you a full report as soon as possible."

"I'd appreciate it."

Over coffee and a late breakfast, Jon updates his old friend on the progress and challenges the team has faced. "You ever hear from our former crew?"

"At first, I tried to put together a reunion, but as my responsibilities increased, it fell by the wayside. You're the only one I've maintained any degree of contact with through the years. I came to realize all but a few have moved on."

Jon puts his cup down. "I want a straight answer, my friend. Why *are* you here?"

"I heard you were in trouble——"

"Let's cut through the crap, Jay. You could not have gotten here this fast from Washington, and you would not have come all this way to only check on my welfare. What's going on?"

He hesitates before he answers. "Your intuition hasn't failed you in your advancing years, but we can't talk about this here. Let's resume this discussion back in your room."

The two men stroll around the cavernous lobby and wander by a surf shop.

Jon grabs J.J.'s arm. "I'll need another swimsuit. Do you mind?" A reach into his empty pocket serves a reminder he has no money.

"Put whatever you need on your room bill. That reminds me, there's an envelope in your room's safe with a modest amount of cash. The desk has a copy of your passport which will help you through the various airports."

"Really? Well, thank you." J.J. gestures toward the surf shop.

Jon walks in and scans the clothes options——racks full of brightly colored fabrics——fluorescent oranges, neon yellows, chartreuse greens, and fuchsia reds. Jon reels until J.J. grabs his arm, "What's going on?"

"Help me out of here."

He sits down on the nearest bench in the lobby.

"Better," he groans lightly. "All those colors ... sensory overload. Too soon for the outside world I suppose. We'd better head back upstairs."

They settle in before Jon aims an inquisitive look at his friend.

J.J. responds. "Okay. You are correct. Paul, Dax, and Eric aren't the only agents we have deployed here. We have men fanned out throughout the entire region. I'm here to tighten up our lines of communication, keep a closer eye on the operations, and coordinate logistical support where needed."

"We're only a part of this, aren't we?"

"Right again."

"But what *aren't* you telling me?"

"My friend, it's good you're back on your feet." He stands and grabs his cane. "Follow your physicians' orders and I promise to touch base with you when this is over."

They give each other a hug along with their good-byes.

Jon has a lot to consider, but it's early and he wants to catch a nap before the car from the base arrives.

Keira nurses her first cup of coffee in the conference room when Steve walks in. She is tired and waiting for the caffeine to kick in. He is upbeat and offers a smile which annoys her to no-end this early in the morning.

"How're you feelin', young lady?"

She responds by raising her cup in a mock toast, "Meh."

He pours a cup for himself, and takes a seat across from her.

"I got the news about your father. I'm sorry you've had to go through that. Any update on his progress?"

She whispers a barely audible, "Not yet."

"You put in a rough night?"

She murmurs. "I'm not awake yet."

Steve does his best to steer the conversation into a more upbeat mode. "I think you'll enjoy the day we have lined up. We're headed to the *Fujikawa Maru*, one of my favorite sites, and I'm sure will end up as one of yours. It offers a spectacular array of marine life which I know you'll appreciate.

"There's also much to do inside the wreck. The cavernous holds are easily accessible and filled with artifacts, both large and small. The ship's cargo of B6N "Jill" bombers and support materials wasn't fully offloaded before the Allied raid hit. Pertinent to your assignment, fuel drums are scattered throughout the vessel. They're on the list for removal if and when the reclamation project begins. Any questions?"

"Where are the others today?"

"After a dive on the *Fumizuki* they'll take some time to snorkel over several remains of aircraft dropped in the battle."

"Who's leading the dive?"

"It's only the three agents, so Andon's sending them out with Alou and Kristian. I imagine Alou will oversee their safety, otherwise they're on their own. So, what's our plan today?"

"I'll meet you at the docks in thirty? We'll talk about the dive en route."

Steve has provided his personal sixteen foot-long Boston Whaler, markedly smaller than Andon's boats. A bench seat spans the center. Steve's equipment is already set up and deposited on the deck space behind the seat and the boat motor. He encourages Keira to prep all of her gear on the dock, and bag her loose items for the transit.

There's no overhead protection from the sun, so Keira covers herself with the beach towel and wide-brimmed hat. It's a distant ride, but the wind-free flat waters allow the boat to skim the surface quickly. A familiar whiff of the outboard motor brings back fond memories of her youth on Maui.

The *Fujikawa Maru*, at one-time an aircraft transport, is located immediately south of tiny Eten Island, which served as the main airfield for the occupying Japanese and the initial focus of air assaults in February '44. The island's currently undergoing another battle, this time with the jungle growth of tropical vegetation which continues to transform Eton back to its original state. By the time they arrive, it's lightly overcast, but will not obscure the beauty of what they're about to explore. Keira peers over the side of his boat and can clearly make out the wreck's expanse.

Steve breaks out a case with his still camera and strobes,

clips the assembly to a ten foot-long drop line and lowers the rig over the side.

She points to the lowered line. "I never got into underwater photography. When did you start?"

"I dove for nine years before I caught the bug. First to develop my skill set, then to learn as much about the marine life and how to safely interact with them. Afterward, our travels centered around diverse destinations. Everything changed when I got into shooting."

Once geared up and in the water, Keira snorkels over the panoramic wreckage while she waits for Steve to join her. From the surface, the ship is spectacular. There's a slight current running from the stern to its bow which serves to maximize the remarkable visibility.

They descend to the port side near the bow. A sizable bright yellow tree branch coral has caught her attention. Although the wreck's fully illuminated in the midday sun, Keira uses her dive light to highlight the rich yellow polyps and discovers a nearly translucent emperor shrimp with a clutch of eggs beneath its tail.

Keira's confidence as a wreck-diver has grown appreciably during their extended stay. When she realizes Steve's lost to his macro photography she continues along the hull. The visuals presented by the marine life serve to dispel any notions of danger diving on a decomposing wreck.

She comes across a curiosity——a single cable bolted to the hull near a spot where corrosion has rotted through the metal. She follows the cable to the lagoon's floor at a hundred and ten feet. It's anchored to a sizable rectangular block of metal. She makes a notation on her slate to bring this up with Steve after the dive.

When they rendezvous, he's ready to move on. They enter the number two hold to inspect disassembled bombers abandoned in the attack. Smaller artifacts are easily accessible, no doubt rooted-out by earlier guides. A pilot's mask, with its intact goggles and oxygen hose. A varied collection of clipped machine gun ammunition sits in the open.

They come across stacks of fuel drums stored in various compartments. Steve's drawings provide precise renditions of each deck. He points out the position of the compartments to Keira on his sketches and she takes special care to annotate them accurately.

Back on *Fujikawa's* deck, Steve directs her toward the bow. She observes the collapsed bulkheads and overheads left by the support beams. A typhoon swept through the islands a short while back and took down an already compromised superstructure.

Steve wants them to continue the tour and gestures toward the six-inch bow gun. At the foremost point on the bow, he points out an oddly placed telegraph, a silent sentinel awaiting orders to relay maneuvers to the engine room. They start back toward the stern along the port side companionway.

Darting in and out of encrusted growth, countless fish animate the aft mast. The innocuous lifeboat davits support sweeping fronds of colorful tree branch coral. Keira notes an exotic regal angelfish, wary of interlopers, but curious enough to stay within sight, only not too close.

They continue to another six-inch gun at the stern where the growth's similar to the bow gun, with one exception——a resident 'slender grouper' unaffected by the bubbly presence of two visitors. After fifty minutes on the wreck, the time has come to start their ascent.

Their next destination's the southeastern shore of nearby Tonoas Island.

It's a short walk from the dock to the Japanese fuel depots targeted by the air assaults. The Allies hit them where they would do the greatest damage——their precious fuel reserves. The area's overgrown with vegetation disguising the circular remnants of three immense storage tanks——each one contained a 17,000 ton capacity which burned for a full two weeks after the bombs struck.

Steve breaks out their lunch. They have much to discuss. Keira opens with, "What happened to the superstructure?"

"It was a victim of a typhoon some months past."

"Weather alone could do that?"

"Weather is a huge factor, but keep in mind these wrecks have spent the last half century in corrosive seawater. Steel and iron cannot withstand the weakening effects of the elements. The sad truth is over time, maybe not for decades, but eventually, they will collapse.

"From what I've observed, Keira, you have excellent buoyancy control. You keep yourself neutrally buoyant and avoid contact with the surface areas. Many divers who visit these waters do as well, but not all. They touch down on the wreck and carelessly handle the artifacts doing inadvertent damage to both. All with an unintended negative effect on the marine life as well. And there are the bubbles."

"From our exhalations? How do they cause any harm?"

"When we, myself included, penetrate the wrecks, our bubbles float up and displace particulate from the overheads. Each bubble trims off a few loose flakes of rust in one place, and exert pressure wherever they settle. Now multiply that by the thousands of dives done annually——all serve to compromise structural integrity. When a heavy storm hits, or a carelessly dragged anchor scrapes over a wreck, the damage to the already weakened structures is catastrophic."

"I never considered the impact we have. I attributed the decay solely to the corrosive effects of water. So our surveys aren't a sham?"

"I'm afraid not."

The idea sobers Keira. *One day the beauty of this place might all become a distant memory——how catastrophic.* "Can anything be done to push back the clock? I mean the beauty ..." The words catch in her throat.

"There're some theories being tested on a few of the wrecks, but all come with a price tag along with the question, 'Who's going to pay for it?'"

"I ran across a cable running from the hull to an

anchorage, on the seabed near the wreck."

"It's a good example of what we've discussed. A noted engineer from Australia has taken a personal interest in the deterioration. He sent a team of volunteers to the islands to do surveys and setup the experiment I believe you discovered. They brought with them the remnants of a car stripped to its metal components and crushed, which comprise the 'anchorage' you found. The electrolysis from the compacted metals interacts with the seawater and generates enough current back to the hull to slow the corrosion."

"It sounds promising."

"True enough. You probably noticed all the abandoned vehicles along the roadside from the airport to the hotel. Theoretically a company could recover and prep them, before they're crushed. The cars provide the raw materials and they have an untapped labor pool to draw from. But it all goes back to money."

"Would it work?"

"At least to the point it could push back the ravages of time." Steve flips through his journal for related entries. "What's more frustrating are the disingenuous complaints from the fishing industry. Did you noticed the depletion of mines from *San Francisco's* forward hold?"

"I did dive the hold but didn't have any reference to go by."

"I guess you wouldn't. A select number of local fishermen have stripped the *Nippo Maru* of its munitions to harvest gunpowder for dynamite fishing. The fish school near the wrecks, the explosions kill the fish which in turn contributes to the wreck's collateral damage. It's a vicious cycle. The government's impotent to stop them and the guilty fishermen are too short-sighted and greedy to understand the long-term impact of their activities."

"Do you have any recommendations?"

"Not without the stringent enforcement necessary to protect the sites. Without the funding, it will never happen. The question remains, who will pay? The local government's certainly in no position."

"We're here at the behest of their government to address the issue. They want our financial support to deal with the potential crisis."

"I promise you, Keira, if the United States sends money to enable this government without independent oversight and accounting, the funds will vaporize."

"How do you figure?"

"Corruption. I've heard rumors the governor's involved in other ventures, which may include your old acquaintance, Brent. I also think he's aiming for one last payday to set himself up before he leaves office. Your team may enable him."

Her voice starts to elevate and cracks, "I hate all this subterfuge."

"I can imagine, but listen. If at any time these people think your presence's a ruse, you may be in jeopardy. It's why I'm suggesting to stick to your role: take your surveys, write your reports, and stay safe."

"That's reassuring," she snorts. "You mean I will need to keep looking over my shoulder the remaining time we're here?"

"Not necessarily, but it wouldn't hurt. They want to maintain as transparent a profile as possible. Best you keep your guard up. Stick close to those you trust."

The subject reverts back to the positive aspect of their dive. Keira starts to go on about her marine life observations.

Steve interjects, "Before you leave, you should dive this wreck at night to appreciate the displays in their full glory. Simply stunning."

"I'm not so sure," Keira reflects, "Whenever I think about diving at night I can't shake the feeling critters wait beyond the limits of my light, ready to pounce."

"Keep in mind whatever's out there fears you too."

"Possibly we can squeeze one in before we leave."

A couple of hours after they return, Dax and Eric seat themselves on either side of Keira. Paul chooses to keep Alou company at the console. They're en route to Andon's home across the channel. Keira's unsure of what to expect, but anticipates a pleasant time with Andon in the relaxed atmosphere of his home turf.

He's waiting at the dock when they arrive, and greets the group with outstretched arms. "Welcome everyone."

As he offers his hand to help her out, Keira answers his oft-seen smile with one of her own. She walks alongside him, arm-in-arm, chatting flirtatiously. Close to the house they can hear the unbridled play of several youngsters.

"Those your children?"

"Some are; the rest belong to neighbors and relatives."

She drops her hand from Andon's arm and glances at him. *'Some are?'*

He leads her to a noisy gathering of animated women who act and sound like they haven't seen each other in years. When they catch sight of Andon and his guests they stop their jibber-jabber. His wife works her way to the forefront. She comes across like they were unexpected. "And who might these people be?"

"Keira, I'm proud to introduce you to my wife, Emiko." Apparently of Japanese descent, she's petite, nicely proportioned, with straight black hair that falls to the middle of her back. The symmetry of her face is perfect, but her demeanor is cold. Keira quickly drops her attentive gaze.

He adds, "Keira is Jon's daughter."

The two acknowledge each other awkwardly and respond in unison, "It's nice to meet you," then share a nervous laugh together with the others.

Andon leaves her in the company of the women and circulates among the men. Emiko rolls her eyes toward the other women. This isn't the first time she's met one of her husband's female admirers. Keira's expression gives away her disappointment. She constantly searches for others at the party rather than the women she's been marooned with.

"May I get you something to drink?" Emiko offers.

"Oh please," she sighs. "The stronger the better."

She retrieves a beer from the cooler. "Sorry, but it's as strong as we have."

"Good enough. Thank you."

The other women acknowledge her politely, but exclude her from their conversations. After a few minutes, Keira wanders away and works her way over to Paul. From the other side of a nearby table, he viewed her predicament with some degree of amusement. She sharply swats his stomach.

He flinches and puts his hand out defensively. "What the——?"

"You knew, didn't you?"

"Of course I did."

"And you didn't deem it necessary to tell me."

When Paul doesn't respond, she wanders off in disgust to find Dax and Eric.

After everyone shares much food and more stories, Paul joins Eric who's holding court with the children. Keira, left alone with her beer for company, eyes him as he ambles over. *Why am I obsessing about him?*

Eric explains the rules before the children take off with the soccer ball to get started.

"You're good with the kids," Paul notes.

"Have a lot of practice with my own. I miss them at times like this."

"Any discoveries this morning?"

One young girl yells at them. "Come play with us, Eric?" Pointing to Paul, she giggles, "You can bring your friend, too."

Eric points his thumb toward the rambunctious kids. "Guess we have orders from a higher authority. How about we continue this discussion back at the hotel."

They rise to follow their leader.

Dax observes Keira's fixation on Paul and Eric. He retrieves a couple of bottles from the cooler and takes a seat at the table across from her. "I believe a fresh one's in order?"

"You or the bottle?" She smirks. "I'm happy you came over. We haven't had much of a chance to talk this trip."

"Paul *has* done a good job of keeping us busy."

The whole time Dax rambles on about his history with the agency, his family, and his long friendship with Paul, Keira never takes her eyes off the men playing with the children. Dax notices her distraction, "… and it ended with China dropping the bomb."

"What?" Keira blushes. She puts her hand on top of his. "I'm sorry." She pauses to find her wording, "Would you be willing to tell me about Hannah?"

Dax is a bit surprised by her question. "I can, but not sure if I should. I don't wish to lose Paul's trust. Why do you ask?"

She glances at him sheepishly. "Why do you think?"

"Oh … bad, huh?" She remains mute. "Hannah. Hmm. Let me give you the condensed version of it. They met through mutual friends. After a time, Paul envisioned their future together, but she had other ideas. It's not much more complicated. They had a painful parting and he hasn't seen her since."

When the game breaks up, Keira stands. Dax takes her forearm and gestures her to sit.

She uncomfortably responds, "What?"

"As a personal favor, don't hurt him, Keira. He deserves some happiness."

She stands. "I don't have that kind of power over him." She leaves him at the table to walk over to the play area.

Dax notices Paul put his arm around her waist and thinks, *Yeah, Keira … you do. You really do.*

The party lasts throughout the afternoon until one youngster runs to her father in tears. When Andon picks her up, she drops her head onto his shoulder.

"I think you need a nap young lady." She turns her face away from his and surrenders to sleep.

Andon beckons the group, "Guess we need to put the kids down for their naps. Time to call it a day. Thank you everybody for spending your afternoon with us."

The guests convey their appreciation and make their way to the boat for the return. Keira takes a seat on the bench opposite Paul only to ignore him during the crossing.

On their walk from the dock, Paul steps up his pace to keep up with her.

Keira doesn't break stride. "I'm kinda angry with you."

"Obviously … but why?"

"You hurt me today. I made a fool of myself, and you sat there and let me. Why?"

"It presented an opportunity for you to get him out of your system before you have regrets later."

"Want to elaborate?"

"If you knew he had such a beautiful wife, would you have wanted to come today?"

"I doubt it, but you never gave me the option." She stops in her tracks and turns to face him. "Now, let me ask *you* …"

"Shoot."

"Are these my interests you care so much about, or your own?"

"What's on your mind, Keira?"

"I need to know I can trust and count on you. After today's stunt, I'm not so sure."

His silence frustrates her, and she leaves him where he stands to continue to the hotel lounge where Dax and Steve agreed to meet.

"Where's Eric?" She asks Dax.

"Paul left him on the island with an assignment. He's supposed to join us later."

He gestures for Sal to set her up.

A short while later, Paul enters the lounge to join the party, and steps up to the bar to order a round.

Sal wants a few minutes of his time.

"Sure. What's on your mind?"

"From what I hear, you've got some pretty serious stuff going on out there."

"You'll need to elaborate."

"Okay. You can't talk to me about it, but let me give you a word of advice." Without encouragement from Paul, Sal adds, "My friend Jon is sitting in the recompression chamber on Guam right now. You think it's an accident he's there? He's been coming here for years. He's too smart and too professional to let this happen to him. Whatever you're digging into, you need to use caution."

"Where're you going with this, Sal?"

"Look, man, word's going around that Vincenté has his eyes on you."

"Who's Vincenté?"

"You shining me?"

"Just answer my question."

He leans over the bar to answer him quietly, "Whatever kind of firepower you brought with you, if he decides to make a move, you'll need every bit of it."

Paul grabs the bottles for the table before he rejoins his crew. "I trust you'll keep me in the loop?"

"Uh huh," Sal mutters to himself.

By now everyone feels pretty good despite the drain the day's activities have taken. The fatigue and cold brews lead them to drop many of their inhibitions. Conversations become more direct without the restrictions of filters, and the resultant gut-laughs are spontaneous and free.

When Eric makes an appearance, Keira stands atop her seat and yells, "Get your butt over here, Eric, and grab a brew."

Amused, he makes everyone clear a space so he can sit next to her, and signals the waitress for another round. Paul gives him an inquisitive glance and he responds with a slight nod.

"Drink up everyone. Last round," Paul announces.

"But Eric just got here," Keira protests.

Paul nods, and adds, "Sorry, but duty calls."

Keira's disappointed but happy she can spend some undistracted time with Steve. He slides in next to her.

"Where's your valise?"

"No notes tonight," he answers. "How about dinner tomorrow. Right here, seven o'clock?"

"It's a date," she asserts, and immediately regrets she didn't choose a better word. "I mean——"

Steve's blurts out, "Don't fret yourself. I need to get home, too. We've had a full day."

"I guess I better turn in." She admits, "I'm just a lit … tle bit tipsy."

As they rise, another set of eyes observes from the lounge's deep recesses. Brent snuffs his cigarette and discretely follows Steve out the door.

Chapter 18
Interrogations

From the air, Tonoas Island resembles the head of a duck with its open beak facing east. Steve's home is located on the island's northern peninsula (beak), upcountry on Unikopos mountain. He's returning after a day of personal investigations into the Consortium's activities. He's tired, and the trek to his house is a steep, graded pathway from the concrete dock, tucked into a recess near the coastal village of Meseran.

Modest by U.S. standards, his house is more than adequate to meet his needs. It has a kitchenette, a modest-sized living room, and two bedrooms. He converted the larger into a studio for his art, which is haphazardly displayed throughout. It's generously lit with several windows, a skylight, and glass double-doors which open onto a lanai and a panoramic view to the lagoon.

He plans to shower, and review his findings before his return to Weno for the promised meet with Keira. He's laden with his field journal, maps, camera, and binoculars. To make things worse, he has lost track of his flashlight and darkness shrouds the path.

He recognizes the apparition approaching him from the shadows. "You're Nededog? I don't recall having an appoint—"

"Knock off the nonsense, Mitchell," Tino snaps. "You're in

possession of some information valuable to us."

Steve notices his house is fully illuminated. Fighting the instinct to rush back to the dock, he turns quickly and runs into BG blocking his path. "What's this all about?" he demands.

"We need to examine your journal for starters."

He attempts another escape down the path, deftly sidesteps BG, before he runs into two of Tino's confederates——young Consortium punks the governor has employed as drug dealers and enforcers. Damon and Miguel hold tactical pistols at waist-level aimed directly at him.

"Mr. Mitchell, please," Tino pleads, "don't make a scene. Let's take this discussion inside, where it'll be much more pleasant for all of us."

By this time, BG has caught up with him and fastened a grip on the underside of his upper arm. He tries to break his hold without success. "I guess you have the advantage here."

Tino asks BG to release him. He points to the two holding guns, and adds, "If you run one more time, my young friends have orders to shoot."

Early in the evening, Paul joins Keira in the sparsely populated lounge. She hopes to use the occasion to break through some of Paul's barriers and get him to open up. She has a cocktail, so Paul catches the eye of Sal, points to her drink, and holds up two fingers. Keira notices the waitress's alluring smile when she delivers a cold Heineken for Paul and slides the other to her without acknowledgment.

"Old friend or acquaintance?"

Paul doesn't respond.

"Oh-kay, let's start with an easier question. How's my father connected with your agency and, well … who exactly are you people?"

He takes his time nursing his brew to sort out an answer. "Where this inquisition leads, depends on your assurance you won't share any of this."

She holds up two fingers, "Girl Scout's honor."

"Cute, but in all seriousness, you cannot repeat this."

"Agreed," she responds tersely.

"We're here to represent the Environmental Protection Agency, but truthfully, the Treasury Department dictates our mission's parameters. When they suspect a petition from another government is 'layered', my team is dispatched to substantiate what's behind the request."

"But you're obviously more than auditors."

"Apparently there's a lot at stake here——not only about the funds they've requested, but the regional stability."

Keira's more baffled than ever. "How did my father end up in the middle of all this?"

"From what I gather, he served in the Navy with my boss. They crewed together and maintained a lifelong friendship. The photo Jon has on the sideboard at his house——"

"I'm familiar with it."

"Well, our director has the same picture on his desk at work. After the governor indirectly contacted your father through Brent, he called our director when he got back to the States."

"I've never heard of this 'director' before."

"I'm not surprised. He keeps a low profile. Ever hear your father speak about a man named 'J.J.'?"

"Vaguely, but he never elaborated. Sea stories and such."

"J.J. is Jay Johnson, the 'Director', but we're not allowed to address him by his old nickname. Apparently, he served as a radio operator and handled a lot of crypto material while in the service." Keira's confused. "Top secret communications equipment and code books. When he got discharged from the Navy he excelled at university, drew the attention of head-hunters at the Treasury Department, and was eventually recruited to put together our group."

"The other day you mentioned 'potential problems' between Brent and my father. What did you mean?"

Paul wrestles with how much more he should divulge. *If I*

do this, it will mean stepping outside our operational guidelines. I did promise Jon I'd keep her safe, but I have to face the fact it's gotten personal.

"We need assurances the government's money will reach the right people and be used for the designated purpose. Along those lines, we believe the governor and Brent may be connected, but unsure to what extent. With only circumstantial evidence, we're tasked with determining the truth behind it."

"You must have a lot on your plate."

His eyes wander.

She nurses her drink, while mustering her courage. "May I continue with a more personal subject?"

"You can try."

As Steve is forced through his own front door, he's shocked by the vision he's confronting. The extent of the disarray terrifies him. The kitchenette has been turned inside out. Every drawer removed from the cabinets, emptied of their contents and cast about the floor. The desk is trashed, and the worktable is an unrecognizable mess of papers, notebooks, and journals. His extensive collection of books and magazines are strewn throughout with their covers torn off and irreparable. Save for a few chairs and dining table, his furniture lays about smashed, cut open and eviscerated. Surprisingly, his artwork is untouched.

He struggles with his emotions to put up a false bravado with Tino, "Did you enjoy tearing my life apart like this?"

"Sit down and shut up."

BG forces him onto the chair facing the dining room's rear wall, and begins to strap him in. His head is bound so tightly his sightline is limited to his peripheral vision. His eyes widen and dart between Tino and BG. Brent stands out of view, in a shadowy corner as far away from the chair as possible, curious to what's happening, but afraid of being recognized.

Damon and Miguel have darkened the windows and wait outside the door in case anyone shows up uninvited.

"Your paintings interest me, Mr. Mitchell. You obviously have a good eye for detail."

Despite his discomfort, he demands, "What do you want from me?"

Tino's eyes move toward BG, who viciously backhands Steve's cheek knocking both him and the chair onto the floor sideways. BG immediately lifts the occupied chair upright.

"Now, if you don't mind, *I'll* be the one who asks the questions." He groans as he tries to clear his head and spits out the pooled blood in his mouth. Tino glances at the blotches of red spittle on the floor before he holds out a packet of black and white photographs. "I'm especially interested in your unhealthy curiosity about our activities. Tell me what you *think* you've found?"

With no response forthcoming, Tino follows with, "What would you do, Mr. Mitchell, if you could no longer practice your art?" He waits for the question to sink in. With his face no further than an inch away from Steve's, he shouts, "Tell me about Miss Hall's involvement! What does *she* already know?"

He uses what energy he has to fruitlessly wrestle against his restraints. "You leave her out of this!" he screams, half out of his wits.

Without a prompt from Tino, BG uses his pistol to knock Steve to the floor. He's out cold and remains so until a searing pain from his shattered right hand snaps him fully awake. Again, BG turns his chair upright. A tightly rolled, wet towel wedged between the jaws of his open mouth muffle his screams. His hand throbs; he isn't able to lift it. He struggles to breath through his nose, rapidly filling with blood and mucus. He stares at Tino through tear-filled eyes, but tells him nothing when BG loosens the towel. Without warning, BG delivers a crushing blow to his sternum. He gasps for air through the moist towel. Tino points specifically to a photograph of Keira standing next to Paul.

"We can do this all night, Mitchell. Why don't you spare

yourself any more pain and tell me about her involvement?" Steve continues to gasp, so Tino gestures the towel be lowered. "Talk to me!"

"Stop, please … I don't have …" Darkness closes in on him. He groans and feels a twinge of light-headedness before he slumps forward.

BG grasps Steve's throat, then jerks his hand away. "Huh." He faces Tino. "His heart musta gave out, boss. I think he's dead."

Tino verifies BG's suspicions. With his hand still in place about Steve's neck, Tino glares at the big man. "You lost control of yourself and killed him, you moron." He drops his grip and starts to pace back and forth. Wildly waving a pointed finger, he barks out a series of orders. "Get the other two in here. Have them use his bedding to wrap up the body. Try *not* to get noticed. Meanwhile, I'll need to think of an explanation for the boss."

BG hates his belittling condescension and glares at the diminutive man before he summons Damon and Miguel inside to dispose of the body. Following the two men outside, he glances back at Tino contemptuously before they start down the hill.

In the darkness, Tino catches distant movement to the right of the house. After taking a slow look around, he shakes off the distraction, bolts the door, and orders a rattled Brent to remove any evidence of their presence, which includes Steve's blood splattered photographs and the variety of graphics he made for Keira.

"You've gotta be shitting me!" Brent screams at him. "You killed him, man! I gotta get outta here."

When he makes his move, Tino quickly sidesteps to block his exit and pushes him back.

"You're now an accessory, my friend! Up to your neck," he gestures accordingly. "It's best you remember who your friends are."

"Howdya figure? I never laid a hand on him!" he yells back.

"Don't try to pull the 'I'm innocent' routine on me. Why if it hadn't been for you, we'd of had a much more difficult task locating his house." He points his finger at Brent with a smug note of appreciation, "You provided an invaluable service when you led us here tonight. Otherwise, it would have cost us precious time and raised all sorts of suspicions if we had to ask around on our own."

The full weight of Tino's accusation hits home with Brent. *I helped them murder him. This will follow me for the rest of my life. How will I ever get out of this mess? The authorities? I'm a dead man either way.* He's so shaken, he's unable to function.

Tino tries to calm him down and pulls out the last upright chair at the table. "Take a seat, Brent … please."

Afraid he's next to go down, Brent holds out his hand. "Thanks, but I think … I think I'd rather stand."

Tino swiftly walks straight up to him, their noses nearly touch. "SIT DOWN!" He reacts as if someone swept his feet out from under him, and drops into the chair. Tino calmly continues, "Now, let's talk about your upcoming dives."

When he's hears the double-s*nick* of Steve's door lock, Eric, who's assigned to get information about the governor's crew, packs up his array and waits for the men to clear the area before he sidles down the hill toward the village.

Eric has already made arrangements for his return to Weno Island, but first he walks west hugging the north shoreline of Tonoas. His head's constantly on a swivel in search of cover. He eventually catches a good spot to view the Consortium's yacht.

Through dense vegetation, he uses his binoculars to scan the boat and observes several heavily armed guards on deck. The crewman catches a glint of light reflecting off the lenses of Eric's glasses. He lets his own binoculars fall to his chest and lifts his rifle to scan the area with a high-powered scope and the potential of getting off a clean shot. Eric notices the growing interest aimed in his direction and immediately crawls to deeper cover. The guard calls two of his companions and the three search in vain. When they give up and return to their posts, Eric slinks back to the village under the protective cloak of night.

With a glance at her wrist, Keira notices her time with Paul is drawing to a close. "Do you have anyone special in your life?"

The directness of her question catches Paul off-guard. When he hesitates, she presses, "I tried with the other two, but got nothing. Dax told me about his wife and blended family, and I surmise Eric's new to your team, which brings up another——"

"What's the question again?"

When she checks the time, Paul states, "Guess I better leave now, huh?"

"Hold on," she protests, "you haven't answered me yet about your special someone."

"You've done your homework. You ought to think about coming to work for us."

She sloughs off his parry. "I suppose that's confidential too?"

Keira waits for Paul to elaborate, *Steve's due to arrive any moment now, but it's the first opportunity I've had Paul open up to me.* "I'm really sorry, but I'm supposed to meet someone here soon."

He playfully responds, "You know, I feeling kinda hungry. I could possibly help with your discussion ... two birds ..."

"Yeah, you're such an engaging conversationalist," she smirks.

They both stand. When he lingers at the table, she pushes him toward the door.

"'Is it Steve?"

"Yes, it's Steve. Now, get out of here."

"You two have gotten pretty chummy. You do realize people talk."

She makes a grand gesture to physically point him toward the lobby. "Out!"

After Paul leaves, an amused Keira returns to her seat and continues her wait.

Paul opens his door to the other two agents who are engrossed in Eric's findings. Dax invites him to sit. "You'd better listen to this."

Eric shares, "Our 'friends' got to Steve and worked him over. I can't tell you who exactly, but I think he's dead."

Paul has a new quandary, *Can I share any of this with Keira.*

"Before you go, there's one more thing we need to discuss." Eric tells him about his interaction with the yacht.

Paul adds, "I had an odd conversation with Sal last night. He took it upon himself to warn me about a man named Vincenté. Eric, I need you to contact Chief Kohper. Get what info you can about this Vincenté fellow. Before you go, leave your binoculars here. Think I'll do a bit of 'bird-watching' myself." Paul heads directly to the lobby and seeks Keira.

"What happened to your date?" Paul needles as he approaches her table.

"I'm worried. We made plans to go over what he's found."

Paul's taken aback. "'What he's found'? He's not part of what we're doing here." When she doesn't respond, he pushes, "Tell me truthfully, Keira, how involved are you?"

"I'd better wait for Steve to fill you in on the details."

"It's best *you* bring me up to speed on Steve's end of things … right now!"

"Well, Jonathan hired him——"

"For what?"

"To begin with, he provided me with all the graphics we've used during the briefings, and the materials I've had with me for the surveys. I really think——" Paul scans the lounge before he holds up his hand to interrupt her.

"Let's take this outside. You willing to go for a walk?"

"Okay," she skeptically responds.

Keira waits for Paul to take the lead. They slowly stroll the shoreline while he uses the time to formulate his next series of questions.

"From what you told me in there, can I correctly assume Steve took it upon himself to do a bit of freelancing?"

"I'm sure he's just trying to help."

Paul has already decided not to disclose what he learned from Eric. "What about you? Did you help him in any way?"

"Not in the field. Only later to mull over his findings. He's trying to suss out some facts to support his theories."

"Yeah, I need to hear what he's come up with." *I'll have to call J.J. and give him an update.* "Where does Steve live?"

"He has a place on the island across the channel from us, but I'm unsure where." She turns toward Tonoas, and ponders, "What's keeping him. He's always been early for our meets, and usually left to wait for me."

"I wouldn't worry too much about it. He may have experienced some trouble with his boat or possibly overslept a nap."

Keira points out lights coming from the dock by the dive shop, and with it a level of conversation unusually loud for this time of night. "Maybe he got hung up over there."

Paul holds out his hand, "Let's go check it out? Andon may have some answers."

They find Andon at the dock, involved in a lively discussion with several of his staff. When he notices the couple nearing their group, Andon addresses Paul directly, "Your arrival's timely. We have——"

"I'm sorry to interrupt, Andon, but can you tell me where Steve lives?" Continuing the ruse, he adds, "He's supposed to meet with Keira for dinner tonight."

Annoyed Paul cut him off, Andon responds, "Our problems here are a lot more important than a broken dinner engagement."

"Why? What's going on?"

"Maybe you could shed some light on this? One of my boats was sabotaged this evening. The boat's easily repairable, but I have one man hospitalized and the balance of my people are frightened." He points his forefinger directly at Paul. "Whatever it is you're involved with, they refuse to go out with you anymore. They feel threatened and frankly, I can't blame them."

Paul drops Keira's hand. Before he can respond, Andon adds, "This could affect your future here as well."

Paul stiffens. "How do you figure?"

Keira wants them to focus on what's most important. "I hope your man's injuries aren't too severe."

Andon's temper calms, but he's tries to keep from breaking down. "When he confronted the intruders, they beat him so badly. He said he didn't recognize either of the two on the boat or see the third person who struck him down from behind. I'm not so sure. We summoned the police, but there's not much they'll do."

"Do you have any suspicions?"

"I do, but nothing more." Paul gestures to Keira they should return to the hotel. When he turns to join her, Andon grabs his arm. "I need you to tell me the truth. What's your involvement here?"

"I've told you all I can right now."

Andon snorts, "But you really haven't told me *anything*!" Paul shakes his arm loose leading to a rare fit of temper from Andon, "Your lame excuses won't fly with my staff any longer, *Agent* Gerhart. I'd hoped you'd come up with a better explanation."

"Shouldn't you stop to answer him?" Keira suggests.

"Keep moving."

When they continue toward the hotel, Andon yells, "And it won't fly with me, either!" He stands defiantly, but unanswered, until they're out of sight.

They pass by the door to Paul's room, and stop outside Keira's. "I have some cold water in the fridge."

"Sorry, but I have to make a call. It's important."

"Oh." She's does nothing to mask her disappointment.

He locks the door to his room, and places a call to Guam.

"Director Johnson here."

"It's Paul, sir. How're things progressing on Guam?"

"If your call is about Jon, he shows improvement daily. I don't expect he'll have to make more than one or two more visits to the chamber. But I need to ask, what did you really call me about?"

"I have a couple of situations I need your advice and approval on. The first entails one of Jon's associates, Steve Mitchell."

"What about him?"

"I gathered from Keira he's been doing some freelance investigation on the Consortium's operations. Woods reported they found him out and dealt with it."

"How so?"

"It's unconfirmed at this point, but he's probably dead."

"Is Keira involved in it?"

"She said 'no', but it doesn't mean they don't have their suspicions."

"Keep in mind, Jon is concerned about his daughter's welfare."

"So am I."

"Do you have anything more?"

"Yes, sir. It involves the owner of Micronesian Divers. Things have turned threatening. One of his men is in the hospital, probably collateral damage from our operation, and he's demanding more information than I feel comfortable disclosing right now."

"At present, I'm way too busy on Guam to address your

issues, Paul."

"Sir?"

"I can't give you more right now."

Paul laughs to himself. *Now I get why Keira gets so frustrated with me.*

"As to your original question, we do have rules regarding disclosure, but they're guidelines not orders. Our best asset in the field is the ability to think for ourselves which gives you a certain degree of latitude."

"Understood."

"Jon tells me he's had a good history with Andon and we should consider him trustworthy. If you're convinced it's necessary and he realizes the importance of maintaining confidentiality, you have a green light to disclose whatever you believe will satisfy him. I trust your judgement completely."

"Thank you, sir."

"The rest of your staff staying safe?"

"So far."

"Good. Keep a close eye on Keira and continue to stay in touch. Good night."

The receiver clicks off. Paul stares at the phone before putting it down.

When he opens the door to check on Keira, she's standing directly in front of him, ready to knock.

"Oh, hi. Finished with your call?"

He steps outside, but hesitates. Stifling a yawn, he says, "It's been a really long day, Keira, can we pick this up tomorrow?"

Without saying a word, she turns back to her room alone, and slams the door behind her.

Andon greets the flirtatious receptionist as he enters the hotel lobby. "Good morning, Anaria,"

"And good morning to you, sir," she enthusiastically responds. "Unusual you here so early."

"Can you tell me if Mr. Gerhart has come down for breakfast yet?"

"Oh, yes, Mr. Andon. He and his two friends come down …" she glances at the clock, "oh, some thirty minutes now."

"And Miss Hall?"

She laughs to herself. "Oh, she never come down early than she have to for their meetings."

"Good to know. I guess you're working the early shift today?"

"I work early shift *everyday*, Mr. Andon."

"I'm sorry, Anaria, I forgot. For this early in the morning, you present yourself … um, very nicely."

She blushes, and gives her handsome employer a quick up-down glance. "And you too look good, Mr. Andon." She giggles and turns away from the counter.

He takes a quick check of his garb——a swimsuit, a pair of worn leather sandals, and an unbuttoned shirt which he quickly buttons up and pats down his flat stomach. Her eyes follow him to the dining room.

When he spots the agents' table, he gestures to an older man who has worked in the restaurant since Andon's youth. Isaoshy's surprised by his employer's presence in the dining room at all, much less this early.

"Is there a problem, Mr. Andon?"

"No, no my friend. I need you to bring me some coffee." He points to Paul's table. "Over there, but not for five minutes, okay?"

Isaoshy nods and quietly returns to his duties at the buffet.

Andon walks over to where the three agents are having a guarded conversation. He remains standing until Dax glances up.

"We have company," he announces under his breath.

"Could I have a word with you, Paul."

Dax looks at Eric. "Why don't we go check out their stock of renowned donuts." They move to another table with their plates and drinks in hand.

Paul points to the empty chairs. "What's on your mind today?"

"I don't feel comfortable with the way things ended between us last night."

"Neither do I."

Andon senses the chill in Paul's tone. "I've spent——"

Isaoshy carefully places a cup and spoon in front of Andon. "Your coffee, Mr. Andon. Black, two sugars. Correct?"

He gestures the older man to wait and readdresses Paul, "can my friend get you anything?"

He shakes his head.

"Thank you, Isaoshy. Please make sure we're left undisturbed."

He bows slightly and claims a spot near the entry.

Paul starts to speak when Andon cuts him off. "Please. Let me continue. We've had a long and profitable relationship with Mr. Hall and I do not want to have last night jeopardize it. I understand your reluctance to share your day-to-day operations, but if it involves me or my people I would appreciate the courtesy."

"I'm sorry, too. You and your staff have supported us throughout our stay. Unfortunately, the ongoing investigation imposes certain constraints about what I can or cannot share. Please don't take any of this personally."

"I need you to make the effort to identify with what *I'm* going through ... when my men get hurt and my business is threatened, I *must* take it personally."

"Trust me, I do. We'll wrap up our operations here soon. I don't anticipate anymore problems."

Dax catches Paul's eye as he and Eric walk by the table. He taps on the face of his watch, which prompts Paul to check his.

"Are you at least allowed to tell me about Jon's progress?"

Paul stands and helps pull out Andon's chair. "Let's talk as we walk."

BG's face lights up when his father descend the steps of United Airlines' 737 mid-morning arrival. Chairman Vincenté greets his son warmly.

BG was not so much adopted as "taken in" to fulfill a long ago promise Vincenté made to a dying friend. In his youth, BG grilled Vincenté's acquaintances about his early life and the horrors of surviving the big war on Saipan. Despite his efforts, BG never heard about them directly from his father. In fact, Vincenté kept a lot to himself, including the story of how his wife died during the war. Occasionally he sought the company of other women, but no one the young boy could call "mom", or experience the love and affection of a mother.

The one and only memory BG has of his father yelling at him was the day he'd left the bathroom door unlocked. BG opened it during his shave. Through the mirror, Vincenté caught his young charge staring at the horrific layers of scars emblazoned on his back——a painful and permanent reminder of an American flamethrower's attack on the cave where he'd sought refuge with his family, which he alone survived. When BG worked up the courage to ask, Vincenté insisted he drop it and never returned to the topic. It's the last time he mentioned it, and the last time his father left the door unlocked.

Vincenté works through the day in his mind. "How much further to the yacht, Benjamin?"

"It's only a mile down the road, sir."

The heavy congestion of traffic ahead dictates a slow drive along the short stretch. Vincenté notices BG's head constantly moving——unusually skittish behavior for his normally subdued son.

"Pull the car over!" Vincenté abruptly shouts.

"What, here? We're a short——"

"Right now," he insists. "I want to have a talk with you, somewhere alone."

BG exhales deeply and searches for a spot to park. He takes a sharp left into the Berea Christian Church's empty parking lot and finds an umbrella of shade. As soon as he sets the brake and turns the key, Vincenté starts in. "What's going on with you, son?"

"What do you mean?" The perceptive man quietly stares at him. BG's reluctant to break the news to him, but doesn't want his father to hear about it from anyone else. "I believe I killed Steve Mitchell last night. He's the man I told you about."

"What do you mean 'you *believe* you killed' him? Why the confusion? You must have had your reasons. Tell me what happened … from the beginning."

"We collared him at his home and questioned him about his activities. I guess I musta over-powered him."

"Who's 'we'?"

"Me, Tino, and two of your boys, Miguel and Damon," as an afterthought, he adds, "oh, and Brent Edelson, too."

"Wasn't this Mitchell character the one sticking his nose into where it didn't belong?"

"He got too close, asked too many questions."

"Who's idea was it to take these steps?"

"Tino's," he responds softly, and quickly adds, "But Mitchell's death wasn't his fault."

"Tell me what happened."

BG breaks eye contact with his father and stares out the windshield. "We tied him to a chair, and I roughed him up while Tino did the interrogation. He refused to answer anything. Tino got more and more frustrated. I guess I overdid it. Mitchell's heart musta gave out."

The Chairman pats his son on his thigh and drops the discussion.

"Will you be here for awhile?"

"I need some time to relax, and meet with a couple of people, starting with your governor. I have a few bones to pick with him and hope to get him back in line with our agenda."

"Do you think there's a chance we'll spend any time together?"

He appreciates his son's interest. "As I mentioned the other day, I'm afraid now's not a good time. After all this settles down, I will send for you so we can spend some quality time on Saipan. Now, tell me where we are headed?"

BG points to the south. "Immediately past the Kingdom Hall up ahead. Not far. We can almost see it from here."

Vincenté tries to stifle a laugh.

"What?"

"You have these houses of worship pretty well checked out. You getting religion on me?"

"No, sir." BG deadpans. "There's less of a chance of interruptions during the weekdays."

"Good call."

Two cargo freighters shadow the Consortium's sleek hundred and fifty-three foot, *Black Moon*. Crews aboard the larger ships jockey for position along the rails to get a better view.

The Chairman admires the ship——the dark brushed-aluminum hull houses three decks, a promenade, an isolated veranda off the main suite, and a smartly appointed interior.

When he was but a Vice in the organization, he played an instrumental role in its acquisition. He hasn't spent any time aboard her since the initial inspection cruise.

Several cars have turned into the harbor's spacious parking lot, and offloaded an unexpected gathering of curious onlookers. Their numbers necessitate shipboard personnel placing crowd-control barriers a good distance from the loading ramp, while carefully screening those attempting to board.

As soon as BG slows to a stop, a coterie of personnel swiftly unload the VIP, take his bags up, and signals BG to move on. He waits until his father reaches the welcoming crew and disappears inside.

On deck, Captain Arroyo's the first to greet the Chairman, "Everything's as you requested, sir. Your accommodations await."

The captain joined the organization along with the yacht, and resents his move to a guest suite. It's not a step down in quality, but hates the inconvenience of the dog-and-pony show.

After Vincenté settles in, he tours the compartment's amenities, and private veranda. "She's exactly as I remember her, Captain. From what I can tell, you've done a commendable job maintaining her."

"Thank you, sir. Have you made plans for your visit?"

As he scans the horizon, Vincenté shields his eyes from the reflective glare off the water. "Where's your normal anchorage from here?"

"About five miles south-southwest." Arroyo points in the approximate direction and adds, "we can make it in less than an hour."

Vincenté glances at the skies and the conditions outside the breakwater. "What if we take the leisurely way around to get there?"

"The 'leisurely way', sir?"

The Chairman turns and faces the shorter man. "Yes, Captain. Don't make me repeat myself. We go north, and turn east around the island. It's a beautiful day, so let's enjoy it. There's no need to hurry; we can share a lunch together on the veranda."

"I'd be honored, sir."

After a couple of hours, the ship drops anchor on the calmer side of Fono Island, north of Weno. As soon as the twin engines shut down, several crewmen scramble for a spot along the rail to fish, while a steward sets a table on the veranda for the captain and his guest.

As a young boy, Atiniui loved to fish these islands with his father and older brother, Asou. He's now in his mid-thirties, uneducated, unkempt, and soft-spoken. These waters served as a classroom with his late father as his teacher. Without much to show for it, he has spent his entire life perfecting his craft. It's a good life, and an important time for him to share his accumulated knowledge and experience with *his* sons, Wani and Inario. Atiniui's father passed down his love for the sea which he, in turn, tries to imbue in his children. His boys are young——too young to understand the region's violent history, but not too young to learn to love and draw their sustenance from them.

Atiniui's proud of both his sons, but especially Wani who, at ten, has figured out how fishing and navigation work together. Wani wants to take on more responsibilities and his father plans to give him the independence he asks for, but not yet.

They start early from their modest home on remote Romonum Island. Their boat is bare-boned by his contemporaries' standards, but it doesn't phase the experienced fisherman. They have the essentials——food, water, and time——everything they need. They plan to fish the north side of Udot Island, an area where they've enjoyed success in the past, three miles east from the dive boats and the intrusion of their tourists.

After an hour at anchor, Wani stands on the bow and points off to the distance. He shouts to his father, *"Sam, sam out there!"*

Atiniui cannot make out what has him so excited. "What's got your attention, boy?"

He leans forward hoping the stance will help him focus more clearly and takes another view. The sky plays tricks with his vision. Stratus clouds pushed by upper elevation winds create a patchwork mosaic on the water's surface. The yellow object's too far away to pick out details, especially when it drifts in and out of the shadows. Atiniui does not want to pull anchor for an apparition they cannot clearly identify. "You wait, son. It'll draw closer."

Wani tries to put the distraction out of his mind, but he can't take his eyes off it. Atiniui glances over to the younger Inario, but he's as much taken in by his older brother's behavior as Wani is by the discovery. It's uncharacteristic for his oldest son to act this way and Atiniui's curiosity is tweaked as well. "Okay, okay. Let's check out what's gotten hold of your attention so early. The fish will have to wait." He has Wani retrieve the bent rebar anchor, coil the line and stow it neatly.

The mystery soon resolves itself——it's a dingy cast adrift. Wani stands at the bow, his hands on his hips, confident this is *his* discovery and soon, *his* possession. When they near the derelict, his demeanor rapidly changes. He glances back at his father. Atiniui notices fear and doubt have replaced Wani's confidence. One more peek inside the boat and the young boy makes his way behind his father. Diminutive Inario has to prop himself up on his toes to discover for himself what's inside. He puts his hands over his gasping mouth. His expressive brown eyes stare at the boat, and through interlocked fingers seeks reassurance from his father.

Atiniui shares the shock that has unnerved his children——

a body, partially wrapped in a sheet, laying in a pool of blood on the deck. The face shows signs of a severe beating and the right hand is crushed, barely attached to the wrist.

When Wani turns to his father, his eyes have gotten as wide as Atiniui can remember. He tries not to cry. "What we do now, *sam*?"

"We cannot leave this boat adrift. Do you follow me?" Inario wants reassurance from his older brother, and agrees without knowing why.

Atiniui covers the body with a tarp, careful not to upset any possible evidence before he retrieves the bowline and ties it off the stern of his boat. Ahead, they face a lengthy trip to Weno Island.

He thinks through his options, before he starts the motor. *How much of a threat does this pose to the boys, or should I drop them off and get my brother's help?* It's an easy decision. He doubles-back toward his home to get more fuel with no guarantee his brother will either be found or available. He tasks Wani with tracking down Uncle Asou while he tops off the gas cans.

When they tie off, Wani jumps off the boat and takes to the west on a bare-footed run. Before Atiniui grabs the gas cans for a refill, he instructs his youngest to stay and keep an eye on both boats while they're gone. Inario nods in agreement while his father speaks, but as soon as he starts up the ramp, the little boy runs after him. When his father tries to shoo him back to the boat, the boy vigorously shakes his head emphatically, 'No!' Atiniui shrugs his shoulders in surrender, hoping Wani's discovery will remain unmolested.

Wani follows the gravel path a half mile past the pier until he reaches the trailhead to Asou's cabin. From there it's a short uphill climb to his uncle's place.

No one's around, so he yells, "Asou, Asou!" There's no answer. He runs further back and tries anew, "Asou, Asou!"

"Over here, boy," his uncle responds from the adjacent neighbor's backyard.

In the past, Wani's been sternly warned to stay away, but

reason wins out and he inches closer before yelling, "Asou, Asou, come here!"

Asou wanders over to his near-frantic nephew. "What's got you so worked up, boy?"

Wani reaches out to take his hand. "You *have* to come with me," he insists.

Asou shakes his handhold loose and jabs his thumb over his shoulder. "Can't you see I'm busy right now." He's with three other men gutting explosives from anti-personnel beach mines retrieved from a deep water wreck.

Wani grabs his hand and starts to yank his arm to follow. "You can do that anytime." He stomps his foot with the pronouncement, "My father needs you right now, uncle!"

Asou scans the other men sheepishly and shrugs his shoulders. "Guess I gotta go see what my brother needs."

One of his friends taunts him, "Asou, Asou!", and the others join in the ribbing.

"Okay," he laughs. "You've had your fun, but I gotta go."

They continue mercilessly until he's out of sight. Asou continues to hear their laughter, but turns his attentions to his nephew. Wani has already started back, forcing Asou to run after him. "I've never seen you in such a hurry. What's gotten into you, son?"

"*Sam* needs you."

"He okay?"

At the mention of his father, Wani picks up the pace. Asou has no choice but to keep up. When they reach the ramshackle pier, Asou places his hands on his knees and gasps, "Your boy, brother ... he's pretty excited. I couldn't get him calmed down enough to tell me about what."

Atiniui steps over to the boat in tow and pulls back the tarp.

"Oh. Where did——"

"Climb in. I'll fill you in on our way to Weno."

Asou pants, "Should I go back and get my gun?"

Atiniui shakes his head. "No time. It's eleven miles to the big island. As things stand, we won't make it back here before dark."

The two boys stand at the dock and wave to their father and uncle as they cast off.

"You two stay close to your mother today. We'll return sometime this evening."

235

Keira wakes up groggy. She put in a rough night filled with worries about her father, Steve's whereabouts, and her growing attraction to Paul. It's a lot to work through, and leaves her unsettled. She glances at the early morning sun starting to make its way through the slats in her partially closed blinds. "I give up," she complains to no one, kicking off the bedding in disgust. She drags herself into the shower before making her way to the dining room for many coffees and a rare breakfast. She's not alone.

Eric towers over her seat. "May I join you?"

She points to the chair across from her, and tries to stifle a yawn, "Please do."

He scans the walls for a clock. "Usually don't notice you here for a couple more hours."

"Rough night," she mumbles. "Where's your sidekick?"

"Paul?"

"No. The short, cute one."

"Ah. A bit early yet. I come here to spend some time alone with my kids."

"Huh?"

He pats his shirt pocket and pulls out a photo and lays it on the table in front of her.

Keira picks up the print and places it in the light to help

her eyes focus. "You have a lovely family. Willing to share?"

He gently taps each image. "My son, Mark, at fourteen has now discovered the opposite sex. The serious one here's Pamela, eleven and already an addicted reader." His voice grows tender. "My sweetie, Mindy, our youngest, recently turned five, and has me wrapped around her baby finger."

"And your wife?"

"Ahh, Alison," he boasts.

"She's very attractive."

"Her beauty runs deeper than what you see in the photo. From the first moment I laid eyes on her——"

"You're a lucky man."

"You won't get any argument from me."

Keira takes a sip from her coffee mug. "Miss them?"

He's sidetracked by memories, before he counters, "Enough about me. What's up with you and Paul?"

She sputters some of her drink onto the table and his family. "Oh, dear, I'm so sorry," she croaks grabbing for her napkin while trying to catch her breath.

He laughs before he lies, "Don't worry about it. I have another copy in the room."

She apologetically adds, "I haven't considered … "

"Testing the waters?"

She chuckles as she echos him. "'Testing the waters', that's cute."

When he raises his eyebrows, she replies, "I can't wrap my head around our relationship, but hold on. I want to learn more about you. Paul said you held down the top cop desk in Denver? What did the job entail?"

"Things have decidedly changed since my time with Denver." His eyes focus on his own mug, and his voice drops to a whisper.

"What's wrong, Eric?"

"I'd prefer not to go there. Same as you, I have some issues to work through."

"If you ever need a friend."

"Thanks, but really I'm fine."

She doesn't press the issue. "You diving with Dax today?"

"Haven't heard yet."

"How 'bout you buddy up with me?"

"Sounds like a plan."

Keira refills her thermos when Andon steps beside her to do the same.

"Good morning," she wears a curious expression. "Surprised you're here today."

"I'm filling another gap in our staff this morning."

"Does that mean you're diving with us?"

He shakes his head, stuns her with the news Brent's covering, and directs her toward the seats.

"Morning all. We'll start out with the *Yamigiri Maru* today for a couple of reasons: she's the closest wreck to the boat docks, relatively easy to negotiate, filled with marine life, and has unusually interesting artifacts. It's thirty feet to the wreck's upper portions, and a hundred and twenty to its deepest."

Eric's curious. "What's so special about this one?"

He points to the mounted print. "The *Yamagiri* has developed into a beautiful and highly popular site in the lagoon. The four hundred and forty foot freighter settled on its port side with its bow's aimed directly at us right now."

Dax points to the graphic. "Is the hole there in the starboard hull the one that sent the ship to the bottom?"

"I understand how you'd think that, but no. She sailed with a convoy in transit from Rabaul to Palau when intercepted at night by the *U.S.S. Drum* in August of '43. The sub fired an array of four torpedos at the ship resulting in this." He points to the hole Dax mentioned. "But she didn't flounder and managed to limp back to Rabaul for repairs. Before the attack on February seventeenth, she either sailed or was taken under tow to Truk for the better repair facilities. The *Yamagiri* stood at anchor when the attack started. During the second day of the raid, 1,000- and 500-pound bombs found their target, which started severe fires followed by secondary explosions. One blew open a thirty foot hole in the bottom of the number three cargo hold. Though not depicted in this drawing, that's what took the ship down, along with twelve of its crew. The only sighting the pilots had in the aftermath was black smoke rising to over 4,000 feet and an expansive oil slick.

"Besides the same marine growth which predominates the more shallow wrecks, the artifacts will captivate and disturb at the same time. I think you'll enjoy this wreck as much as I do."

Keira can clearly make out the wreckage from the boat as they secure the tie-off. Brent's the first over the side. She and Eric follow close behind. The three wait for the team to enter. Lateral visibility's fifty feet today——not the best, but adequate.

Keira and Eric start toward the bow, but Brent holds them back and signals the first two holds are empty. He redirects the team toward the superstructure's remnants. Keira's stunned by the degree of growth, undulating gorgonian sea fans and the stunningly colorful tree branch corals.

Swimming aside the main deck, Keira signals Eric and points out the overgrown beams which span the entry into the number three hold. Ambient light illuminates the structural latticework, also backlit by the opening in the boat's keel, ripped apart in the final explosion.

Brent directs them toward the engine room. The ship's smokestack remains in tact with circled Y's welded into each side, identifying the Yamashita Kisen Kaisha shipping line. They peer into the engine room through the skylights adjacent to the funnel. Ladders and catwalks surround the twin banks of engines, their aspect skewed ninety degrees by the ship's final position at rest. Dax holds back to observe Brent's activities from a distance.

In the back recesses, Brent waves them over with his dive light and with its bright beam directs their eyes to the sight above. The violent blast which took the ship down, flung a crewman into the starboard bulkhead. His helmeted skull embedded into what was soon to become the overhead when the ship rolled on its side. As time and nature took their toll, his remains eventually disengaged from the head and dropped to a shelf directly below. The remainder of a fire-blackened skull is now coated with a veneer of orange and oversees the visiting divers.

Keira hears an audible gasp from Eric's regulator followed by his hasty exit from the hold. She locates him in open water holding tightly to the kingpost; his rapid breaths leads her to place a hand on his shoulder. She waits until his exhalations gradually slow to a relatively normal rate before she signals if he's okay. He releases his hand hold to join the others as they exit the compartment.

Eric opts to slowly surface alone, while the group continues into hold number five. A new sight tweaks Keira's curiosity——a mound of artillery armament en route to support the Imperial Japanese Navy's battleships. Not the more common four and five inch ammunition found on several wrecks, but each measures over three feet in length by fourteen inches in diameter. The cataclysmic sinking violently redistributed the shells into their current disarray. She's dwarfed by a stack clumped together, each encrusted with blue sponge and sea squirts.

Deeper into the hold, twenty more rest, shelved in orderly fashion, four per metal container, each mounted on its own narrow-gauge rail cart. Keira grabs her slate and writes, "Won't they still explode?" Brent shakes his head to reassure her there's no danger. He signals her to follow him to the next hold further aft. En route to the exit, they glide past the remnants of a steam roller intermingled with the decayed remains of equipment used for road construction.

In hold number six, Brent shines his light toward the

stacks of fuel drums and several more strewn about the sea bed. He writes on her slate, "AvGas and oil." She continues her tabulations.

Brent gives the signal it's time for everyone to ascend.

On the way to the line, Keira passes an oversized medusa jellyfish in transit, its gelatinous bell undulates around its train of organs, which slowly propels the critter alongside the wreckage. She takes her time to work her way to the bow, reveling in the diversity of life which congregates in and around the voids——the countless schools of fish and variety of growth could fill a marine biologist's library. Her dive computer shows their profile hit ninety-five feet at the deepest point. At the fifty minute mark she ascends to her sole decompression stop before she surfaces.

Onboard, Keira makes it a point to touch bases with Eric who has sequestered himself aft to breakdown his gear.

"You alright?"

"Thinking about the shocking remains in the engine room, I imagine he never knew what hit him. Why his bones are still there puzzles me."

She pats him on the shoulder and joins Brent who's seated by himself with a recently lit cigarette. "What can you tell me about the artillery shells?"

Knowing her aversion to cigarettes and those who use them, he peevishly contemplates his smoke and with a scowl, flings it overboard.

"From what I've read, the IJN ear-marked the shells for eight of their battleships, but not the two super battleships, *Yamato* or *Musashi* as earlier assumed. A Canadian film crew corrected the misconception with accurate measurements taken for their project."

"You're obviously comfortable with divers' safety around them."

"Oh sure. They'd need a separate detonator, which fell to

the ships' gunnery officers on site."

"I've been told fishermen recover the mines from cargo holds and use 'em for dynamite fishing. Why not take these, too?"

"Each one weighs close to fourteen hundred pounds."

"Oh."

Eric and Dax join them.

"Where to next?" Eric leads.

"Th*e Kensho Maru.*"

Keira adds, "What's her story?"

"An earlier attack disabled her, which necessitated her transport here under tow." He points east toward Tonoas Island. "She anchored on the island's west side to undergo repairs when the attacks hit. The survivors escaped in lifeboats only to witness her go down from the nearby shoreline. Six crew died in the attack."

Paul mentions the shift in Brent's attitude, "You come across as not remotely enthusiastic about this wreck, or the day for that matter."

"Well, the *Kensho* isn't exactly one of my favorites. It's considered a "dirty wreck."

"How so?"

"Its location." He gestures to the nearby islands. "She's layered with silt, which renews with runoff from each rainfall. You'll see what I mean when you go below."

As they clean and stow their gear after the dive, Paul and Keira chat about their experiences.

"Well, what did you think?"

"Loved it!" she answers with unbridled enthusiasm.

Paul doesn't share in her zeal. "How so?"

"It took me back to the exhilaration and freedom I felt on my first dive ever. Did you make it to the engine room? I did a free-float descent from its overhead catwalk——a sensation akin to flight." She holds her arms out to pantomime the descent and grabs onto Paul's forearm as she continues describing her experience. "I loved it. Brent took me to the deck below the engine and illuminated a bulkhead which displays a unique arrangement of spare parts. It could pass for a work of art."

He feels her hand tighten on his arm, but stoically responds, "You got excited about spare parts."

"I appreciate the artistry of order———each piece conveniently sorted by size and stacked, available for the engineer's easy access. No wasted space. The entire arrangement's fused together in a heavy blanket of monochromatic rust. I think it's beautiful."

Paul doesn't continue the inquiry. By this time, her hand has slid into his, "What stood out to you?"

"A couple of things. Those intact panes of glass leaning against the passageway's bulkhead."

"I know, right? How do you think they survived the sinking intact?"

Paul shrugs his shoulders. "How about the oversized binoculars by the descent line? They must weigh close to twenty-five pounds. I image they were mounted on a pedestal affixed to the deck."

"You did see the rubber boot next to them?"

"Kind of a sobering reminder of the event."

Keira points to Brent, "He's apparently impatient to get back … more nervous than normal this trip."

"I noticed."

As they draw nearer to the dock, two boats from the shop pull close alongside, both manned with armed police.

Brent has Alou slow the boat and yells over, "Any problems officers?"

They ignore his inquiry. When Alou cuts the throttle further, the officers gesture he's to continue to the marina.

Paul sidles over to Brent who closely monitors their

activity. "What's going on?"

"Why ask me?"

"Does this have to do with your behavior today?"

"What?"

"You're more distracted than usual."

"Why do you care?"

"A police escort to the docks doesn't hold any concerns for you? Leads me to believe you're the reason they're here. I might be able to help you out."

Brent scoffs, "Yeah, right."

After their boat makes dockside, he ties it off, grabs his gear bag, and takes a speedy jaunt to the dive shop before he discreetly makes a rapid exit from the premises.

The police chief and his subordinate sit in a well-used silver truck with POLICE painted in foot-tall bright blue letters on each of its front doors. Their eyes follow Brent's movement until he's out of sight.

His partner wants direction. "Think we oughta chase him down?"

"His address is on file; we'll deal with him later. For right now, I have some questions for the young lady."

Paul's curious about the contingency of officers questioning several of Andon's staff. "What's with all the cops? Did someone get hurt?"

"I need you to come with me," Andon demands.

When Keira hears their interchange, she puts down her dive bag to follow. He adds, "Alone," loud enough for her to hear. *I hate it when they're so dismissive.* Within minutes, the chief and his partner corral and escort her to the truck to start their round of questioning.

Paul stares as she's led away. Andon has to grab his sleeve to get his attention. "Steve Mitchell's body was recovered earlier today."

Paul gazes at the truck. "By whom … where?"

"A local fishermen and his two young sons found his boat adrift west of Udot Island. His body is at the coroner's for autopsy. Apparently he was tortured."

Paul has concerns the event may shift unwanted attention to his operation. "How many people have heard about this?"

"Besides the fishermen and the police, no one." He points to the truck and Keira. "But word will get around fast enough."

"They breaking the news to her?"

"I think right now they want to hear about her whereabouts last night. You'll probably need to come up with a credible cover."

Paul heads toward the chief's truck when Andon stops him. "Hold on a minute."

Paul turns to face him. When he doesn't respond, Andon pleads, "Talk to me, Paul. Do you think we're vulnerable?"

"I know as much as you do."

He starts to walk away when Andon grabs him by the shoulder and forces him to turn around. Paul acknowledges his grip with a gaze. Andon drops his hand, but insists, "You *will* give me some answers, or I'll shut down my participation! No boats, no gear, no guides!" he yells. "We've had enough excitement around here since your arrival and I need the truth. No more secrets or our time together is over!"

Paul notices Andon shaking with repressed anger——time to let him in.

"You have someplace where we can talk ... privately?"

Eric and Dax intercept Paul as he leaves Andon's shop.

Eric opens, "Has word gotten out about Steve?"

"Apparently."

Dax follows-up. "How?"

"Andon told me some fishermen found him adrift in a dingy."

Before they continue, Paul points toward the police truck. "Listen guys, I need to have a talk with the chief. Give me a few minutes and I'll catch up with you in the lounge."

Kohper stands next to his partner by the front fender

filling out reports, when Paul arrives. "It appears you've had a busy day, Elias."

He rises from his paperwork, and gestures his eyes toward his partner, and responds curtly, "It's *Chief Kohper.*"

When Paul starts to apologize, he interrupts, "What's your involvement here?"

"None."

"But you did know" he quickly interrupts. "Didn't you?"

Paul hesitates before he answers, "Not directly."

"What does that mean?" Paul doesn't answer, but leans his head toward the chief's partner. Kohper asks him to allow them some privacy.

"You know I can't give you all the details of our work here, but one of my partners made observations last night which raised similar suspicions."

Kohper lifts his eyebrows inquisitively.

"I couldn't report his findings, because we had nothing solid to go on." Paul hesitates before adding, "If I share any of this with you, Elias, it could compromise our investigation."

Kohper concedes the point.

"You can't honestly believe Keira had a hand in this?"

As the chief rereads his report, a wry expression overtakes his face. "As you've made abundantly clear, 'I can't compromise——"

Paul starts to chuckle, "Fair enough. Later, *Chief.*"

Kohper's rejoined by his partner. "Do you think he's being straight with you?"

The chief points to his notebook sitting on the hood. "Grab the book, and get inside. We need to track down Edelson."

247

Chapter 21
At The Water's Edge

Keira catches up with the three agents who are standing in the crowded lounge discussing the day's events.

Her voice is filled with heartbreak as she approaches Paul, "Did you hear about Steve?"

Paul's response is to hold up his bottle and four fingers toward the bartender.

She stares at him quizzically before the realization hits her, "You knew Steve was dead last night, didn't you?" Her voice is fragile, loud, and filled with astonishment.

Paul gently takes her by the shoulders to steer her toward a recently vacated table. She shrugs him off.

"Tell me this, did you have anything to do with it?"

The agents are shocked. She has the complete attention of the now silent room.

Paul says, "What in the world would make you think——"

"All these secrets you've been keeping and your attempts to distract me," she says heatedly.

"Keira."

"Look, I'm angry … I'm confused, no thanks to you, and … and I'm just …" She breaks down and buries her head in his chest and sobs, "Of all people … why Steve?"

A few more minutes pass before the waitress delivers their order and tactfully makes a quick retreat. When Paul leads her over to their table, Dax and Eric take their drinks to the bar leaving them alone. "You've trained them well," she quips while reaching for a napkin to blow her nose. "Why didn't you tell me?"

When Paul hesitates again, she impulsively exits the lounge. He quickly gathers his things, and chases after her.

Keira reaches the middle of the hotel grounds before he is able to catch up. When she ignores him he stops and pleads, "Keira, please."

She reluctantly turns to face him. "I need you to tell me the truth, Paul. What's going on?"

"Some local fishermen found Steve's body adrift in his boat near Udot Island, which I'm sure you already know. What you may not have heard is how he died."

"Meaning?"

"At this point anything I say is purely speculative. I'll know more when they give me the results of the autopsy, and I promise I'll pass them along as soon as I get word."

It's a good start, but her look tells him she needs more. "Did you know about this the other night?"

"Nothing that could be verified."

"Why are you still hiding behind all this double-talk? Why won't you be honest with me?"

"I didn't want to unnecessarily upset you."

When she starts to object, he raises his hand. "Keira, for your own sake, I have to find out how deeply *you* were involved in his activities."

"Why? Am *I* in some kind of danger?"

"Possibly."

The lack of hesitance in his response alarms her.

"But if you are," he adds, "we can protect you."

"Really. You think I'll feel safe after what they did to him?"

"Trust me, Keira. We know what we're doing. I would be happier if you sat out this next dive, though."

"How will I be protected with the three of you on a dive at the far side of the lagoon? And how will you maintain my cover story when I am not there to do 'the survey'?"

"I imagine you already know they're are not our primary

concern."

"Steve surmised that early on. I wish you'd have let me in——."

"I couldn't."

She reaches out to gently touch his arm. "I guess I've never appreciated the burden you've had to carry throughout this trip."

"Regrettably, it comes with the job."

She nods toward the shoreline, and demurely asks, "Will you walk with me?"

"Where to?"

She takes his hand. "How 'bout down by the water."

They wander along the edge of the shoreline until they find the seat on the bench palm. Keira looks over the lagoon.

His arm is around her shoulder; hers is wrapped around his waist. She is still for a long time, which makes him wary. "You're unusually quiet. What's going on?"

She continues to stare at the water for countless seconds, until she turns to face him. "Hold me … close?" She loses herself in their embrace, nestles her head in his chest, then turns to face the lagoon. "I love the beauty of this place … but then, I've always been happiest when I'm by the sea, and its tranquility. It's forced me to think about my work at the institute. I've gotten so wrapped up in what I do, that I've lost track of what's really important to me. I've used it as an excuse to stay away from my father and any semblance of a social life … more importantly a close, intimate relationship." She takes a pause to gather her thoughts and how to put them into words. "I've turned into someone that I've come to dislike, but it's been so long that I can't seem to find my way back to a time and place when I was really happy."

When she looks up, Paul gently caresses her cheeks to wipe off her tears, then lifts her face up to his. She intercepts his hand and holds it close, "Kiss me," she whispers.

With his eyes locked on hers, he kisses her lips softly … then with more passion. When she moves in for more, he breaks their embrace. "Keira. I'm sorry, but …" He catches himself. "With all that's going on, I need to keep a clear head. Can we just leave things at that … at least for now?"

She has her own reservations, but still feels vulnerable and needs his reassurance. She shifts her position and leans her head back onto his chest. The intimacy of him placing one hand around her waist to rest on her thigh sends a ripple of anticipation down her spine. When she places her hand atop his, she closes her eyes and lets the sounds of the water have their effect. He feels the tension in her body slowly give way. They lose track of time, quietly enjoying the serenity of the gently lapping water along the shoreline.

Keira is first to notice the distinct drone of multiple boats and looks east. Paul follows suit. They see the *Black Moon* in the distance silhouetted against the backdrop of Tonoas Island. It's cruising at a relatively slow speed, and there are two inflatable Zodiacs running escort with three armed-men in each.

When she asks, Paul hands her the binoculars. After taking several scans of the small flotilla, she gives them back. "Seems like a lot of fire-power for a pleasure cruise."

Paul glasses the boats to get a better picture, first to the armed men in the lighter boats, then shifts for a more complete scan of the yacht.

She asks, "Why do you think they're so heavily armed?"

"The stepped-up security tells me they have someone aboard who is important to them."

"Any idea who?"

Once the ship passes the southeast corner of the main island, the Chairman makes his way to the flying bridge for a better view for the last leg of their journey. Captain Arroyo stands next to his chair. Vincenté orders the Zodiacs to return to the ship before they pass by the hotel. The ship slows to take aboard the crew and extend the two booms to hoist the runabouts and retract them into the overhead storage.

An armed guard approaches. With deference to the captain, he adddresses Vincenté, "I've had my sights on a couple along the tree line who are taking an unusual interest in our activities."

Vincenté leans close to Arroyo. "Summon Antonio and Francisco right away."

Arroyo's surprised at both the request, and the idea that he's familiar with their first names. Along with their shipboard duties, both have been trained in a wide variety of weaponry from handguns and semiautomatics, to high-powered, scoped rifles that individually cost the same as a modest SUV.

Arroyo skeptically asks, "What do you have in mind?"

"Now is not the time for questions. Have them come up on deck right away."

"As you wish," he says. *Wonder what thoughts are rolling around in that head of his?* It takes several minutes for him to find the two. Antonio has crew duties, which he hands off to one of his mates. The second, Francisco, is catching some rack time and needs to make himself presentable.

When they report, Vincenté impatiently huddles them together with the captain.

"I want you to find the ship's Master-at-Arms, then——"

Vincenté notices Arroyo shaking his head. "Out with it, Captain. You seem to have some objection to my plan?"

Arroyo swallows hard. "I … don't think this is a very good idea, sir. I think it will draw attention to us that we neither want nor need right now."

Vincenté is irritated with his impertinence. "Some of your guards have relayed their observations of others spying on this vessel. I want to put a stop to it right now by sending them a strong message."

Arroyo still disagrees. "I've gotten the same reports, but the step you're proposing——"

Impatient with his subordinate, Vincenté adds, "If you don't have the stomach for this, *Captain*, maybe I can find you a different position in this organization. Something on land perhaps?"

"I only have the interests of the Consortium at heart, sir."

"You let *me* worry about the Consortium's interests, and *you* concentrate on this ship," he says, continuing to focus on the shoreline. "Do we understand each other?" When Arroyo relents, the Chairman adds, "Now, get outta my sight."

He seeks a spot outside the bridge, toward the stern, but within full view of what's going on.

Paul lifts his binoculars again to watch the yacht as it passes. On signal from the Chairman, both snipers stand in unison. The shorter of the two, Antonio has his sights locked on Paul; Francisco's are on Keira.

She grips Paul's arm tightly. "What are they doing?" she shouts.

"They're drawing a line in the sand."

She wrestles her way out of Paul's arms. "They're doing more than that. Let go of me!"

"No. Keira don't!"

She takes off toward the hotel.

"Get down!"

She ducks when he yells, but continues on the run.

A family of four tourists emerge from the hotel, and stop in the doorway when they see her panicked approach.

With the crack of Francisco's rifle, Keira goes down face-first. A spray of dirt and grass settle on her outstretched arm and shoulder.

Paul immediate yells, "No!" And takes off on an all-out run to reach her.

The mother of the family wants to help Keira, but her husband gathers her and their children to shuttle them back inside.

Jumping up Vincenté immediately yells, "Stand down!" Then bumps Francisco's arm as he discharges a second shot. Together the gunmen lower their rifles and wait for further orders.

Paul drops atop Keira when he hears the second discharge. The bullet pierces the hotel's door as it closes, crumbling the glass within the steel framework.

Keira raises her head and spits out sand, dirt and a few blades of grass, then does her best to catch her breath.

"We're you hit?" Paul asks.

"Not that I know of." She continues to spit out remnants.

"Can you make it up, or should I carry you?"

Amped up from the excitement, she throws her arms around his neck, and draws him close.

"I'm okay, Paul. I'm okay."

He cranes his head to catch sight of the activity on the ship as it passes by.

Arroyo runs back to the Chairman and asks, "What were you thinking?"

"Relax. Things got a little out of control," he says without lowering his binoculars.

"'A little out of control'! Were you *trying* to have them killed?"

"Be careful of what you say next, Captain. Besides, I thought I told you to get out of my sight."

"You wanted me to worry about the interests of this ship, sir. Well, I'm worried."

The Chairman silently eyes the captain up and down. *At*

least he has more backbone than I give him credit for.

Vincenté relaxes from his watch and gives the riflemen a dismissive nod.

"Thank you, men. That'll be all."

Arroyo acknowledges his men as they depart, but he thinks, *You reckless idiot. This'll get us all killed!* He continues to stare at the Chairman when he asks, "What else do you have in store for us … *sir?*"

Vincenté notes the attitude, stands, stretches, and points to the west. "Enjoy the beautiful sunset, Captain," then leaves for his quarters.

Chapter 22
Black Moon

By 11 a.m. the Restaurant On The Wharf is nearly empty. The breakfast traffic has thinned out, and the lunch crowd has yet to hit. Paul arrives with Dax thirty minutes before their scheduled meet with Kohper. The waitress delivers coffee and menus as soon as they're seated.

Dax taps Paul. "Where'd you hear about this place?"

"Keira and I had a sit-down here the day Jon was flown to Guam."

"How's she doing by the way?"

"Sleeping in. I checked in with her earlier and she's surprisingly non-plussed by the whole situation."

Eric arrives twenty minutes after the others and takes the seat next to Paul.

"How'd you make out?"

"No problem." He slips an envelope into his hand, which catches Dax's eye.

"What's going on."

Paul shows him the spent cartridges Eric retrieved.

"More detective-ing." Dax mutters.

"Before the chief gets here, I want to talk about bringing him in on this."

He's interrupted by the early arrival of their guest and greets him at the door. "Good morning, Elias. Let me introduce——"

"I need to talk with you, outside and right now," barks Kohper.

Paul looks at the other two. "I'll be back shortly ... hopefully."

"What's on your mind, Elias?"

"Call me Chief Kohper. This is an official inquiry."

"What now?"

"You wanna tell me what's going on? My phone hasn't stopped ringing since late yesterday afternoon. First it was the hotel, then tourists, and now my boss on Pohnpei has gotten wind of it. All I've heard about is rifle shots, 'it's like a war zone out there', and tourists with their families in danger, packing to leave the islands. The one call I did *not* receive was the one I should have gotten ... *from you!*"

"Sorry, Eli ... *Chief*, but I——"

"'Sorry' isn't going to cut it, Gerhart. I told you before, this is my island, and these are my people, and now they're afraid. Do I have to arrest you to get some straight answers?"

Paul points to the front door of the restaurant. "I have evidence and some ideas in there, but you need to calm down before we carry this shouting matching inside. Think you can manage that?"

"Don't press your luck."

"Please ... let's go inside and work this out together, as a team."

"This better be good."

The four take their seats. A cup of coffee's brought to the new arrival and refills all around. Each orders a sandwich before getting down to business.

The chief sets his cup down when Paul hands him the cartridges. "Eric dug these out from the crime scene."

Paul takes his time to retell the details of the encounter he and Keira had with the *Black Moon's* crew the previous afternoon.

"They discharged a weapon at the hotel grounds?" Kohper's louder than anyone at the table is comfortable with. "You should've called me." He swats his notepad for emphasis.

Eric adds, "We have a solution I think can help all of us."

"Please, I'm all ears."

Paul picks up the discussion. "How about you take one of my men here to accompany you aboard their vessel … under the guise of an investigation about the reported shooting … use it as an excuse to inspect their onboard armory." Paul glances over Eric's way, which the chief doesn't catch, but Eric does.

He ponders the offer. "Why aren't *you* the one going with me? And whatever makes you think they would allow us onboard?"

Shaking his head, Paul answers, "They'd recognize me from yesterday's encounter, but they haven't gotten a good look at either Eric or Dax. Think a court order would get you admission onto the boat?"

"It may work." He sorts through his notepad. "The courthouse is less than half a mile from my office. Let me call my brother. He can pull some strings and get things moving with the judge. Who'd you have in mind?"

"You're already familiar with Eric, and he's the most experienced of the three."

Dax tosses his napkin aside and shoots daggers toward Paul. "You wanna tell me why I'm even here?"

Paul glares back. "Can we have this discussion not here and not now?"

Dax huffs.

Kohper hands Eric his card. "This has my number and the address to my office. Meet me no later than seven a.m. Do not keep me waiting. I'll need to find you a uniform before we head to the dock."

The three men stand when Kohper leaves.

Eric follows him out. "Obviously you two have some issues to work out. I'll wait in the car."

Paul tosses him the keys. "Thanks."

He turns to Dax, "Go ahead. Spill it."

Dax stares at Eric walking to their vehicle and realizes, "I was out of line and I'm sorry. I'm not used to holding down the third-wheel spot."

"I have a lot on my plate right now, Dax, and I need your support more than ever. I have to make decisions on what I feel's best for our team. You're still my primary go-to-guy, but right now Eric's background dovetails nicely with our mission and I need to feel I can utilize him without having to worry about your toes."

"I guess."

"Before we leave, tell me we're okay," Paul insists.

"If I can help, in any way …"

Eric and the chief motor toward the *Black Moon's* anchorage in an older, modest plywood boat Andon made available for them. At first, neither man speaks, their exposure to each other was limited to the Hetiback woman, and neither wants to start out their day with unpalatable posturing.

As they draw closer, Kohper suggests, "Let's circle around her to get a more well-rounded perspective."

"My pleasure. She is one beautiful boat," admires Eric.

A crewman on the top deck follows their approach closely. He's armed with a rifle which he keeps slung over his shoulder, and a pistol in a chest-mounted holster. The teak decking leads him by the enclosed bridge where Arroyo monitors the guard's movements. He taps on the window and opens the hatchway. "Think you'd better come out and get a take on this, Captain."

"We've got company," notes Eric.

The chief's wave at the two on the uppermost deck goes unacknowledged. "Hopefully they won't feel threatened," Kohper says as he steers toward the fantail. "We have a lot of private pleasure craft visit us, including several under sail, but I have to admit, this stands out among all the rest. She's what? A hundred and fifty feet?"

"Fair guess, but considering the weaponry, this isn't a

pleasure cruise. Why do you think they're so heavily armed?" When Kohper doesn't answer, Eric adds, "There's money behind it, and I mean a lot. Any idea what would bring them here? Maybe related to what we learned from Mrs. Hetiback?"

"Hopefully we'll have some answers soon enough. Let's get to it."

The Chairman's on the veranda with his second cup of coffee since the crew bussed his breakfast dishes. He hears the drone from the chief's boat, when a rap on his door elicits a response, "Enter."

Captain Arroyo ducks his head in, "We have company."

"You're expecting someone——"

"No, sir, but after the other day …"

The Chairman snorts his contempt.

"It's the police chief and one of his officers. They gave us a pretty thorough look-see before attempting to tie off."

"Find out what they want," Vincenté directs, *"before* you let them on board."

"Will do." He closes the door.

The behemoth yacht dwarfs the chief's. They're having to wait for a crewman to give them a hand with the line, and permission to board.

One leans over the railing. "State your business."

Kohper tosses his bowline up to him, but he ignores the attempt and lets the line drop into the water. Kohper leans over the railing to recover the line.

"What's your business here, Chief Kohper?" asks Arroyo.

Squinting up, "How're you aware of my name?"

"I make it my business to know the local authorities on all the islands," he boasts.

"I haven't had the pleasure——"

"I'm the captain of this vessel," Arroyo proudly answers.

"Yeah, and I'm the captain of this one," he gestures. "You gotta last name?"

"I do, it's Arroyo." Kohper notes it in his pad. Arroyo continues, "Again, what's your business here?"

Kohper holds up a folded sheet of paper. "I have a court order to inspect your ship."

"What for?" The reckless display the Chairman ordered still eats at Arroyo. *Vincenté needs to know this is on him.*

"You brought this on yourself. You and your crew managed to upset a lot of people." Kohper yells up.

"I admit we do carry arms, but they're strictly for our own protection. Isn't that enough information to satisfy your curiosity?"

"You sufficiently demonstrated that already, so now we'll have to inspect and account for of all your weapons. We need to see proof of proper licenses for each piece you have onboard."

Arroyo concedes. "Toss up your bow line, and we'll lower the ladder."

When they reach the fantail's deck, Kohper hands the court order to Arroyo, who instructs them to wait in place while he walks off.

Arroyo gives the attending crew the task of chasing down the requested documentation while he informs the Chairman.

He holds out the paper toward Vincenté. "It appears in order." He notices the man sitting in the far corner of the compartment before he turns his attention back to the Chairman. "They're here to inspect all of our onboard armament and corresponding paperwork."

Vincenté ponders, "In your opinion, would he respond to, oh, say a contribution to his retirement fund and just go away?"

"I think we're past that point. Don't you? Word has it he's pretty much a straight-arrow."

"Why do you … oh, never mind. Who's with the chief?"

"He didn't introduce himself, possibly one of his deputies."

"You sure about that?" the stranger interjects.

Arroyo does a quick glance to BG and back to Vincenté.

"Not at this time, and I apologize for my negligence." He gestures toward the man. "Would you introduce me to your guest?"

"He's my son. He lives on the island, and came aboard last night for a visit."

"I usually hear about new guests when they——"

"You have more pressing concerns right now, Captain. Focus your attention on them."

Vincenté directs the next question toward BG. "Why have I not heard about this new deputy? And whatever happened to the boy at the dive shop we paid for this kind of information?"

"We haven't heard from him since Edelson's first encounter with Gerhart."

"That's unacceptable!" Vincenté seethes. "Take my son here with you, Captain. If he can covertly put eyes on the deputy, send him back to me right away. I need any information the two of you can get."

"Will do." When Arroyo gestures to BG, he's shocked at the size of the man when he stands.

When they turn to leave, the Chairman adds, "Need I remind you our presence here is strictly confidential?"

"Understood."

Arroyo points to an anteroom off the lower deck, adjacent to the armory. "You'll have a good view from here."

Accompanied by the two crewmen who produced the requested paperwork, Arroyo takes a quick scan through the binder before he hands it to Kohper. "It appears all's in order."

Kohper firmly requests, "Show me where you keep your weapons."

"If you insist."

"I do."

"Follow me," he impatiently mutters. He leads the way quickly past the anteroom en route to the munitions locker. As they walk, he sorts through a ring crammed with keys. Unlocking the double padlocks, one high and one low, the heavy gauge steel door opens smoothly with a slight tug. Before he enters, Eric checks out the door's mechanism, and catches sight of BG.

Arroyo tries to distract him. "The light switch is on your right officer."

Eric's hit with the distinct odor of oil when he enters. His hand gropes along the wall until it brushes across the switch. He shades his eyes when the fluorescents kick in, then quickly scans the racked rifles lining the compartment. An insulated cable runs through the trigger guard on each weapon.

Eric initiates the audit with the four drawers of a floor cabinet, where they keep their stash of handguns, a minimal amount of ammunition, and a few cleaning items.

He opens the top drawer of the cabinet with the hand guns and inspects each one——fifteen FN Five-seveN tactical semiautomatic pistols.

Kohper whistles as he copies all the information into his notepad.

"Why do you need to copy all of this down?"

"Let's instead talk about why *you* need all these weapons," Eric responds.

"Standard operating procedure for our own security."

Eric smirks, "Expecting an invasion?"

Unamused, Arroyo directs his response to the chief, "You, of all people, should sympathize with the challenges we share for procurement in our remote locale."

"What's your point?"

"We have high-profile clientele who occasionally make their way here, and they need to feel we have the means to adequately protect them."

Kohper retrieves his notepad and pen. "Unlock the cables, please."

"Is this really necessary, Chief? We're cooperating aren't we? They're all right here in front of you."

"We have to identify each weapon against your records," Eric qualifies without making direct eye contact, "and we can't do it without verifying the serial numbers."

Arroyo addresses Eric, "I'm sorry, but I didn't catch your name."

"Officer Woods, sir." Eric takes the first rifle from the rack, feels its heft, holds it up as if to aim it, locates the serial number and passes the information to Kohper who crosschecks each against their respective documents. "AN-94, assault rifle, serial number …"

After accounting for the first twelve, Eric turns to the opposite wall and the six Heckler & Koch PSG1 scoped sniper rifles. Arroyo quickly secures the cable on the rack of twelve. When Eric finishes his inspection on the second rack, he informs Kohper and Arroyo the rack should remain unsecured.

"What seems to be the problem officer?"

Eric glances at Kohper, who responds with a nod, then answers, "All your rifles have been cleaned and well lubricated except this one," pointing to the second from the last he inspected. We'll need it to complete some tests for our reports, which we cannot do here."

"I don't understand. What are you thinking?"

Kohper steps in, "Ballistics. We have to send it off-island to a facility that can accommodate us."

"Where——"

"Guam," Kohper's quick to respond.

"I can't allow that."

"You have no choice in the matter," Eric interjects. "This is a criminal investigation." He attempts to avoid an argument, "I couldn't find much ammunition to support your armory."

"We keep the bulk of it in a safe box below decks."

"I'll follow you."

"Have it your way," Arroyo grumbles. He leads them to a double-locked door, which opens to a hatch in the deck. Arroyo drops down to the next level and has to bend completely over to make his way to the lockbox. Eric's the only one who follows him down. He scans the area to visualize their relative position in the ship.

Arroyo flips the light on before opening the combination lock. "Over here officer."

When Eric reaches the case, he's surprised by the sheer

volume of ammunition: three different types segregated by the weapons they'd support.

Lifting the lid of a sizable wooden crate in a nearby shadowed recess, Eric immediately drops it shut when its acrid odor draws burning tears, nearly gagging him. His flashlight doesn't help to identify the contents. "What's in here," he rasps, "and what is that stench?"

"Some of our boys retrieved the contents from a local wreck. The fishermen use them."

He continues to wince and painfully coughs, "For what?"

"They're a couple of mines left over from the war, which is what I think you're smelling. We haven't taken the time to address them yet."

Eric recognizes the fetid odor of picric acid, and has to restrain himself from telling them about the toxic and volatile dangers they've allowed onboard. "And you're planning on doing what with them?"

"You must be new to the islands," he dismissively snickers. "We hope to hire a local fisherman to show us how to disassemble them. Give us an easier way to fish. We supplement our food stocks with fresh-caught. You familiar with weaponry from the war, officer?"

"Enlightening, Captain. Thank you for your cooperation."

"We do what we can to support our local authorities," Arroyo snidely answers. "Now if you don't mind," he points toward the exit. "I have a ship to run here."

"Not so fast." Eric interrupts. "We're still missing one rifle and a handgun."

"I believe it's currently with our crewman on deck."

When they reach the ladder to the lounge area, Kohper inquires, "Mind giving me a tour while my deputy verifies the last of your guns?"

"Hold fast. Your court order only covers what you've already seen. I'll send the guard down here, followed by your immediate departure."

When the deck watch arrives with the unaccounted weapons, he's not alone. Chairman Vincenté and Captain Arroyo are close behind.

While Eric compares the two weapons against the logs, Kohper already has the Heckler & Koch slung over his shoulder.

Vincenté forcefully steps around the guard. "I'm afraid I can't let you do that, Chief."

Eric seeks to qualify, "And you are?"

"Francis Vincenté——"

"*Chairman* Vincenté," Arroyo quickly interrupts.

Eric calmly closes the log and sets it on the table. Kohper's intimidated by the encounter with the legendary Chairman. Eric is not. "We're attempting to clarify some facts for our reports on the incident two days ago. You are left with *more* than enough armament aboard your ship. This will only be a minor inconvenience until our tests are complete and the rifle is returned to you. If we have any further questions, how can we contact you directly?"

Without an answer, Vincenté turns to Arroyo in disgust. "Let 'em have it, and follow me back to my quarters immediately after they're off our ship." He walks away.

When they finished their count, a guard escorts them back to the fantail. They re-board their boat, which now feels a whole lot smaller. The crewman unwinds their line from the cleat and drops it indiscriminately into the water before he backs out of sight.

"Thank you, and thank Paul for me," the much relieved chief says to Eric. "I'm glad you were along," he asserts while retrieving the line.

"Who's the new man?" demands Vincenté.

Arroyo hesitates when BG returns and answers his question. "His name is Woods, Eric Woods. He came over with the team from D.C."

"An agent," Vincenté surmises.

"I think it's a pretty safe assumption."

"And now, captain, you've bared our soul to them. As soon as they leave, find what's his name … Francisco?"

Arroyo nods.

"Get him in here."

After Eric returns to the hotel, he makes a beeline for his room. He settles in to record his findings and details of the encounter while still fresh in his mind. A rap on the door interrupts him. It's been left slightly ajar, and Dax walks in, "How'd it go, inspector?"

Eric points to a chair next to him at the table. "I'm tabulating a weapons' count and roughing out a diagram with a location of where they're stored. Give me a minute to finish this, and I'll tell you about our day."

Paul joins them a few minutes later. "Sounds like you've made a new friend," he says to Eric.

"Oh?"

"I just got off the phone with the chief. Couldn't say enough good things about you."

"Uh huh," Eric mutters dispassionately while he continues writing.

"In fact, he said he'd make a place for you in the department if you wanted to relocate."

"That's nice," never lifting up his head to engage.

"Got anything to drink in this place?" Dax interjects.

"Check the fridge and help yourself."

"I see a partial case of bottled water and a six-pack of beer." Cracking the tab, he offers, "You guys want one?"

"Sure," says Paul, "thanks."

Eric remains focused on his notes. Dax brings over three cans, and sits until he's ready.

Kohper makes it back to headquarters in the municipal building by mid-afternoon. The desk officer intercepts him with a stack of new calls to follow-up. Located on the second floor, the spartan office has a surplus military desk with an adjoining table scattered with files in no particular order. A bench seat butts up against the wall to the right, next to three four-drawer file cabinets filled with case records, pay vouchers, and a clean change of clothes. At the opposite far corner, a makeshift jail cell is currently occupied by a familiar drunk Kohper encountered the night before, passed out on a bench.

Kohper unslings the rifle, and leans it against the wall before he places a call to the central headquarters on Pohnpei.

"Officer Panuel speaking. How may I help you?"

"Hey, Eiken, Chief Kohper."

"How goes it, Elias?"

"Busy as ever. Would you patch me through to Kyota?"

"Sure, gimme a sec."

The line rings several times before the phone is picked up.

"Kyota here." He's near the end of his shift, and has trouble stifling a yawn.

"Afternoon, Chief. This is Kohper on Chuuk."

"Sounds like you've been busy, Elias."

Kohper elaborates on what they discovered aboard the yacht.

"I already heard."

Kohper disregards his comment and continues, "Do you remember your offer to send some men to assist me?"

"Tell me more about this inspection you felt necessary to make."

"We're responding to the complaints you called me about earlier."

"Anything out of order aboard the *Black Moon*?"

"With the exception of a few contraband mines recovered from one of our wrecks, everything's properly accounted for.

However, we did procure one of their rifles, we'll send to Guam for a ballistic's match."

"Then what's the problem, Elias?"

"I'm a bit overtaxed right now."

"Listen, if you can't handle the job——"

"Okay, I hear ya. Sorry to disturb." Kohper slams down the phone.

Kyota follows suit, thinks a minute, then picks up the receiver to make a call of his own.

A crewman working the *Black Moon's* communication desk taps Vincenté's door, "Mr. Chairman, sir, we have a call for you from Pohnpei."

"Did he identify himself?"

"He did. Said his name's Kyota, pardon me, *Chief* Kyota."

"I'm on my way."

When the Chairman returns to his suite, he pages the captain, "Get in here. We have a problem."

After hearing Eric's account, Paul opens the door to the room's balcony for fresh air, and to find the yacht's current locale. When Eric stands to join him, Dax catches his arm. "Keep your seat. He needs time to sort this out on his own, alone and undistracted."

A short time later, Paul walks through the room and out the door leaving it slightly ajar.

"Should we follow him?"

"He'd have invited us," answers Dax staring at the open door. "I imagine you're hungry. Let's get something to eat. I'm interested in hearing more about what led you to us."

Kohper grabs a quick bite at the nearby Island Mart, before he returns to his office and a ringing telephone. It's the deputy from the front desk. "Yeah," he answers.

"There's some men coming up. I tried to stop them, but they barged straight through."

"Got it." He reaches into the top right-hand drawer of his desk and readies his handgun, then turns on an old window-mounted air conditioner which slowly grinds into operation.

"Chief Kohper," the first man forcefully pronounces as he reaches the top of the landing.

"Well, Damon. Haven't seen you in these parts for awhile."

"That's a good thing, isn't it?"

"Not necessarily."

"Hey, Chief!" yells the cell's occupant. "When're ya gonna let me outta here?"

"Okay," he laughs, "Sounds like you've slept it off."

He motions the four uninvited men to take a seat while he signs off the paperwork. Francisco discretely notes the location of the rifle before he joins the others.

"Come over here, and sign your release."

"Don't ya hafta unlock my cell?"

"No need."

When the inmate tests the door, it opens freely with a slight nudge. "Well, I'll be. You mean all this time——"

Kohper stoically acknowledges.

"I'll be," he chuckles, then catches himself on the door to keep from falling after he stumbles out.

Damon remains in front of Kohper. The inmate faces off with him and scans him toes-to-eye level. "Step aside, youngster."

Responding to Damon's gesture, Miguel and Ryley each grab an arm. Francisco jumps up before they forcefully seat the old man on the bench next to the exit. When he starts to object, Miguel gets in his face. "You're interrupting the business our main man's having with the chief."

"I don't ca——"

"One more word outta you old man and you'll take a quick trip downstairs."

The threat attracts Kohper's attention. "Leave him alone, fellas."

He gestures to the inmate, "Better go home and try to stay out of trouble tonight."

The disheveled man stands and draws up his pants so they stay in place over his paunch. He starts down the steps muttering, "Young punks, don't show no respect to no one, no more."

The chief walks over to the doorway to ensure he makes it down safely. He turns back to his visitors. "Okay, now what brings you here?"

"Heard you paid a visit to the *Black Moon* today."

"From who?"

Without answering, Damon counters, "Who was the man with you posing as an officer?"

"A deputized assistant."

"We keep track of all the flunkies you have on standby here and he's doesn't fit the mold."

"Good to hear, but it's none of your business. Anything else?"

Damon sticks out a finger toward Kohper which he immediately slaps aside. "I believe you have something that belongs to us."

The chief instinctively glances at the rifle.

"I'm instructed to give you fair warning, Chief——don't go stickin' your nose into things of no concern to you," securing a look at the rifle, he points to it. "Now if you'd be so kind as to return our property."

Kohper doesn't skip a beat, "Let me give you a different set of instructions. You ever come into my office without a police escort, or a personal invite from me, I'll arrest you on the spot." Damon signals the others to start their descent down the stairs, "Don't say I didn't warn you, *Chief.*"

Kohper returns to his desk, ticked off and more demoralized than tired. He holsters his pistol, grabs his bagged meal, and shuts down the office. A short way down the steps, an explosive blast and wave of heat propels him down the remainder.

Kohper ends up face-down on the bottom step. Shattered dry wall, and splintered studs are scattered throughout the second floor hallway and onto his concussed body. A dense cloud of dust fills the entry and spills out onto the sidewalk.

Outside, several car alarms are jarred to life. Shards of shattered glass, bricks, and splintered wood litter the parking lot and the street fronting the building. The air conditioner, mounted in its metal window sleeve, precariously sways over the sidewalk, tenuously held in place by its frayed cord still plugged into the office outlet.

In the confusion, Francisco runs past Kohper's body on his way back up the steps, while the others wait in the car. He waves his hand in the dust-filled air to clear a sightline to the rifle, which he roots out of the rubble. He's careful to negotiate the detritus on the stairs as he makes his way back to their car, tosses the rifle in the trunk and dives into the back seat.

The agents, on their way to meet with the chief, arrive on the scene. Paul rushes into the smoke-filled stairwell where Kohper lies unconscious.

He directs Dax to the clouded office downstairs. The only one in the building is the young deputy who reported on duty an hour earlier. He's seated by the front counter in a state of shock, and uncommunicative.

Eric takes a position at the center of the main road trying to direct cars around the wreckage while urging the rubber-neckers to keep moving.

Within minutes, two trucks from the fire department arrive from their station near the airport. They unroll the hoses and begin to spray down the second story. Surprisingly, there's no fire as a result.

Paul solicits Dax to give him a hand escorting the chief to

his Jeep. After Dax returns to collect the deputy, Paul rushes them to the hospital.

Eric's left in place. The firemen equip him with a helmet, and a pair of coned flashlights as the sun starts to set. As one of the cars slowly passes the scene, its four occupants break out in laughter as soon as they clear the mayhem.

The next morning, Paul walks downstairs to find Keira waiting for him in the lobby. "This is a pleasant surprise," he offers in a monotone.

"What happened to you last night?"

"A bomb blast at police headquarters injured Kohper and his deputy. It made for a rather long evening."

"That's terrible!" she remarked, "Were you able to get any rest?"

"A bit."

She takes his arm and steers him into the dining room where he'd planned on meeting with his partners.

At their approach, Dax grabs an empty chair from the adjacent table, but Keira has other ideas. Paul shrugs at the two with a look of, 'I'm not in control here.'

She leads him to a recently vacated table. After it's bussed and coffee is served, Paul submits, "I'm all ears."

She places her hand atop his forearm. "It's about the other day. I feel guilty about questioning your integrity regarding Steve's death. I knew you had nothing to do with it, and I'm sorry. I let my emotions get the best of me."

"There's no need to apologize; he was your friend."

"How do you plan to deal with what's ahead of us today?"

"Hopefully we'll have a chance to relax on the way to the site. As I mentioned yesterday, I think you should sit this one out."

"Not going to happen," she pleads. "Hanging with you is all I'll need to feel secure."

"Okay, but if you change your mind——"

She emphatically shakes her head. "I won't ... but ..."

Paul checks his watch as he stands. "I'm sorry, but I have a prearranged appointment with Andon."

She reluctantly lets him go, and watches him until he's out of sight.

Dax and Eric invite Keira to join them, which she readily accepts.

As the group files in, Paul and Andon are still engaged in a quiet discussion by the whiteboard. Paul moves to the podium when Andon takes a seat with the others.

The rudimentary sketch on the easel depicts a ship broken in two. "We won't need this until later," he says as he flips the graphic over. "I have a couple pieces of news before Andon gives the brief. An attempt was made to sabotage his boats the other night which landed one of his people in the hospital. As a result, some of his staff have opted out."

Eric squirms in his seat. "Do you think we should still dive today?"

"This is our last scheduled day with Andon. Not holding to our original plans will serve no useful purpose. Besides, we have to make way for another charter arriving the first part of next week. It'll give him the time he needs to get all of his boats back on line."

From his seat, Andon reinforces Paul's response. "No problem, Eric. We can easily repair the boats and still have the two you've utilized during your stay. I'll pilot the lead boat today, and Alou will man the second."

Paul continues, "*And* this means Brent will lead one of the teams." Anticipating their reaction of moans and groans, Paul holds up his arms. "All right, let's move on. Eric and I will dive with him today." It's another bit of news which adds to Eric's increasing discomfort.

Andon stands to tell the crew about *Oite's* final voyage. His demeanor is more serious than usual. He's normally so soft-spoken everyone has to pay close attention. Today's different. He speaks loudly enough for everyone to hear. "Thanks, Paul. I'll try not to belabor this, but the ship and its men deserve their story be told ahead of our visit to the wreck. I'll occasionally need to refer to my notes, and detail artifacts you're likely to find on the wreck.

"Supporting the attack in February of '44, the submarine *USS Skate*, set sail from Midway for the Caroline Islands, in an area approximately one hundred and sixty miles northwest of Truk.

"The evening before the main assault, the sub intercepted three transiting enemy ships, en route to the navy yard at Yokuska, Japan: a crippled yet nevertheless prized light cruiser, a small submarine chaser, and an older, three hundred and thirty-six foot Kamikaze class destroyer, the *Oite*.

An up-and-coming officer, Lieutenant Yasuhiko Uono, had taken command of her the previous October. He was to report for his next assignment as staff officer at the naval base and with it a promotion to lieutenant commander——both personal honors, but he was painfully aware they faced a slow and perilous voyage of over 2,000 nautical miles escorting an impaired vessel in submarine infested waters.

"With periscope raised, the submerged sub cautiously approached the slow-moving ships. At a range of 2,400 yards the commander targeted the cruiser with an array of four Mark 14 torpedoes fired from the forward launch tubes. He immediately ordered the periscope down and his boat to depth. They did not have long to wait for the tell-tale report. Traveling at forty-six knots, three explosions rapidly signaled their success.

"The blasts from the torpedoes had blown up its boilers, knocked out the power, and killed one hundred and seven of its crew. The loss of power disabled Damage Control, taking with it their ability to fight the resultant flames. Dense steam and smoke completely shrouded the stricken *Agano*. Screams arose from men suffering from their injuries and others trying to issue orders over the ensuing chaos.

"The sub's skipper could not rest on his laurels. The destroyer had begun its pursuit. Though way past its intended use as a frontline combatant, and viewed by the IJN as obsolete by the onset of hostilities, the allies still considered the twenty year-old man-o-war a formidable opponent. Its crew of one hundred and forty-eight officers and men, served a deadly combination of deck guns and light antiaircraft guns, as well as eighteen depth charges deployable from either of two projectors or rolled down a pair of rails off its fantail.

"After the attack on the *Agano*, one of Japan's newest light cruisers, her Commanding Officer, Captain Takemutsu Matsuda, transferred seven officers and one hundred and eighteen men to *Submarine Chaser 28*.

"Back from its unsuccessful hunt, the *Oite* returned to the stricken vessel where it remained the night and following day to render assistance. Matsuda ordered its remaining fuel transferred to the destroyer. Listing heavily to port, the surviving crew of twenty-nine officers, including Matsuda, and four hundred and thirty-two men sought refuge aboard the *Oite*, crammed into any available space below decks. Despite having more senior officers aboard by rank, Uono retained command.

"Out of immediate danger from the destroyer, but without confirmation, the *Skate* turned back to determine the stricken cruiser's status. He found his affirmation as soon as the periscope broke the surface. After the vessel rolled to port and slipped beneath the surface, the *Skate* left the scene undetected. For the surviving Japanese, the travails continued."

"With both the *Oite* and *Submarine Chaser 28* dangerously overloaded, Uono messaged for assistance. Dispatched to assist with their burden, the light cruiser, *Naka*, also met her fate thirty-five miles west of Truk, from a bomb and a torpedo.

The cruiser broke in two and sank with two hundred and forty of her crew. Left on their own, the *Oite* and *Submarine Chaser 28* set a course for Guam.

"Uono messaged Truk, '… picked up survivors … we are very full … request permission to proceed Saipan.' But the allied assault had already begun.

"Uono received a reply, 'Truk under attack … return with the survivors.' Taking precautions to enter via the North Pass, Uono displayed special recognition signals to the coastal artillery emplacements to deter their nervous gunners.

"When questioned as to why he returned, Uono tersely responded, 'I'm following orders.' A countermand redirected the *Oite* to Saipan. Before he received confirmation, the message traffic stopped. Without further instructions the *Oite* continued south at high speed toward Dublon Island only to come under attack by the Navy's F6F Hellcats.

"Diving from an altitude of 12,000 feet, the aircraft began the first of four strafing runs on the hapless vessel. The attacks focused on the bridge and midship areas. Effective gunfire tore through the bridge killing Lieutenant Uono and ignited fires aft of the stacks. The gunnery officer from the *Agano* took control of the bridge and directed her into standard evasive S-turns. A subsequent round of strafing killed him as well. *Agano's* Captain Matsuda assumed command.

"When *Oite's* gunners returned fierce fire with the shipboard anti-aircraft guns. The Hellcats radioed for assistance. Five TBF Avengers began a well-coordinated attack toward the ship's stern. Matsuda initiated a thirty knot, three hundred and sixty degree turn to starboard. The Avengers fanned out. At the apex of *Oite's* turn, one of the torpedoes struck her amidships. The tremendous explosion lifted the ship until it broke in two and immediately sank, taking with it the entirety of *Agano's* crew and all but twenty of *Oite's*. The survivors desperately struggled to stay afloat in shark-infested waters while evading the smoking pools of burning oil.

"The two sections of ship plowed into the sandy bottom two hundred and ten feet below. The aft section hit fantail first and settled upright. Thirty feet away the bow section came to rest upside down."

"Decades later, a researcher in Japan ran ads in the country's major newspapers and interviewed four survivors to update the accuracy of reports and coordinates where the vessel was last seen. A search commenced in February of '84. The efforts proved fruitless until he solicited help from my father. Dad knew a local fisherman named Lilipas who had a front-row seat to the spectacle. In the subsequent years, he had fished the general vicinity where the ship went down and often noticed globules of oil percolate to the surface from the wreckage.

"Pin-pointing the wreck's location fell to my father and me. Five days later, we got a potential read-out from the Fathometer. When we entered the water to confirm the discovery, upwards of fifty sharks greeted us!"

An undercurrent of astonishment and angst filters throughout the conference room. Andon does what he can to lessen their anxiety.

"Not to worry. Their numbers thinned out dramatically as we dove deeper. No one was hurt.

"On the first of March 1986, forty years after she went down, we confirmed the wreck's location."

Andon carefully collects his notes, tamps them down on the table top and places them in the folder. "Let's take a break."

While the team refreshes their drinks, Andon flips over the *Oite's* graphic, and invites the group to move closer.

Eric lightly grabs Andon's elbow and points to the images. "This all belongs to the one ship?"

"It does." He holds his fists out and pantomimes a stick

breaking in half. "Same ship, but snapped in two."

"Let's talk about our dive plan. We'll spend twenty minutes on the wreck and sixty-six on the ascent for decompression."

Eric leans in close to Dax's ear. "He serious? Over an hour on our ascent?"

With little patience, Dax points toward the podium. "Yes. Pay attention. This is important."

Andon continues, "The extreme depths will necessitate the same accommodations of extra tanks, regulators, and staff."

He points to the graphic, "Though only thirty-two feet away, the bow's completely upside down, turned in the opposite direction from the stern and a waste of our precious bottom time exploring it.

"We also need to discuss the approaching weather. The forecast calls for heavy rains and brisk winds. Plan on a rough ride to the site."

"Great," Eric mutters to himself.

"Set up your equipment at the docks, and make sure everything's stowed securely. The boat crews will take extra measures to ensure your gear is battened down properly. The reduced ambient light will necessitate you carry your dive lights.

"Because the remote locale and depth of *Oite's* wreckage have restricted access to all but a few professionals, you should feel privileged to be making this special dive."

Paul takes Andon's spot at the dais. "Adding the latest weather report to our already eventful day, this will be our most stressful dive. When we arrive and secure the anchor, our boat will undoubtedly continue to roll with the waves. Help each other gear up and use extra precaution as you move about to prevent losing your balance. Even though we're in two teams, we'll start our descent together. Wait for the signal from Andon before you start.

"Then after the dive, please help each other with your gear and take special care to hand it up to the tenders. Any questions?"

Eric speaks up. "How much time will the boat ride take to get there? Will it be safe to go down? With the sharks and narcosis. I mean … two hundred plus feet. What kind of effects will it have on me … I mean us?"

Paul answers, "You dove on the *Aikoku Maru* without any difficulty, didn't you? She was considered a deep one as well. If you didn't have a problem then, you should be fine on this one."

Intimidated by the questions, Eric thinks, *At a hundred and forty feet I felt anxious, and not in control. He must have forgotten I begged out of their series of deep dives.*

Keira stands when she addresses Andon, "You haven't dived with us since we got here."

"Yeah, sorry, but with everything going on … regardless, I'm all yours today," he says with a smile. Everyone in the room laughs.

Keira's aware of smirks and snarky laughter. "Oh, shut up." She sits down to a loud round of applause.

Andon closes the brief. "One last, and important item—unlike the other wrecks in the lagoon, *all* the sailors' remains are still onboard. Please respect the site as an open war grave—do not disturb their bones."

Chapter 24
The Dive

Mornings in the lagoon are usually clear, crisp and beautiful with each new day's sun reflecting deeply off the waters in the horizon. This is not one of those mornings.

On their way to the dock, Dax grabs Paul's attention and points to the sky. "If it gets much darker this could turn into a night dive."

With no break in the approaching storm front, Paul concurs.

Keira inhales deeply. "Andon was right; you can smell the rain. Did either of you notice how worked up Eric seemed?"

Paul's fatigue leaves him little patience. "Forget about Eric," he snaps. "He's my responsibility. I'm more concerned about how *you're* going to handle a dive this deep."

"You don't have to worry about me. I can take care of myself. But——"

"Listen to what she's saying, Paul," Dax interrupts. "He made a beeline for the boat as soon as he left the conference room."

"I know *that*. He mentioned getting an early start on his equipment. And I can't imagine he'd appreciate the close scrutiny from you two. I certainly wouldn't." Before Keira can resume, he adds, "And yes, Keira, I *will* give him the opportunity to bow out … gracefully."

After Eric secures his rig, he checks his dive light. "Uh-oh. Hey Alou, do you have an extra set of batteries? Looks like I left my light on after our last outing."

"No problem."

Eric tries to act nonchalantly, "So what have you heard about the weather today?"

Alou looks up then does his best to downplay the threat, "Oh, we've gone out in plenty of rough conditions before ... lot worse than what's in today's forecast."

"Sounds good, I suppose."

As the team boards and begins their prep work, Paul takes the seat next to Eric. "Tell me how you're doing, buddy. You seemed a bit ... well, on edge this morning."

He tries to mask his agitation, "Among our issues with Brent, the depth, the trouble with Andon's people, and now the weather... it's a lot to deal with."

Paul agrees. "I get it. I do."

Eric's steals a glimpse at the others as if they can hear his conversation. Paul notices too, draws closer, and speaks quietly, "Would you rather sit this one out? It's totally your call."

Eric considers his offer before he responds, "I don't think so. I don't want to let the others down."

"We have a pretty flexible group. Nobody will think less of you——"

He interrupts, "Let me get back to you once we're onsite. It'll give me some time to think about it."

Paul pats him on the shoulder as he stands. "It's your call. Let me know by the time the anchor is set."

Within fifteen minutes of their departure, the wind-blown waves have grown from a light surface chop to deepening troughs. The crews roll up and secure the canvas tops to prevent them from acting as sails in the growing winds. The clouds continue to blacken and eventually lose the fight to hold back the rain. It's delivered in heavy sheets. The boat slaps down with each successive wave. Unsettled passengers fumble around to find a tighter grip on their seats or each other for the bone-jarring trek. Equipment not properly stowed is tossed about until quickly secured by the crew.

Paul carefully works his way forward to Andon, and though he stands next to him, has to shout over the laboring twin boat motors and formidable weather. "Should we consider turning back?"

Andon's forced to keep his attention ahead while he yells his response, "We've experienced worse. It'll get better once we start our descent. Please return to your seat and hold on."

As soon as Paul sits back down, Keira grabs tightly onto his arm. "Do you think we're safe?"

He tilts his head toward Andon. "He's been through this before."

The troughs continue to deepen and Paul can't help but harbor his own doubts, which he keeps to himself.

It's well over an hour before the throttle's cut back. The rainfall veils a clear view to the islands and reduces the visibility between the two boats. The conditions make it difficult for Andon to get a good fix. He needs several minutes for a visual alignment on the indistinct landmarks for a pinpoint anchor drop. Foamy waters mask the usual telltale rivulets of oil on the surface. He directs his crewman, Kristian, to drop anchor and lets the boat drift to allow it to catch. With the failure to take hold on the first attempt, Andon has to reposition the boat for another try. On the third attempt, the anchor takes a good bite. Kristian yanks the line to confirm it's hold. His nephew follows suit with the second boat and anchors fifty feet away to give the boats room to sway without colliding in the rough waters.

Unnerved, Eric's faced with a choice, *Should I blow off the dive and stay on board? If I do, I'll end up getting battered about this thing for the next couple of hours.*

He nudges Paul. "I think it'll be easier to dive than stay topside."

"Okay then," he answers with a thumbs up. "Give me a couple of minutes to help Keira gear up, and I'll get back to you."

Brent takes care of himself and makes his water entry without assisting anyone. By his way of reckoning, he's done everyone a favor by staying out of their way. It's a thought no one else shares.

Paul and Dax work together to help Keira with her rig, escort her back to the transom, and hold her steady until she times the waves' cycle to safely jump in. The two turn their attentions to Eric before they suit themselves up.

Once in, the divers bob atop the surface swells. Andon gets okay signs all around, before he signals to descend.

Andon, Keira, and Dax drop down first. She fights the pull from the surface, which draws her up then pushes her deeper with each wave, leaving her feeling like an awkward marionette on the descent line. Staring through the water column to locate any object below to focus on, they see it's dark green, indistinct, and foreboding. Both Keira and Dax have second thoughts until Andon comes alongside for reassurance. They continue down together.

In the other team, Brent descends so fast he's quickly out of sight. Paul ignores him and stays close by Eric.

Thirty feet down, the effects from the storm have noticeably abated. The only clue to the severe surface activity is the anchor line's cyclical tightening and slacking. Everyone's much happier at depth than those stuck topside. At a hundred and twenty feet the water's current-free, and the outlines of wreckage come into view. There's another sixty plus feet of descent to reach their target.

Two of Andon's staff verify the anchor's security, tie off the spare tanks, and monitor from a distance before they make an early return to the boats.

At depth, Keira gives Andon an enthusiastic okay, and the three begin their exploration amidships to where the explosion ripped the ship apart. Torn, jagged, and rusted hull plates visibly define the devastation of the torpedo's impact; the wreckage appears to have been disemboweled. A large mound of bones spilled onto the sandy bottom from the stern's open maw——an amalgam of ship's company with the *Agano's* crew who sought protection below decks. Dax thinks, *He didn't exaggerate. We're in an open grave.*

At two hundred and five feet, Keira's uneasy, and focuses on closely monitoring her air, depth, and time. Dax observes her fidgeting and offers his forearm for security. She rests her hand atop his wrist.

Andon points out how clearly visible the inverted bow appears. Narcosis has now muddled Dax's thoughts and he starts to lead Keira in that direction. Andon quickly stops him and emphatically points them toward the stern.

Oite's aft-section came to rest with a slight list to starboard. When Brent's team reaches the deck at a hundred and seventy-five feet, Paul checks how Eric's handling himself. A couple of short taps of air added to his b.c. for neutral buoyancy is a reassuring sign he's thinking clearly.

Eric chooses to hover slightly above the deck while Paul and Brent drop over the stern to view the ship's propellors; her twin screws buried to their hubs in the sand. Eric's head already pounds, exacerbating his uneasiness. With the other two clearly in view, he's decides to stay at his current depth, and minutes later, the three rendezvous on deck.

Fighting his own fatigue, Paul points out the pair of rails used to guide depth charges rolled off the fantail. A large canister lays balanced against the port side rail, where a grotesquely eerie sponge took root and shadows the unexploded ordnance.

Moving forward they come across a heavily encrusted, rectangular-shaped ready-rack fully loaded with depth charges——launchers used to 'throw' the canisters over the port and starboard rails. Paul attempts a series of hand-signals to convey the equipment's role, but Eric's too narced to comprehend and Paul's too tired to try further.

Before they continue, Eric taps on his wrist to gesture if it's time to surface. Paul checks Eric's pressure gauge followed by his own, and answers him with an emphatic shake of his head. He points ahead where Brent stopped to wait for them.

They pass by a deckhouse supporting a pair of antiaircraft guns both pointed to port. As the encrustation of corals and sponge remains relatively light, compared to the more shallow wrecks, Paul can easily identify the twin-barreled Type 96, 25mm machine cannons. The main 4.7-inch deck gun is their next stop. A nearby open ammo box displays a complete load of sixteen cartridges.

Brent impatiently beckons his team to the port side, specifically to an uncovered hatchway. Two skulls preside over the foot and a half square opening, one balanced over the rim's edge and the other kitty-corner to it. Brent illuminates the contents below the hatch for Paul, who has inadvertently blocked Eric's view of the two skulls.

After a long look, Brent nudges him aside to allow Eric access to the scene. He first sights the two skulls which stop him cold. *He warned us of bones, but ...* narcosis has a solid grip on his psyche. Transfixed by the image, he hallucinates, *they're watching me.* He closes his eyes for a few seconds in hopes the visions go away. They don't. When he backs away, Brent immediately grabs his vest and pulls him to the rim of the hatch. The beam of his light directs Eric's eyes to the site within——an endless field of skull caps, in countless numbers, which extend as far forward and side-to-side, as the powerful beam can reach——more remains of men forced below during the attack. With only the tops of skulls visible, terror is in full control of Eric.

He raises his left arm, and slashes down violently enough

to break Brent's grip on his vest. With the heel of his hand he stiff-arms Brent's second stage into his top two teeth. The focused impact tears open the regulator's rubber mouthpiece, and cuts his lip while it cleanly breaks off one tooth, and loosens the other. Brent yells in pain and backs away. He's left sucking water with each pull for air, difficult enough in shallow depths, but at nearly two hundred feet of depth, he's in serious trouble.

Paul has been examining a corroded break in the hull to get a better view of the contents, and missed the spectacle of their encounter. When he turns back, he assesses the jeopardy Brent's in and quickly retrieves the extra second stage of Brent's regulator assembly. After Brent secures the intact mouthpiece, and resumes breathing normally, Paul seeks Eric.

Feeling completely alone, and in the throws of panic, Eric fixates on ending his dive. *I'm outta here, Now!* He focuses all his attentions toward the surface. Frantically swimming away and up, he yanks open the clasp of his weight belt which slides down his legs and drops onto the ship's deck.

Unless Paul can intercept him, he realizes Eric's done for. With hopes to settle him down and provide an escort up the anchor line, Paul reaches out to grasp his legs. With the heal of his fin Eric kicks Paul's face mask nearly off his head, forcing him to stop, reseat and clear the water inside his mask, precious seconds that allow Eric to break away and continue his perilous ascent alone.

Paul's held in place by an maddening pull on his elbow until he recognizes it's Dax, who takes out his regulator and yells in his ear, "Stay ... you'll die, too." Paul surrenders to the futility. *Eric!* He stops to make a concerted effort to calm down and collect his thoughts. *This wasn't an accident. Brent knew exactly ...* but he's lost sight of him somewhere in the dimly lit waters.

During Eric's escape, the surrounding water pressure

rapidly decreases. The resultant expansion of air in his vest squeezes his chest and increases his rate of ascent. He can't get air fast enough. Losing any sense of reason, he rips the regulator out of his mouth, tears the mask off his face, and propels himself upward as fast as possible, past the anchor line, the emergency tanks, and suspended regulators, until he jets waist-high above the surface, startling the tenders.

The expanding air he holds in his lungs creates a severe tear resulting in lethal circulation blockage to his brain. He deeply gasps then settles face-up and unconscious. Blood from his ears, nose, and mouth is diluted and washed away by the overlapping waves. Starved of oxygen, his heart stops minutes later. His limp body bobs atop the heavy surf and drifts away from the boat.

Kristian dives in to retrieve him before the waves push him too far away to safely recover. He gags from a large gulp of sea water and pauses to catch his breath and quell the nausea. The turbulent surface conditions obstruct his vision. He's lost sight of the body. His throat burns as he yells for assistance. With constant updates from Jayvee, he's pointed in the right direction. Somehow he manages to reach him, but faces the herculean task of towing him back against the wind-driven swells. It's an exasperating trek while pulling the dead-weight of a fully-geared diver.

From the escort boat, Nathaniel notices Jayvee breaking out the bodyboard from storage. He swats Alou in the arm and points. "What's going on over there?"

"They must be in trouble. Go ahead and swim over to give them a hand."

Nathaniel's adamant. "I'm not strong enough to swim in these conditions."

Painfully aware of his responsibilities, Alou grimaces in resignation, leaves the boat in the care of Nathaniel and dives in. He swims past the lead boat and reaches Kristian to help him tow the body back. Kristian is completely spent and gratefully hands him off. When he reaches the boat, Alou frees the equipment, hands up the bulky assembly to Jayvee who precariously reaches out from the surging transom all while maintaining a secure handhold on the ladder. As they struggle to keep themselves afloat, the two men secure Eric to the bodyboard while fighting their own fatigue. Kristian needs help boarding while the remaining two work in tandem to hoist the body up and onto the boat, a monumental task in the surging seas.

After doing their best to perform a futile attempt to resuscitate him, they cover his body with a blanket before anyone boards. The wind soon snatches the cover and carries it well past the point of retrieval. Exhausted, Alou drops down to the deck alongside Kristian.

The rhythmic pull from the surface swells inhibit the returning divers ability to maintain a steady depth for their lengthy decompression stops. Paul is haunted by thoughts of Eric and the awareness he's faced a disastrous outcome. He searches for Brent, but several divers remain deeper and the light absorption makes it difficult to distinguish one from another.

Andon and Keira break the surface an hour after Eric. They help each other struggle out of their equipment. Andon tends to his two downed crew before he checks Eric's body. Paul's next to surface and stays in the water to help the others while keeping an eye out for Brent. There's no sign of him.

When Paul does board, he approaches Keira kneeling by Eric. She's holding one of his cold hands and weeps convulsively while trying to wipe the seepage of blood off his face. Paul puts his arm on her shoulder and she places her hand atop his——the security of his touch calms her. Keira can't help but stare at Eric's face. Her mind floods with memories of her brother.

Preoccupied with another, Paul paces nervously, obsessed with locating him. "Has anyone caught a sign of Brent yet?" He quizzes everybody: the crew, those already onboard, newly surfaced divers. There's no response. He's torn between his personal guilt over Eric and his building rage.

While the divers make their way aboard, Brent takes a distant path to surface near the back-up boat's opposite side. He eases around to the stern with hopes no one catches sight of him, but the improved visibility reveals activity clearly visible between the two. Nathaniel helps Brent up the ladder and turns to stow his tank when Brent throws a sharp elbow to the back of his neck. His head snaps back, and he drops Brent's gear before he collapses. Half-crazed, Brent quickly slides him overboard, and yells to Kristian, who stares at the drama unfolding before them, "You're not laughing at me now."

Paul signals Dax to retrieve the boy before he dives in to swim toward the other boat. Brent has already cut the anchor line and thrown the tanks with the drop lines overboard. He fires up the motor and hits the throttle, barely missing Dax with Nathaniel in tow. Paul has to make a quick dive below to avoid getting run over. Brent laughs as he circles for a second precariously close pass before speeding out of sight.

Paul yells to Andon, "Can you call this in? Have them intercept his return?"

Andon focuses on where the radio is usually found. "No." He points to the boat Brent has taken. "He has the only working unit."

En route, Brent unscrews the two knurl nuts holding the radio in its mounted bracket, yanks it from its wiring harness, and tosses the entire assembly overboard.

Andon realizes the futility of any pursuit. They must wait for everyone to board, which includes carefully handling an unconscious Nathaniel. They're seriously overloaded and their dilemma is exacerbated by the weather. The reality of extra people, equipment, and inclement conditions, means a safe return to the dock necessitates an excruciatingly slow pace. Brent easily has a twenty minute head start and his faster transit will widen the gap considerably before their eventual arrival.

Brent uses the storm's cover to drive past the marina and the hotel. He ties off the helm with a weight belt to hold a straight course seaward, grabs his rolled up clothing, and leaps off the moving craft as it passes by an inlet close to his destination. The boat continues eastward, and will do so until it either runs out of gas, grounds itself on a fringing isle, or passes through to the open ocean. *This will give them another distraction to deal with after they return. I need to make tracks.*

Under the cover of foliage, he strips down to his swimsuit, carries his clothes, and starts running. Constantly glancing back, he pushes himself as fast and far as his adrenalin can carry him.

After Keira has sufficiently calmed down, she pats Eric's forearm, awkwardly stands up, and navigates the crowded boat until she can squeeze herself between Dax and Paul on the bench. When she rests her head on Paul's shoulder, he repositions himself to wrap her in his arm. "What will you do about him? You can't let him get away with this."

"I won't," he avows. "I have an idea where he's headed. After we get back, Dax will cover the arrangements for Eric, and I'll make a house call."

"Alone?"

"Alone!"

The hotel grounds remain soggy from the earlier storm. Aware of the slick footing, Paul has to negotiate the gauntlet of puddles to the parked Jeep. He's surprised to find it unlocked. Keira's inside holding the keys. "You dropped these on the boat."

"Thanks." He reaches out the palm of his hand, but she doesn't respond.

"Come on, Keira, I'm in a hurry."

"Fine." She hands him the keys. "Let's go."

"But you can't——" He stops himself short, realizing he won't win this argument. "Better hold on." She buckles in as he guns the accelerator.

After a seemingly endless drive through dark roads avoiding potholes filled with rain water, they reach their destination. The gate to the governor's driveway is slightly ajar. Paul leaves the Jeep to open it all the way, then navigates the wet drive to the manse.

In response to the lights circling the driveway, BG steps out front while Tino ducks into the security office.

Paul focuses on the big man waiting to greet them. He tells his uninvited companion, "For your own safety I think it's best you wait here."

She's already on her way to the house when she snorts, "Fat chance."

"An unexpected pleasure. Miss Hall; lovely as ever. And Mr. Gerhart, what brings——"

"Stow it, BG. This isn't a social call," Paul interrupts. "We're here to see the governor."

BG blocks the door. "What makes you think he's here?"

"Because you are. Now get out of my way." He wants to shove him aside but knows it's an exercise in futility. BG steps aside, leaving the heavy door for them to open.

The governor instructed Tino and BG he was to be left undisturbed for the evening. Looking forward to some quiet time alone, instead he finds himself in a heated argument with Brent who seeks sanctuary in his home. He is about to evict the unwanted fugitive when Tino interrupts him.

"Looks like two more have arrived at the door, Governor," he announces.

"Who is it this time?" he asks, directing his annoyance toward Brent.

"I'll get a better view," Tino responds while he manipulates the camera's remote. "Okay, here we go, it looks like ... Gerhart and ..." with a tone of surprise, he turns his chair to face the two men, "and the Hall woman."

Brent leans in to get a look at the monitor, when the governor grabs his face and pulls him close. "What did you think was going to happen by coming here tonight? Don't you realize you're no longer welcome here? Look at the trouble you've brought down on us. You better come with a good explanation for all of this."

When Brent tries to speak, the governor sternly orders him to, "Shut up," then points to the back corner of the office, "and stay out of our way."

He has to compose himself before he faces the two. He quickly scans the monitor, before he asks, "What are they up to now?"

Tino selects the control for the internal view. "Miss Hall is engrossed in your collections."

"How about the other one?"

"He stands next to her apparently focused on the rear part

of the room."

"Is he holding a weapon?"

"Doesn't look like it."

"Good. I'll lose them soon enough."

He glares at Bent before he leaves, "And you stay put until you hear from me. Understand?"

Brent stays out of the governor'a way until he leaves the room, then moves to Tino's back shoulder to observe the monitor.

The governor does his best to put up a good front for the unexpected visitors. "Mr. Gerhart and Miss Hall. What brings the two of you here at this late hour?"

BG enters and takes a place next to him.

"It's no mystery why we're here, Governor." Paul raises his voice. "Where are you hiding Brent?"

"He's not in this alone," Keira quickly adds.

"I think you have the wrong impres——" The governor hasn't finished his sentence before Brent walks into the room unconsciously twirling his knife in one hand.

The governor rolls his eyes, *Not yet, you fool.*

Brent never takes his gaze off Paul and stands next to a grim-faced BG. "I'm right here, *Agent* Gerhart. I didn't realize you'd miss me so soon."

"You have to answer for Eric. I'm taking you in——"

"Hold on a minute," interrupts the governor. "You have no authority to come into my——"

"Shut-up!" Paul and Keira yell in unison.

Suppressing a laugh, Brent adds, "Chill out, Gerhart. We have a score to settle and I can't think of a better place than right here, in front of these credible witnesses."

Keira takes an aggressive step forward. "You mean accomplices."

Paul grabs Keira by the shoulders, "Stay behind me."

As he turns to make a move toward Brent, the governor steps aside allowing BG to block his path. When Paul hesitates, BG reaches around his back to retrieve his handgun, but has to lean slightly forward to maneuver his bulky, muscular arm. Facing eye-to-eye with him, Paul braces his feet, and slams the point of his left elbow into the right side of BG's face. The impact staggers him and before he can regain his balance, Paul shifts his stance, stiffens his right hand and powerfully cuffs BG with a heavy chop slightly below the back of his left ear. The combination of moves sends the behemoth down. His chin solidly hits the tiled floor stunning him senseless.

Paul quickly peels the weapon toward the back of BG's hand, but the big man's finger is jammed in the trigger guard. BG lets out a groggy yelp of pain as the gun fires wildly, then drops to the floor. The shot sends the startled governor to his knees. Struggling to get himself up, he notices a trickle of blood down his right arm from a grazed shoulder wound. Feeling faint, he grabs the sofa's edge to keep from falling back.

Brent immediately flings his knife at Paul who dodges the projectile and takes Keira to the floor with him. The knife misses her by a thread, smashes through the display's glass door, and shatters several pieces of china, before it's tightly embedded in the rear of the cabinet. The perilous distraction gives Brent the opportunity to retrieve the gun and focus it on Paul.

The governor groggily yells at Brent while he points to the two, "What're you waiting for? Shoot them both, starting with him!"

Brent moves to grip the trigger, when Keira screams, "Brent! No!"

Startled, he redirects his attention and weapon on her.

She holds out her raised hand and pleads, "Think, Brent, you have a choice."

He hesitates.

Pointing to the governor, she adds, "Don't you see? You're in over your head because of him."

With the assurance he's holding the only gun in the room, Brent figures he has nothing to lose. "It wasn't me. Tino noticed Eric scoping out Steve's place——"

Regaining his senses and finding his voice, the governor yells, "Shut up you fool!" Holding his limp arm he pleads with him. "Quit babbling and kill them!"

Brent ignores him and continues to focus on Keira. "Brent, you don't have to be one of his puppets anymore."

He starts to speak, when the governor again yells, "If you can't keep your mouth shut, I'll have it shut for you!" When Brent doesn't react, he adds, "You're going to regret this, boy!"

Brent peevishly responds. "I'm not deaf! I understand exactly what you want."

Keira flinches at the discharge of the weapon. The bullet enters below the governor's right jaw and passes through the upper left side of his skull. Brain matter, blood, and pieces of bone splatter the wall to the left of him. He's dead before he hits the floor.

Brent's no stranger to handling firearms, yet he stares at the piece in disbelief. His self-satisfaction comes as another surprise. Paul quickly reacts by knocking the gun out of his hand, and kicking it back toward Kiera. An immediate right jab to Brent's throat, though not a solid hit, triggers bronchial spasms. When Brent recovers he's facing a steel barrel with Keira holding the trigger.

He stops in place and holds up both his hands shoulder high. After several attempts to clear his throat, he rasps, "It's your choice now, Keira. You gonna grant me the same mercy I just gave you?"

She holds the gun firmly with both hands. "It depends. Did you take part in torturing Steve?"

Brent shakes his head and glibly replies, "I already told you I had nothing to do with it."

"But you knew? Didn't you?"

Brent stays silent, his eyes shift between the two.

Paul cautiously approaches Keira holding out his hand. "Keira, give me the gun."

When she glances toward Paul, Brent bolts toward the front door. Keira quickly takes aim and Paul reflexively drops out of her line of fire. With the discharge of two rounds, the bullets fracture the thick wooden frame and completely shatter the door's heavy glass while Brent forces it open.

Paul stands to reach for the gun, when Keira's face reveals a newfound horror. "Paul!" Her warning's too late.

BG's oaken arms come down together on the back of Paul's shoulders with a crushing blow which knocks him into Keira and both of them to the floor.

Staggered, BG fixates on the grotesque sight of the governor's body lying in a growing pool of blood. He turns his attention back toward the other two. Paul's still dazed, but Keira sits upright on the floor with a firm grip on the weapon zeroed in on BG's face. With hands raised shoulder high, he stands in place. She slowly lowers the gun so it's no longer aimed directly at him. He warily drops his arms and takes a single step backward keeping his eyes locked onto hers. When she finally drops her arms, he runs to the remains of the door, never taking an eye off her. He carefully negotiates the apron of shattered glass, and with a final glimpse back at the two, steps through the opening to the outside landing, and makes a quick turn toward the garage.

Keira helps Paul sit up and eases his back into her. She wraps her arms around him and he drops the back of his head onto her shoulder.

When he regains his senses, Paul scans the room until he locates the governor's body. "That could've gone better," he groans. It's a struggle for him to regain his footing, yet manages to help her up as well.

"You okay?" she asks.

He holds out his hand for stability. "Help me out here, Keira. I need a phone."

Tino monitors the scene as it plays out through the camera feed in the security office. When the governor goes down, he picks up the phone next to the radio tuner.

The Chairman has settled into his quarters to entertain a

number of visitors within the organization, when he's beckoned by an intimidated crewman. "I'm sorry for the interruption, sir."

"You have my attention. Spit it out."

In a low voice he informs him, "We have a call for you on our ship-to-shore from someone who claims he's a Mr. Nededog."

"Tell him I will reach him after my meeting."

"He said it's vital, sir."

Vincenté's out of sorts when he stands and excuses the imposition to his guests. "This'll take but a minute."

The seaman hands the phone to the Chairman who waits until the room's vacated before he responds. "What's so important that you've interrupted——."

Tino frantically breaks in, "The governor's … he's been shot, sir … I tho——."

"Calm down, Tino," Vincenté speaks with a soothing voice. "How serious——"

With staccato-fast precision he immediately responds, "I saw the whole thing through the security feed. It's bad, sir."

"Tell me exactly what you saw."

"The four of them, sir: BG, Brent, Gerhart, and the Hall woman. They had a scuffle and now the governor's dead on the floor."

"You're sure he's dead?"

"Considering the amount of blood everywhere and the fact he hasn't so much as twitched since he fell, I think——"

"Can you personally confirm the extent of his injuries?"

"It's not possible at the moment, sir. The agent and the woman are still there. They're armed and on the phone right now."

BG enters the security room where Tino's in mid-conversation. He takes a few minutes to get his wind back, before he rifles through the desk for another handgun.

"Anyone else in on this?" Vincenté pushes.

"Brent's already left the scene. In fact, *he* did the shooting."

"What about the others?"

"The agent took a heavy blow from BG."

At the mention of his name, BG interrupts, "You talking to the police?" Tino shakes his head as he covers the mouthpiece.

Vincenté hears the sounds of a muffled conversation, and loses his patience. "Who's in there with you?"

"Sorry. It's BG. He's managed to make his way back here."

"Listen Tino, you need to find Brent. I want this mess settled. We clear on this? Tell me now I can depend on you to do the right thing?"

"Yes, sir."

"Make sure of it."

Tino disconnects his end and thumbs BG in the ribs. "We don't want to be here when the authorities arrive. Let's get out of here, now."

"Where do we start?"

"The boathouse."

Vincenté orders the guard outside communications, "Summon the captain, without delay."

Within minutes, Arroyo knocks on the door. "Mr. Chairman, you sent——"

Vincenté opens the door, but does not let him in. He speaks in a voice low enough so his guests won't hear. "Get Damon's team together. I have an assignment for them in town. Have them wait outside until I'm finished here."

Andon and Alou wait at the dock to help the fishermen cast off. They recognized and recovered Andon's boat floating derelict off the east side of Weno. Andon promised them he would make a run to the bank the next morning for a finder's fee. He planned to deliver the payment later in the day. Andon retrieves his checkbook from the safe. Alou sits facing him. "How much did that cost you?"

He slides the register with the signed withdrawal slip back to him. "Whoa. Why so much?"

"Cost of doing business. We'll take the hit."

"But——"

"It'll help them out, and I'll have a reliable ally in the future."

After they've taken the time to discuss the tragic events of the day, and Andon has consoled Alou, they have to prepare for the upcoming week. Andon slides another sheet of paper over to his nephew. While he scans the list of maintenance gripes, Andon adds, "We only have a couple of days to get the boats, equipment, and shop back in order before the new charter group arrives." He walks over to the window to read the skies. "The rains have passed and it's getting dark. Why don't you call it a night. Your mother'll be happy to have you safe at home."

The young man heads out the door, then turns back to his uncle. "Before I go, I'll run the boat over to the depot to refuel it, and hose it down. I'll be back first thing tomorrow to start on the rest."

Andon pats him on the shoulder as he walks out the door. "Give my sister a hug."

"Will do."

Alou unties the boat. It's out of fuel, so he uses a pole for the short trip around back to the concrete dock at the fuel station. He loops the fore and aft lines to the cleats, tosses the pole onto the dock, and starts filling the tanks.

While he reattaches the overhead canvas, three men arrive. Their appearance startles him. They remain in the shadows so Alou doesn't immediately recognized them. "Can I help you?"

"Did you think you could hide from us forever, Alou?"

The voice sounds familiar, but he has to take a closer view in the fading light before he realizes who called him out. "Damien," he whispers to himself. He can't identify the other two, and continues to tug at the last corner of the canvas.

The three group together on the dock. "We haven't heard a word from you for some time now."

"Just leave me alo——"

POP POP

Alou hadn't notice Damon's pistol. The blow from the impact, knocks the wind out of him. He remains standing for several seconds until his legs go limp and he crumples to the deck.

Damon gestures to Miguel and Ryley. They hop aboard and rifle through the storage bins under the seats. Ryley locates the weight belts and lead. He carries three belts to Alou and drops them by his feet. The young man's eyes open wide in terror. He tries to yell for help but can't. He's helpless to fend them off, and struggles to breath. Ryley forcefully untangles Alou's legs, stretches them straight out, wraps the belt around his ankles, and cinches it. Alou barely has the strength to lift his head. The other belt's wrapped around his arms at the elbows and tightly secured. When Ryley leaves Alou to get some line, Miguel places the third belt above his hips, this one threaded with six pounds of lead. It's not much, but enough.

Alou's head moves side to side when Damon kneels next to him.

Alou whispers, "I can't catch my breath."

Damon gazes down at him sympathetically and places his hand atop his head. Alou can no longer feel the touch. "Don't worry, my friend. This won't last much longer."

Alou's eyes dart to Ryley who has the yellow line. It's quickly wrapped through the belt holding his ankles together, and tied off the aft cleat. The two men drag him up from the deck and slowly lower him over the stern headfirst into the water. His struggle is over in minutes.

Miguel starts to slash the overhead canvas with his knife. Ryley pulls down the aluminum support poles one at a time until they crimp at the base. Damon removes the console's base plate for access to the steering linkage and throttle controls and discards it overboard. He does as much damage as he can cutting cables and wiring. The other two disconnect the outboard motors, cut the connecting lines and mounts, and let them drop into the water. On their way out, they remove the fuel nozzle from the tank and drop it into the water to flow freely.

An hour later Andon wants to moor the boat to the dock for the night.

Loud banging on Paul's door startles him out of a deep sleep. "Paul, it's Dax. Get up."

The banging continues until he hears Paul slowly work his way to answer. It's been a couple of hours since he dozed off. His arms and shoulders ache as he unlocks and opens the door.

Paul points toward the bathroom. "Before you get started, let me take some aspirin."

Dax patiently waits at the table while Paul soaks his head in a wet towel. He walks over to his partner and hands him a note from the hotel desk. "Sorry, bud. They've tried to get ahold of you for close to an hour, and collared me when I returned from the coroner's."

"You get Eric situated?"

"I did." He nods as he holds out the paper. "I think you better read the note."

Paul sits down, wipes his head and tries to focus before he returns it to Dax. "I'm too tired. Go ahead and read it to me?"

Dax hesitates until he has Paul's attention. "'Urgent for Paul Gerhart. Please meet me at the shop as soon as you can. I'll wait for you there. Please hurry. Life or death. Andon'."

Paul doesn't react. "What's your next move, boss?"

Paul tries to shake off the fatigue. "Guess I need to get dressed."

"Want some company?"

"You're pretty tired yourself."

"I'm okay."

"Glad to have you along."

They arrive downstairs where Keira's waiting. He

grimaces when she throws her arms around his shoulders, and draws him close. "What's wrong?"

She breaks her hold. "You're kidding me, right? How are you?"

"A bit stiff."

He tries to stretch out his shoulders, but stops when she speaks, "I want to talk about what happened."

Waving the note, he pleads, "I would love to hear what you have to say, Keira, but at a later time. Right now, there's an urgent matter I must follow up with."

She takes a step back, confused at his indifference.

"Will you be alright here?"

"I'm not sure," she answers defiantly, "I'm alone and I'm afraid."

Paul gestures to Dax, and the three head to the now-empty bar where they can talk privately. "I seriously doubt you're afraid. You kept your head earlier when both our lives hung in the balance."

"This sounds interesting," Dax interjects. "What happened?"

Paul waves off the question, "Stay with Keira. She can fill you in." He checks the time and apologizes, "I gotta go."

Keira isn't satisfied "Before you run off, Paul ... Brent's out there and has my room number ... not to mention his associates."

"Take this." Paul reaches behind his back, pulls out his gun and hands it to Keira, which stuns Dax. "When I get back, I want to hear more about where you learned how to handle these. Why don't you plan to spend the night in my room tonight."

"I beg your pardon."

Paul shakes off her implication. "I'll stay in yours. Anyone comes for you will have a rather unpleasant surprise."

The suggestion doesn't quell her angst. "If you're going after Brent, there's no way you'll find him."

"I don't need to. I'll leave it up to the local police and the others flying in to assist with the manhunt. He'll eventually resurface at some point, but right now …" He taps on the note. "Dax will keep an eye on you."

Keira follows him into the lobby. "Where are you going, Paul?" she yells, but he's already out the door.

Dax is still left in the dark. "Would you please tell me what's going on."

Paul cups his hands on the window of the darkened building. The door's locked and he sees no movement within. He raps carefully on the glass with his room key. Andon approaches him from outside. "Thank you for coming, Paul." His face is red, and puffy with bloodshot eyes.

"Your note sounded urgent."

"Follow me."

He's wearing heavy boots midway up his calf that reek of fuel. It's a short walk to the depot. Paul's shocked by the sight.

"When did all this happen?"

Andon leans his back against the cinder block building and slides down to the deck sobbing. Paul sits down next to him and doesn't speak. The two men sit until Andon settles down, Paul tries to reassure him the agency will cover the cost of repairs.

Andon soberly states, "What about Alou?"

"Alou did this?"

Andon shakes his head and sobs, "No. No. We've lost him, Paul … *I* lost him." He tries to wipe off his new stream of tears.

Paul stands and makes a closer inspection of the boat and stops at the pool of blood near the stern. He returns next to Andon.

"I am so sorry."

"What can I do?" he sobs. "How will I ever tell my sister?"

307

Mid-Channel amid Fefan, Tonoas and Weno Islands

Brent has done scores of wreck dives at night, particularly on the Kaidai (large Admiralty) Class submarine, *I-169*, known as the *Shinohara*. At one time he led daylight tours on the sub, but penetration dives became restricted after the death of a diver who lost his bearings beneath a grated deck and ran out of air. The restriction dovetails perfectly with the late governor's operation.

A couple of times a week he would send Brent to the wreck for a night dive to retrieve a sealed case left by an entity known only to the governor. Brent harbored his suspicions about the contents in the locked case, but they kept the cargo a secret from him. He'd deliver the item to a third party, and collect an adequate finder's fee from the intermediary along with the warning his presence was no longer welcome.

Tonight he's on his own and headed for the boat's war-time anchorage due south of the hotel. Locating the wreck at night has inherent difficulties, but he's learned to navigate the channel's waters after dark, an invaluable skill for his extracurricular activity. He eventually locates the surface marker and ties off.

2 April 1944

The *I-169* floated at anchorage in Truk Lagoon while its captain, Lieutenant Commander Shigeo Shinohara, was on shore to coordinate the boat's resupply. Word of an inbound Allied air raid sent the sub to its current location at the channel's bottom, one hundred and thirty feet below, to wait out the attack——standard practice for submarines in a port with no sub pens.

After the raid, it failed to resurface. Speculation circulated that in their haste the crew most likely left an upper valve in the storm ventilation tube open causing the control room to flood.

A diver checked for survivors by using a sledge to rap on the sub's hatch covers. He received responses to his metallic inquiries from four of the five areas he signaled. The rescue team returned with a barge outfitted with a winch, and steel cables to place around the hull. The attempt to raise the sub ended in complete disaster. The ill-fated boat had taken on more water than the rigging could handle, and the cables gave way from the extra weight. Subsequent rapping by the diver yielded no more responses from within. Afraid the Allies might re-float the submarine, the Japanese destroyed it with depth charges. The blasts crushed the bow, tore the conning tower from the hull, and wrenched the propellor shaft. Thirty-two bodies were recovered from the forward compartments. The remains of the crew left in the wreckage was recovered in 1973 and burned as part of a Shinto ceremony.

Present Day

Due to the residual nitrogen he has in his system from the earlier dive on the *Oite*, Brent feels a sense of urgency to make this dive as short as possible. He quickly begins his descent down the yellow nylon line to the wreck of the submarine, and notes the faint whirling buzz from a number of small boat propellors cutting through the lagoon far off in the distance.

The warmth of enveloping waters and the familiar surroundings serve as calming influences from the day's calamity——Brent begins to relax.

He descends ninety feet to the ill-fated boat's forward hatch where the marker's tied off. His path's illuminated solely by his dive light——an old but reliable heavy-duty yellow aluminum housing with a beefy plexiglass plate which puts out an intense beam of light.

The sub's wooden and thinner gauge steel deck plates have long since disintegrated. Leafy, green sea lettuce algae coats the exposed exoskeleton of support beams which encircle the inner pressure hull. Brent has no trouble working his way to the rear hatch. He passes over the boat's distinguishable conning tower——twisted and face-down on the seabed. From there it's an easy swim to the triad assembly once used to support the long-wire radio wave antenna which ran from the conning tower to the boat's aft-most section and displayed the sub's flag when in dock.

Brent's not there to sightsee; he heads directly to the short mast. It marks the access point immediately in front, an encrusted hatch topped with a smaller wheel normally turned to unlock the cover. Corrosion tightly seized the wheel which now serves as a utile handhold for leverage when opening the heavy lid.

To minimize the effect of his fins stirring up the silt inside, he removes and clips them to a line he places at the portal. He carefully enters the compartment feet first and negotiates his way through the potential snag hazard of cables which hang down from the overhead.

His light illuminates the port-side instrument panel. Its dials are encased in housings with a bright patina of rust, and still readable though frozen in time. His light tracks along the deck grates leading aft, now closed out by a heavy dune of silt. To the right stand two banks of engines silenced by rusted works and powdered with silt, algae, and flakes of steel. The tops of its cylinder heads have distinctive hexagonal nuts which appear ready for adjustment, but remain tightly fused in telltale orange.

Brent's routine is to retrieve a sealed, waterproof case planted by the Consortium for the governor, but on this one last dive he believes the case and its contents are now his to keep. As expected, it's in the usual location——behind the port engine furthest from the entry, securely wedged in place. The container is slightly buoyant by design. If for some reason a carrier loses the grip, the case would float on the surface for easy retrieval.

Brent's curiosity has gotten the best of him——he's compelled to find out what's inside. He pulls his dive knife from its sheath on the inside of his left calf to break off the padlocked polypropylene latch. Brent stuffs the pieces into his vest pocket, unclips the remaining latches, and carefully opens the lid. The influx of water replaces the escaping air, causing scores of bottles to rattle against each other, reminders of *Sankisan's* cargo hold.

He carefully places the case on the grated walkway and retrieves one of the sealed, cobalt blue bottles to examine it closely with his light. With the rush of a perceived windfall, he grabs a handful of the containers, *I'm holding a fortune here.* When a couple of vials get away from him and plummet through the deck, he clumsily stoops to retrieve them knocking several more through the grate, into the accumulated silt. *Close the lid you idiot.* He awkwardly reseals the case.

It's time to go. He slowly glides between the two engine banks toward the exit when an unnerving *CLANG* reverberates throughout the hull causing Brent's guideline to go slack. It's his only clue to the sound's source. He shines his light side-to-side and top-to-bottom to assess what happened. Flecks of rust and algae drift down from the overhead. *Are the support beams starting to collapse? Hmm. I've got nothing. Refocus.* With his quarry in hand, Brent takes up the slack guideline and continues his return through the engine room's passageway. Though clouded, the hatchway's easy to locate——straight up from aft end of the starboard engine bank. There he finds the answer. The hatch had somehow closed!

Needing both hands, he lets the case go. It rises to the sub's overhead and stays in place near the blocked exit. Brent tries to brace himself for leverage. He exerts all his effort into opening the heavy hatch cover, managing only to push himself down and away. *This isn't good. I should have an easy out. Now what?*

Anxiety starts to disquiet him. To survive, he has to use reason rather than surrender to panic. He pokes around for a device he can use to pry the hatch open, but any help within the sub is either gone or irretrievably buried under silt. *I gotta get leverage to push it up, if only a bit.*

In an attempt to establish a handhold, he wedges the blade of his knife through the slit where the hatch does not fully seal. He pulls down on the handle. To overcome the initial resistance, he applies all the force he can until the blade snaps, ripping his knuckles across the circular metal frame and knocking the knife handle loose. He screams through his regulator, cursing himself and the situation he's been forced into. The bubbles from his outburst silently collect at the overhead and dislodge more particulate. *This should be an easy routine retrieval. Same as all the rest. In-and-out and I'm home free.* He takes a deep breath. *Calm down and get it together. Work the problem and get yourself out of this.*

Brent comes to the realization his chances of escaping the submarine alive dwindle by the minute. He checks his remaining air. *At this rate you have some fifteen more minutes before you'll start to feel the pull of a near-empty cylinder. Slow down your breathing. THINK!* With adrenalin spiking, and panic taking control, desperation dominates his rationale. His inner voice screams, *Get outta here!* He beats on the hatch with his dive light until it smashes apart, floods, and goes dark. Now he's completely alone in the black confinement with his fear. He desperately claws at the hatch with his fingers until they are torn raw, too painful to continue.

Startled by the brush of a loose cable from the overhead,

he overreacts to its light contact with his cheek, and yanks his head aside smacking it into the engine's corner. His head bounces away from the solid surface, his face throbbing and bleeding. With difficulty he reorients himself, and settles on the grated deck. Using his bare fingers to feel his way around, he grovels along its surface until reaching the smooth feel of metallic cabinetry. He rapidly lifts himself straight into the instrument console's sharp underside, knocking his mask askew and filling it with water. *I'm losing control here! Stop moving and THINK!*

With painful fingers, he clears his mask and gingerly fumbles around the pockets of his b.c. to retrieve a ChemLight——a translucent plastic tube about the size of a fountain pen. He bends it in the center and breaks the internal vial with a crisp *SNAP*, a signal to shake it. *Light, I have light.* It only produces a minimal green glow, but it's enough for him to draw a gratifying amount of comfort.

His anger escalates. *I'm not done; not yet.* With only the dim light stick to work with, he gropes around the overhead until he puts hands on the case. He reopens the latch, grabs two bottles, and scatters the rest which are eventually swallowed up in the silt. He locates the starboard engine bank an arm's length away, leaves one bottle on top of it, and tucks the other under the sleeve of his wetsuit. *They'll get the message.*

He works his way back to the hatch, yanks off his b.c., removes the tank with the regulator, and packs the vest under the hatch. He fills its bladder to capacity with air from the tank before he disconnects the inflator hose with hopes the vest's increased buoyancy will suffice to open the hatch——it doesn't. *"This isn't fair! I finally got my chance to break free from these people and now——I'M TRAPPED!"* He hears a muffled voice, but who and from where? Anoxia clouds his psyche——the sounds belong to him, speaking out loud.

Light-headed, he laughs maniacally until the deepening pull of his regulator forces him back to reality; his tank's close to empty. *What can I do? I can't end this way. Air. I've got to get air.* He remembers the vest, which contains breathable air he hoped would help lift the hatch. His chest pounding, he feels his way back to where he left the vest bunched in the portal. He groans with each desperate moment as he fumbles through the maze of material, straps, and velcro, searching for the inflator's mouthpiece. With a euphoric rush, darkness closes in on him.

BG returns to the hatch two hours after he wedged it closed——a sufficient margin for Brent to have exhausted his air supply. His light catches a glint of Brent's broken knife blade outside the rim. He warily removes the bar he used to secure the hatch. Though powerful on land and afraid of no one, BG's not in his element when below, alone, and especially at night. He uses his dive light to take a prolonged search around him, fearful someone or thing might hover nearby. After he reassures himself he's safe, he lifts the hatch. Brent's buoyancy vest bursts through the opening in an explosion of bubbles, eliciting a yelp from the startled BG. The entangled body of Brent follows, his mask in place, his glazed eyes open, and wearing an eerie expression. He's dragged through the hatch by the vest's upward pull. BG backs away from the apparition, and paddles as rapidly as he possibly can with both his hands and fins while yelling expletives into his mouthpiece. His huge lungs pull air as fast as the regulator will feed it to him.

He's past the precipice of reason and with both arms wrapped tightly around a support stanchion, he squeezes his eyes closed until the wave of panic subsides. After a number of seconds, he slowly opens one eye, a peek at first, before he scans his surroundings. Feeling more secure, he focuses on the hatchway where a flurry of bubbles drags Brent's lifeless body upward until it abruptly breaks the surface tension and slowly drifts with the slight current.

BG fights his initial impulse to follow his body to the surface, but he's there for a reason, the same as Brent. He takes several more minutes for his nerves to settle until he starts to think rationally. Unclipping Brent's fins from the line, he has another moment of insecurity as he drops them over the edge of the hull. His head jerks upward for reassurance Brent won't return for them. BG replaces them on the line with his own and with one last scan, drops into the pressure hull feet first, past the cable hazard, wary of what might await inside. He's startled by the sight of Brent's exhausted aluminum tank floating upside down, held midwater in an inverted position by the weighty tank valve and regulator. BG angrily sweeps it out of his way and begins his search for the case. He shines his light along the overhead until he comes across it, but not in the condition he expected. The case is open and empty save for its dimpled liner. A quick scan with his dive light reveals no sign of the blue vials except the one Brent planted atop the starboard engine bank. Holding the solitary bottle, BG can imagine the little weasel's laugh. *The rest must lay somewhere within the silt. We'd need a dredge to sift them out, which would attract too much attention. The governor wouldn't approve, but he's not with us anymore.* He retrieves the buoyant case, slips the solitary bottle under the liner, closes it, and makes his way though the hatch.

Back on the decaying deck, he dons his fins with his one free hand, but in the process loses the case. It slowly floats up.

As soon as BG breaks the surface, he quickly pulls his mask off, lies back and deeply inhales several lungfuls of fresh air. It's a number of minutes before his anxiety subsides and his breathing returns to normal.

"What the hell took you so much time?" yells an impatient Tino. "We can't stay here all night. Gimme the case so we can get out of here!"

After the ordeal BG experienced below, all of Tino's carping exacerbates his frustrations. He retrieves the wayward container and swims it over to him. With a powerful thrust of his fins, he boards the boat, dive gear and all.

The broken latch arouses Tino's suspicions. "What's this?" he yells to BG.

"It's empty."

"I'm not blind, you fool. What happened to the contents?"

Aggravated to the breaking point, BG stands up in the rocking boat which amplifies any movement, and stumbles to one knee.

"Careful you clumsy oaf," Tino yells, "or you'll tip——"

BG quickly grabs Tino's throat, forces him onto his back, and centers his weight on his handhold to keep him down. His hand easily spans the smaller man's throat, and the downward pressure of his weight inhibits Tino's ability to breathe, or speak.

He lowers his face to within inches inches of Tino's, and with great restraint, articulates, "I'll let it go this one last time, Nededog, but don't ever call me an 'idiot' or 'moron' or any other demeaning name which enters your pea-sized brain!" His voice calms, but the pressure on Tino's throat does not. "People have fed me crap all my entire life and I don't need to put up with it now, especially from you. If you can't respect that, we're going to have issues."

Tino's face continues to redden, his eyes start to bulge, and he fears for his life. BG releases the pressure, which leaves him gasping for air. When he recovers enough to speak, he focuses on the big man still leaning on top of him.

Still infuriated, BG yells, "Tell me now you agree!"

If he doesn't, he knows he's a dead man. "Yeah, yeah, now get off me."

BG takes his time to comply and sits back on the bench.

After he collects himself, Tino resumes fishing around the case. He locates the one bottle BG retrieved from atop the engine, and holds it up to him. "Where's the remainder?"

"I think Brent intended it as a message."

Tino slams the case down on the deck, "Double-crossing li——"

"What'll we do with his boat?" BG interrupts.

Tino has to think for a minute. "Pull the stern line over and we'll set the charge."

To orient himself facing forward, BG swings his legs over

the bench, and reaches over the bow to grab the line. When he leans back to coil it up, a quick *POP* produces a searing pain at the base of his neck which paralyses him. With another *POP POP* the line and his body go limp and slumps forward. His body involuntarily quivers as Tino leans over him, and shouts in his deaf ear, "Who's the man now, you imbecile!"

Tino shakily stands, and nearly loses his footing while he climbs over the unwieldy hulk. He wraps the line around BG's ankles, returns to the stern, starts up the motor, and throws it in reverse, pulling the line taut. The motor labors against the resistance. With Tino's assist, BG's mutilated body eventually slides over the bow into the lagoon and floats by the stern of Brent's boat.

At three a.m., a fireball emanates from the moderate explosion aboard the abandoned craft. Tino is nowhere nearby.

At daybreak, a crew of local fishermen reach the anchorage scatted with frayed ends of yellow nylon line, charred wood, fiberglass, and cushions. In their search, they retrieve a b.c. among the flotsam and are shocked to discover Brent entangled in it. They eventually come across what's left of BG's remains. It takes the entire crew to recover his body and lay it alongside Brent's, and with whatever equipment they could retrieve. When they reach port, the men turn over everything to the authorities.

Hagåtña, Guam

Jon's awakened by the rap on the door to his room.

"Pack your bags, Jon. We're heading to Chuuk," J.J. speaks through the door.

Jon opens the room. "Some kind of an emergency?"

"You could say that."

"What's going on?"

J.J. thinks awhile before he decides to break precedence.

"Dax called to tell me one of my agents is down, followed up by a ship-to-shore intercept … the governor's shot and presumed dead."

"Who's down?" Jon's in a near panic. "How's my daughter?"

"It's the new man, Woods, the one I asked you about earlier. Apparently it happened on their last dive."

"And, what——"

J.J. dismisses Jon's question before he finishes.

"It's all I have right now. Paul and Keira may have been involved in the governor's death."

"Keira!" yells Jon. "I told Paul I didn't want her endangered." He starts to frantically pace around the room.

"Take it easy, Jon. They're both fine."

"What are you going to do about this?"

"I can't make any decisions until I get a complete pass-down."

Jon's agitated and anxious to get underway. He needs reassurance of Keira's safety. "When do you think you'll get some info?"

"Paul's picking us up at the airport. As soon as we brief, I'll decide from there."

"Whatever you're planning to do, J.J., I want in."

"It doesn't work that way, my friend. You're a civilian."

"But now it's personal."

"All the more reason."

He grabs J.J.'s arm. "They tried to kill my daughter."

"Calm down, Jon. This isn't helping."

"Please, J.J. She's all I have left."

"We have the flight ahead of us, I'll think about it on the way and present your suggestion to Paul. He'll lead the operation … and make the final call."

"Good. He's a reasonable man."

Yeah, big mistake! J.J. regrets disclosing his intentions.

The parking expanse to the new hospital consists of unmarked gravel with no designated parking. The ambulance has a reserved spot, but is blocked in front and back. The same goes for the hospital administrator's space. It's a pressing issue which needs addressing sooner rather than later.

Paul parks alongside the road near the lot's entrance.

The building is long, wide and white inside with wooden bench seats running the corridor's length. Paul makes his way to the admitting desk. A young woman in scrubs responds from her seat. "May I help you?"

"I'm Agent Gerhart. I spoke with the Medical Examiner a few minutes ago. He's expecting me."

She picks up the phone, but first has to answer a nurse's inquiry before she can dial the number. After hanging up, she motions Paul to follow her. They take a right, down a ramp to the lower floor at the corridor's end, where the woman points to the sign outside a set of double doors:

PRIVATE
NO ADMITTANCE
WITHOUT PERMISSION

Two policemen stand at the doorway.

"Push the blue button to the left. Dr. Earle's waiting for you."

Paul thanks her before he depresses the oversized square activating the doors which swing outward. Two men hunch over a clipboard. He's familiar with one, the Chief of Police. The other's new to him. "Doctor Earle?"

"Agent Gerhart." He's wearing a three quarter length white coat with a hard-to-read black name tag. "May I verify your identification?"

Paul takes a quick visual around the room as he hands him his wallet with his ID card and badge. He acknowledges Kohper.

The morgue has six bodies on separate tables or gurneys

covered with sheets. "You've got your hands full," Paul addresses the doctor.

"Rumor has it that you are either directly, or indirectly involved with this?" Kohper speculates.

"Glad to see you're back on your feet, Elias."

The chief bristles, and the doctor interjects, "His question isn't out of line."

"One is Agent Woods," Paul concedes, "and I know about the governor and Mitchell. Who're the others?"

"Let me give you a quick tour."

"Could you verify the identifications with me?"

"I'll do what I can to help."

He uncovers Brent first.

"What took him out?"

"I hoped you'd give me the answer. It appears he drowned. Some fishermen brought him in along with the next one over here."

At the next gurney, it's difficult to view the grizzly remains of BG. "Three gunshots to his head." His face is charred and torn apart. "Any chance they're from your gun?"

Paul shakes his head.

One by one he unveils the remaining tables, and confirms the identities with Paul before he quickly replaces each cover and moves on. The chief has leaned his back against the counter to observe Paul's reaction to each revelation.

After pausing for a moment with Eric, they move to the final table. "Our latest arrival."

Paul presumes it's Alou, but braces himself with a deep breath before the reveal. It's especially difficult to view someone so young who has lost any chance for a tomorrow. He pulls his chart to read the cause of death.

"Drowning? Andon told me he was shot!"

The doctor points to the two entry wounds in his upper thorax. "He took two small caliber bullets here. Not enough to kill, but enough to put him down. No way he could resist what followed."

Paul has trouble maintaining. "What do you mean 'what

followed'?"

The doctor clinically explains, "They found him tied off at the ankles and elbows, weighted down, and suspended head-first in the water. He was alive when they lifted him over the stern, and lowered into the lagoon. The bullets didn't kill him, the water he inhaled did."

"We hoped you could shed some light on this," adds the chief.

The memory of Alou's infectious smile turns his sorrow into rage. Paul quickly wheels around, his back turned to the table and stares through his tears at the coroner's chart notes. Kohper notices Paul's complexion turning red as he fights his emotions. A thread of veins in his forehead noticeably swells. When he remembers Alou telling him about Tino luring him into their web, he slams the clipboard onto the floor and barges from the room, knocking over an unsuspecting officer outside the door. The chief quickly follows, but stops to help the protesting deputy back to his feet, while Paul continues to negotiate a fast-paced circuit out of the building. It's a running trek over the graveled driveway to his Jeep. Before he can fully open the door, the chief slams it shut.

"What?" yells Paul turning to face him.

Paul blindly reacts to the chief's attempt at placing a hand of consolation on his shoulder by brushing it aside. The chief makes another attempt at calming him, "I realize you're angry Paul, and you have every right, but I'm going to need your help."

He's inconsolable, but Kohper continues to plead with him, "It's gotten way beyond my department's capability. I can't do this with you rushing off half-cocked for revenge."

Paul gently, but firmly, forces the chief aside and climbs into his vehicle. He rolls down the window and tells the officer, "I'm on this. Don't worry about your manpower issues. We'll cover this ourselves."

"Do you need a reminder you're an officer of the law?"

"Not here and not tonight, Elias. Now get out of my way."

"First thing tomorrow morning, I'll need you to meet me

at the airport. We'll be in the Security Office, and wait for you there."

Without acknowledging him, Paul starts the Jeep, hits the gas, and pops the clutch laying down a path of smoke and rubber. Kohper has to duck as the vehicle kicks up a spray of gravel until it gains traction on the macadam surface. Paul doesn't slow down until he reaches the airport and its tarmac.

It's after dark when the government jet touches down at Chuuk International. J.J. and Jon disembark and recognize Paul's vehicle as it screeches to a stop. When Jon catches sight of him, he rushes the unsuspecting agent and throws a solid right cross which catches him squarely on the chin, putting him down on the tarmac.

"What the hell, Jon!" yells J.J. as he runs over to Paul.

Standing, Paul assumes a defensive posture and glares at Jon while he wipes his chin with the back of his hand——no blood. "I presume this is about your daughter!" he yells at Jon venomously. "We're both *fine* by the way! Thanks for asking."

Rubbing his sore right hand, Jon yells, "We had an agreement! You were to *protect her*, not place her right in the middle of your heroics!"

"Will you relax. Keira's safe, unharmed, and surprisingly resourceful."

Jon takes another step toward Paul, which prompts J.J. to place himself between the two.

J.J. speaks directly into Jon's ear. "Can we continue this *discussion* where it's a bit less public?"

"What do you think you're doing?" responds Jon.

J.J. stares at him with incredulity. "Frankly, I'm protecting your dumb ass. He'd drop you in a heartbeat. For your own good, you'd better calm down and quickly."

"OKAY! Okay … I'm good," Jon relents, but glares at Paul.

After everyone cools down, Paul leads them to the vehicle. J.J. stays close to Jon until they get in the back seat. Paul drives them to a hotel near the airport where they'll have some privacy.

It's a quiet walk through the lobby and up to the room. Jon's anxious to pick Paul's brains, primarily about the safety and welfare of his daughter, and hear the details about everything since his medevac.

Moving his jaw side-to-side Paul concedes, "You know for an old guy, you throw a helluva punch."

"Yeah. Sorry. Guess I over——"

"No apology necessary. She's precious to me too and the last person I would want to place in jeopardy."

Jon reacts with raised eyebrows, and points his thumb toward J.J. "You have any idea what he's cooking up over there?"

"Not at all."

J.J. sets down the phone and turns his chair to face the men. "You two kiss and make up yet?"

"We're good," Paul chuckles. "What do you have in mind?"

"I already have things in motion. I'm putting together an assault team."

"For——"

"The Consortium has become too dangerous and widespread. We need to take them out."

Paul needs clarification. "How? By direct assault?

J.J. gives him a silent assent.

"I think it's the wrong tactic."

"Oh, really?"

"They're heavily armed and well-trained, sir. We could … no, we *would* lose a lot of our men attempting a direct assault. Not to mention the potential for collateral damage."

"You have a better idea?"

"Whatever you've planned, I want in," Jon anxiously interrupts.

"It's your call, Paul," The director throws his hands out to the side. "You're heading up this operation."

A light rapping on the door springs Paul to his feet. He

opens it to Andon, who knew about their pending arrival. "Good timing. Come on in."

Jon strides over with his hand extended. When Andon takes it, Jon pulls him close for a gentle hug. "I'm so sorry to hear the news about Alou."

Andon bites his lower lip and takes a deep breath. "Thank you, Jon. Glad to have you back."

Jon keeps hold of his hand and turns to J.J. "I'd like you to meet my friend, Andon."

J.J. takes his hand and extends his condolences. "Paul filled us in. My heart-felt sympathy to you and your family."

They take seats around the room and spend the time getting caught up on events. Jon brings Andon up to speed. "We're discussing what to do about the Consortium."

Paul answers Jon's earlier request. "Thinking about your offer, Jon, I appreciate it, but I'll have to pass."

Jon notices J.J.'s nod agreeing with Paul. "Why?"

"We have a different plan in mind, and honestly I need someone who can keep up with me."

"But——"

"No offense, but you're returning from six days in the chamber."

"This isn't because I popped you one?"

"Ah, no." Paul shakes his head. "Listen, I invited Andon here for a reason. Let me tell you what we have in mind."

Chapter 27
Reckoning

Captain Arroyo reluctantly knocks on the Chairman's door and is gruffly acknowledged. "What brings you here so early?"

Arroyo's holding a message he received from a nurse on the organization's payroll. The captain does not make eye contact, but holds the paper out to his superior. "It's from one of ours, sir."

He stands mute while Vincenté starts to read it. The Chairman gestures toward the chair, but Arroyo remains standing.

After reading a few lines, Vincenté glances at Arroyo. "Good, good. We won't have to deal with Brent anymore."

"I think you'd better keep reading, sir."

Vincenté tries to get a take on the captain who continues to stare at the floor, and believes he's withholding. Once he reads the complete message, he furiously wads up the paper, then loudly inquires of the captain, "Have you confirmed this?"

This time Arroyo looks at him directly. "Yes, sir. I called the medical examiner personally. The report's accurate. Agent Gerhart positively identified Benjamin's remains."

"Why was Gerhart brought in on this?"

"The medical examiner said they're over-whelmed. The agent was there to see to the disposition of Agent Woods, and offered to help identify the rest."

Vincenté squeezes tightly around the ball of paper. With whatever control he can muster, he orders, "Contact the three we sent ashore. Explain the situation to them. Tell them," he self-consciously wipes a tear off his cheek with his sleeve, "tell them to *finish* the job! No loose ends."

Arroyo closes the door. As he leaves for the communication's room, he can hear the muffled pain of a father who has lost his only child.

Tino sits alone on a concrete bench in the open-air lobby to await the announcement of his flight's departure. A nondescript orange photographer's case festooned with a collection of decals from various locales is straddled between his legs, a common sight with groups of traveling divers. Caressed by the tropical breeze, he closes his eyes and puts the events of the previous day behind him.

Paul's approach startles him. "Interesting case you have there, Tino." He's accompanied by the Chief of Police and three other officers. "Sunset House, Grand Cayman ... Dive Taveuni, Fiji ... Desert Divers, Dahab, Egypt." Paul shakes his head in mock wonderment and disbelief. "Have you *really* visited all these destinations? ... You 'diplomats' ... you must roll in it."

Dismayed by the unexpected encounter, Tino scowls.

Kohper, impatient to get on with the process, intercedes. "We have a report of a theft from a hotel, Mr. Nededog. We need to inspect your case."

Tino scans the five men confronting him, and scoffs, "Lotta manpower for a trumped-up theft report."

The chief ignores the comment, holds out his hand, and responds, "Your case, sir."

Tino grasps it tightly and holds it closely to his chest. "In fact, I do mind. I'm on my way to the consulate in Saipan with classified diplomatic documents."

"Mr. Nededog, you've given me no other choice but to

detain you for questioning. Please accompany us to the Security Office. I don't believe you'd want your classified documents to be seen here in public."

A dozen or so people stare at the commotion. Tino directs his attention back to the chief. "Under what charge, Officer?"

"For starters, how about several counts of murder," Paul interjects bitterly.

"You're out of your jurisdiction," he smugly accuses Paul. "And you, Chief Kohper, you've left me no other choice. Our consulate will exonerate me of this illegal detention, and you'll lose your job for this. I'm under diplomatic immunity."

One of the deputies takes hold of Tino's arm and leads him to the door marked SECURITY OFFICE. Once inside the confined room, the chief directs him to place the locked case atop the table.

"Now open it up … please!" Paul orders with disdain.

Tino doesn't move, but defiantly states, "You have no authority over me." He scans the room. "As a matter of fact, none of you do. As I mentioned earlier, I'm under diplomatic protection."

"You're a broken record, Tino. There's no immunity for murder here. Either you open this up, or we will. Afterward we'll give you the pieces of whatever's left."

Paul moves over to where Tino is seated and leans in until they're face-to-face. "And please, Tino … I beg you … continue to resist."

The chief signals two officers to force him to his feet. He begins rifling through his pockets. Tino relents, "While you continue to get your jollies pawing around in there, you're not going to locate whatever you expect to come across."

Paul takes control. "Let's play it your way. Get undressed … your shoes first."

"You're kidding me, right."

"Quit wasting our time and get started," Kohper concurs.

Tino reluctantly kicks them off, one at a time. Paul picks up his left shoe first, raps it on the table with a loud, *THWACK*, which surprises everyone in the room. A nickel-sized key falls onto the table. Paul holds it up for Tino, then states, "Thank you," before he shoves the shoe forcefully into his gut. With a loud, *OOF*, he stumbles onto the chairs.

Paul unlocks and opens the case. He empties it onto the table, along with the dimpled foam rubber inserts used to protect the contents. "Where's all the so-called 'classified documents', you claim to carry? Oh … hey, this is interesting." He holds up an envelope with an unusually fat stack of cash.

Tino stands. "I imagine it would be for someone in your profession," he goads Paul. "How much does a government agent make these days?" Paul anticipates his next move. When he lunges for the envelope, Paul lures it out of his reach with one hand and reactively grabs his throat, and applies pressure to shove him back down.

Rubbing his throat, Tino rasps, "As far as the money you're holding, today is payday for our envoys throughout the Marianas and Micronesia."

"And I take it you're the disbursing officer?"

"Yeah, you got it," he mocks, "I'm the dis-purse-sing officer."

Paul fans the padded envelope. "And you deal only in cash?"

"We do this to save our associates the trouble of bank transactions and conversion rates."

"And taxes, I presume."

Paul carefully inspects the disarray on the table. "I think your 'associates' will have to cope with an unexpected disappointment today. I can only imagine that when word gets out, it won't go well for you." He leans over the items spread about the tabletop, and adds, "Let me repack this."

Tino stands quickly. "No problem, I can do it."

The chief forcefully sits him back down. "For your own good, I think you better stay put."

"Don't burden yourself," Paul adds. "It's my mess, and I do clean up after myself."

He starts by patting down the dimpled liner with his fingers. "What's in here?"

When Paul holds up a cobalt-blue bottle found tucked into a razor-cut slit, Chief Kohper points it out to Tino. "Tell me about this."

"It was a gift from my friend, the late governor."

Paul's astonished. "Huh. You called him the 'late' governor, when the news has yet to be made public."

"Kohper can attest to stories of that ilk circulating rapidly on an island this size," Tino responds. "And a story of *this* magnitude … well, I can imagine it's already reached certain ears in Washington by now."

Paul reaches into his own pack and retrieves a test kit——a quart-sized transparent bag containing a vial of liquid. He breaks the seal on Tino's bottle, pours its contents into the bag, reseals it, snaps its internal vial, and rapidly shakes it. The liquid from the vial mixes with the powder and turns blue. Paul anticipated the results, but shows the chief the color card from the kit which identifies the contents.

"Heroin," Kohper mutters while holding the card up to the bag for comparison.

Paul confirms.

The chief orders his men to cuff the suspect, and read him his rights. Tino's continued protests fall on deaf ears. A deputy lays a stack of evidence bags on the counter for the cash, his passport, airline ticket, and wallet, the blue bottle, and the heroin test kit.

Paul closely inspects the outer case. He reaches into his pocket and pulls out a jumble of pieces which easily align with its broken latch. He holds them up. "We found these in the pocket of Brent's compensator vest this morning, along with another bottle in the cuff of his wetsuit which matches the 'gift' the governor gave you. He had it on him when the fishermen recovered his body."

Tino remains silent.

"Add these to your collection, officer." Paul hands the items to the policeman who continues to label the evidence bags.

Paul turns his attention back to the prisoner. "I'm curious,

Tino. Why didn't you react when I mentioned Brent's death?"

"I'm not surprised. Whatever happened to the punk, he had it coming."

"I thought you two were tight. Business associates right?" The chief inquires.

"I want to speak to my attorney."

"Good idea," Paul responds. "I hope, for your sake, he's a good one."

By mid-afternoon Paul's back at the hotel. He needs a quick nap before dinner, but is intercepted in the lobby by Anaria. "Mr. Gerhart, we have another message for you labeled 'Urgent'." He grabs the note without reading it, seeks a table in the lounge and orders an iced tea from Sal.

Keira's hand gently rests on his shoulder. "Mind if I join you?" He slides out a chair with his foot. He wants to read the note, but welcomes the interruption.

"Did you speak with Andon yet? What's Nathaniel's prognosis?"

Paul turns back to the note. After a few minutes she waves her hand close to his eyes. "*Hellooo*," When he stops reading, she adds, "Well?"

Paul places the note face-down on the table. "Sorry, I'm not ignoring you, just a bit distracted. To answer your questions, Nathaniel's recovering well. He'll need to rest a few days, and limit his lifting, but he'll be back on the job soon."

"At least there's some good news today." She points to the paper on the table. "What's got your attention now? It apparently isn't me."

Paul rereads the note and hands it to her. "Anaria gave me this on my way in. I think you'll appreciate the contents, but I need to address it right away."

He registers the disappointment on her face, and holds out his hand. "Got some time? I'd like you to come into town with me."

She smiles, stuffs the unread note into her pocket, and takes the offer of his hand. "Let's go."

Paul throws a five spot on the table as they quickly leave.

When they reach the desk he orders a cab. Anaria points outside, "There's already one waiting for you."

She's read the note, Paul thinks.

"The hospital and fast," he tells the cabbie.

After reading it, Keira stuffs the paper in Paul's shirt pocket.

"I thought Kohper arrested Tino this morning?" she whispers.

When she points out the driver turning an ear in their direction, Paul leans in closer so they can have some semblance of privacy, "What's with the hospital visit?"

"Apparently someone got to him after I left the station this morning. He's requested my presence, and I expect a more talkative prisoner this time."

She comments, "Tino's in the hospital? You're right. It is a better day."

"We're here to see Hostino Nededog," Paul informs the admitting receptionist.

She telephones her supervisor, retrieves his chart, and hands it to the older head nurse who scans through his chart notes. After setting down the paperwork, she makes eye contact with the waiting couple, and emphatically declares, "Mr. Nededog is not allowed any visitors right now."

Paul holds out his wallet to reveal his badge. "We're not here on a social call; this is official business."

Keeping her eyes on Paul, she slumps her shoulders and points her thumb at Keira. "Is it necessary for *both* of you to go in? He's in critical condition."

Without hesitation, Paul gestures toward Keira, "Absolutely. My associate has information vital to this investigation."

When the nurse turns away, Keira pokes Paul's ribs and rolls her eyes.

The nurse bends over to whisper to the receptionist, then addresses them, "Follow me." As they leave the admissions desk, she picks up the phone.

They're led along the lengthy hallway to the door where a security guard is seated. "Please make this short," the nurse warns Paul as she opens his room.

From the facial swelling and bloodied bandages, it's apparent Tino suffered a severe beating. He's on oxygen and hooked up to a morphine IV infusion pump.

Paul addresses the nurse, "This shouldn't take too long," and directs his eyes toward the door. She closes it gently on her way out.

"Agent Gerhart," Tino speaks haltingly, "and Miss Hall … "

"Looks like you should have stayed in custody today."

"I guess they got the news about BG."

"What news? Who's 'they'? What about BG?"

Although Paul had already viewed the man's mutilated body at the morgue, he needs to hear him acknowledge it.

"They must have put two and two together."

"Were you involved in his death?" Paul raises the question.

Tino pushes the oxygen feed from his face to answer him. "I thought you were smarter than that *Agent* Gerhart."

Paul has to laugh. "Touché, but then which one of us is the patient here?"

"The mistake I made … not checking out BG's background and relationships … I met him through the governor … didn't feel the need. The Chairman sent the three men to educate me."

"The same three men you sent to 'educate' Alou last night?"

Keira eyes curiously probe Paul.

Tino starts to cough. Bloody sputum dribbles from the corner of his mouth. He's too spent to clean himself, and neither of his visitors care to.

"We worked for the same people."

"You don't work for the governor?"

Tino tries to suppress his laughter which triggers another coughing spasm. When he catches his breath, he adds, "Too stupid and greedy … him and Brent … one and the same."

Coughing continues to interrupt Tino's testimony. He needs to speak slowly, but wants to cooperate. Paul gives him time to settle down. "How did you end up in this fix?"

"They met me outside the police station." He still struggles to breathe. "Vincenté arranged for my release … afraid I'd talk … guess he wanted payback for his son."

"His son?" Paul proclaims. "BG?"

Tino nods to confirm. "The fools … they left me for dead. Didn't finish the job … too bad for them …" he gasps.

"I want to hear more about *them*."

Tino lifts his eyebrows. "Some cheap locals … on the Consortium's payroll." Paul raises his eyebrows. "You must have observed their yacht by now … hard to miss …"

Keira places her hand on Tino's, but it's cold and limp. "How deeply you involved here, Tino?"

"On Chuuk? You believe you've uncovered some great criminal enterprise on this island … with the governor maybe … or *Brent*?" he faintly smirks.

She jerks back her hand, and bitterly follows, "Meaning what?"

He can barely lift his finger to point at her. "You need to broaden your horizons. Brent … the governor … they were a front. Same as you. We knew from the start you didn't need any 'official' survey to measure the wrecks' decay … or the ramifications over a bit of spilled oil." Keira eyes him with a puzzled expression.

"Oh, don't act surprised, pretty lady … we did our research, too. You think the governor's activities amounted to a whit? Pocket change. We used *him* as a ruse to keep you off the real scent."

Keira tries to sort it out. "What led you to take these

actions against us? My father? Eric?"

"You can thank Brent for that. Well, I guess then you can't anymore, can you?" he smirks.

She loudly reacts to his arrogance. "What about Steve!"

"Ask BG."

"Too bad he's no longer here to defend himself," Paul interjects.

"You have no proof ..." His eyes start to flutter. The interrogation is taking its effect on him.

Keira shakes his bed, "What about Brent?"

He slowly opens his eyes to reengage in the conversation. "We couldn't control him. Try as we might, he wouldn't listen. But Steve ... now *he* got peoples' attention. He wanted to play detective ... become a hero and solve the 'caper' for you ... in the process of helping you with your 'investigation', he got other peoples' attention ... the wrong people ... dangerous ..." He closes his eyes. After a few seconds Paul nudges the bed. Tino returns with a disoriented, worried look. When he can refocus on Keira, he settles down.

"You mentioned Steve," she reminds him.

"Yes, Steve ... apparently he made the Consortium nervous. When we realized he'd share his results with you ... we had to intercept him."

Paul notices Keira's fist clench, and places himself between the two. Holding his arm out to keep her in place, she yells around him, "You tortured him! You killed an artist you ba——."

Tino whispers, "Artists die too, dear."

Keira's scream is answered by the nurse, who's been listening outside the door, bursts through with the security guard.

Paul continues his agenda. "Did you have a hand in Alou's murder?"

Keira's head violently turns toward Paul. "Alou!" she yells. "He's dead?" She starts to sob, "That sweet young boy."

The nurse steps in. "That's it. You're through. I insist you leave here, immediately."

Paul holds out his arm to stop the nurse in her tracks. "One more question, please."

"It better be the last one," she concedes.

 They both stay to listen.

"Where can I find this 'employer' of yours, Tino."

He gestures with his hand to draw him closer, shoots a wary look at the nurse, then lifts his head slightly to whisper, "Everywhere," and collapses back onto his pillow. He closes his eyes to signal their interrogation's finished.

The nurse moves between them and the bed, and checks Tino's vitals. "Okay. Your 'visitation' is over. I want you out, now."

The guard takes Paul by the arm to escort them out.

"Unless you want to share the bed next to him I suggest you get your hands off me." The guard complies. "Thank you."

As they exit, Keira thinks out loud, "I hope he dies."

Paul doesn't break stride. "He won't survive this."

"Good. Why didn't you tell me about Alou? What happened?"

"I'm honoring Andon's wishes. He hasn't broken the news to his family yet."

On the *Black Moon*, the three men stand in front of Chairman Vincenté who's seated. "I sent you to do a simple job for me, but I just got off the phone with one of my people at the hospital. I'm told Tino's not only alive, but being interrogated by Federal agents! Would you care to explain yourselves?"

When no one responds, Vincenté points to Damon at the far right. "I held you responsible for this detail. Correct?"

"Yes, sir."

"Tell me, how's Tino still able to breathe? Your assignment included ending him!"

"We," he pauses, "*I* presumed he'd die. It's not possible he survived the beating we laid on him."

"All evidence to the contrary. Did we not issue you weapons and ammunition?"

"You did, sir," he responds in lowered tones.

"Apparently you didn't remember when and how to use the guns we issued." He taps on the desktop with one finger. "Place yours here on my desk. You won't need it anymore. I'm sending you home, without pay."

The other two glance at each other, and step aside while he leans forward to lay down the pistol. "You two get out of here, and you," pointing to Damon, "sit back down. We have some expectations to review."

Captain Arroyo intercepts Miguel and Ryley as they close the door. "There's a boat waiting for you at the stern. The Chairman wants you to to go to the hospital and *finish* the job. And you best not screw it up this time."

As Miguel steps into the Zodiac, he flinches when the crack of a gunshot echoes through the lagoon. "I think we just got our severance notice. Let's wrap this up."

The receptionist phones the head nurse when the pair arrive. They're aware of Tino's whereabouts and continue past the desk without breaking stride or acknowledging her. The patient's aghast when the guard steps in and holds the door open for the two men. Miguel signals the guard to vacate the area. When Ryley steps over to the bedside, Tino takes a deep breath and closes his eyes.

The next stop for both men is the airport, a short jaunt, a couple of minutes away. As they exit the building, Kohper is waiting with two of his deputies, handguns aimed at the ready. "Don't think!" Kohper yells. "Just place your weapons on the ground!" Pointing to his truck, he adds, "Slowly place your hands flat on the hood of my truck."

"To hell with you," yells Miguel. He drops down and grabs his weapon.

Ryley panics in the confusion and fumbles his attempt at retrieving his gun. Kohper drops him with a round through his neck. Miguel stands and wildly returns fire, spurring a return of several volleys from the three officers.

Kohper confirms his men are okay before he orders them to cautiously approach Ryley. His weapon lays next to his lifeless body. Kohper kneels over him to feel for a pulse. *I hope you thought it was worth it.*

Outside the hotel, Keira sits alone on the palm's bench. She aches for Paul's company. The sunset cloaks both the sky and waters below with an orange filter until the stars win their competition with the light show. It's a new moon and the only light reflecting off the water comes from the *Black Moon* at anchor. It's the second time Keira notices the armed guards patrolling its deck. The Consortium's presence and threat gnaw at her, but she knows Paul has jurisdictional limitations.

She misses the men she's spent the last several weeks with. Her father continues to recover on Guam, Dax's escorting Eric's body back to his family, Steve and Alou are dead, and now Paul's missing in action. She feels lonelier than ever.

As the light fades, broad-billed flycatchers break the silence as they sweep the skies for airborne insects. She makes a vain attempt to catch a glimpse. "At least you're here to keep me company tonight. Guess it's time I turn in."

"It's too quiet around here," exclaims the concerned Chairman. "This place ought to be swarming with agents. How many boats do we have patrolling right now?"

"None," responds Arroyo. "I expected you'd want a lower profile after the news of the governor's passing gets around."

"You're right, I suppose. Have you heard back from the hospital, yet?"

The captain shakes his head. "What would please you?"

"For now we sit——"

The ear-shattering blast tears through the cabin sucking the oxygen from the compartment and the lungs of its inhabitants. The bulkheads flex upward and outward as expanding, superheated gases continue throughout the overhead, projecting shards of wood, metal, and fiberglass through the guards on deck, and flinging all into the lagoon. The sleek yacht is transformed into mangled wreckage and plummets to the depths carrying with it the last remnants of the Consortium.

Keira's facing the hotel when the flash of light reflects off the lounge windows. The entire region's rocked by the explosion. The blast shakes the hotel windows and rattles the patrons. A wave of heat nudges the back of Keira enough to turn her toward the lagoon and to view the fireball's ascent which reignites the skies in a white, yellow, and red upwelling. Particulate radiates from the blast center to shower the waters with debris. An empty skiff formerly tied alongside the *Black Moon* floats aimlessly in the anchorage.

Startled and curious guests either vacate the hotel to gather by the shoreline, or stand at their balconies for a safer view. Keira selects a place on the lawn to sit, and leans her back against the hotel's rough exterior. She studies the people milling about, and follows the boats heading to the area in search of survivors. Their lights slowly scan the waters for an hour before they stop for the night and motor back to their homes. By this time the guests have lost interest, and already returned inside. Keira eventually does the same.

The conversations in the lobby, dining area, and lounge grow louder, filled with misinformed speculation. Keira's bored with all of it and heads upstairs. Passing by the door to Paul's room, she hears movement and decides to knock. A minute later, wet feet pad across the tile floor. Clad in a hotel towel, his wavy tousled hair wet from the shower, Paul opens the door slightly.

"Come in and take a load off. I'll be finished soon. There's an open bottle of red on the end table. Help yourself."

She closes the door behind her and allows her eyes to follow him into the bathroom. His wet footprints on the tile floor direct her eyes toward a bundle outside the bathroom dripping into a growing pool of water. A quick tug on its cover of towels reveals unfamiliar equipment.

"Hey, Paul … what's all of this?"

She's startled by a voice from the dark recess. "They're a couple of rebreathers, Keira Lynn."

"Daddy? What——" She strides over to give him a hug. "When did you——"

"I know, I know we have a lot to talk about, but let's wait for Paul."

With the latest news about her son, Lorleen Hetiback has been struggling to find something good in their lives. It hasn't been easy.

Two months ago, a biopsy at the clinic verified she has stage three breast cancer, and was told she must fly to Guam to meet with a Surgical Oncologist for a mastectomy followed by radiation and chemotherapy. Until now, she's shared none of this with her husband. The stress and concern over their finances, and her life-threatening cancer, has finally overwhelmed her. She tearfully shares it all with him now.

The couple is startled by unexpected raps on their door. "Yes," she shakily responds, "who is it?" With no answer, she turns on the outside light, and opens the door slightly keeping its security chain in place. After a quick glance, she turns toward her husband who hasn't moved from the living room sofa. Together the couple open the door to a dour-faced Kohper.

"What brings *you* here this time of night, *Chief*?" he bitterly asks.

"May I talk with both of you for a moment?"

When neither makes a move, he adds, "Inside, if I may?"

The two remain standing near the door, and face the officer once he works his way in. Kohper squeezes past them and points toward the kitchen table. "Please let's take a seat together. I have something to give you."

They reluctantly follow his suggestion while the chief pulls an envelope from inside his jacket. "I believe this is rightfully yours." Lorleen peers inside, drops it, and breaks down. Her husband looks at Kohper, snatches the packet off the table, and thumbs through the several thousands of dollars confiscated from Tino earlier.

Ryley's father is stupefied when he looks back at the chief. "It belonged to a business associate of your son. I believe it was meant for you."

With nothing more said, Kohper gently closes the door on his way out.

Sal sends a round of beers over to Jon and Keira who sequestered themselves in a secluded corner. They left Paul in his room to make a couple of calls.

Jon picks up his glass, when he realizes Keira is impatiently staring at him. "Alright," he starts, "Let me address the obvious question first. I returned yesterday."

"Why didn't——"

"It's better no one knew. Yes, I feel fine——symptom free. The physician gave me a dictum not to dive for the next couple of weeks."

Keira questions her father for more information about his time on Guam and to get reacquainted.

After a while, Paul pulls up a chair to join them, catches Sal's attention, and circles his finger around the table to order another round. He takes a draw from his bottle before he speaks. "I got word Tino died about an hour ago. 'Officially' from internal bleeding … unofficially from a low-caliber bullet to the base of his brain. Kohper and his deputies intercepted his killers."

"Will they provide you with more information about Vincenté or his Consortium?"

"They won't be testifying to anything."

"Oh." Keira crosses her arms and slumps back in her chair. "I'm not sorry for any of them. What's your next move?"

Jon lets Paul speak first. "Tino didn't exaggerate when he said they operated everywhere, but unbeknownst to me, the agency knew their operational extent before our team arrived."

"Why didn't anyone——"

Jon takes hold of her hand. "The less people knew, dear, the better."

"Yeah, yeah, I think your response has gotten pretty thread-bare by now. Don't you?"

Paul tries to fill in the blanks for her. "Their operation was already well-established in the Marianas: Guam, Saipan, Rota before it spread throughout the Micronesian chain. They exerted heavy pressure on all the local governments through influence peddling, subterfuge, and whatever they could do to destabilize the leadership and replace them with their own people. The governor represented the Consortium's front man on Chuuk, but when he heard about their request for federal funding he got greedy and careless. He didn't coordinate his request through the organization. It got our attention and the excuse to look deeper into their activities. We deployed agents to verify the reports, and shut down their entire enterprise."

"Doesn't sound like I was even necessary, so why did you drag *me* into this?"

Jon quickly answers, "We needed a credible cover and it gave me the opportunity to reconnect with you. I want you back in my life."

"You seemed to have pulled that off," she smiles. Keira recognizes he's struggling with his emotions and gives him a reassuring hug. "It's something we both needed, Daddy. It just took me longer to realize it."

Paul adds, "While they focused their energies on controlling the operations here, our director used the opportunity to move other agents throughout the islands. Brent turned out to be the wild card we were worried might botch the whole thing up ... and he came close to pulling it off."

"When we started out, I hoped he'd work *with* us," she offers.

Paul responds with disgust. "Brent worked for nobody but Brent. We feared he might force them to either pull out or expose them before we got all the evidence we needed and could move on it."

"What role did Tino have?"

"A bit player. He served as a go-between, a messenger boy and cheap enforcer, nothing more."

Keira's about to query her father how he got so deeply involved when two men enter the lounge who draw an unusual amount of attention. The local man is enthusiastically greeted by Sal from behind the bar. Leaving Keira alone, Paul and Jon quickly make their way to the new arrivals, finish their introductions, and escort them back to join her.

Paul starts, "Keira, I'd like you to meet the new governor of Chuuk, Solomon Enap. This is Jon's daughter, the young lady you've heard so much about."

Governor Enap takes her hand, "Thank you for all you've done for our people."

She's a bit self-conscience when she stands to return his greeting. When she looks at the other stranger, Jon steps in. "And my dear, I'm proud to introduce you to my friend and old radio operator from the Navy, Jay Johnson."

J.J. extends his hand, which she takes warmly. "So you're the infamous 'Director' I've heard so much about."

With a sly smirk he looks at the others then places his free hand atop hers and replies, "In the flesh, my dear. Nice to finally meet you," which elicits chuckles from the rest of the party.

After they all sit, Salpasr makes his way to the table to take their drink requests. When Jon follows him to help with the order and cover the tab, Keira quickly engages J.J. in a muted conversation.

Paul leans over to the governor. "Will Elias be joining us?"

"Not tonight. He has a difficult house call to make."

"He mentioned something about it on the phone."

"He's known the Hetibacks for a long time, and feels terrible about the way things went down. He also knows they're in serious need of help, and made a compelling case with me to redirect the funds."

"Your brother's a good man——he always showed us his first loyalty is to the people of Chuuk. I don't think you have to worry about him succeeding in his role."

The governor gives an appreciative nod to Paul when Jon and Sal arrive with the trays.

The group raises a toast to the new governor, and pays tribute to Eric with their second.

Afterward, they spend a most enjoyable evening laughing at the embellished sea stories J.J. and Jon share about their time in the service almost three decades ago. The director then embarrasses Paul with a few of his team's misadventures with the agency.

Listening to the camaraderie and laughter the men share, Keira remembers the fuss she made when they coerced her into coming along. In retrospect, she wouldn't have missed this at any price.

When she notices her father stifle a yawn, she slides her arm around his shoulder. "You feeling okay?"

Jon takes her other hand into both of his. "Never better, dear." He gazes at her face and recognizes his wife's eyes gazing back. "Think it's possible you could start coming around to visit your old man again?"

With a tender glance toward Paul, she leans in and whispers, "May I bring a friend?"

They that go down to the sea in ships,
… see the works of the Lord,
and his wonders in the deep.
Psalm 107:23&24 AKJV (paraphrased)

Truk has been a personal obsession since early 1972. During my squadron's deployment to the Naval Air Station at Sigonella, Sicily, I shared a villa in Trecastagni, at the southern foot of Mount Etna. When the latest issue of *Skin Diver* magazine arrived, its cover featured the discovery of the *I-169*, a World War II Japanese submarine at the bottom of Truk Lagoon.

Segue to April 1987; Kathy and I were afforded the opportunity to visit the islands for two weeks. Diving every day, we were stunned by the variety of wrecks, their artifacts, and the fabulous profusion of marine life.

There are several operations, both land-based and live-aboard, that run charters in the islands. Our personal time was spent with Blue Lagoon Dive Resort. They provided a thoroughly enjoyable, rewarding experience, leaving us with a lifetime of memories.

Gradvin Aisek served as our personal guide during our entire stay, showing us the best the islands had to offer, along with filling some requests we made that were outside the boundaries of normal sport diving limits. Gradvin's father, Kimiuo, had been one of the major factors in the development of diving in Truk. He did everything he could to accommodate our visit., and eventually served as a translator between us and a researcher from Tokyo who was instrumental in the discovery of the *Fumizuki*. Twenty-six dives, eighty five rolls of film, and fifteen days later, we reluctantly returned to the real world, with the only regret we couldn't stay longer.

To both Gradvin, and his late father, we owe a sincere debt of gratitude for their cooperation and support. The islands of Chuuk are every bit as exotic as a visitor could hope for. Its wreck diving is world-renowned. There are no words, photos, or videos that can fully convey the remarkable offerings. You have to experience them first hand.

It *is* hoped that readers who wish to safely share all the adventures the sport has to offer, (which I highly recommend) will seek out and complete formal certification classes conducted by qualified instructors who are sanctioned by internationally recognized organizations. Scuba classes cover a wide-range of topics from equipment, to physics, physiology, maladies, marine life, decompression and most importantly safety.

Sport diving has evolved dramatically since the mid-90's (the setting for this book) including the use of exotic gas mixtures which allow for safer deep-diving, but comes with its own specialized equipment and requisite training.

The solo diving (without a dive buddy) by a couple of characters in the narrative is neither safe nor endorsed.

It has been eighty years since the attack on Truk Lagoon by the Allied forces that sent the ships to its sandy bottom. Time and interaction with the sea is taking its toll on the historic wrecks. The concerns about the consequences of their decay are very real, and efforts are being made to address the issues.

There have been a number of books written about the historic islands and the diving. I recommend the following in chronological order of their publication:

Lindemann, Klaus. *Hailstorm Over Truk Lagoon*, Belleville, Michigan: Pacific Press Publications, 1982. For several months before our visit, and throughout our entire time there, I lived in this book, to soak up as much information about the wrecks that was available at the time.

Bailey, Dan E. *World War II Wrecks of the Truk Lagoon*, Redding, California: North Valley Diver Publications, 2000. This remarkable publication has updated and amplified not only the wrecks' individual stories and condition, but also the development of the facilities of the Japanese occupational forces. The hardbound book contains 518 high gloss pages, with 173 maps and drawings, and 101 black and white, as well as 150 color photographs.

Macdonald, Rod. *Dive Truk Lagoon, The Japanese WWII Pacific Shipwrecks*, Caithness, Scotland, UK: Whittles Publishing Ltd., 2014, reprinted with revisions 2017. This publication provides the most up-to-date reporting on the wrecks, an informative overview of the battle, with superb maps, and drawings. This hardbound book (265 pages) should be in everyone's dive bag who visits the islands. Macdonald has also posted some very high-quality videos on YouTube that are great for an introduction and orientation on what visiting divers can expect to encounter.

Accessing more than one of these references will give you comparative descriptions of the same wrecks and their condition, which I found interesting. The descriptions presented in Klaus Lindemann's book in 1982 are far different than those published by Rod MacDonald in 2017.

To give you an an example, my wife and I were the first Americans to dive on the *Fumizuki* the day after it was discovered by a Japanese team led by researcher Tomoyuki Yoshimura, on 26 April 1987. We were afforded the privilege of experiencing a pristine wreck, with the pilot house/bridge still intact and the ship in relative order. The most recent footage of the wreckage tells a vastly different story: the pilot house has collapsed, the bow section has been torn from the main body by what appears to be a large anchor, the impact of divers over time, and reports of dynamite fishing that has damaged the stern of the wreck. We noticed, first-hand, the damage to the starboard rear quarter of the hull. Yoshimura told us it was the fatal blow of a torpedo that took the ship to the bottom. The balance of the wreckage now, compared to what it was, is barely recognizable.

Strong, Diane M., *Witness to War: Truk Lagoon's Master Diver Kimiuo Aisek,* Diane M. Strong, 2013. This book takes a different slant to tell the story of Truk, focusing on the development of diving in Truk through the life of Kimiuo Aisek, a man whom the author got to know over the years, and filled her with many stories of his personal witness to the battle, and life growing up in the islands when he was still a teen-ager.

Several people contributed to the completion of the manuscript: I attended Cindy Hiday's adult education classes on Creative Writing for a number of years. She was gracious in allowing me to share some of the passages of this book during class exercises. She is an accomplished writer of numerous novels, and actively involved in publishing new works. Her website can be found at www.cindyhiday.com.

One of my classmates, Mac McRedmond, is a retired police officer, who coached Paul on how to fight defensively, and the use of test kits for identifying drugs in the field.

A team of beta-readers read through the initial, very rough drafts contributing many helpful suggestions. Many heartfelt thanks go out to Jan Macdonald, Loie Matthews, Steven Wright, Gayle and Ralph Higgins, Rich and Nancy Canham, and my wife Kathy.

While on a road trip to Central Oregon we spotted an industrial complex in the distance with a very distinctive profile of a U.S. Navy P-2V Neptune aircraft parked on the tarmac. The P-2 was the predecessor to the P-3 Orion, both anti-submarine patrol craft. I crewed on P-3's for nine years, so the sight of this craft inspired further investigation. What we discovered was the Erickson Aircraft Collection, on 2408 NW Berg Drive, in Madras, Oregon.

Contact information is: 541-460-5065

www.ericksoncollection.com

info@ericksincollection.com

Housed in a spacious facility, the aircraft in the museum's collection are all flight worthy, and frequently participate in air shows.

Many thanks to Michelle Forster and David Reed for all the personal assistance and accommodation given us during our visit.

Kath and I shared the experience at Truk. She was by my side, both above and beneath the surface for every dive and activity. She has relived this adventure with me throughout the development of the novel, with insightful suggestions, and tons of encouragement. She has my heart, and my deepest gratitude.

351

About the
Author

Rod Canham has a diverse background with nine years in Naval Aviation and twenty as a professional diver and underwater photographer. He has had more than fifty articles published on travel for international dive magazines culminating in *Hawaii Below*, a guide book for diving the Hawaiian Islands.

His most recent book, *the Artillerist, a Civil War novel*, recounts experiences in the Civil War through the eyes of his great-grandfather.

Rod and Kathy make their home in the Pacific Northwest.

About the Author